A MELODY OF CRIMSON REGRETS

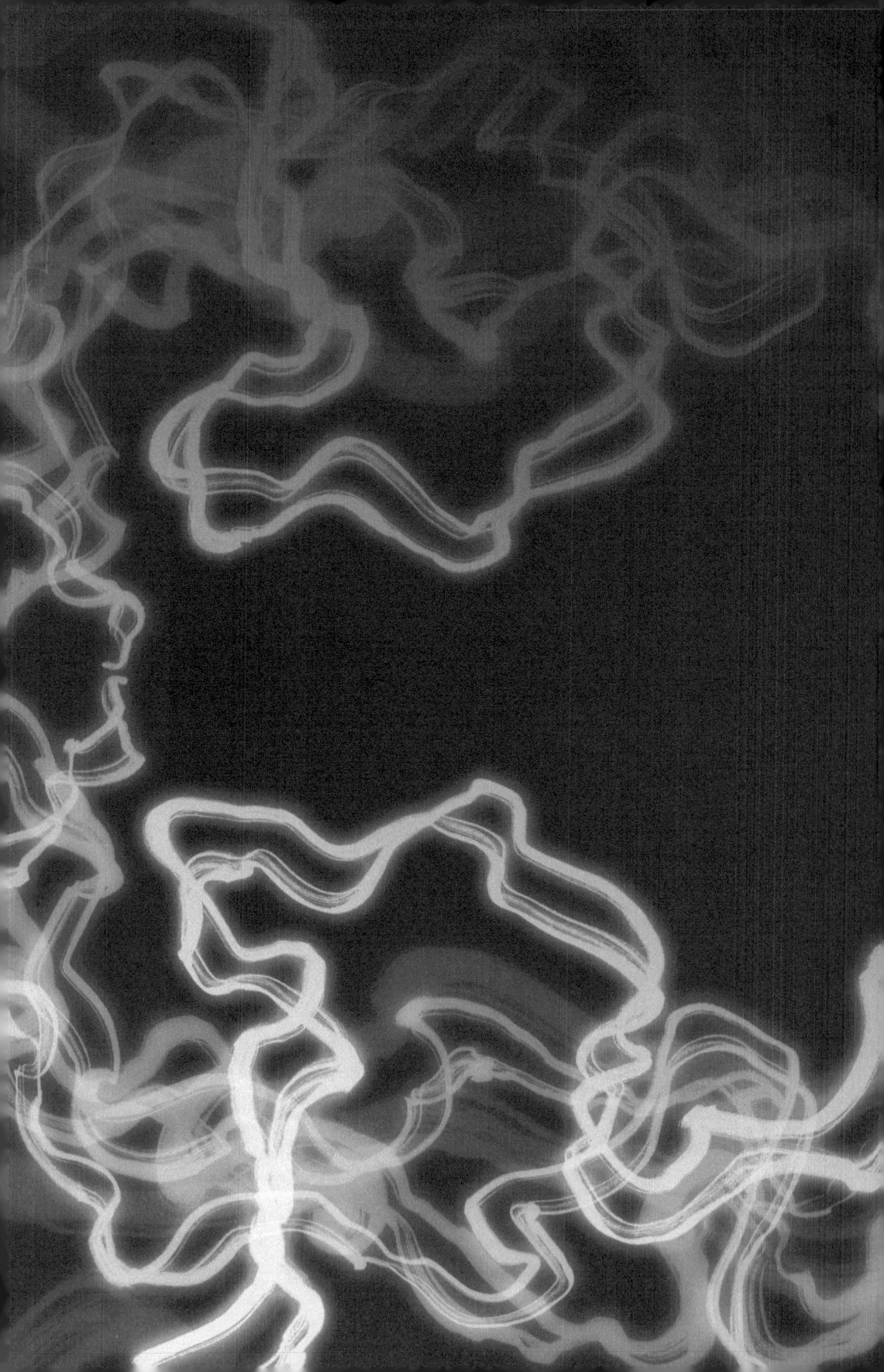

A MELODY OF CRIMSON REGRETS

MANUEL CACHO

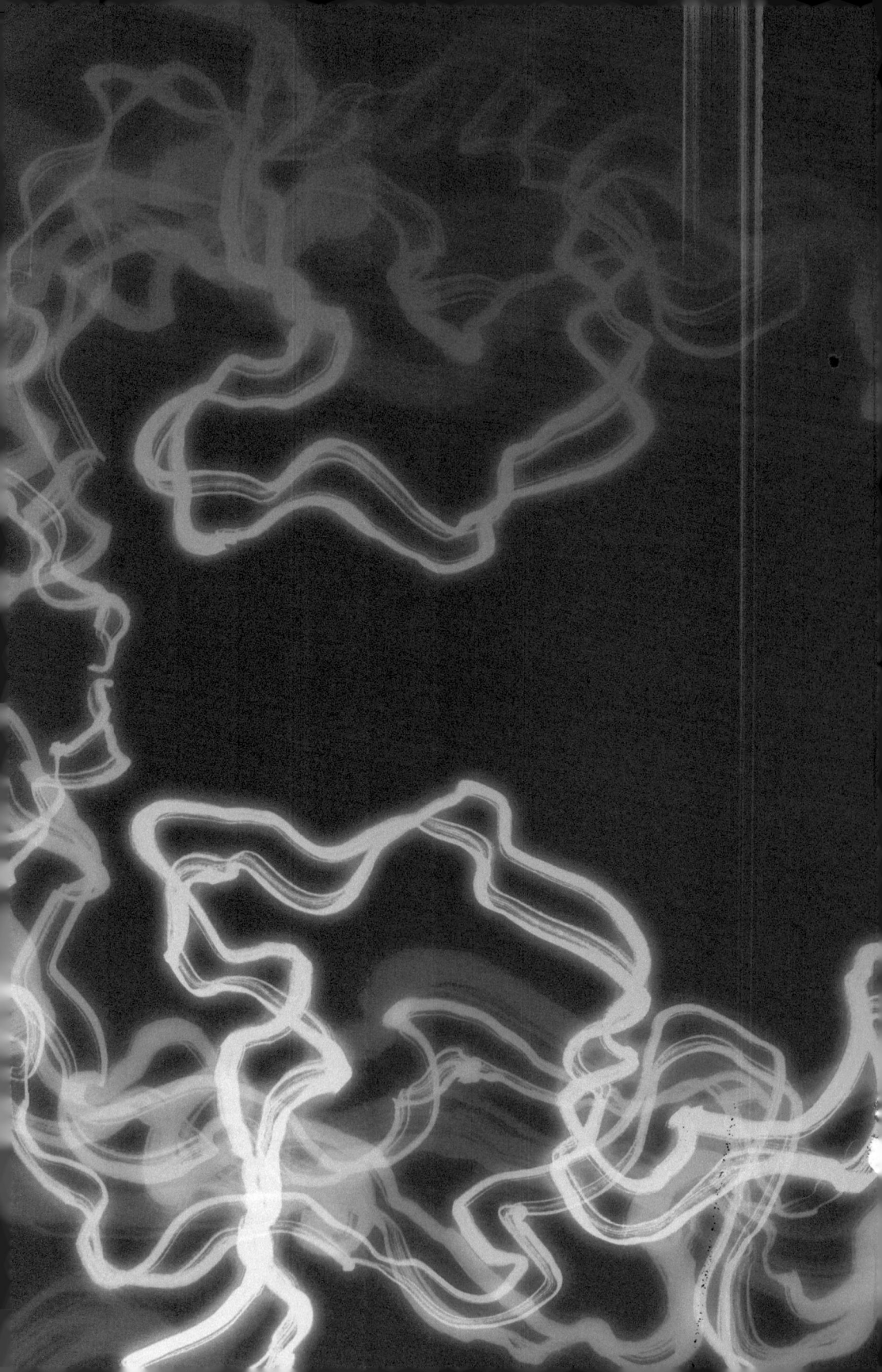

A summer bead, dressed in white,
It dreams of wings, child take flight.

The crimson spots, like crimson eyes,
A springtime gaze will agonize.

A hanging threat, a vermilion fear,
Run or suffer, fall's accursed premier.

A winter breath is flapped away,
Nigredo wings bring black decay.

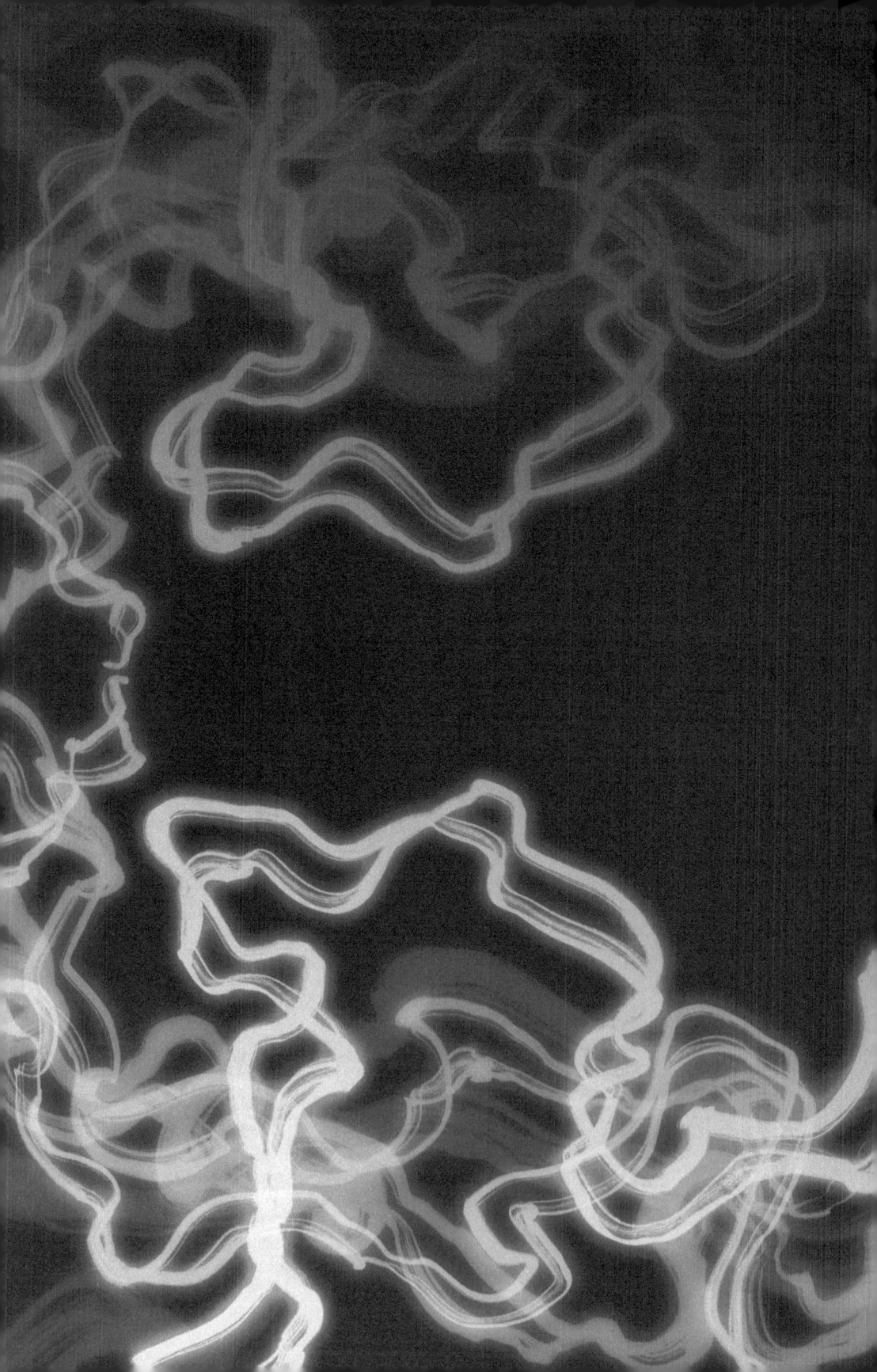

FIRST REGRET

"I should have known better."

-ANTOINETTE KATHERINE
SCHOFIELD

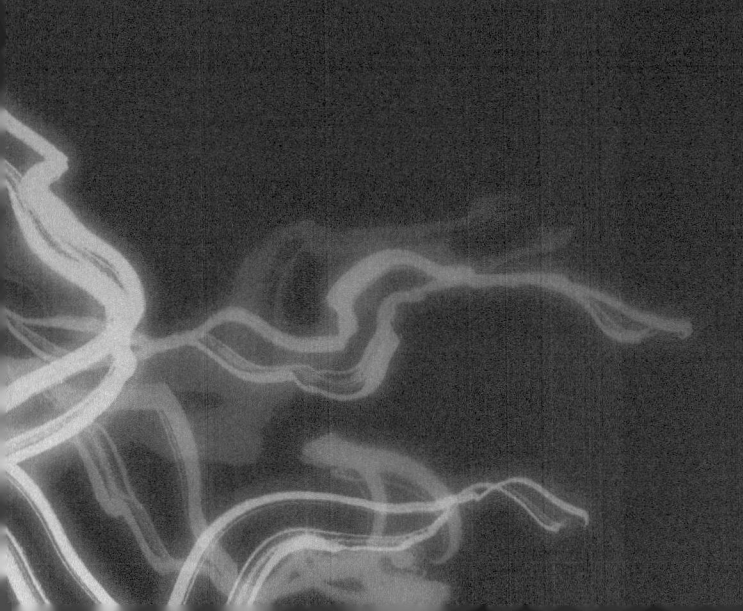

1

THE ONLY LIGHT THAT POURED INTO THE BLACKSMITH'S SHOP
came from a window that rested at ground level, low and long, adjacent
to a flurry of footsteps silhouetting onto a furnace in heat, hungry for
the vampire's steel. Across the blaze, a blackened table waited for the advent
of another weapon, ready to add the reshaped steel to the collection of swords
that neatly wallpapered the room, resting on their cast-iron hooks.

A man's head popped into the shop, the crackle of the blaze reflected in
his eyes as he looked around for a moment before letting himself in, paying
no mind to the rattle of the bell over his head. The visitor had to squint in
the darkness to make out the swords, waiting for an acknowledgement as the
craftsman continued working while the man browsed.

"Are these for sale?" he asked, breaking the silence and running his finger
along a sword with a topaz gem on the handle, brushing the soot off the blade
as he did, revealing a playful edge that sliced through him with ease, threatening
to draw a drop of his blood.

The craftsman struggled to hear the question over the blows from his hammer and the throb of his forge, trying his hardest to ignore the faint scent of blood as the man pocketed his sliced finger, hiding a slight flush on his cheeks. "Not that one... hasn't been for a long time," he whispered with a quiet smile before continuing with his work.

"Does anyone even use swords nowadays?" the visitor asked, pacing around the room. "Or are they just ornamental?"

"If nothing else..." the vampire struck, not making eye contact, "...they're a symbol... and symbols have always had power."

"I don't see the appeal." The stranger rubbed his thumb against his index finger in his pocket, squinting to make sure that the slice hadn't been deep enough to draw any blood. "But if you decide you want a change," the man called out loudly, competing with the unending blows, frustrated that he couldn't hold the vampire's attention, "...give me a call," he added, withdrawing a business card from his wallet, placing it on the table, and taking his leave.

Hours after the visitor had left, the blacksmith finally paused, wiping the sweat from his brow, letting the echoes of his hammer die down and the embers of his forge cool, beckoning a reprieve and inviting him to review the scrap of paper the man had left. A printed name was stamped above the word 'realtor' and a phone number below. His fading blue eyes washed over the card. "A change..." he mumbled to himself as he looked around the room before squaring the card against the corner of the table. "...It's not that easy... there's still work to be done."

As the vampire returned to his station, the clang of an old bell atop the exhausted entryway sounded for the second time that afternoon, stricken by the brash opening of his door once more. The speed and strength behind the entrance kicked up layers of dust and ash which folded into a doorstop that snapped the blacksmith from his fiery thoughts, hinges reeling at the force. The vampire didn't need to turn around to know who stood in his doorway. In the two centuries that he'd been alive, only one person had ever so unapologetically made herself at home wherever he was: Antoinette Katherine Schofield.

The woman pressed the black lace of an elegant dress against the silk vermilion layer beneath, hugging the dress against her body to squeeze past the door frame and into the shop, releasing it once she'd crossed the threshold, letting it expand in the shop. With a single finger she forced the door shut with the same power she'd used to open it.

The blacksmith watched as she unwrapped her shawl to hang from a dusty hook on the wall, removed her large-brimmed hat, then finally took off her sunglasses, revealing stark green eyes that danced upon his welding goggles before darting away.

"Christian..." she said with a nervous smile, voice trembling, a broken fang just visible as her lips moved, "...Something happened..."

Her eyes avoided his, looking to the swords along the walls as he pulled the tinted goggles off his forehead, revealing tired eyes which admired his former lover with a solemn joy. In the silence she reached forward for him inviting him closer, taking his head upon her bodice when he approached and stroking the hair of a man who looked like he could have been her father. She wrapped her arms around him, holding him tightly as he removed his heavy gloves, revealing a faint scar on his left wrist, taking care not to dirty her dress

He tried to pull away from an embrace that lasted longer than it should have but she wouldn't let him. She didn't want his eyes to judge her. "Something happened..." she repeated with fear in her voice, failing to keep the blacksmith pinned against her, looking away when he managed to break free. She rubbed a nervous right hand that hid a terrible secret. "I Turned someone..."

Antoinette didn't know where to begin. Coming to his shop was as far as she'd thought this out, and Christian Nikolai Dusk, like a patient father remained silent, leaning his head forward, almost as if to provide her with his undivided attention, when in fact, the opposite was the case.

Any onlooker would have thought it was to hear *her* better, but it wasn't. To all but a few, the voices of the dead were mute. She didn't have his curse. She couldn't hear what he could. The dead could speak to him.

They elaborated her bitter crime through a warbled and piecemeal cacophony of fragments. Soundbites of facts and observations flooded his ears. In his mind only, to his ears only, did the departed legion profess; and when she opened her mouth after a long pause, he could see the word *Christian* on her lips, competing with an orchestra of voices at his ears.

"*Quiet!*" a woman's voice from the world of the dead rang crisp, only audible to him.

"Silence," he professed, loudly but sharply. Antoinette flinched as he spoke, his decree snapping him back into this reality, back to the silence of the room, quieting the flood of noise so he could hear the woman who stood in his shop.

"I Turned someone... and killed someone too..." she added, tears welling up in her eyes as she recalled, wanting to tell him everything, wanting to tell him the story herself, hoping beyond hope that he would be there for her like he always had been.

The dead could report to him. The dead could replay what they had seen. But the dead didn't know what thoughts raced through her head, and just like humans and vampires, the dead could lie.

"Albedo. That was his name. The one she Turned." A voice whispered to him and others echoed.

"Albedo."

"Albedo."

"Albedo?" Christian declared the name of the human she'd bitten, seeing her nervous nod and prompting a pause. His voice usually built her up, but today his disappointment carved into her like one of the swords on his walls.

"Arrah. Her housemate. The one she killed." the first voice whispered again.

"Killer."

"Murderer."

"Betrayer."

"Arrah?" Antoinette nodded again, her eyes filling with tears as she recalled the vampire she'd killed.

"Brother..." the voice of the woman who rang crisp whispered solemnly into his ear, *"...Orpha is making her way to Evan Blood..."*

"Orpha has fled. She's on her way to the Coven."

Antoinette's lips quivered. She said something, but he wasn't focusing on her. He was fixated on the whispers from the dead. He was trying to hear them retell her story, but it was difficult. Concurrent accounts told two stories: one where Antoinette had bitten Albedo and killed Arrah, and the other where Orpha was making her way to the Evan Blood Coven to report the crime. He couldn't separate them. They were drowning him.

His powers weren't what they used to be. Now he caught only fragments of the events that had led up to her decision, fragments of words between folds of static.

"Albedo... Turned... Command..."

"Murdered... Schofield."

"Justice! I will have justice!"

"Approaches Castille..."

"Kill yourself."

"Enough!"

"Did they hurt you?" he asked, frustrated at not knowing. The woman pursed her lips, unsure of how to answer, reaching to steady the trembling of her hand as the clouds rolled in and the rain began to fall.

2

LAST NIGHT

ANTOINETTE STARED AT HER REFLECTION IN THE MIRROR. HER features were mostly the same, unchanged in the two hundred years since she had become a vampire, though few would have known it. Her green eyes still held their same curiosity, her face still carried the pride her mother had forced her to don, and her posture was still immaculate. She had no one left to impress now, but the shadows of her childhood still clung to her.

In this night's reflection, Antoinette spotted something new—a defiant wrinkle emerging on her unblemished face, daring her to move forward while her vanity tried to bury the notion. *With a drop,* she found herself thinking, *with a single drop of blood I could erase this wrinkle.*

Christian was on her mind as she contemplated what to do. She had visited him more frequently in these last few years, slowly approximating the familiarity she had once had with him. Each time she had seen him, he'd looked older. He was aging, slowly letting himself die, and, despite it all, he seemed at peace with the prospect. *With a single drop I could erase this wrinkle... or it could be the first of many...*

Her train of thought was interrupted by a boisterous giggle that spilled through the neighboring wall.

"Take it," a man said.

Antoinette tried to discern the voice. It was a voice she had heard, but not one of her housemates.

"I know what you are," the man continued as the woman's giggles combined with a third person's snicker, immediately recognizable as belonging to one of her housemates: Arrah Iona Roda.

"Oh really?" said the giggling voice, small and sharp, not unlike the proprietor, Orpha deReville.

"I've been watching you..." the man said from the other side of the wall, piquing Antoinette's curiosity. "I see you all... most nights... I see you."

"Sounds like we've got a little voyeur," Arrah said.

"Mhmm," Orpha added. "Lucky for us he's cute."

Antoinette had no interest in continuing to eavesdrop on her housemates and whatever game they were playing in the next room. Instead, she stood up and headed towards the hallway of her second-story home, bound for the kitchen on the first floor when the whiff of blood tickled her nose. She took in a shallow inhale. It was human blood.

In the neighboring room, Orpha's giggles and snickers were roaring and it was clear that they were about to feast. Antoinette tried to put it out of her mind until the scent overwhelmed her senses, making her eyes water. It was a nauseating amount of blood that filled the air and drew her curiosity to push the slightly ajar door open, her eyes drawn to a man clutching at his neck.

He was young. He was barely a man. Yesterday he could have been a boy.

The man sat on Orpha's sleigh bed, propped against the headboard with claw marks on his neck, barely visible beneath an ocean of blood that poured from them, running down his naked torso. Two women had their mouths wrapped around him, sucking at his neck, pinning down his arms, trapping him in place.

The smaller woman, Orpha, had long brunette hair that thinned as it fell over her muted peach body. An opaque-yellow nightgown precariously hung over her, the translucence showcasing her curves and leaving little to be imagined. Her devilishly refined facial features were buried in the river of blood that streamed from the twitching man's neck.

The other woman, Arrah, had matte eggshell skin with short hair that complemented her rounded face. Even on her knees beside the man it was clear that she was much taller than both Orpha and Antoinette. Her eyes were shut as she lapped up the man's blood.

He was young. He was barely a man. Yesterday he could have been a boy. Tomorrow he would be a corpse.

The man, too petrified to register the assault he was being subjected to, simply stared at Antoinette who tried to subdue her own instinct to join in, the perfume of his blood a delight in and of itself.

"Antoinette," he mouthed, though only a small gasp emerged.

Her eyes narrowed curiously as he spoke her name, and Orpha came up for a breath, turning to her. "Breakfast?" She slid to one side to make room, playfully hitting Arrah when she didn't do the same.

"Who is he?" Antoinette asked, a hastening breath giving life to a feeling of dread in her heart at the wrongness of seeing a man who knew her by name bleed out.

"Some creep. He was watching us when we were coming home last night... even knew our names," Arrah said brazenly. "Won't know much for long."

"Albedo," the man mouthed to Antoinette, sensation leaving his pinned arms as Arrah grabbed his hair and forced his head back, helping herself to seconds.

He tried to struggle, but Arrah and Orpha pinned down his legs. His black eyes pleaded with Antoinette and her heartbeat quickened. She recalled eyes like his and a feeling of powerlessness that had overtaken her. He reminded her of someone, someone she hadn't been able to save, someone who still made her heart ache.

"Wait!" Antoinette stepped into the room, remembering who the man was. She reached forward to brush Orpha off, but Arrah's hand intercepted her with a growl. In a quick motion, Arrah shoved Antoinette across the room, sending her crashing into a dresser with ease. "He's our neighbor." Antoinette righted herself, more worried than fazed, remembering the times she had seen him walk by her house. "It's the doctor's kid."

He was young. He was barely a man. Yesterday he could have been a boy. Today he was on the verge of dying.

"The brat with the braces?" Orpha asked, sticking two bloodied fingers in his mouth to pry it open. "I don't see it." She squinted, rubbing the blood off his neatly aligned teeth and sucking on her finger.

"He's breakfast now." Arrah grinned, ignoring the glare that Antoinette gave her. "Besides, it's just a stupid kid."

Antoinette pursed her lips, hiding the offense she took behind a balled-up fist turned singular punch that collided with Arrah's face, propelling her into the opposite wall. "I'm stopping this. He can still be saved..." Antoinette tried to convince herself.

"Yeah, no," Orpha said, donning a half-face of blood like a sacrificial priestess. "We'll let you save the next one if you're all high-and-mighty then." She paused. "Not like you cared the last time." An emboldened grimace met a thunderous slap as Antoinette rounded the bed and sent Orpha tumbling into Arrah.

As Albedo continued to bleed out, Orpha and Arrah composed themselves. "He's a goner," Orpha spat, watching Albedo try to cup the slices on his neck, unable to stop the torrents of blood running down his chest, his dark eyes shaking in their sockets. "Best to enjoy our meal while it's still warm..."

He was young. He was barely a man. Yesterday he could have been a boy. Now there was only one way to save him.

Antoinette's two fangs protruded and she sunk them into his wrist.

She wouldn't let him die.

She wouldn't powerlessly watch him die like she had been forced to with her son.

She could do for him what she couldn't for her own family.

She could save him.

3

ANTOINETTE'S TWO FANGS SUNK INTO ALBEDO'S WRIST FOR JUST
an instant before Orpha reappeared at her side, a freshly manicured set
of silver-colored nails wrapped in a fist all her own that sent her flying
across the room.

Antoinette cupped her mouth, tongue lapping at the cracked fang which
broke off and fell to the floor, her eyes looking past Orpha to Albedo, whose
body writhed as his wounds began to heal.

It was a longshot to bite him, and in this case, the reward was instanta-
neous: the beginnings of a transformation that compelled his Turning body
to attempt to heal the deep gashes on his neck.

As the human-turned-vampire healed before their eyes, so too did Arrah's
face, her fractured jaw resetting itself, her tongue running dry as she downed
the blood that still coated her mouth.

"You can save the next one!" Orpha repeated as Arrah headed for the man.

Albedo's hands reached towards his neck with uncertainty. The blood
loss was slowing, but the momentary relief he felt turned to fear as Arrah

approached him, shattering a nearby glass of wine and holding the stem like a sharpened stake, her palm wrapping around the base. One strike, one precise strike to the heart would kill this man. But as she swung, his hand caught her wrist.

Powerless as a human, now he stopped her swing, unsure of his own newfound strength as he held her off. Arrah's weight shifted as she hovered over him, a wicked smile delighting in the challenge. In a day, or in a week, or in a month, his physical strength could have overpowered her, but today, he could do little more than struggle to hold her in place as his body focused on healing. He had just been Turned, and the blood he had lost was not so easily replenished.

Antoinette writhed as Orpha restrained her, her small hands pinning Antoinette against the wall, the bloody breakfast she had consumed temporarily enhancing her strength.

She could do little more than struggle and look on as Arrah's might began to overpower Albedo's, her smile growing wider as his strength waned. His dark eyes implored mercy as his two hands struggled to fend off Arrah's one, bulging with a muscle, propelling the crystal stem glass towards his chest with a cackle. "I don't want to die," he pleaded, first to Arrah, then to Antoinette. "Please... stop them!"

A ring of red flashed in Albedo's eyes, mirrored in Antoinette's as he uttered the command.

Antoinette stopped struggling. Her expression turned vacant. She cocked her head back and slammed it into Orpha's shoulder, crunching against it. Orpha reeled, trying to shake away the stun before Antoinette launched a surgical chop with five fingers that amputated arm from shoulder.

Orpha dropped to her knees in shock, looking at her severed arm, limp on the floor beside her. She met Antoinette's eyes for a stunned moment, seeing a cold obedience in the lusterless green of her eyes.

Before Orpha could warn Arrah, Antoinette had moved across the room with daring speed, wielding another strike that broke all five of Antoinette's fingers as she penetrated Arrah's back, her ribs, and ultimately her heart. Arrah had no time to realize what was happening, no time to process a countermeasure as she wielded the crystal stem, and no time to avoid it.

The force of the strike was more than Albedo could handle, and the crystal stem in Arrah's hand shifted, piercing his neck as Arrah went limp, collapsing in a geyser of Albedo's blood. In a panic, Orpha took haste to escape, leaving her best friend and her severed arm behind.

Antoinette felt the command subside and finally registered the pain that came with five broken fingers, washed in the crimson blood of the dead housemate beneath her. She backed away from Albedo who reached out for her fearfully, a conflicted terror in his eyes as he rolled the body of his would-be assassin off the bed and onto the floor with a distinctive thud, the crystal stem of the wine glass still lodged in his neck.

Of course he didn't know it.

He didn't know the price a vampire paid for biting someone was giving them complete control over you. It was why hardly any vampires Turned anyone of their own free will. And even though Albedo had no idea how he had made her protect him, her insides twisted as she realized that she had given another man complete control over her. The compulsion was absolute, to be followed at all costs, and only one vampire, Genesis Blood, had ever broken free of the Executive Command on his own.

He was young. He was barely a man. Yesterday he could have been her boy. Now she could only see her abusive husband.

"Antoinette." Albedo coughed blood as she cowered, as she crawled into a corner, afraid to look at him, afraid to listen, afraid to exist, the memories of the last man who she'd Turned twisting up her insides, making her sick while the thoughts of the boy she had just saved tried to make up for it. "I..." Before he could finish that thought, he passed out.

The adrenaline had faded and, like most Turned vampires, he would sleep until his strength was restored. If he survived the Turn he would wake, and if he did, he would learn that he could make this woman do anything he wanted. He could make her reveal all her secrets. He could make her his slave. He could make her kill people she loved. Sooner or later he would learn, just like her husband had, the truly terrifying power of the Executive Command.

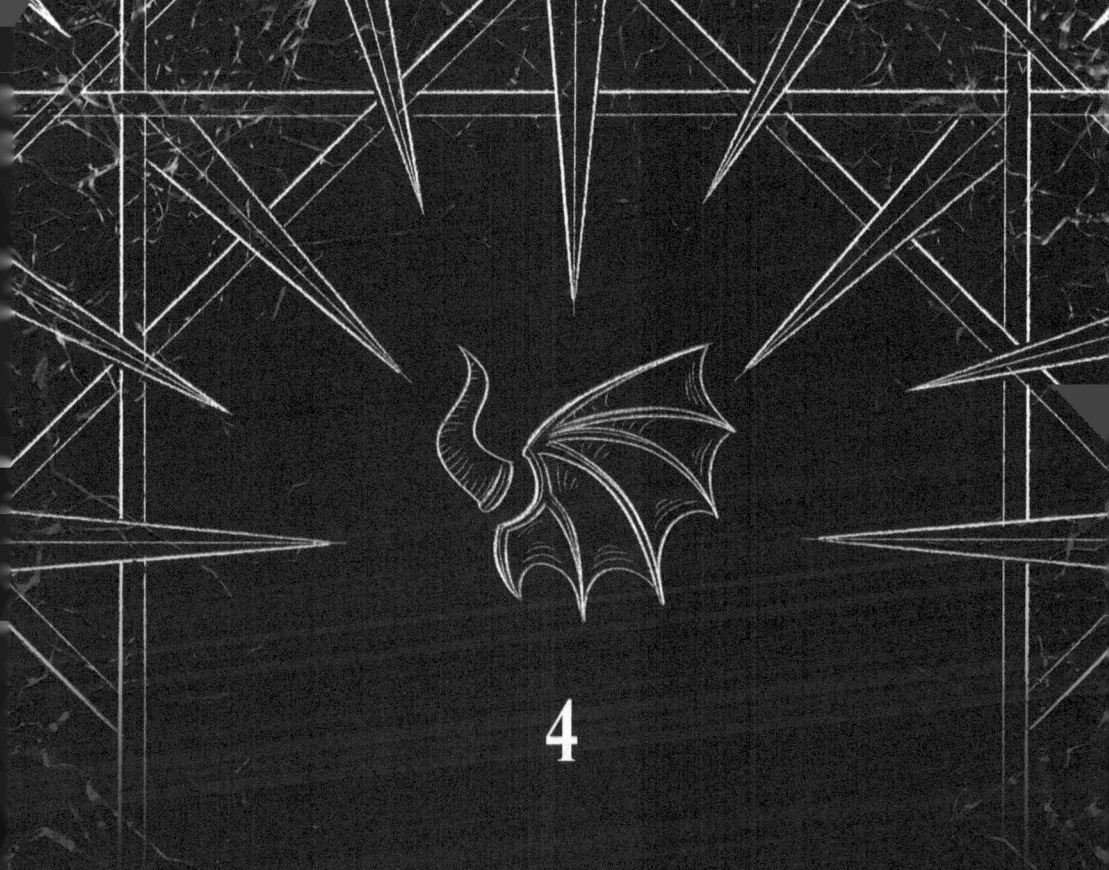

4

AN EMPTY BOTTLE OF PILLS STARED AT ANTOINETTE FROM THE medicine cabinet as she gripped the sides of her bathroom sink with a wince. The very notion of breathing was labored in the hours that followed the events of that morning. When Albedo slept, he reminded her of her son: soft and fragile. Antoinette had withdrawn the glass stem from his neck and wrapped his wounds as best she could with her one good hand.

It was an accident, she repeated all morning, *he didn't do it on purpose. He's just a boy. It was an accident.*

As she stared out the window, waiting for evening to come, she watched the clouds on the horizon and flexed her hand, finding the bones had fused back together. The memory of the pain still lingered. The thought of her dead housemate beside a sleeping Albedo made her want to vomit again.

From the comfort of the first floor of her two-story Victorian home she waited, covering as much of her body as she could, preparing for the journey into the light of the evening, knowing that Christian Nikolai Dusk had always been a creature of habit.

A storm was at her back as she left her home, steadily approaching. A shawl strangled her neck while dark lens-fitted sunglasses ensnared her face, shielding her eyes until the clouds could take up the mantle. Her look wasn't subtle. Anyone with half an imagination would have heralded her a vampire, but she didn't care. Her worry was already consumed by the events of that morning, and the lighter dress she had wanted to wear had been stained by her bloody hands as she had tried to get it on.

Albedo hadn't been the first man that she had Turned. Lifetimes ago she had Turned another, her husband, Michael, a man who still haunted her dreams. With one word, with one command, he would paralyze her. He would starve her, control her, punish and ridicule her—and she was helpless to do anything. He would turn her into a ragdoll of a woman until she could take no more, and then the cycle would begin anew.

With a single command, Albedo had forced her to kill Arrah. *It was an accident*, she repeated, *he didn't do it on purpose.* He had never seemed like a threat as their neighbor, she reassured herself as she recalled a smile from afar or a wave on the streets. There was no malice. He wasn't like Michael. Michael had been evil from the beginning.

Even as she tried to humanize Albedo, the thought that he could command her to do anything overwhelmed her. The idea that Albedo *could* become like her husband terrified her. It was the reason she had vowed so many lifetimes ago that she would never Turn a human again, and yet *he had his eyes.* His eyes were so much like her son's.

The possibility that Albedo could become like Michael bred a worry that made her stomach churn. She thought her other friends would have been more understanding, but a disgruntled disgust was rife on the faces of her two other housemates when she tried to explain what had happened, when she tried to justify why she had saved Albedo and killed Arrah in the process.

Antoinette had tried to explain herself, but Orpha had already fed them her side of the story. Her housemates and so-called friends mustered an average of one suitcase and one word apiece: 'Goodbye, Antoinette.'

In one day, with one brazen decision, Antoinette Katherine Schofield had lost her friends, her freedom, and soon, her House. Now all that she had left was one person, the one person she knew would never betray her—the person she loved most in this world, the blacksmith who resided in the neighboring town of Iespēja, her once-loyal servant, Christian Nikolai Dusk.

5

TODAY

WITH THE EVENTS OF THE DAY RECOUNTED, THE BLACKSMITH watched Antoinette shift uneasily atop the table in his workshop, absent any chairs to invite anyone to stay long. Her black dress, now settled in ash and dust, reminded him of when they had been young, when Antoinette's mother would scold her for tarnishing her clothes. But that was a lifetime ago, before she had founded the House of Schofield, before they had joined the Evan Blood Coven, before they had lost their child, before they had been Turned, when her only worry was a curt word from her mother, and his a lashing from the Head Servant.

"Christian, won't you say something?" Antoinette urged softly.

His eyes avoided hers. Sometimes it hurt to look at her, to look upon the woman who he still held a candle for, a candle which wavered at the reminder of the child they had lost. When he struck the iron he thought of them, those that had died, and those that had lived their lives with regret. He tried to hammer out his own, but the steel was too weak. *Did she still think of their son as often as he did? Did she still say his name aloud?* It was an old wound that they'd never been able to get over: the prospect of a family, fractured by a death, irredeemable as vampires, unable to have another.

"After Michael, why?" Three words summed up his nihilistic existence. Three words summed up their distance. Three words summed up her current predicament and she tried hard to fight back the tears. Her housemates had asked the same question. If she had just let Arrah and Orpha have their way, Antoinette wouldn't have Turned a human, Orpha wouldn't have lost her arm, Arrah wouldn't be dead, and those two housemates wouldn't have turned tail. All she had needed to do was nothing.

"I knew him... and if I didn't do something he would have bled out. He would have died in that room! He's just a boy... he has his eyes."

Christian had been away when she'd lost their child. He had been powerless to save his family then, and now, a new reality of powerlessness threatened them again, and just like it had been so long ago, his disappointment was apparent.

"*You haven't always been this rational, brother,*" Claire butted in, a crisp and clear voice only Christian could hear. "*You've acted on a whim too. Do I need to remind you of her name?*"

The Elders called it the Red World, the world of the dead, beyond the Divide between life and death, where vampires and humans alike went when they died. It was a world that only a few select vampires, Listeners, could hear. The voices from the Red World were varied. Some were quiet and others were loud. The stronger the will, the clearer the voice, but as the aging vampire looked to his visitor, his weakened state meant that he was unable to quiet them for long. Without the blows from his hammer to drown them out, the voices often overwhelmed him.

Still, there was one voice that sliced through them all with crystal clarity, one voice whose connection with him was intricately woven into his own, always whispering in his ear, his dead twin sister, Claire Sefira Dusk. Even in death, even from the Red World, she wanted him to experience joy. Few were the times she had seen him smile in earnest or known him to be happy, but this woman had brought out that side of him. "*She needs you.*"

"Now you need me?" he asked quietly.

Antoinette reeled. "I've always needed you! But you..."

"...*sulk and brood*," Claire whispered.

"...you cling to the past, you..."

"*Take your anger out on scraps of steel.*"

"We could run away." She reached for his hand. "You and I, like we talked about?"

"The Coven's area of influence is wide. If you flee... he'll hunt you down." Antoinette's face fell.

"I can't stay..." She looked past the wall, in the direction of her House. "I can't be alone and wait for him to command me... or Jason to come get me... or Orpha to come back and fight me."

"*There might be another way,*" Claire whispered, soothing her brother from beyond the Divide, reminding him of an option that he had long since abandoned, of a choice he had long since postponed, urging him to walk back down the road that he had paved so long ago. "*You won't forgive yourself if you lose her too.*"

He had looked for a sign in this hollow existence. Every day he had looked for a sign that might justify taking an active role in the world again, and all the while he'd found none. One day he stopped looking. He stopped trying. He moved on with his life, but today the choice was on his mind, and the decision sat atop his table, quivering with fear, playing nervously with a business card, her tongue catching the jagged edges of her broken fang, waiting for his scolding, seeking his comfort, but finding only a terrifying silence.

He let out an exhale and turned his lips into the softest smile he could. "There might be another way." She raised her head timidly. "Perhaps you're right... perhaps I need to move on. Perhaps I can try again... we can try again," he said as she nodded nervously, letting her bury her head in his chest as she sobbed.

6

ANTOINETTE'S HANDS GRAVITATED TOWARDS THE FALLING DROPS on the window outside, eager for a distraction as she pressed her hands against the glass, yearning for their tapping upon her body. The glass would share no cold, but she quivered nonetheless: one part excitement, one part dread.

The four other vampires who had held together the House of Schofield were no more: one had been killed, another maimed and fled, and two departed of their own free will.

"Are you almost ready?" Antoinette found herself asking as the menacing clouds dropped a gentle rain.

Christian tidied his stations carefully, setting each tool in its place and seeing the forge to its quiet slumber. "Almost," he said, packing a small bag in the corner.

"Thank you, again," She said softly, listening to the rustle and clang as he packed.

"After what happened with Michael..." Christian began, cutting down the woman that he cared for with the memory of the man who had broken them, "...I didn't think we'd ever be here again." It wasn't anger, it was disappointment and declaration. Even though Turning Michael had been its own predicament, the risks for Turning someone, should they survive, were always the same.

"I know." It disgusted her that she'd made this bed.

"Jason will aim to dismantle your House..."

"...*and kill her*," Claire whispered into her brother's ear.

"Unless we find a way out," he continued.

"How did it end... the last time you dealt with him?"

"As well as I could have hoped for."

A lifetime ago, Christian had been the Head of the House of Dusk—the first House in the Evan Blood Coven, and one of the wealthiest Houses formed. The fall of his House had been warped into a lesson in humility for others. Still, Christian's early adoption and special circumstances had allowed him to escape a punishment that might now threaten Antoinette.

"Could he forgive this?" she asked, turning her focus to him. "Possibly?" she hoped.

"*It's unlikely.*"

Despite the Evan Blood Coven's consolidation of power over the past two centuries, the House system remained a thorn in Jason's side. An extension of the Coven in theory, numerous House issues had resulted in a flurry of problems for the Coven which Jason had been forced to address, one by one. Too proud to acknowledge his creation as a failure, Jason had slowly managed to bring the Houses to their knees. Only a few remained, and the House of Schofield was one of those privileged few.

"Not by choice." Despite Jason's stronghold on the Coven, the Evan Blood Charter served as the bible for the rules of governance. His actions were still subject to oversight by the Coven Elders.

"*We can best him at his own game.*"

Christian eyed a few blades, lacking a hilt to call them daggers, placing two of them in his bag. "The same Charter that gives Jason Castille his power as Head of the Coven also prescribes the penalties associated with... oversteps."

"Oversteps...?" Antoinette repeated, following the blades from wall to bag and watching as he slipped a single coin into his breast pocket. *Was that what killing Arrah was? An overstep?* A knot in her throat was hard to swallow and a tear at the edge of her eye was hard to hold in.

"You'll need loopholes. If not ones that Jason offers, ones the Elders force him to accept."

Christian had read the Charter when he'd been High Listener at the Coven. He'd read the Addendum when he'd been granted his own House. "The language provides the answers... and regardless of what's changed in the past two centuries, you will be called to a hearing to plead your case." He picked up his bag and threw on a shale-lined coat. "Jason loves his theatrics."

"He could try her for anything..." Claire whispered.

"Kill yourself," interjected another voice from the Red World.

Christian paid no mind to the other voice. "We'll need more information, but there *is* one problem we can solve..." Antoinette's gaze grew uneasy as she looked around the empty room. "The bylaws state that a House requires two or more members. A House of one is a House Fallen." Antoinette felt the shivers spread as he approached her, bag in hand. "A vampire must pledge themselves to the Coven before joining a House."

"Albedo?" Antoinette said under her breath. *Was that his plan? To convince a human-turned-vampire to join her House?* The choice didn't seem all that better: a man who might control her forever and a Coven that might end her life tomorrow. *He probably wasn't like Michael... but what if he was?*

The blacksmith's tired and swollen eyes hid a gentle hue of sapphire, a merciful light that shone weakly, perceivable only to someone close enough to him to interpret it: a caring gaze that tried to hold her. "I belong to no House, but I have pledged myself to the Coven already." His frayed hair stretched from his head madly, as though ready to fight against the rain that began to build up at his doorstep. "Will you let me serve you again, Lady Schofield?"

And there it was, a few words that came from between his cracked lips, offering her instant relief. "I've waited so long to hear you ask that." She nodded eagerly, feeling a tear well up in her eyes.

"The path forward will not be easy."

"When has it been?"

Christian wrapped the shawl around her head. "But we've faced greater odds."

The shivers subsided as he cast open the door, taking the lead up the stairs, shades of his former self emerging as he climbed up from his basement-level shop. To anyone else, he was a tired old man emerging from a long day's work, but to Antoinette, he was a survivor, returning to the fray, returning only for her, to protect her once again.

The pair walked in silence down the main road, past rows of ground-level shops and past a grandfather leading a worried granddaughter through the rain. They walked past the sign that marked the entrance to the town, dilapidated and fractured, bearing the strange name of the town Christian had called home for over a hundred years, Iespēja.

"Brother, about the man she turned..."

"I know," Dusk whispered under his breath.

"Christian? Did you say something?"

"Nothing... just talking to Claire." He offered her his arm and she took it.

7

CHRISTIAN HAD ALWAYS BEEN CAUTIOUS. HE NEVER RACED IN IF IT could be avoided, but today a problem had perched itself upon a table in his shop, clothed in an elegant dress and embellished by eyes in distress that pleaded with him to help—and he was powerless to say no.

He knew that if Antoinette tried to flee, Jason Castille, Head of the Evan Blood Coven, would hunt her down and kill her. He was her only hope now, and though the candle he held for her sometimes wavered at the thought of the child they lost, the candle was forever lit. He was prepared to die for her— even in the moments the candle burned quietest.

A maimed Orpha's journey to the Evan Blood Coven was nearly complete, but the details from the dead voices in the Red World were fractured. They came in bits and pieces, and the former High Listener could do little more than plan for every uncertainty in the hope that it would matter.

His abilities weren't what they had been. He had starved himself for so long, deprived himself of blood for years, and, with it, the full extent of his powers. He had resolved himself to age so that he could live out what life he'd been cursed with, in as much peace as he could afford. The idea of a family had long since been cast aside, but every time Antoinette showed up, a glimmer of hope crept to the surface.

He hadn't planned to take in blood anymore; he hadn't planned to amplify his powers; he hadn't hoped to ever pursue being suffocated by the noise from the Red World again. But today a problem perched itself upon a table in his shop, and his own convictions wavered for hers.

The details from the Red World were sparse—and the former High Listener needed blood to hear more and protect the woman he loved.

Antoinette walked slowly at his side, unaware of the weight of her problem upon his shoulders. She didn't give a second thought to his slow and deliberate movements, nor to the voices from the Red World teasing him with drops of information when he longed for a storm, unease filling his every step.

"He'll kill … too."

Not all the voices from the Red World wanted to help him. Not all wanted him to succeed. Not all cooperated with him. The echoes from the Red World, just like the humans or vampires they had once been, could do their own damage. It was a harsh truth he'd learned long ago.

"Finally, you'll join us." A sinister voice in his ear sighed with glee.

"Christian?" Antoinette interrupted his inner dialogue, catching an empty smile as she said his name. "I wondered…" A feeling of dread washed over her as they approached her Victorian home, eyes looking up towards the second story where she'd left Albedo sleeping, his bandaged neck wrapped by one of her scarves, and the dead body of her housemate cool to the touch beside his. She had been avoiding talking the entire walk. The rain was loud around her, but her mind was not so silent. *What do we do about the boy I Turned? We can't kill him, but I'm afraid of him controlling me. What will we do? What will you… do?* "We haven't talked… about Albedo…?" she trailed off, feeling a knot in her throat as she did.

She had always felt safe when she was with Christian, whether it was as children when he'd served her family, or when they'd frolicked in her room as forbidden lovers, or when they'd slept in his House nearly two hundred years ago. She had always felt the safest with this man, the one who had always tried to protect her, even from herself, but today she didn't know what he was planning, and the thought of Albedo made her heart quicken beneath her bodice.

"Will you be ... for his ... too? Or will you hide behind ... sister?" the sinister voice hissed from the Red World.

"Don't listen to her, brother," Claire soothed.

"If not for you he wouldn't have done it... always manipulating him... leaving him to ... the fallout of your schemes."

"Christian?" Antoinette bit her lip.

"I wouldn't have Turned him..." The words were cold; the words were calculated; and any onlooker worth their salt understood the disappointment he carved into each one. Antoinette tried to remove her arm from his, hoping that he would reach out for her, but he didn't. She pulled away and he let her. He'd always been like that. It was always Antoinette who had to come to him. He had always been there to clean up her messes. This wouldn't be the first time he'd have to make a problem like this one disappear, but the last time his methods had been more savage.

Those who had tagged along for his journey from beyond the Divide flocked to his ears as his sister tried her best to silence them.

"Kill him."

"Save him."

"It should be me!"

Claire couldn't always keep the voices at bay. They were like a row of inmates eager for blood and itching for a show. They rattled on their cages, egging him on, hoping to influence their Listener.

"...I wouldn't have Turned him... but I understand why you did." A forge-beaten hand with a singular scar on its wrist reached towards the front door of the House of Schofield where Antoinette lived. It reached towards the life he'd abandoned, standing in the shadow of the structure he had ordered built. But that was a lifetime ago, before they lost their child, before everything became so complicated.

"An open invitation you never accepted," Claire said, sensing his hesitation. *"It could still be a home where you have a family. Where you both move on... together."*

Christian inhaled, closing his eyes. "You wanted to protect him? To do for Albedo... what you couldn't do for our son?" Antoinette's wistful smile watched as his breathing slowed. His hand retreated, caressing his temples.

"*You can still find happiness here, brother,*" Claire tried to cut through the eager dead that crowded his ears.

"They're louder here... aren't they?" Antoinette asked, seeing him clutch at his head. "Is she here too?" Her eyes shuddered. "Arrah?"

"*Bitch!*" Arrah boomed from the Red World. "*If you had just... your fucking business!*"

The Red World erupted.

"*Quiet!*" Claire commanded, humming softly despite the voices attempting to drown her out.

"She's angry. I just need a moment." he mustered, focusing on the soft vibrations of his sister's voice, tuning out the others as best he could. Not all wanted him to succeed. Some wanted him to suffer. And his sister could only do so much.

He turned away from the door, gripping a discolored portion of the patio's railing, taking a moment to compose himself. A second deep breath was all the fuel he needed to face the door again and push it open, focusing on Claire's hum so he wouldn't be overtaken by the current of noise. "Thank you, sister."

"*It used to be so quiet... didn't it?*"

When Christian had chosen to break ground on this spot, long before the house stood, long before Iespēja was a town, there had been silence in this place. He had chosen this spot deliberately because it was quiet. Now the house stood in a row of others. In the two hundred years since it had been built, some who had called this street home had died, and others had been killed. Most dead clung to something, and for many that was the place they had died.

"*Brother... if you can't handle this... perhaps...*"

"I wish it had mattered..." His pair of sapphire blue eyes looked from the house back to Antoinette who didn't quite register the words, the Red World growing silent, as if to listen to him. "I wish Albedo had survived the transformation to prove that he wasn't like Michael."

Antoinette's jaw opened nervously as she looked to the man she loved, catching glimpses of the boy she'd grown up with, in the body of the man who could have been her father. She looked into his eyes as she tried to comprehend his words, then at his back as he turned around, staring at him, unsure if it was just his cloak that was sopping. "He... Albedo... he?"

"*Is... alive!*" the sinister voice boomed.

"Didn't survive..."

"*You disgust me.*"

Antoinette rubbed a thumb against her index finger as she took a nervous step back, foot slipping on a small puddle. She would have toppled, but Christian's outstretched hand caught her, slowly lowering her to her knees, a storm in her eyes and a downpour at her back. "He was... he was alive... I saved him..." Her chest rose and fell nervously. The collar of her dress felt tight. "I saved him. I pulled out the glass stem... he was still breathing."

"*Silver nail polish... brother... if you need an excuse.*"

"He was..." Christian dropped to his hunches in front of her. "When Orpha sank her nails into his skin, they were lined with silver. His body tried to heal. All day it tried... but he died when you came to see me... He tried to heal, but couldn't."

The Red World erupted, but one sinister voice boomed through them all. "*Disgusting. You... your sister. He can... wake up!*"

"I... no... I..." *Not like you saved the last one,* Antoinette recalled Orpha's words. "I saved him..."

"He's grateful you tried." Dusk looked up to the staircase. "I'll give him a proper burial. You shouldn't have to see him like that."

Antoinette watched the man she loved ascend the stairs in silence. The Red World quieted for a second time, like the hush after the flicker of theater lights just before the curtain would rise. They knew the plot, but still they waited with bated existence to see if the former High Listener would execute.

"*Remember, he would already be dead if she hadn't bitten him, brother.*"

"*A disgusting justification...*" The sinister voice followed Christian and Claire into the room where Albedo slept.

The Red World may have been split on whether to kill or spare the man who laid on the bed, body still trying to complete the transformation, but Christian Nikolai Dusk was not. A weathered hand wielded a weathered blade while another hovered over the boy's mouth.

Today a problem perched itself upon a table in his shop, and the only solution available was the one where her ignorance protected her from knowing what needed to be done.

"You may not deserve this..." he whispered, "...but so much of what I've loved, I've lost. I won't lose her too. She's my family."

The Red World grew louder, and Antoinette was none the wiser.

8

TWO BODIES WERE WRAPPED IN WHITE SHEETS THAT FOLDED ATOP themselves, failing to obscure the blood as the blacksmith descended the stairs, each step as measured as each blow from his hammer.

Antoinette needed only one glance to see her former lover carrying the two bodies over his shoulders before she felt her stomach drop, before she shut her eyes tightly and turned away, heading to open the back door for Christian, struggling to see through her own tears.

"This is how much he still loves you. He wouldn't do this for anyone but you," Claire whispered to a woman who could not hear her, watching from the Red World as her brother carried the bodies to the backyard.

Christian had dug enough graves in his life to know how big it ought to be. Something about a burial, no matter the circumstances, made him connect with his emotions more, made him feel more human.

The ash handle of a rarely used shovel fit nicely in his working hands. The spade slicing into a grassy area near the rosebushes made him feel at peace. The dirt was soft as the rain continued to fall.

"It was raining when you buried me too, wasn't it, brother?"

Antoinette stood on the threshold, from the safety of her home, watching the man work through the night, avoiding looking at the corpses that lay at his side as he dug, one shovelful of dirt at a time, eventually dropping into the muddy holes himself to ensure the bodies could be completely buried, lost in the mundanity of the task.

The voices of the Red World judged him. Some praised him. Some cursed him. He tried his best to ignore them, tried his best to focus on the sounds of the world: the slice of metal into dirt, the pitter patter of rain around him, the shallow breaths of the woman in the house watching him toil.

It wasn't the first grave Antoinette had seen him dig, and she wasn't the only one who felt a strange nostalgia as the earth parted at his commandments.

In the moments between his thrusts, he recalled burying his sister, burying what had remained of a beloved housemate, and burying Michael. These graves weren't like those. As hollow as it was, these graves didn't carry the meaning that the others did.

"You could rest..." Antoinette called out to the backyard, breaking up the silence. "It's almost morning."

"Soon," Christian said, crawling out of the hole to look at her, covered in mud from head to toe, a monster emerging from his swamp, the sapphire in his eyes peeking back at her. "I'll join you when the work is done," he added, attempting to restore some humanity to the moment.

"I'll run a bath for you..." Antoinette said lowly, "...like you used to for me," she trailed off, turning away and disappearing into the house, feeling guilty for not raising a finger to help. *Even if I had wanted to, he wouldn't have let me,* she confessed as she ascended the stairs.

Outside, Christian paused, the hard part done. He turned his head up, letting the rain fall directly on his face. "I thought I was done with things like these," he confessed to the Red World. "I thought that's what living like a human meant."

"That's what living like a sheep is," Claire responded.

"Perhaps you're right," he sighed, backfilling the hole, assisted by the rain.

"You don't have to be a sheep. There are still some who know, like I do, that you could be anything. When did you forget that?"

"When you lied to me sister. When you betrayed me."

"Like you lied to Antoinette? Like you lie to protect her?"

He pursed his lips as he cast another shovelful of earth into the hole, bringing down the muddy hill atop the void.

"You could rise up and take what's yours. You could stop asking and start commanding. There are still those who would come running if you called."

Christian cracked an empty smile, looking at the patchy graves, almost filled in now, and to a sliver of a white sheet where Albedo's head was. "I'll protect Antoinette, sister. That's always been our charge. That's enough for me."

"Protect her from what? Death? The Coven? Loneliness?" Claire paused as her brother worked. *"Your half-measures confuse her. Your inaction curses her. Let your penance be over, brother. Take this as a sign—start living again. Be a part of a family like you've always wanted, even if its without a child."*

"He can't. He's a coward!" the sinister woman's voice boomed as a gust blew, sending ripples over the spots where water was pooling. *"A coward ... for my death. A coward turned killer for you. And I'm not the only one ... thinks so."*

"You're a coward," Albedo repeated sadly from the Red World.

"Perhaps..." Christian murmured, unable to drown out their other voices, "...perhaps I am. Perhaps that's how I've always lived."

"Kill yourself."

"... a coward."

9

LISTENING WAS AN ABILITY FEW VAMPIRES HAD, SOUGHT AFTER BY Covens since the times when the Old Religion was at its zenith and the teachings of the Six Gods proliferated. The clerics claimed it was the Gods at one of the first Conclaves who first called it Listening and coined the term: Listeners.

Listening was an ability that took a toll: the power to hear the dead and, in tandem, the inability to hear silence in any place where they clung. The voices of the dead echoed from beyond the Divide, from the Red World, where lives went, where events were recorded, and ultimately, where he too would go one day.

Some carried their entire histories with them into the Red World, others took their regrets, still others, nothing. Some could learn beyond the Divide, but most were a broken record, repeating their last living moments, recalling their final circumstances, unable to say anything else. Some voices were louder, and others quieter. It was a coin toss as to what Christian could glean from the Red World. Some would help, some would not. Some could be commanded to help, others could not. Some persisted, others slowly faded into nothingness, eventually disappearing from the Red World entirely.

Regardless of who the voices belonged to, when they knew an ear listened, they converged. As Christian had approached mortality under the guise of a blacksmith, many of the transient voices had quieted, but not his sister's, not Claire's.

Unlike most of the dead who clung to an object or a place, she clung to her brother. In the times when the voices overwhelmed him, she soothed him and, in the times when the voices rang out too loud, she lulled them. She was his shield unto the madness and his beacon of sanity for the curse that he carried. But she was also a daily reminder of what he had lost.

As Christian shoveled the last bit of dirt over Albedo's face, he was reminded of the punishment he had exacted on the last man who Antoinette had Turned, her husband, Michael Escoté. It was a monster's punishment, doled out by the same, but it was a mantle he was willing to accept. His years of serving as an executioner hadn't numbed him to the ideas of the lives he'd destroyed, Albedo's included, but it had prepared him for what followed: living with the decision. He had mourned only two people: his child and his sister. Everyone else had simply moved from one plane to another, some by his own hand.

"*Coward,*" Albedo's disappointment was fresh as he was buried, a tinge of sadness in the insult. "*You're a coward,*" Albedo repeated, a whisper drowning amidst the other voices.

"I might be," the gravedigger responded.

Albedo wasn't like Michael, evil from the onset. Instead, he was simply an untested variable. But in that unknown existed the possibility, regardless of the improbability, of malice: a spark that needed to be snuffed out before it had the chance to grow. The blacksmith had been burned too many times to not know: never trust a fire that you didn't start, and never stoke a fire that you couldn't put out. Albedo was the former, and to him, he'd apply the rule of the latter.

"*... a coward. She was... to save me! You cowarded me. I would still be a coward if you hadn't cowarded me.*" Albedo repeated. "*You stole my coward!*"

"Trapped in that thought?" Christian asked, leaning the spade against the side of the house.

Not every soul that went to the Red World remained whole. Even Christian, whose Listening abilities were better than any, knew that the transition from one side of the Divide to the other took a toll. Not all remained whole, and, for most, the journey to the Red World meant being stripped of almost everything.

"Co...wa...rd... you..." the voice repeated, as though trying to say something else, but unable to. "*I will always co...wa...rd,*" Albedo floundered, somewhat incoherently, incapable of forming any other words. "*I didn't coward to coward!*"

"I'm sorry Albedo..." the rain tamped his words as he withdrew a small blade from his inside coat pocket, letting his blood wash off and wiping it clean against his coat sleeve, "... for what little it's worth."

He slipped the knife back into his pocket, stepping onto the mat inside and closing the door to Albedo, leaving him to stand watch over his grave. Carefully, and with more balance than it seemed possible, the blacksmith pulled off his boots, brimming with mud like a man who'd been digging for clams, setting them upright beside him. He removed his pants next, then his soaked coat which he hung from the doorknob. His buttoned shirt came off next, and then his undershirt. His clothes were a combination of muddy, wet, or dusty, but with each layer he took off, he revealed more of his form.

The blacksmith stood only in his dark underwear, his massive forearms swinging him forward towards the staircase he'd descended. His hair was drenched, and water raced down his body. His short hair crested over his face; and his hands, tired, cold, and muddy, were a stark contrast from the rest of him.

At the top of the staircase, Antoinette stood, with hardly the time to mourn the death of Albedo or Arrah before her fear was replaced with relief as a half-naked man ascended. Her heart skipped a beat as he reached the second floor, standing next to her, looking up at her with a gaze that said, '*order me.*'

"The bathroom is..." she began, feeling an inappropriate blush as he pressed on, wanting so desperately to reach her arms around his body. "I'll show you."

"*The bitch... her man and I don't even get a bitch!*" Arrah's voice raked Christian's ears, heading down the long hallway, towards a stained-glass window at the far end that Antoinette had stared out of for hours when she'd first arrived. Gradients of rose-colored glass were arranged in a mandala that hid in the shadow of an obelisk that always seemed to be a world away.

Before they arrived at the end of the hall, she stopped. The last room was hers, and the bathroom was an ensuite through it. A light fog from the steam of the bath spilled into the hallway. "I can wait out here," Antoinette said, stepping aside, *or I can come inside?*

The blacksmith hesitated, about to say something before deciding against it. The whispers from the Red World were quieter near her room.

He took a step forward, his feet guiding him through her room without a care, to a pool of water in a clawfoot tub of the adjacent bathroom. Antoinette remained in the hallway, taking a step towards the stained-glass window when she heard an article of clothing fall to the floor, then his body sink into the water with a subtle slosh.

"Antoinette?" he asked quietly from the bathroom, like she were at his side. He wasn't loud, and if she wasn't by the door, she wouldn't have heard him; and if she hadn't, he wouldn't have called out to her again.

"Yes?" she said, taking a hesitant step into her room, towards the bathroom door that was still ajar, trying to temper her excitement and her frustration, catching a glimpse of herself in the vanity. The wrinkle she'd contemplated over was gone now, her makeup had been thrashed by the storm, and her lips reminded her of blood.

"Am I a coward?" Albedo's judgment didn't wash off as cleanly as the mud. Antoinette felt relief at how he spoke, at his question, at the boyish curiosity and awkwardness he had always had, as she wiped away the smudges of her makeup. "You've known me since we were children... you would know best."

She pressed her back against the wall beside the bathroom, eyes fixated on her bed. "Who called you that?" she asked, leaning her ear towards the movements within the tub. "What poor soul felt the need to insult you this time? Katja?"

"I've called him worse... deserves it," the sinister voice chimed in.

"It doesn't matter," Christian said, feeling more vulnerable than usual as he cupped the water, pouring it over his head, feeling the steam break through the layer of cold from the rain.

"A coward... is afraid to do what must be done," she said. "You're never afraid, but..."

"You hide... coward, you hide."

"But?"

"You only do what must be done."

Christian opened his mouth, then paused. "Claire said something similar."

"Great minds," Antoinette inhaled. "You're brave when you need to be. You're strong when you need to be. You're not a coward... but most people haven't seen what you can become." She bit her lower lip nervously. "It's hard for us... for Claire Bear... for me... seeing them look at you like you're nothing, when we know you aren't... and you won't fight for yourself. You're not a servant anymore."

"I fought... for a while," he confessed. "But it ended poorly... for all of us."

"It wasn't your fault... it was mine... it was Claire's... but it wasn't yours." Antoinette looked down at the floor sadly. "I want you to be happy... coward or not... with me or not. I want to see you smile like you did at the ball when you stood proudly beside Hecate and Freya. After Claire Bear died... after our son..." She paused, looking up and batting away a tear. "I didn't think I'd see you smile like that again... smile like when I told you I was pregnant," her voice trembled. "Are you happier now... not fighting? I want you to be happy Christian, but I don't want to force you."

"I..." *think I want that too, but I don't want to risk losing it. I can't handle losing my family again*, he admitted to himself, rising from the tub, reaching for a nearby towel, wiping off the excess water and remaining mud before tossing it aside.

Antoinette took a deep breath at hearing the towel fall. *I'm no coward either!* She gulped, rounding the wall and standing in the doorway of the bathroom, face-to-face with a naked Christian.

Her heart was beating quickly as he looked at her, locked in the body of a person who'd given up. His naked figure stood daringly before her, unashamed, almost unfazed. Her eyes were crying out to his, waiting for an invitation he wanted so fearfully to extend. She couldn't wait for him to do only what needed to be done. "I'm no coward either," she declared out loud, taking a daring step forward, reaching a hand for his face, and pulling him in for a kiss.

"Coward!"

With a single word he could have stopped her. With a single slight everything could have reverted to how it had been. He could have said *no* when she deepened the kiss and pulled him into her room, pushing him up against one of the four bedposts. He could have said *no* when her hand wrapped around his naked back. He could have said *no* when she ran her hands along his chest, traversing every blemish from the weapons he'd burned himself on over the years and fixating on a deep scar near his heart. During any of these times, he could have said *no*, but she was right. He just wanted to be happy too before the sadness could consume him.

Christian pulled his head away from her kiss for a moment, just long enough for him to flare his hungry fangs and sink them into her neck. Her gasp was louder than the whispers as he took in her blood, as he fumbled to remove her clothes.

She wasn't the same girl she had been when he'd last left her, nor was he the same boy, but there was something complementary about these two beings, fractured by their pain, joined in a common space, realizing that there was just enough of themselves to make the other feel complete.

Both had been too preoccupied with Albedo or Arrah to hope or even plan for something like this. Antoinette didn't match her underwear with her bra and Christian hadn't completely removed the mud from his hands. They didn't know that today would be the day that she would walk into his shop and walk out with him. Last night she was terrified, and now that terror was buried beneath her excitement.

Her half-naked body pushed the blacksmith to her bed, starving to be broken in, watching as his body changed beneath her, as her blood worked its way through his body, restoring his youth. His hands gripped her hips, strongly, passionately, caringly, and her unbroken fang caressed his neck as they lost each other in the nostalgia of their passion.

10

The Christian that slept in Antoinette's bed was not the man she'd approached hours ago.

When she looked down at him as he stirred, she noticed how his features had changed. It had started when he'd bit her last night, when he'd taken in her blood, and when she'd spilled into him. His hazy sapphire eyes had grown more vibrant, the bags under his eyes had disappeared, and his skin had cleared up. Between the love they shared that night, decades of neglect were cast aside, and a chiseled body had emerged, complementary to her youth. But Antoinette didn't care how he looked. The love she felt for him ran far deeper than his flesh.

The sun was high in the sky but failed to penetrate the blackout curtains from her room. Two beings lay unabashed, two bodies on full display between the four posts of a lavish bed sitting in the middle of a room in disarray. Antoinette's clothes had been littered to the corners of her room; the crimson covers had been tossed aside; and a broken leg from the vanity lay just beside where it should have been, unable to bear the weight of them both. She was too shaky to sleep, but she willed herself to try, burying herself next to him.

Hours later, when he finally awoke, he raised his free arm, noticing the manicured hand of his youth that had returned. It no longer showed signs from the years of missed swings when he'd been a blacksmith. The burns he'd suffered from his craft were gone, taken by his indulgence, erased by her blood. Now only two scars remained: one was thin and shallow on his wrist, the other deep and thick near his heart. Wounds from silver never fully healed.

Dusk slid his arm away and rose, walking over to the vanity, accidentally kicking the broken leg, sending it to the back wall with a soft tap that caused Antoinette to stir.

As he looked at himself in the mirror, he put a finger to his lips, still red from his lover. Something about her blood in particular was a rush, a callback to the times in his life when he'd felt invincible, when he shed the fears and insecurities of the past, when his cowardice melted away and propelled him towards a future with her, a future with a family.

"Christian?" she called to him from the bed, watching him turn, measuring every sculpted feature of his body as he walked towards her, the chains of the mundane cast off, and a newfound spark daring to be different as he kissed her. Her girlish grin was splayed on her naked body, broken fang restored, and his taste was still fresh on her lips. "I've waited so long..." she began before an interruption.

Thunk. A bang entered the room and Antoinette froze as Christian turned to face the door to the hallway.

Thunk. A second bang climbed up the stairs he'd descended with a body over each shoulder.

Thunk. A third bang. A distinct clash of brass on wood echoed through the house—its origin revealed: the front door.

Antoinette's bliss turned to panic.

Dusk slipped into the bathroom to put on his underwear while she found herself running to the closet, tugging at the first dress she could find, slipping a well-loved sunflower floral over her body, unaware that the tag stuck out.

Thunk. A fourth bang. Louder than the first three.

"Claire?" Dusk's voice was a whisper as he looked around the room.

"A man," his sister's voice said, sounding clearer than ever before. *"Sent by Jason."*

"A threat?" Dusk stepped out of the room and headed down the hall, not waiting for Antoinette, half-naked, most of his clothes still caked in mud beside the back door. The blade he'd used to kill Albedo was still safely tucked in his coat pocket.

"No. A messenger." Her voice came from in front of him, almost as though guiding him down the stairs and looking back at him.

"A vampire?"

"A human."

"You'll need to translate," he whispered. "Antoinette?" he called out louder, hearing her stumble, hearing her falling over herself trying to run a brush through her hair or find underwear. "It's just a messenger... but you may want to join me," he said, arriving at the landing and reaching for the doorknob to the front door.

Antoinette barely made it to the top of the staircase before a fifth knock. She ran her hands through her long hair, trying to straighten up before their visitor, standing tall, unaware that the teachings of her mother, Navara Schofield, still demanded compliance. "Open it."

Dusk opened the door.

The unwelcome visitor who stood on the doorstep basked in the mid-morning light that Dusk shied away from. As Claire had reported, the visitor was not a vampire, but a man who wore the crest of the Evan Blood Coven on the collar of his grey polo: a black wing with a single horn.

As Dusk looked to the visitor's soggy hair and wet shoulders, the whispers from the Red World were an orchestra to his ears, too loud to ignore.

The man opened his mouth to introduce himself. Dusk saw it move; he followed the man's lips with his piercing sapphire eyes, then watched as he mouthed: *Could you be, Christian Nikolai Dusk?*

Antoinette heard the man as she descended, but before Dusk could say a single word, she brushed him aside. "Please, come in."

The human stepped over the threshold as Dusk took a step away, leaving Antoinette to speak to the visitor. He hadn't forgotten this sensation of powerlessness, and even after all these years, the feeling was still as eerie as it had been then.

Being a Listener of the Red World had its perks, but as Dusk watched the pair converse, he heard only Antoinette speak, then silence as the man responded, then her voice, then more silence.

A Listener had always been destined for such a fate. Dusk couldn't hear humans speak anymore.

While the man and Antoinette conversed, the whispers from the Red World interrupted, interjected, or screamed. Some voices parroted parts of the human's words like a poorly dubbed production. It wasn't the same, but it was what was available to him, a luxury only available to him, envied by Listeners who weren't as connected to the Red World as he was.

It was too jarring for Dusk to try to focus on the conversation, so he turned his back to it, letting the voices of the Red World tell him what they so deemed, rather than trying to read his lips and filter out the noise from the Red World's added commentaries.

"Brian Keet..." Claire said, one against a dozen other voices. *"Sent by the Evan Blood Coven... by Jason."* A pause as Claire collected their thoughts. *"Orpha is with Jason now... it sounds like he has a soft spot for her..."*

As Dusk focused on Claire's voice, he felt a hand graze his shoulder, prompting him to turn. Brian's lips continued to move, but Dusk couldn't hear a single word of it.

As with other Listeners, Listening begat the onset of a selective deafness from humans. Most vampires had known Listening only as a progressive disease. Most Listeners hadn't fasted from blood, certainly not like the years he had as a blacksmith. Even after decades of fasting, hearing humans had been hard; he had to strain to do it, but it was a relief altogether that he could. It was one of the few perks of his return to humanity. *Was.*

Now it was gone. With a single drop of blood, he was deaf to them all again. His curse had returned in full force, and the Red World spoke as clearly as it ever had, while Brian Keet, or any human for that matter, could have bellowed into his ear and it would have been for naught.

"He can't hear you..." Antoinette said, mediating the conversation, "...but I can tell him what you're saying."

"I should have known that. I studied him. The former High Listener under the reign of Bruce Alazar," his mute words rang out, repeated by Antoinette.

"I've looked into his face in the Hall of Houses a hundred times. I've seen yours too, Lady Schofield. He looks... exactly the same."

"Is that right?" Antoinette asked nervously.

"Oh yes, and once I've served my time..." he rubbed his arms, hiding the needle marks from his hazing, "...the Coven will make me a vampire too."

"They won't," Dusk and Claire said in unison.

"Lord Dusk... I have Master Castille's personal assurance," Brian said optimistically, hoping the promise he'd been fed wasn't a lie, prepared to trade one life of servitude for several of something more.

"They won't," Claire said again, but Brian wouldn't have accepted it. He didn't have access to the Red World's compendium of knowledge. He couldn't hear the voices from other humans who'd been made the same promise, now laughing at him as he fell for the same lie, despite attempting to warn him against it. *"At least the slaves under Bruce were never fed such hope."*

Brian looked on with envy to the vampire who stood in his presence, past the one he was here to summon, this messenger for the Evan Blood Coven who had studied and memorized the lineage since the time of Exodus Evan Blood, nearly a millennium ago. For most, the task of studying the more acclaimed vampires who'd existed was daunting, but when they came attached with a portrait, and when these were Listeners, Brian's ears perked up.

He wanted to be a Listener, this human. He wanted to be the one percent of vampires who could don such a title. But Listening was not a skill to be learned, instead it was one you were Turned with. It was a trait that developed as soon as the transformation occurred, something that couldn't be taught or handed down, something without rhyme or reason... or at least it appeared to be.

Listening was a distinction, a beautiful and exceptional distinction, that brought with it untold power—historically respected—and untold pain. A human who had only lived some twenty plus years couldn't begin to understand it. Even Dusk, after two hundred years, struggled with the idea of his brand of uniqueness. Brian may have begged to differ, but it had been resolved long ago: becoming a vampire was the beginning of a miserable reality for Christian Nikolai Dusk.

"Is that for her?" Dusk finally asked, noticing a sliver of parchment bound with a single red thread clasped in his hands.

"It is," Brian said, standing taller, clearing his throat and handing her the rolled-up document. "By order of Jason Castille, Head of the Evan Blood Coven, Antoinette Katherine Schofield, Head of the House of Schofield, you are hereby issued this summons and ordered to return with me to the Coven."

Dusk spent the day in quiet meditation with the voices of the Red World bombarding him. He Listened to the collective memories and events that had occurred, taking him on a journey through the years, through the lives of those who still remained in the Red World that had encountered the Coven in the past, through powerful victories and crushing defeats.

The memories of the Red World stretched back to the beginning, to the time before necromancers, to the time before humans, some even claimed to come from as far back as when the Gods walked the realm. Luckily, Dusk needed only to piece together the last two hundred years since he'd left the Coven.

But the further back he went, the harder it was to focus; the further back he went, the more the voices faded into the ambient white noise. Few voices remained themselves after thousands of years of being alone with only their thoughts. The stubborn ones stayed; the rest faded away.

"Coward!" an errant voice screamed at him from behind a crowd of other voices that tried to provide information.

Filtering out the noise wasn't always easy. Some voices boomed as they retold their life stories, while others blathered on about their lives of failure, rife with regret. The majority just repeated a choice few words over and over again, like an echo, slowly fading from its origin, slowly becoming less and less of itself.

The voices of the loud would regularly drown out those who would otherwise answer him. The conversation could quickly turn into a screaming match. The louder voices were plentiful. To really hear what Dusk wanted to hear, he had to focus.

The voices of the dead who'd cared for him when they were alive were his only saving grace from the madness that drove so many other Listeners to kill themselves.

"Quiet!" Claire's voice always rang out clearly. She wasn't the only person who soothed him. His friends also tried, as did the people that he had loved, and even some who he'd known only after their death, like Renata. When they were around they did their best to shield him from the deafening screams of the unintelligible dead. It didn't always work, but without them Dusk would have gone mad already.

Listening was a double-edged sword: knowing that he could access the knowledge of the world and be sidetracked time and again, his simple questions taking roundabout paths that dead-ended. But today more so than other days, it was time he didn't have to waste.

"Not even a day," Antoinette mumbled somewhere in the room, invisible to his closed eyes. "Not even time to rest... We must be on the road by nightfall."

"Who needs to... before an execution?" a sinister voice belonging to a woman named Katja whispered to a woman who couldn't hear her. *"She can rest by my... when it's done. I'll... her like I do you... until you join us."*

"Christian? Do you need anything?" Antoinette asked.

"His bag," Claire said from the direction where it sat, neatly tucked under a wooden chair that Brian Keet had found himself sitting on near the entryway to the house. *"A set of clothes,"* she called from the direction of his muddy pants. *"Another day to think,"* she added before finally piping down.

"Sister."

When Dusk pressed his ear to the Red World, he could perceive its shape, tangled, like a spider's web overlaid on the world, made of rich threads. He couldn't see it, but Saya had told him what it had looked like many years ago.

There were parts where it had broken. There were parts where the threads that represented the people were thin and the whispers were almost inaudible. There were parts where the threads were never to be undone: rich, rigid, and loud. There were paths everywhere; some roads were narrow, and others were wide; some had no outlet and others folded upon themselves like knots or roots. Finding the path forward was never a straight line; not all of the voices wanted to help him, and not all of them had the sanity to.

"Clothes," Dusk said after finding himself down another dead-end, leaning back on the edge of the bed, his muscles glistening in the artificial light. "Do you have any?"

Antoinette jumped at hearing someone other than herself talk. "I'll look in Mark's closet... see if he left anything behind, or maybe Arrah has some in her closet..." Antoinette suddenly remembered Albedo. *How could she have forgotten about him, even for a second?* "...I'll find some."

"Keep an eye on her brother... you weren't there when my nephew died... you didn't see her spiral..."

Some lives had mattered more than others; some were solidified in the Red World, like pillars in the afterlife, holding it up and keeping it taught, loud and crisp. It was around these pillars that the most threads wrapped around—a spike through a chaotic web—the arteries that seemed to keep it upright and living.

Other lives straddled the opposite end of the spectrum: threads that dangled, dead ends that would eventually rot away and fall into the nothingness below, slipping from people's minds altogether, quietly withering, desperately wanting to matter again, but without a single soul to vouch for their worth or relevance, or too young to know how to hold on.

A minute later, Antoinette placed her hand on Dusk's shoulder and watched his eyes roll open, looking vacantly past her for a moment, then finally focusing on her, regaining some humanity as he did.

She carried an ornate suit in her arms which she began to fit over the blacksmith. A pristine white shirt with lace cuffs and a high collar paired well with a maroon coat. An ornate golden stitch trimmed the coat with two triangles at the bottom which hung before his thighs. Antoinette wrapped her arms around his neck, swinging a matching golden ascot over it. His pants were thin and sharp, practically made for his body, and the shoes bore golden aglets that screamed bespoke.

"Wow," Antoinette and Claire said in unison.

"It's very..." he began.

"Charming," Antoinette said, blushing as his eyes fixed on her.

"*Elegant,*" Claire added, as he stood up taller.

"*It's alright,*" another voice chimed in playfully from the Red World, "*but nothing like the coat I made for you.*"

"It's uncomfortable, isn't it?" Antoinette watched him stand taller.

"That might be why he left it," Dusk continued, looking at himself. He hadn't dressed like this in years, not since the ball at the House of Dusk. It felt unnatural to see himself like this again. Every day for a century he'd seen his face age in the reflection of a gleaming blade in his shop.

"I could get you something else," Antoinette said, watching his eyes measure the stranger in the mirror.

A day ago he was a blacksmith: hardened, old, and quiet. Today he was a young stranger, a vain stranger who looked back at him, daring him to be more. "It's fine," he said with a bleak smile, finally turning to look at Antoinette. "How else would I be fit to stand by your side?"

She stood before him the picture of beauty. A long black dress with dark red accents hugged a crimson bodice and filled out beneath her hips. Her dark satin gloves raced up her arms, almost ensnaring the crimson choker that she wore. Her hair was down, neatly brushed, falling just below her exposed clavicle. "How do *I* look?" She asked, wishing the girly coyness would subside.

He measured her up and down, then turned to look at the vanity, messy with various makeups and perfumes, righted after their night together. He opened the top middle drawer unapologetically, then the right drawer, and finally the left, finding what he was after. "I think it will look better up," he said, handing her a pair of hair pins which clinked, heavy in her out-stretched hand.

Antoinette looked at the metal hair pins. They didn't match the dress, they didn't match his outfit, but they were long and sharp and they matched the occasion. "I think you're right," she said, nervously twisting her hair around and inserting them into the bun in an x shape.

"Perfect," Dusk said, leaning forward to kiss her.

"Perfect," Antoinette sighed happily.

12

JUST AFTER THE SUN HAD SET, AN UNDERTAKER'S CHARIOT BEARING the sigil of the Evan Blood Coven arrived. Two black stallions stood at the helm, a driver clad in gray held their reigns, and Brian Keet stepped out of the house first, holding open the door for the pair.

As they rode, Dusk slept. His humanity had been cast aside, but his years of being a human still told him that night was a time to sleep, and the journey ahead would be a taxing one.

While he dreamt, Antoinette stroked his head upon her lap, unaware that the voices of the Red World flashed by, failing to cling to the former High Listener, diffusing into a garbled white noise that was as close to a respite as he could hope for.

For the first few minutes of the ride, Brian tried to make small talk with them. He wanted to be a Listener that could rise in its ranks like the man before him.

"What a fool you are," Claire whispered to the ether, the only one paying attention to Brian, her voice emanating from the space next to his body in the four-person carriage.

After Antoinette didn't engage, Brian tried his hand at changing the topic, aware that Dusk couldn't hear him without her interpreting. "How is he alive...?" Brian tried to recall exactly what other scribes had written about him.

"Did anyone claim he was dead?" Antoinette thought out loud, wondering if perhaps his accompaniment might catch Jason off guard.

"Not exactly," Brian said, "but it's strange. And Master Castille isn't keen on strange."

"We're aware," she rubbed her thumb against her forefinger, turning to watch the scenery change before her eyes.

"Can I ask..." Brian raised his brows hopefully and, absent a *no*, continued, "...who Turned you?"

"Me?" Antoinette continued looking out the window.

"You... and Lord Dusk. It isn't in the ledger."

"The ledger?"

Brian paused, his eyes shifting nervously. "We keep a ledger now... a lineage of who Turned whom. Perhaps it's not as old as you..." Brian felt the words spill out of his mouth before he could catch them, casting a sideways glare from the woman who could have very well been his sister, no older than thirty, and not the two-hundred-year-old vampire she was. "I didn't mean..."

"I know." Her smile relaxed. "Perhaps one day I'll tell you... but not today." She stroked Dusk's hair on her lap.

"And Lord Dusk? Who Turned him?"

"A monster."

"No one knows."

"No one... knows?"

"A stranger. An act of madness. On a night not unlike this one."

"A vampire who willingly bit a human... for no reason?" Brian scratched his head. "That doesn't make sense. Biting a human isn't something that's done on a whim."

"I agree and yet... years searching for him and nothing. No trace of the man who made my brother the monster others purport him to be."

"The monster... guidance turned him into..."

"It just doesn't make sense..."

"...Wake us when we arrive," Antoinette whispered, deliberately closing her eyes and bringing quiet to the carriage.

A COBBLESTONE ROAD TURNED INTO A DIRT ONE, THEN INTO HARDLY A
road at all. Tightly knit houses grew further and further spaced apart, and the
lights that illuminated the town were replaced by stars. Nearly two hundred
years ago the distanced had seemed greater. Antoinette had excitedly made
her way to a house Christian had erected for her in a place that seemed a
lifetime away, heartbroken when he wasn't there, heartbroken when a friend
revealed that last time she had seen him he'd been beside himself in tears.

Today, hours after their departure, hours into Antoinette's restless dreams
of the two boys she failed to save, and hours into the following day, the
farmers who rose before the cock crowed watched a familiar carriage stroll by
with an air of death they turned their eyes away from.

Four enduring wheels traveled past their fields and off a beaten path, aside
wayward oaks and towards a parcel encircled by a wrought iron gate. The axles
of the carriage bore the hypnotic crest that also adorned the carriage door:
a bat's wing with a single horn defiantly stiff, a symbol which drew looks of
contempt and disgust from the human onlookers.

The locals knew that there was something amiss about the Evan Blood
Manor that hid just behind the apex of the tallest hill. A row of staked iron
rods marked the boundary between where their harvests would flourish and
where they would flounder. A copse of trees thinned as the carriage climbed,
hearty and healthy at first, then bleak and lethargic, beckoning for the waste-
land of a courtyard the mansion called its own. The wheels stabilized as they
passed between the markers, eventually gliding over paved roads.

Four spires that had once promised to hold the falling sky had long since
been reduced to two, but the fortress that a thousand villagers were forced to
build still remained. Four walls, as tall as four roads wrapped the skeleton of
the castle tightly, and with each rotation of the axle, the castle came into focus
and the Red World erupted.

"*He returns.*"

"*A murderer.*"

"*Here to betray... one who trusts you?*"

"How could you?"

"Exciting. Exciting."

"I shouldn't have killed her."

"Who are they?"

"What happened?"

"Not fair."

A tidal wave of voices knocked against Dusk's ears and woke him from his slumber. He tried to steady his hands while Brian and Antoinette drew the velvet curtains to look outside.

The sunrise was upon them and the rainfall had broken. Somehow the absence of a storm made the air feel even more ominous than before. The rays of sunlight chased the visitors into the Coven and a flurry of armed guards, human for the most part, operated the main gate and bid the carriage in.

Dusk reeled from the voices, sitting up uneasily, Antoinette locking her fingers with his. *"Steady yourself, brother,"* Claire said crisply. *"Focus on my voice."* He took in a deep breath, feeling the panic turn to unease, attempting to calm himself, reaching for a coin in his pocket, careful not to crush it.

"It's worse now."

"I know brother. Focus on my voice. Remember the massacre at Red Crescent. It overwhelmed you at first too."

At the edge of the main entrance, the carriage began to slow, but before it could stop, the door was flung open and another member of the Coven, another foot soldier in Jason Castille's army, reached for and took Antoinette by both her arms, her hand unlinking with his as she was swept towards the front door. "Christian!"

"Pomp and circumstance, brother. He loves his entrances."

There was no need for the theatrics; she had come willingly. But Jason Castille had always enjoyed making a game of his conquests. The slaves had learned of it shortly after he'd arrived, and Dusk knew it all too well. Even his own sentencing had felt like a production.

Antoinette attempted to regain her footing as she was pulled, but the awkward way in which they walked made her unable to do so. She let herself be half-carried, half-jostled, down an imposing hallway to the inner sanctum lined with portraits.

"After you," Brian mutely said to a Dusk who took the initiative without the invitation.

He followed behind quietly, walking on his own accord, keeping his arms at his side, taking in the all-too-familiar scenery of the narrow entryway, lined with portraits as far as the eye could see.

"The Hall of Houses," Claire said, leading him forward. *"That's what they call this now... not like we knew it. Not like Jason would have left it as it was... Too many memories."* Claire headed towards Antoinette as she reached the end of the hall.

She was right. Under the rule of Bruce, before Jason's coup d'état, the hall had been lined with paintings of members of the Coven. Those paintings were gone now. Most of those vampires were gone now. Instead, what was present now were paintings that were an homage to Jason's origins or portraits of Heads of Houses.

Dusk looked down the long row of portraits, in various shapes, dimensions, frames, styles, and colors. It was the vomited design of an overzealous grandfather whose pride and joy were the achievements he was too weak to undertake himself. He could imagine that somewhere between the spires of the Coven there was a map with tiny pins marking the location of each House, not unlike one a king might have, to see the bounds of their territory, or at least what they purported their territory to be.

It must have been easy now: Dusk and Bruce conquered most of the Covens and fought the hard battles. The occasional skirmish was all Jason needed to quell, and he had more than enough allies to do so.

Near the end of the hall, Antoinette attempted to compose herself while Dusk made his way forward.

The smiles in the portraits were sparse. At least three out of every four carried a thick-brushed red X across the face. As he walked down the hallway, the ratio grew and the number of portraits without a red X were fewer.

"The older the House, the lower the chance they survived," Claire said. *"Ant's is the oldest now."*

In the falling light of the candles at the end of the hall, a ladder blocked the way forward and Dusk caught up to Antoinette and spied his own portrait, the spitting image of the version of himself that stood in this moment, frozen in his twenty-something year.old state, his full name on a plaque beneath the painting, and beneath that, the word *Fallen*. A red X was prominently slathered across his face.

"*Fallen?*" Claire blurted out, still unsure of what her brother would do. "*I wonder if that gave him a chuckle?*"

"Move your ladder!" One of the men hollered at an old man who blocked the narrow path forward, ascending a ladder perpendicular to the hall, only a few feet from the double doors at the end. "We have orders."

"And I have orders too," the old man said with a sigh. He climbed the ladder hesitantly, with no haste, an accentuated hunched back shaping his outline. "I'm sorry Lady Antoinette... but they come straight from the horse's mouth." The old man avoided her living gaze and instead stepped up the ladder, face-to-face with a painting of her, the last one without a red X before the end of the hallway.

"Don't be... Ilovo," Antoinette said nervously, looking up at the painting of herself. Her face sat in an ornate oval, the same face, encumbered by an out-of-place hairstyle, framed in bronze. The Antoinette of the past looked down at her future self with pride and hope, while the one below looked up with disappointment and fear.

The old man, Ilovo, reached for the bowl atop the three-step ladder as one of the men took an angry step around it, hugging the wall as he did. He picked up the ladder and rotated it with Ilovo still on it. He reeled at being carried, holding the bowl steady as he was placed back down, now parallel with the hallway. He held the small bowl while one of the other men took two steps forward and knocked forcefully on the doors that led to the Great Ballroom.

The bowl held within it red ink, and as the ink settled from the jostle, he withdrew a thick calligraphy brush from his inner pocket. "The House of Schofield... is no more," he eulogized, looking to the woman whose portrait was surrounded by Fallen Houses.

"*Kill yourself.*"

He stirred the ink in the bowl and Antoinette clasped his ankle to stop him. "Ilovo, wait. That's not true. My House still stands. I have a trial, Ilovo. I'm here for my trial," she said as a ridge of fear rippled over her skin.

"*The trial is already decided brother. Tread cautiously.*"

The old man waited for the echo of the knocks to dissipate. "I'm sorry Lady Antoinette... these are my orders," he continued stirring the ink, slathering it onto the brush as the guards took Antoinette's hand from his ankle and urged her towards the opening doors.

"Hold off," Dusk said from a few steps back. "The House of Schofield lives on. I have come to stand by her side... to support the Head of the House."

The old man held the paintbrush an inch from the portrait and turned slowly to look down at the voice that came from the ghost in the hallway, illuminated by the dying light of the candles. *Surely it must have been a ghost, for the man who spoke was long thought dead.* "It can't be...?"

"Or would you continue? Do you doubt the former Head of the House of Dusk?"

The old man squinted and looked to him with his gaunt eyes, then past him, to the wall behind where Dusk's portrait had been hung and his face crossed out. He froze to see that face standing in his presence. A drop of paint fell onto the pristine floor below. His old eyes went wide, sinking into his weathered face as he looked down to the former friend he had betrayed. A withered finger reached nervously for a small scar on his own neck, nearly faded, but feeling more pronounced than ever in the presence of this man.

"No, Master Dusk. I will wait to see what comes of this," the old man said humbly, setting down his paintbrush and descending from the ladder, struggling to remember how tall he'd felt standing by his side. As the blacksmith passed him, Ilovo felt a breath of life fill his soul for the first time in over a hundred years.

13

JASON CASTILLE, HEAD OF THE EVAN BLOOD COVEN, STOOD AT the center of the split-level ballroom beyond the double doors from the Hall of Houses, watching as dozens of his people fanned out and around him, corralling Antoinette to the center and leaving Dusk to stand just behind her.

The man who stood before them, un-aged and frozen in his thirty-something-year-old state wore a manicured blonde bush atop his head and a helter-skelter smile that plummeted towards his left dimple. Ornate purple robes reflected his inflated sense of opulence.

He looked past Antoinette and directly to the blacksmith, raising his head higher, puffing out his chest more, standing only a hair taller than them, stroking the place where a mustache could have been.

"Silence." He commanded with a snap as those around him began to whisper upon seeing Dusk, an unexpected addition. Those who knew of him had begun to tell those who didn't, but the room quieted at Jason's command.

Jason's eyes, thin slits of a somber blue, couldn't contain his excitement at seeing the former Head of the House of Dusk standing in his presence again; after all, the last time that Dusk had set foot in the Evan Blood Coven, he had been forced to bend the knee.

"Well, well, well..." Jason began, making his way forward, not unlike how a suitor might inspect a prospective bride, the circle getting tighter. His nose sniffed the air around him, taking in the musk that was still etched in his skin from standing over a forge for years on end. Dusk's body might not have aged a single day, but his face, even behind its newfound youth, still told a story of suffering. Jason's mouth unzipped, "The prodigal son returns." His ragtag Coven sneered in unison, half unsure of why, mirroring the twisted delight of their leader.

"*Slit his throat!*" a voice screamed from beyond the Divide, unclear who it was referring to.

"Many thought you dead... but not me..." Jason Castille said with a grimace. "A vampire like you doesn't go out in a whisper... you go out with a bang. Or was it a series of bangs?" A wicked smile that few had been around long enough to interpret graced his face. "I'm finally getting around to rebuilding atop the ruins you left for me... and after all I offered you." He paused, returning to his initial spot. "But is the shoe finally on the other foot for the last member of Bruce's inner circle? The once-revered High Listener?"

Dusk mustered an empty smile.

The room was mostly unaware, but once upon a time, it had been Dusk who had cast a judgment upon this man from a position of power. Once upon a time, the roles had been reversed, and it was Jason Castille who was staring down great odds. The former Head of the Coven had underestimated him, and in that window he had found allies, puppets that positioned him for this role, to carve out a new future where he would rise.

"As I recall, Bruce gave you an opportunity then."

"As you'll recall... I made the most of it." He brushed his palm against his sash, as though shining the fabric emblem of the Evan Blood Coven. "And I believe I returned the favor... along with three slaves and one messenger... that you returned... damaged." Jason looked beyond Dusk to the old man who'd held the paintbrush, to Ilovo, who cowered behind the masses, feeling smaller than ever, his left leg throbbing.

For the second time in two hundred years, the two men stood before each other, amidst the same conditions, positions reversed. The irony of the situation wasn't lost on Dusk. The thrill wasn't lost on Jason. The last time, Dusk had escaped only by the intervention of others who wagered on two horses. His eyes scanned the room, unsure if there were any allies left.

"And you..." Jason said, turning to Antoinette. "So gracious. Saving us the time. Saving us the resources. Saving us the chase." He looked at Dusk as he added this sentence, taking in a deep breath. "As a gesture... we won't drag it on. Despite the formality it will be quick."

"We've come to plead our case," Antoinette's voice finally interrupted, carving through his judgment as others in the circle began to snicker. Her chin was high, nobility proliferating, shades of her mother peeking through her fear as she braced herself for the penetrating glare he'd set on Dusk to fall on her, but it didn't come.

"I see..." Jason clapped, like a master would for a dog, and the circle of his followers parted. The empty space created a clearing which led to a prepared dining room table that looked like it could seat fifty. "I suppose we can hear it then..." Jason confidently showed his back to Dusk and led the way, taking his seat at the head of the table, inviting his two guests to join him on one side.

"He's too calm," Claire fought through the voices of the Red World to relay the message.

As the couple moved forward, Dusk's eyes measured the room, searching through the masses while the cult-like mob closed the space behind, ushering the group towards their final meal.

"The Elders are on the second floor."

Dusk's eyes shot up. From the second level balcony, from the same place where Bruce Alazar, former Head of the Evan Blood Coven had cast judgment upon Jason Castille, did the swaying brown robes of the Elders give away their positions. His eyes searched through the Elders, measuring each one of the faces that looked down, finally finding the one who'd helped him so long ago, locking eyes with his. They shared a glance for a moment before the Elder broke the gaze.

"They think you've come to die."

"Come come..." Jason insisted, watching as Antoinette and Dusk each took a seat at the ornately decorated dining table. Antoinette sat beside Jason, and Dusk sat one chair further down. The group set upon this three-stair stage as members from the Coven gawked and awed, watching as though a play were unfolding, hanging onto every word.

"*Something's wrong... I'll find out what.*"

"Now I *am* curious..." Jason began, "what would bring *you* out of hiding and into my home?" Again he ignored Antoinette even though she sat beside him. He also paid little mind to the brown-robed men who descended from the upper level to take some of the available seats, listening to the discourse, intrigued.

"I think there was a misunderstanding..." Antoinette broke the silence again, seeing the expressionless stare on Dusk's face as he Listened for what they weren't telling him, a feat that was harder to do when no one but Claire knew what he was thinking, "...Lord Jason."

The Red World was vast, and Christian Nikolai Dusk had an ally that made accessing the world of the dead easier, but just because he could Listen, didn't mean he knew everything. The dead were ever present, but they weren't encyclopedias to be looked up. Some witnessed events, some remembered them, others didn't. Everyone who had ever lived had slipped into the Red World, but not everyone remained. Just because he could access the world of the dead didn't mean he was omniscient.

Before Antoinette was able to elaborate on the misunderstanding, the seat across from her, immediately beside Jason, shifted, and a somber girl stepped into the artificial light. "Orpha..." Jason smiled as she sat. "So glad you could join us."

Orpha deReville donned a velveteen short-sleeved dress that emphasized the amputated arm that Antoinette had sliced off while under Albedo's command. Antoinette looked away as a bandaged stump shied away from her former housemate, attached to yet another puppet in Jason's theater production of *Schofield*.

Orpha took one look at Antoinette and cowered, leaning towards Jason in her seat for protection. "She won't hurt you anymore..." Jason spoke to her like a little child, kissing her forehead, bringing her chair closer to his.

"*But* he *might*," Claire added with disgust.

The subtext of the price for refuge was not lost on the whimsical deviant that was Orpha. Her thigh sat excitedly beneath his clammy hand as she attempted, with difficulty, to handle the steak that had been brought out with her non-dominant hand.

Jason stroked Orpha like a pet as his glass was filled with dark red liquor, matching the rare steaks on the plates before them. "We're waiting on one more... but we can get started. Now, what were you saying, my dear?" His eyes looked from the silent Dusk to Antoinette.

The Red World grew louder before the former High Listener. The voices recounted the numerous glasses of blood wine that had been served, the countless appeals, and the singularly cruel fate Jason had cast at the very table they sat, on the very stage they played. Not one vampire put on trial had left without a death sentence. Antoinette didn't know this, but she was the only one. It was why the Coven gathered. They were hungry for something else and like it always did, the Red World spectated, eager to see if anything would be different this time.

Empowered by the shell of her protector who searched for an answer in the silence, Antoinette did as they had planned, feeling the futility with each rehearsed word. "There has been a misunderstanding about what happened, My Lord." Jason beckoned with his fork in a circular motion, sipping the blood wine in his chalice as a bandaged human refilled it. "The House of Schofield has not Fallen. Christian has joined my House and..." She pulled out a small slip of paper, scrawled in Dusk's handwriting, "As stated in the House Charter... *Houses will find another member within thirty days.*" She gulped. She hadn't had to rehearse line deliveries since her mother had forced her to as a child. "And I was able to do just that." Her hand wrapped around Dusk's and jarred him out of his trance.

"Is this true *Christian*?" Jason asked childishly. "Have you, former Head of the House of Dusk, joined the House of Schofield?"

"I have," Dusk repeated curtly.

The grin that began to form on Jason's face couldn't have grown more taught if he had used his hands to stretch it himself. It began with a curl, and with each moment became more and more sinister. "Tragic... the demise of the House of Dusk. You founded it, built it up into one of the greatest houses under my Charter and then... poof... gone. I didn't believe it at first..." He slid a piece of meat between his teeth, chewing as he spoke, "I thought it a ploy, so I had someone check up on you periodically until you finally settled into your miserable little shop. Everything crashed down around you after your House fell, didn't it? Even your housemates scattered to the wind," he chuckled and everyone laughed. "Even Ilovo came crawling back to us like the worm he is." Dusk couldn't see the old man who'd held the paintbrush hang his head in shame, far removed from the onlookers, all by himself in the entryway. "You're a thinker Christian, like me, and I don't care much for other thinkers. After your House fell, I amended the House Charter. The House of Dusk may have escaped its punishment on a technicality, but no more. A House of one, is a House Fallen. End of Story."

14

T HE ONLY SOUNDS THAT EMERGED IN THE MOMENTS FOLLOWING
Jason's statement came from the cutlery, metal on glass, as Jason devoured
the steak the same way he had devoured their hopes. Antoinette sat
frozen in fear and Dusk frozen in thought.

*"You can kill him brother. Take Antoinette's hair pins. Or take the knife. You
planned for this."*

Each second felt like an eternity. Dusk shook his head lightly. Some might
have thought it was to free himself from his own thoughts, but it was a silent
response to his sister.

"What a meal!" Jason professed as others nodded and whispered in agreement.
"Some might even say fit for a final meal." A human approached, recognizable
to Dusk through the silence as their lips moved. They took Jason's plate, then
Antoinette's and Dusk's, neither having a bite taken from them. "I will say
though... I do commend your knowledge about *my* Charter. After you left... I
became much more of a thinker too... You see, some rumors started circulating.
Nasty rumors. Dangerous rumors about another loophole, also patched."

Antoinette noticed that the blood wine inside the chalice before her was beginning to ripple. Dusk was rapping his fingers underneath the table. *"He's a politician brother... we planned for this possibility... stay calm..."*

"According to the Evan Blood Charter, leniency will be granted for first-time offenders of the Coven." His crisp words punched the air. "Or has that changed too?"

Jason tilted his head back and forth until it popped. All eyes were fixed: the Elders watched the expression of Jason and admired the tenacity of Dusk; Orpha looked to her savior, and Antoinette to hers; the mob watched them all in a bated silence. If it could have gotten quieter before his response, this was the time. "How sad... a Listener operating on antiquated information. That section has *also* been removed from the Evan Blood Charter," he scoffed. "Honestly... is this how you ran your House of slaves and vagabonds? You spin a good yarn, I'll give you that, but leniency considering the crimes? I could forgive her for not adding a vampire she Turned to the Lineage Ledger in a timely manner... whatever his name is...?"

"Albedo," a voice squawked from a distant part of the Red World.

"...But leniency for maiming her housemate? Leniency for killing another? Leniency for her House Falling... Her crimes are many and your argument is leniency? Sad. Bruce didn't offer my brethren leniency." The room chuckled as Antoinette reached under the table for Christian's hand.

"He offered them a choice," Dusk's eyes narrowed.

"Born from hubris or weakness... a mistake that doesn't warrant repeating." Jason clicked his tongue. "You know Christian... a little birdie told me back when you were a human, you were just as weak." He scratched his chin. "Was it Claire? Was that your sister's name? What were her last words? What words haunt you? You couldn't save her either, right?"

"Go to hell!" Claire growled, not noticing the subtle change in her brother's face.

"Nothing to say? Nothing to add? No statement of fact...?" Jason egged on as Dusk reached into his coat. Everyone tensed up hastily, on edge, until he withdrew a small book that calmed all their fears.

Dusk smiled slightly as they jumped. "Are you afraid of me?" He placed a leather-bound book on the table, moving his glass out of the way so he had enough space to open it. His smile broadened as he looked down to everyone settling. "You're right to be."

The mood changed instantly; Jason's smile was stripped from his face, and even Antoinette didn't know how to react to that statement. It was like something had snapped inside of him. But to him, it was like something had reignited, something that she hadn't ever seen before: a part of him he bred in preparation for getting revenge on her husband, Michael, so many years ago.

Antoinette looked down at the book, then whispered in his ear, "Christian?"

From the corner of the room, Ilovo's eyes twinkled as his back straightened, hand on his hip, reaching for a small knife he always carried with him. His Master was returning. Not the shell of a man who had walked in minutes ago, but the Master he had served as Head of the House of Dusk. A beam of pride was on his face as he recalled serving under him, a tinge of regret at his betrayal, and a small hope for an opportunity at redemption.

Dusk's gaze narrowed on Jason, now slightly more serious. "Bruce ruled with an iron fist and yours has always been a rule by the letter of the law—your law."

"I beat Bruce at his own game... you think you can beat me at mine?"

"I have here a copy of the original Charter, drafted under Exodus Evan Blood, which states..." He opened the book's pages, tired and brittle, old and delicate, smeared and all-knowing, "...that..."

"You said it once already Christian." Jason shook his head aghast, feeling a bit silly for having been remotely jarred by his statement. "'Leniency to first time offenders,' and I said that that had been done away with. The fact that you have a copy of the original Charter means nothing. Like you, it's outdated."

A few laughed.

"That..." Dusk continued, ignoring his words, "...a change in the Charter can only be made by the rightful Head of the Evan Blood Coven." Jason smiled and clapped his hands; Orpha nearly fell onto his lap as he snorted, the Coven joining him in a laugh. "The Charter states that the Head of the Evan Blood Coven can only be one of two people: Exodus Evan Blood, founder, or a rightful Heir." Jason smiled at him for a moment before Dusk's eyes looked up at him. "You usurped your place as Head of the Coven. You are not allowed to make any changes to the original Charter, including the clause about leniency."

Jason's smile cracked and he quickly rose from his seat. "That's absurd," he chuckled. "I am the Head of the Coven. Everyone knows that. The Elders acknowledge it. I can do what I want."

The Elders weren't so entertained. The bravest among the five old men spoke out first. "The High Listener is *technically* correct."

"Technically." The others nodded, reaching for the book which Dusk handed off to them.

"Perhaps we should revisit this."

"Is this not our role?" another said.

"A valid claim."

With each Elder's comments, Jason's smile grew increasingly contorted. "I am the Head of the Evan Blood Coven! My changes supersede the old laws."

"But not by right, My Lord," boomed another Elder. "The original Charter is maintained by us... appeals to the laws fall under our purview."

Jason, upon his stage, with the Coven of onlookers below, was shaken. He bent over slightly, leaning against the table slowly, contemplating his next move, keeping his eyes on Dusk the entire time, ignoring the relief that washed over Antoinette. "Don't think she will get off this easy. Regardless, crimes were committed. Crimes!" He jabbed his index finger into the table. "Even *if* leniency is granted, I will still hold a trial." Jason stood back up. "Or is that too outside my scope?" He spat at the Elders. "And you! You will be put on trial too Christian. I will hold you accountable for your crimes. Don't think you will both get off scot-free."

"And what is my crime?" Dusk asked as Antoinette found herself silent, reaching from the empty goblet before her to the full one in front of Dusk. "I warn you against putting me on trial, you don't know the things that I know."

"Clearly you don't know everything." Jason pushed off the table and lunged across the empty space. He launched a blow against Dusk, who dodged in an effortless manner, making Jason stumble forward awkwardly.

Antoinette took a step back while Orpha scurried to a safe distance beside the onlookers. She had never seen Dusk fight, but at a glance, he didn't look any different. "Lucky dodge." Jason composed himself, fixing his sash before he swung again, this time colliding with Dusk's closed fist.

Two sets of knuckles met in midair and Jason's hand folded as it met Dusk's.

The Head of the Evan Blood Coven let out a yelp and sucked in air through his teeth.

The room grew quiet.

The Red World hushed too.

"Did you forget what I used to look like? Don't let this body deceive you," Dusk whispered as he puffed out his chest, his head sitting prouder atop his borrowed suit, gold accents from the trim catching the light with pride. "I once stood beside Bruce Alazar."

Jason's eyes bore into Dusk angrily, not into the man that was before him today, but the one that he had let scurry off so many years ago. This version of him was not the mammoth who once stood proudly in his House, nor was he the frail purveyor of reason he purported to be. His physique was not the same, but his body still remembered how to fight. His hand was shattered, just like Jason's, but the blacksmith didn't wince. There was still a warrior underneath his shell, but Jason had only ever been shell.

"You..." Jason snarled, shaking his fist.

"Enough of this!" an Elder called out, guards appearing who interposed themselves between Dusk and Jason. "A judgment without a trial will not be permitted this time. A trial will settle the allegations brought upon Antoinette Katherine Schofield."

"...You and her..." Jason wagged a finger, righting himself, "...joined at the hips..." He looked past the shield that was Dusk to Antoinette who stood behind him. "Today it will be your undoing..."

"Lord Jason!"

"Calm yourself, Armand," he said to the Elder. "A trial isn't complete without all the victims... Almir..." he called to a stranger in the crowd with a sinister twist, "bring out our special guest before we continue any further." A shuffle of footsteps echoed, loud at first, then more quietly as the standoff continued, as the guards relaxed their posture. "The stage is set for a trial... so a trial we shall have... but not before one more joins us."

The first set of footsteps hurried back, then behind these, another approached.

"No..." Claire whispered in awe before the circle broke, before the second pair of feet took its place just inside the circle. *"How is this possible..."*

The footsteps belonged to a man who looked from Dusk to Antoinette. The black of his eyes was muted, as though it had been drained, and a hollow shell of a man, pale and weak, aged just like the Elders, with spilling white hair stepped forward defiantly. His frizzled hair attempted to cover up his face, old and withered, almost skeletal. "I've waited for the day, wife."

Her eyes narrowed on the man. In her mind the puzzle pieces of his appearance assembled as he spoke. She tried to take another step back, but was against a wall now.

Jason wrapped an arm around the man, "Michael... so nice of you to join us."

Antoinette's gaze shifted from Dusk, who balled his hand in a fist, to Michael, the same man that Antoinette had Turned, the husband who had tortured her, the one who had been responsible for the death of their child.

She didn't understand it. "How...?" *How are you alive? Didn't Christian kill you?*

15

"T*HERE'S TOO MANY OF THEM*," CLAIRE WHISPERED. "*YOU WON'T reach him before they get you.*" She measured Dusk's stare, for the first time in a long time, a drop of emotion turning into an ocean of hate.

"You must know Michael Escoté," Jason said as Michael looked on, trying to stand a little taller, avoiding Dusk's gaze. "You three grew up together... as I understand it?"

Antoinette tried to convince herself that what she was experiencing was a dream. Even as she looked around the room that she knew to be within the Evan Blood Coven, she still found herself in a state of denial. Even having Dusk at her side didn't relax her.

"The tribunal is here... Antoinette Katherine Schofield... will you step forward?" Jason asked. "Will you stand before your...?" He scratched his chin. "Husband... as I recall... so that we can collect the facts which you seem so keen on presenting. Unless the Elders have any objections?" The old men quieted, and Antoinette stood frozen, trying to sink into the wall, to hide in

Dusk's shadows as her thoughts raced. "Earth to Antoinette...?" Jason joked. "Honestly. Michael, do something about that."

"Antoinette, step forward," Michael commanded with an air of defiance.

"*Bastard!*" Claire screamed.

A red ring flashed over Antoinette's eyes as those words left Michael's lips. She stepped forward mechanically, emerging from the shadow and standing beside Dusk. When the red ring faded, she cowered.

The Executive Command was absolute.

"No no no. Not again." She reeled, trying to find some composure, reaching for Dusk's arm, still tensed.

"Good." Jason clapped, turning to look to the circle of vampires behind him, almost as though searching for a rating of approval. Some of the Elders looked away, other members looked on with awe, and when Jason was satisfied, he continued. "Now then..." He took a step forward, as though standing in front of an imaginary podium. "Antoinette Katherine Schofield and Christian Nikolai Dusk, based on the attitudes that the two of you exhibit towards each other, I will combine this matter into a single trial. The outcomes may be different, but rest assured, I will keep things in accordance with the Evan Blood Charter." He sneered at the Elders while Antoinette tried to slip nervously behind him. "Antoinette, if you continue to hide, we may be forced to command you again."

The members of Evan Blood crowded forward for a better vantage point, including Brian Keet and Ilovo. "I'll start with you, Christian. For attempted murder against a fellow vampire, Michael Escoté, Christian Nikolai Dusk, how do you plead?"

Dusk looked at Jason, realizing his plan: to get him for his past sins. Of course, he didn't know that Dusk had recently killed Albedo. "Does it matter?"

"*Kill yourself.*"

"Not really, no," Jason said. "Not when we have someone who can tell us how it happened. Michael?"

"*They're going to put you back in the Silver Cell,*" Claire added, as Michael began to speak. "*Be ready to blow out your ears if he knows.*"

"He blindsided me..." a hoarse Michael began, cowering from his own words, hiding a wicked smile in Jason's shadow, "...and when I awoke after he'd barged into my house, I was chained against a wall!" Dusk stood taller, prouder as Michael revealed the truth. "His minions said I would suffer. They said they wouldn't let me die... They threw me in a hole and left me to rot... him and his bastard servants... for over a hundred years!"

The crowd gasped.

"Disgusting, Christian. Not even the decency to kill him," Jason tsked. "You speak of leniency but this torture... it reeks of Bruce. Perhaps he tainted you too."

"He deserved suffering," Claire said pridefully. *"He deserves more."*

"He needs to pay for what he did to me!" Michael claimed before an interruption from another in the crowd.

"It wasn't him." The old man with the paintbrush stepped into the circle, coming to the forefront, standing in between the four members of the trial. "He didn't condemn you to that fate." Ilovo tried to right his back, tried to stand tall, but struggled all the while. His legs trembled. "I was there too. It was my idea."

"Ilovo? What are you saying?" Jason asked impertinently. "It was Christian who did this. It was Christian who did it! It was his House. He is responsible!" The rage on his face was building as he shook his broken fist.

Ilovo looked on with deep remorse. "When I served in the House of Dusk, my Master offered me everything. I had every opportunity to succeed... and when he confided in me that a man turned vampire had hurt a woman he cared for, Lady Antoinette, I saw the opportunity to repay him. Master Dusk did not condemn that man to that fate—it was I who did it. He only turned a blind eye to it." Jason's mouth began to salivate. "I take full responsibility."

"Ilovo," a sad whisper from the Red World echoed.

"You... will... be tried for this..." Jason said, raising his eyes with a fiery passion. "Our leniency Ilovo... and our patience for your screw ups has come and gone... there will be consequences if what you say is true. You could be executed for this."

Ilovo bowed his head nervously. "...It is the truth."

"Restrain him." A snarl could not hide Jason's rage as a guard stepped into the circle and grabbed Ilovo by his shirt collar. "I always knew you were pathetic..." Jason whispered in his ear, "...but I didn't think you were stupid too." The man made no attempt to fight or flee.

Michael tried to butt in. There was more to the story. "But...!"

"We have a crime, a criminal, and a judgment. Michael..." an Elder in a brown robe smacked his teeth. "Rejoice that you get any justice. Rarely does the Head of the Coven extend the rules of vampiric protection to a non-member."

"He still regrets it..." Claire whispered to Dusk as he watched the guard take Ilovo away, *"what happened that night."*

"I suppose we have to move on." Jason's eye twitched as he turned his attention to Antoinette. "Stand up," he commanded, and she did, fearing that he would have Michael issue the command if she didn't. "Antoinette Katherine Schofield, you are accused of the murder of a fellow housemate, Arrah Iona Roda, and the brutal disfigurement of another, Orpha deReville. What do you have to say for yourself?"

Antoinette looked to Dusk and gulped, "I... I didn't have a choice."

"Explain yourself," said one of the Elders, interjecting himself in the farce that was unfolding.

"Arrah and Orpha were about to kill a human. I saw an opportunity to save him. I bit him, and he commanded me to save him from them. Through that Executive Command I ended up killing Arrah and cutting off Orpha's arm."

"A vampire made me do it?" Jason scoffed. "A newly-Turned vampire, fearing for his life had enough wherewithal to issue you an Executive Command to brutalize people?" He chuckled. "That's your defense?" He looked at the crowd who mumbled at his summary. "In any case, let's ask the other party... Orpha deReville... step forward."

A hobbled Orpha stepped to Jason's left while Michael stood to his right. She grabbed at the stump of her shoulder. Jason put an arm around her, forcing her head into his armpit. "Orpha... tell us in your own words what happened..."

"Arrah and I were in my room... having some fun with a human when Antoinette came in and saw us..."

"Came in? Did you invite her in?" Jason asked the gathered court, measuring Antoinette and Dusk's reactions.

"No."

"No?" he mused. "Hmm... interesting. So, an uninvited Antoinette walked into your room... continue."

"Albedo... the human... he was bleeding..."

"Was he on his deathbed? Was he moments away from dying?"

"No. He was just bleeding..."

"Antoinette said you and Arrah were about to kill him. Is that true?"

"No," Orpha said a little more confidently. "We were just having some fun with him. We've done it before."

"And Antoinette has been fine with that? She's known and allowed it to happen under her roof? In her House?"

"Yes!" Orpha nodded.

"And things turned sideways when Antoinette barged in?"

"Yes!"

"You had it under control until then, right?"

"Exactly."

"Curious." Jason stroked his chin. "So..."

"Enough of this," an Elder interjected. "To what end do you drag this out? Arrah's death occurred. Antoinette does not deny it, nor does she deny having a hand in it."

"To what end...?" Jason asked with a feigned insult, taking a step forward, still out of Dusk's reach. "To make her understand." He pointed to Antoinette. "To make them both understand... all they needed to do was stay out of the picture. All they needed to do was stay out of sight from Evan Blood. We could have all coexisted if Antoinette hadn't murdered a fellow vampire, or if Christian hadn't been complicit in self-served justice, or if the two of them hadn't come here to try to best the Head of the Evan Blood Coven at his own game... but here we are... and as you say Armand, the facts are the facts. Ilovo will get his punishment, Christian has escaped his, but now it's time for hers."

"Death..." began one of the Elders.

"...is not something you will condone. I know. I know. And Arrah is dead. But Orpha is here and wronged. There must be *some* justice."

"*Brother...*"

"Orpha, you loved your arm. Didn't you?" She nodded woefully. "And Antoinette stole that from you. So, tell me, former member of the House of Schofield, what is something Antoinette loves? What has she revealed in the decades you have lived with her?"

Orpha's face twisted, just as it had when she had held Albedo against the headboard, blood spilling from his neck before Antoinette had Turned him. "Him." She pointed to Dusk. "She loves *him*."

Jason folded his arms childishly. "Well, I believe I have an equitable solution." Antoinette felt a cold shiver run down her body as Jason leaned over to Michael and whispered something in his ear, something that made his lips curl with delight. "Michael?" he asked gleefully.

"Blow out her ears brother!"

"I command you..." Michael began as Christian reached for the golden hairpins in Antoinette's bun, catching her eyes as he did, welling up with tears, "...Antoinette Katherine Escoté..."

"Run." Antoinette's eyes locked on Christian's for a moment as he reached for her hairpins, a ring of red in her eyes that caught his, that stopped him in his tracks. A ring of red that was mirrored in his eyes for an instant that forced him to bolt towards the door.

"Brother!"

Christian darted so quickly that no one realized. He flashed down the Hall of Houses, anger in his eyes, pain in his soul.

Run, she had instructed.

The Executive Command was absolute, and just like she had commanded him lifetimes ago, Christian Nikolai Dusk was powerless to do anything but obey.

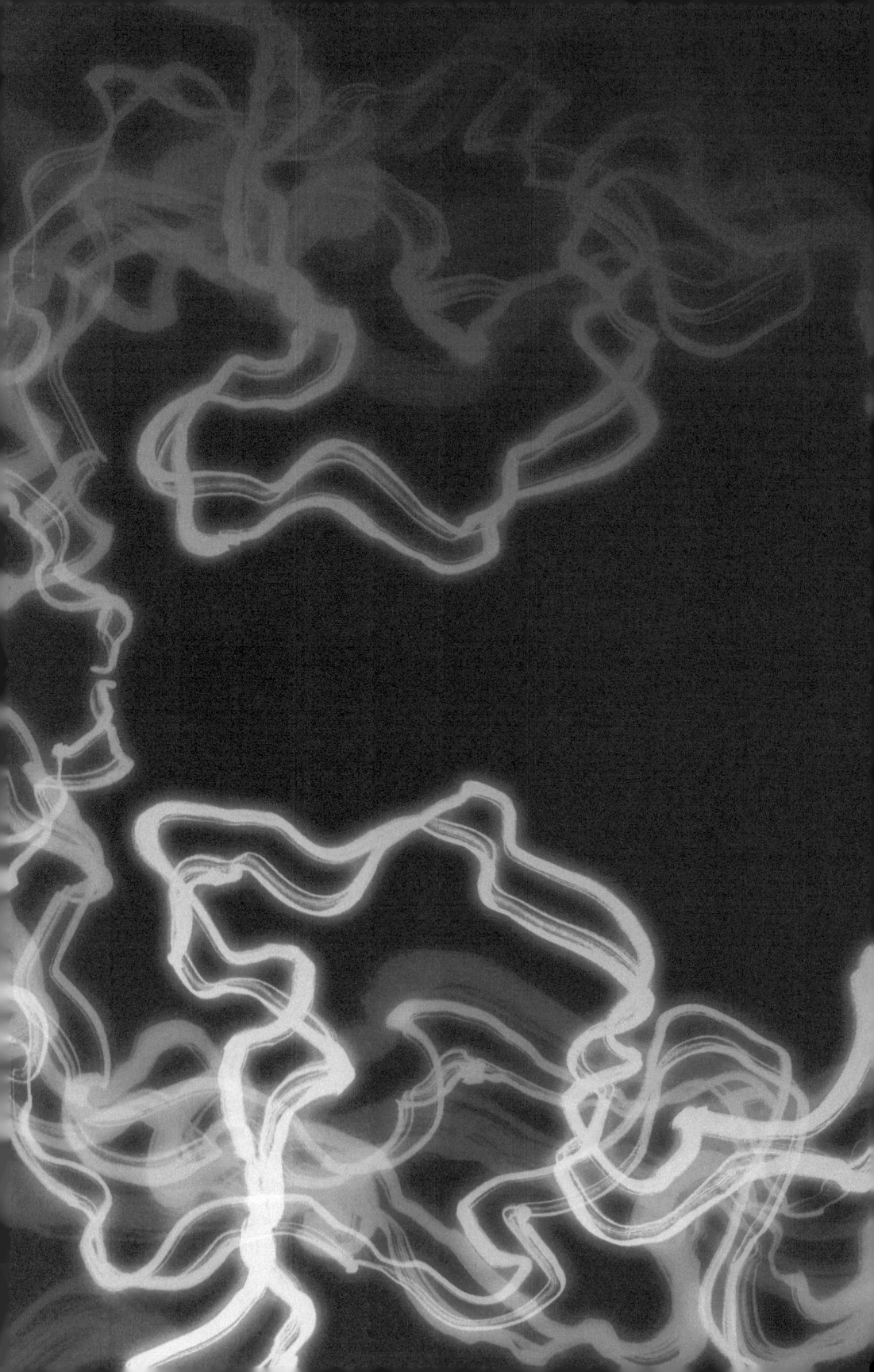

SECOND REGRET

"I should have confided in you."

-CLAIRE SEFIRA DUSK

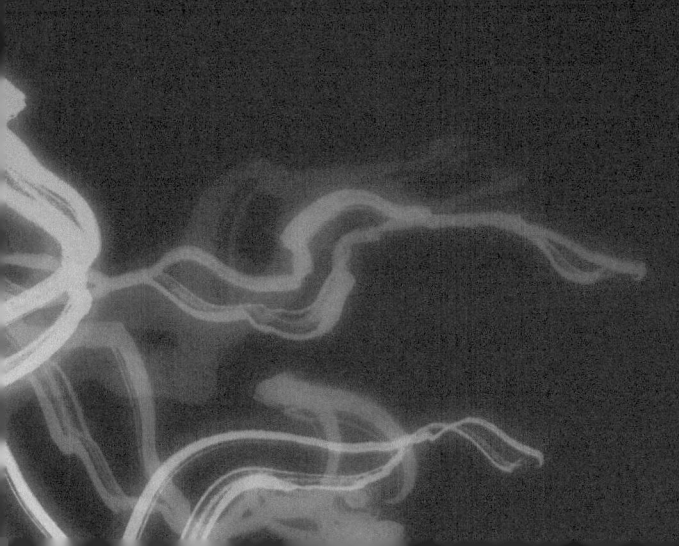

16

ONE HUNDRED NINETY-TWO YEARS AGO

"**Y**OU WILL ADDRESS ME AS MISS EVELYN OR MISS WEBSTER. While you are in the Schofield Manor you will not engage in any activities that bring shame to me, or my station. You are servants, not animals." A woman of thirty-five with elegant brown hair and thin lips walked with a powerful stride, forcing the eight-year-old twins, Claire and Christian, to hurry. "You're no longer with mommy and daddy. You are here to work, and only to work. If you are woken at midnight because a stone looks dirty, you will wake up and clean it. Dust doesn't take a day off. Neither do you. You do not stop until the work is finished." She stopped and looked down at Christian, the memory of his sobbing mother still fresh in his mind from the days before. "Did you hear me?" He nodded, hands behind his back as Claire put her arms around him. "Did you hear me?"

"Yes, Miss Webster," Claire said bravely.

"What do you have in your hands?" Christian shied away. "Show me boy," she hissed until he held out his right hand and opened it. There was a coin in his hand, a single grimy copper coin that Evelyn picked up with a curious eye, running a thumb over the face before flipping it over to see the shield on the reverse—helter-skelter, half-imprinted, impossibly jagged.

She dropped the coin to the floor, rubbing it into the dirt with the heel of her polished shoes. "You'll end up like your mother if you're caught with that." Christian watched as it fell, his hands weak as Evelyn took them, dusting them off with a handkerchief. "Honestly..." she scoffed, pulling him forward, "giving me problems already."

"Sorry," he cowered.

Claire picked up the coin when Evelyn wasn't looking, catching up to the pair and wrapping Christian's free hand around it when she took the lead.

"You are servants of the Schofield Family now. You are not slaves. There *is* a difference." Her ego grew. "It is a privilege to work in the Manor. Can you imagine the people you might meet?" Her dreams were loftier than theirs. "You will not speak unless spoken to, you will do the work assigned to you and you will, under no circumstances, speak with anyone who does not work in the Manor, not without them speaking directly to you first."

Evelyn paused as the cobblestone street continued.

A three-story building was before them, much larger than any of the houses around. The road bowed down into a servant's entrance in the basement beneath the Manor. Above the basement, the first floor was stone, stacked high and proud while the second was a combination of wood and towers. From afar it looked like the house had been built in two distinct phases. Still, the walls were clean, the exterior well maintained, and a tall tree climbed high against one side.

As Christian and Claire followed Evelyn down to the basement, to what they would learn to be the servant's floor, they approached a large, rounded door that swung on its hinges. A boy just older than the twins held it open and lowered his head as Evelyn passed, turning to measure Christian and Claire. His features were thin and pallid, and his clothes were muted shades of brown.

"You two will be silent, like the night..." Evelyn added, leading the pair down the main pathway that wrapped around the lower level.

The servant's level, like the first floor, was laid with cobblestones. While most of the moss was gone, the amount that remained between the stones made it pungent. It wasn't the type of smell that could be cleaned away; it was the kind that occurred when wood and stone married dirt and mud. Still, to Christian and Claire who had known struggle, having four walls and a roof, regardless of the smell, was a blessing against the elements.

"Come girlie," Evelyn said as they reached a door down the hallway. The door creaked and Evelyn shoved Claire inside quickly. "I'll be back for you."

"Claire!" Christian reached for his sister's hand but was denied her touch.

"The women sleep in this room, and the men in the one on the opposite side." She pulled the door behind her with an echoing bang, leaving Claire stupefied, continuing down the hall with Christian.

"*I* have a private room on the first floor. Only a few of the servants are live-in, like we are, but don't you go making a ruckus unless it's an emergency. I'll have one of the other boys show you around when they come finish their chores."

Christian nodded. "Yes ma'am."

"Yes Miss Webster."

"...Yes, Miss Webster."

Connected by the same corridor, but on opposite sides of the basement, the door to Christian's room was similar to Claire's. Just as abruptly as his sister, he was shoved inside and had the door pulled behind him, unsure of what fate awaited him. It was dark, but there was a window at ground level, low and long, open just a crack, airing out the room and letting in some natural light. There were four heaps of rags he rightly assumed to be beds.

When Christian opened the door to look around, he could hear the sniffles of his sister coming from the opposite side of the basement. He listened as Evelyn's footsteps dissipated, and, coin in hand, dared to leave his room when the footsteps of the matriarch sounded from the floor above. He crept through the basement hall as silently as he could, coming to her room and pushing the door open slowly.

"Claire?" he whispered, poking his head inside.

The two rooms were as different as possible. Claire's was bright and open. She had a proper bunk bed instead of a heap of rags to sleep on. The window in her room was larger with more light pouring in. A weathered dresser with a vanity and a chair were neatly placed in the corner with the most light. It was a proper bedroom.

Claire sat on the edge of the lower bed, and her body collided with his in a warm hug when he opened the door. "I wish mom could have come with us," she said sadly, holding her brother. "I wouldn't have minded sharing a bed."

"I know," Christian said, looking around the room, "but we'll get back to her...?"

"And we'll all be together again one day."

"Promise?"

"Promise!" Claire said with a weak smile.

"But... for now... it's just us..."

Claire shook her head roughly. "For always it's us. I won't leave you. No matter what happens. Family always sticks together."

"Promise?" He held out his pinky.

"Promise!" She locked her own and shook.

17

IN THE EVENINGS, EVELYN BARETT WEBSTER WOULD MAKE HER rounds. Christian shared a room with three other boys, Akolai, Chase, and Darius, who would all line up to be inspected. Unlike Christian and Claire who had joined as live-in servants only months ago, the other boys had lived at the Schofield Manor for three years.

When Evelyn would approach, everyone would line up to be inspected. The ones who did not meet her standards for cleanliness were forced to shoulder a makeshift shower courtesy of a large bucket with cold water. The first time that Evelyn had inspected his dirtied nails and thrust the shower atop him had been the worst. He hadn't stopped shivering until the following day. It was to their benefit to do their chores as cleanly as possible, even when the job itself wasn't.

Christian was assigned to maintain the bathrooms, often in the evening hours when the family would be winding down and preparing for bed. The Schofields would normally bathe in the morning, and he would be responsible for draining the tubs, wiping down and drying the floors, tending to the latrines

and keeping the facilities presentable for the following day. Some days, however, there would be a function the following morning, a formal gathering or
the occasional party, and the family would instead bathe in the afternoon or
evening. If Christian was lucky, the water wouldn't be too cold and, when it
was time for his chores, he would be able to take a lukewarm bath without
anyone noticing.

Claire, on the other hand, bathed daily after Evelyn. Unlike her brother,
she had been assigned as the personal servant for the sole daughter of Ivar and
Navara Schofield, Lady Antoinette. Each and every morning after bathing,
Claire would spend the entire day with her: shadowing her, assisting her, and
tending to her every need.

As the days turned to months, the schedules of the twins meant that the
only real time that they could be together was in the late evenings, after Claire
had readied Antoinette for bed, but before she needed to get ready herself.

Some days, she would tag along with Christian while he worked. "Do
you think mom will ever come visit?" Claire sat at the edge of the tub as
Christian scrubbed the floor. She wore a black dress and a lace apron. The
apron might have been white at some point, but the threads were more crème
now. It was an oversized dress meant for a woman that was pinched to fit her
smaller frame.

"I don't know if she's allowed," Christian said, scrubbing the cobblestones.

"Yeah... no one's come to visit any of us live-ins since we've been here...
Not Chase or Darius or Akolai either, right?"

"Yeah..."

"You ever wonder... Miss Evelyn is the only grown up live-in that lives here."

"Chase said it's cause we're all rejects... rejected by the orphanage or our
parents..." He shrugged.

"We weren't rejected. Mom chose to send us here so we could survive..."

"She still rejected us, right?"

Claire raised her hand and slapped him. It should have been harder than it
was. It was filled with more anger than translated, but she didn't want to hurt
him. "Being a grown up is doing hard things sometimes." Christian continued
working, ignoring the slap. "But she loved us... she made the best decision she
could... not like dad."

Christian looked up to see his sister's teary eyes. "Maybe he made the best decision he could too..."

The twins paused for a moment, hearing the faint sounds of footsteps approaching. They quickly stood up, straight and tall, arms at either side as they drew closer, steadily growing louder.

As the twins assumed, the footsteps belonged to Evelyn, whose eyes looked around the unfinished bathroom. She was normally stoic; she was normally cold; and in the months that the twins had been at the Schofield Manor, she had never looked shaken, but on this day, that changed.

She cleared her throat while standing in the master bedroom, not entering the bathroom where the twins stood tall. They waited to be dismissed, praised, struck, or, more likely, chastised. None of these came.

"There's been a development with Chase and Darius. Lord Ivar overheard that they had been... acting out of turn, and he was not pleased." She took a measured pause. "They have been... dismissed, as of this evening. You won't see them again."

"Right..." Claire said slowly.

"Okay," Christian said as Evelyn began to turn around, thinking about his two roommates.

"Miss Webster," Claire raised her voice nervously. "What does dismissed mean?"

"It means you won't be seeing them again, ever." she said, a little more confidently. "We shall see about replacing them, but for the time being, it will be all hands-on deck." She took a step forward, the tension in the air palpable. "I'll inform Akolai as well. He knew them longer."

"One more question, Miss Webster..." Normally she would have been furious. Normally she would have ripped them apart for one question, let alone two, but in the silence of the moment Claire found approval to ask. "Is Lord Ivar planning any trips? Lady Antoinette said that..."

"Yes. He'll be going out at the end of the month for a few weeks. He's very busy fighting for us. Remember..." she paused for an eerily long while, "...a servant should stay out of sight. You'd both do well to stay out of sight from Lord Ivar."

18

"THE ROOM SEEMS BIGGER WITHOUT THEM, DOESN'T IT, AKOLAI?" Often the punchline for the *dismissed* Chase and Darius, Akolai was a mute boy that had been a live-in servant in the Schofield Manor for several years. Though he would not return Christian's conversation in the traditional sense, Christian knew that he enjoyed being spoken to. Akolai would often return the sentiment with a smile or a gesture to communicate. This time it was a nod: solemn, worried, and pensive.

The room of four servant boys was down to two, and neither one of those who remained quite knew how to react. There was a bit of sadness, but there was also a bit of relief. Chase and Darius weren't bad, but they were often exhausting to be around, feeding off each other's energy, pulling pranks on one another that had resulted in an errant lashing coming down on all four of them on more than one occasion.

The settled silence needed a change, and it fell to the only one who could speak to do so. Christian rolled over on his rag heap to see Akolai actively listening from his own pile of clothes. "Claire's learning to read and write with Lady Antoinette. She's teaching me. I can try to teach you if you want. You might be able to say more if you can write."

Akolai's face beamed as he sat up.

Christian went over to a corner and picked at the wall, letting a small stone chip off. With the thin chip, he began to write on the stones. "This is the alphabet," he said after scratching the characters crudely onto the stones. "Claire taught me all the letters... You can't make the sounds, but you can hear them." Christian began to pronounce the sounds as his hand moved over each stone. "We can practice together... and Claire can help us even more. She gets to be around Lady Antoinette when she takes classes... and she's always been good at paying attention to that stuff. If Claire goes back into town to pick up books for Lady Antoinette... I can ask Miss Evelyn if we can go with her, if you want?"

Akolai's glow continued with an eager nod.

THE NEXT TIME CLAIRE MADE THE JOURNEY INTO TOWN, AKOLAI AND Christian accompanied her. The bookseller was at the edge of the marketplace, a forty-five-minute walk from the Schofield Manor. Few knew how to read more than a few identifying words, and fewer were those remarkable enough to read books for joy.

The bookshop blended into the space between lined houses, shoddy shops, and a house formerly used to worship the Old Gods. A dusty window with books piled high was the only identifying marker. If Claire hadn't known specifically where it was, the trio could have easily mistaken it for a messy house and walked right past it, but Evelyn had taken Claire once, and once was enough for her to memorize the route.

"Alex?" Claire called as the shop door opened, a small brass bell announcing their arrival. "Alex, it's Claire."

A young girl emerged from a corridor made of books. "Claire?" Her blonde hair twisted as it fell past her shoulders. In her hand was a book almost too thick to stretch her thumb and forefinger around. She smiled broadly as the trio walked in. "And...?" she asked, taking a step closer to Akolai and Christian.

"This is my brother, Christian."

"Alexandra Globaria. Pleasure. You can call me Alex."

"This is Akolai. He's a servant too, just like me and my brother."

"Pleasure."

"He's mute," Claire added as Akolai waved weakly.

"Fascinating." Alex looked him up and down. "Deaf too?" Akolai shook his head. "Strange... most mutes are also deaf. Were your vocal cords damaged?" Akolai looked to Claire and Christian for some help as the girl, about their age, questioned him, taking his slender jaw and lifting it up to the sky. "Did you hurt your throat as a baby?" Akolai shrugged. "Can you make any sounds?"

"You know..." Claire said, interrupting the one-sided inquisition and removing Alex's hand from Akolai's chin, "Akolai and Christian want to learn to read."

"With Lady Antoinette?"

"Uhmm..." Claire said sheepishly.

"Oh..." Alex said with raised brows. "Under the cover of night. Incognito. In secret," she added, seeing the confusion on their faces.

"So, we were wondering..." Christian and Akolai looked around the room as Claire talked.

"We can't let you borrow anything," a man called from the back. "Not without payment," his voice came closer. He was an older man with thick spectacles. He didn't introduce himself as Alex's father, Vincent Globaria, the owner of the shop, but he didn't need to. "We're not running a free library here..." He took one look at the three children, then to Alex, then rolled his eyes and returned to the back room.

"Sorry about my dad..." Alex said lowly. "Books aren't exactly flying off the shelves... Luckily, the soldiers pay us to write to their families. What do you got there?" Claire passed her a note and a handful of coins, perfectly round, perfectly imprinted. Alex looked at them for only an instant, then at the list of books, heading into the back. "Let's see... these three books for the Schofields... here's the payment," she told her father in the back room as Akolai bent his head over a book at the top of a heap, the cover displaying a sketch of a bird.

The book was dense. Akolai rubbed his palms against his pants and then opened it carefully. It was filled to the brim with words and with the occasional sketch of a bird's skeleton. He couldn't read a single word. Even the single-letter words like 'I' and 'A' were scrawled so awkwardly that he couldn't recognize them. Despite knowing the entire alphabet, it meant nothing.

Alex emerged with a pile of books which she handed to Christian. The books were well-worn, but polished leather bindings were a testament to their care. Her eyes turned to Akolai. "You can't read that," she said factually. "It's in cursive. It's not the sort of thing most people can read. Even nobles struggle with that."

"What's it about?" Christian asked, seeing the curiosity on Akolai's face.

"Ornology. That's the study of birds."

"Ornithology," her father corrected from the back room.

"That." Alex nodded. "It's like a... so you know there are different birds... each area of the world has different kinds of birds. This book is just the ones from a certain place. It's not really a story... it's called a catalogue." Alex scratched her head, trying to dumb it down.

"Like a list of birds and what they look like?"

"Yes! And how long their feathers are, yeah." Akolai closed the book slowly. "Yeah... not the most exciting thing in here. We also have novels... stories, you know? Fiction and non-fiction. Books about love or epic adventures, scripture, even some about the occult, like necromancers or vampires... and..."

"Aleeeeeeeeex?" Vincent called, stretching out the 'e' in her name.

"I should get back," Alex cleared her throat and fanned herself to work off the blush that had come on after her father had cut her off. "We're going to a book fair in a few days to try to sell some things, but those should keep the Schofield Manor busy for a little while."

"Ok, thanks," Claire said, patting the stack of books. "Thank you, Mr. Vincent," she called to the back.

"Right-o," the man responded. "Give my best to the Schofields and to Miss Webster... watch yourselves out there... some folks have been seeing strange things at night."

"Yes sir. Thank you, sir. Bye Alex," Claire said as Christian and Akolai waved and exited the shop, catching a devious wink from Alex.

The trio were a block down the street when Claire stopped Christian, "Claire?"

She picked up the books Christian was hauling one by one. "A-ha." Beneath the bottom two books she found a thin-leaf paperback. She grinned with a smile. "Look what Alex snuck in for us." She pulled out the book. On the cover was a picture of a bat. The text on each page was large and neatly printed. The words were short and easy to pronounce. "A book for you two. Take it. We'll sneak it back in next time."

Akolai reached forward, rubbing his hands against his pants again. He opened the book to the first page gingerly, careful not to crack the absent spine. There was a picture of a bat on it moving around in a circle. He stared at the animal, then looked down to the first four words like they would attack him. Christian and Claire stood over his shoulder, their eyes scanning the single sentence on the page: *I am a bat.*

"Follow my finger..." Christian highlighted the words, one by one, watching his friend's face as he did so. A nervous nod was the signal to continue to the next word. Akolai moved briskly from *I* to *am* to *a* then paused at *bat.* His eyes looked over the word for longer than the others. The voices of strangers on the street seemed to get louder as he tried to focus on the word, feeling his face flush as he thought. Claire's finger joined her brother's on the page, pointing at a cartoonish bat flying over a spire, then tapping on the bat twice.

Akolai's eyes went wide as he looked at the sentence again. *I am a bat*, he thought to himself as the twins watched him, one goofy grin turning into three. He patted his chest and flapped one of his hands eagerly.

"I am a bat?" Claire looked over at the book. "Did you read that?" Akolai nodded eagerly as Claire gave him an encouraging side-hug.

"He sure did!" Christian grinned, patting him on the back. "Should we go to the next page?"

19

Evelyn Barett Webster had forbade the other live-in servants from speaking with the Schofield family or their guests without invitation, but in the months that Claire had been assigned as the personal maid for Antoinette, a bond grew, and in the moments when Claire and Antoinette were alone, the two were more akin to friends than servant and Master.

"Your brother hasn't ever said a word to me, you know," a nine-year old Antoinette told Claire as the servant brushed her flowing black hair.

"Neither has Akolai," Claire said with a grin.

"That's different and you know it," Antoinette pouted, turning around to scold her with her vibrant green eyes.

"Christian isn't..."

"...isn't?" Antoinette turned from the small, padded bench in her room to face her.

"...chatty," Claire finally said, putting her hands in her white apron, pulling out a red string and spinning Antoinette back around to face the mirror. "He talks with me... but we're family... we're all we have."

"I guess... but it wouldn't kill him to say hi or smile... Even when I pass him in the hall... he just stands against the wall and looks down."

"Like Akolai?"

"I guess..."

"Or like I do when Lord Ivar or Lady Navara walk by?"

"I guess," Antoinette conceded with a sigh, picking up a quill at her desk, dipping it into the ink slowly and tracing out a line on blank page in her booklet. "I wish I had more friends. We could all be friends, but maybe he doesn't want to be..."

"I don't think he thinks that at all... he's simple," she said with a sincere smile. "He doesn't want... things... you know. He's happy with what he has... Wait... do you...?" Claire raised an eyebrow as she brushed out a knot.

"Never mind!" Antoinette turned quickly, hiding a blush. When she spun around, she was caught by the brush, unsteadied, and dropped the quill. In doing so, the ink from the well spilled, drenching a corner of the booklet. "Ah!" she exclaimed, standing up so the ink wouldn't fall on her as Claire ran across the hall and came back with some rags to soak it up.

"Apologies, Lady Antoinette... but at least it didn't fall on your nightgown. Then we'd be in trouble."

"My booklet is ruined." Antoinette leaned over, noticing the ink had spread to about a third of the book.

"It's still salvageable," Claire said, picking it up by the inked parts. "See... these other parts are still fine... if you don't mind the ink blots."

Antoinette's smile widened until she let out a hearty laugh. "You're so funny!" She took the book from Claire's hands and dropped it in the waste bin next to her. "I have another one in the closet. One that's new."

Claire's eyes fixated on the one in the trash. True, half of it was useless, but the other half, despite its awkward stain, was perfectly usable. "I have an idea..." Claire said, retrieving it from the garbage. "For tomorrow. If you do it today, he'll know..."

"What's that?" Antoinette asked curiously as Claire whispered her plan.

"CHRISTIAN!" EVELYN BARETT WEBSTER'S VOICE BOOMED IN FRONT OF her before she arrived. Without a knock, she stormed into the boy's room. Where once there had been four heaps of rags, there were now two larger ones. She looked to Christian who sat up on instinct. "There's a mess for you to clean up in Lady Antoinette's room. Bring some rags."

"Yes, Miss Webster?" Christian asked as Akolai looked away. "My sister..."

"Is on an errand in town."

"But..."

"Be quick about it boy. And don't dawdle. Make haste while there's work to be done and don't leave it unfinished. Lord Ivar is due to return soon... best to resolve this before he arrives." She paused. "And no funny business."

"Yes, Miss Webster," Christian said, putting on the cleanest shirt he had and heading to Antoinette's room nervously.

The door was slightly ajar when he arrived on the second floor. He had been inside her room a handful of times when she had been away, but because Antoinette wasn't on trips nearly as often as Lord Ivar, her room was one that Claire kept tidy as part of her duties. Although they were about the same age, considering how Chase and Darius had been dismissed, Christian thought it wise to stay away as much as possible.

He knocked twice and waited.

Silence.

He knocked on the door once more.

"Come in," a voice said. It was a young voice, unmistakable and striking; it was the voice of the person who would one day be responsible for untold joy and untold suffering. Today it was filled with hope, but the stern warning of Evelyn Barett Webster kept him from engaging.

Antoinette Katherine Schofield, a girl of nine years old, stood beside her desk in an elegant blue dress. A well of ink was tipped over and a booklet was swimming in fresh ink. "Something happened..." Antoinette said sheepishly, standing off to the side so he could see.

Slowly, like a mouse heading for cheese in a trap, he approached. "Yes, My Lady. I'll clean this up," he said curtly, taking one of the folded rags he had in his hand and saturating it with the excess ink, curiously noticing how easily the rag mopped up *some* of the ink, but not all of it.

With the first rag soiled, he placed it in the waste basket, pausing for a moment to look down at the stain. Some of the ink was fresh atop her vanity, but there was another layer which had settled in nearly the same place that he had to scrub at to remove. *She must be clumsy,* he found himself thinking.

"Claire talks about you a lot." Antoinette watched him wipe down her desk, lifting the booklet as he did, noticing the broken quill snapped in half and placing it upon the book. "She said you're twins." Christian remained quiet. "You can talk to me too... when it's just me and Claire, we talk." She leaned against one of the corners of her four-post bed.

"Miss Webster said I should focus on cleaning up, My Lady," he responded quietly.

"I could command you to talk to me..." Antoinette said a little more confidently, "I could command you to be my friend, and you'd have to be!"

His vacant eyes turned to look at hers, a subtle panic rippling through his blue ponds. "Is that your command, My Lady?"

Antoinette thought for a moment, then sunk her head and looked down. She turned around hiding a frown. "No... I would never force someone to do something they don't want to."

A wave of relief ran through his body. "I'm almost done here... I'll ask Claire to polish your desk, but for now, the ink won't run further, and the mess won't spread."

"You can take those too..." She pointed at the stained book, broken quill, and the inkwell. "You can take them with the dirty rags."

Christian rifled through the book. Only the first few pages had been used, and the ink had saturated only a corner on the rest. "My Lady... half of this is still usable," he unknowingly parroted his sister. "And the quill's tip is still in working order... and the inkwell is low, but..."

"Mother will buy me a new set. You can take those aways" she said, gripping the book by an unstained corner and dropping it into the waste basket. She was about to do the same with the quill and inkwell when Christian intercepted them, his hand catching hers for a moment, taking both gently and placing them in the wastebasket slowly.

"My Lady... if I may be so bold..." he gulped, "...there is another servant. His name is Akolai. He is mute but learning to read and write. With your permission, I would like to give these to him. Damaged as they are... they would be more useful to him than in the trash."

Antoinette hid a coy smile. The trap had been set, and just like Claire had predicted, Christian had been caught.

"On a condition..." Antoinette reclaimed her boldness as she spoke with crossed arms. "Claire says a lot of good things about you... and I don't have a lot of friends here... I know you're our servant... but if we can also be friends... I think we'd be good friends." She rubbed her arm. "You don't have to if you don't want to... but Claire doesn't say 'My Lady' when it's just us... if you want to try to be friends... maybe one day I can just be *Antoinette* to you too."

Christian watched as she lowered her defenses to offer him her friendship. He held the waste basket tightly, like a shield between them, wondering how to reciprocate. "My sister... Claire says good things about you too... My... Antoinette..." The pair found a mutual blush graze them. "But uh..." he continued, clearing the air, "about the book and quill...?"

"I already told you..." Antoinette said with the smile he'd fall in love with, "you can take those."

20

NINE YEARS LATER

After years of servitude to the Schofield family under their belts, the servants' leashes grew longer. In their teens now, accustomed to the routine of their chores, older and more dexterous, they completed tasks more quickly than ever, and found themselves with a commensurate amount of free time and a pittance of money that was more for show than pay.

In the years that had passed, Akolai's desire to read and write flourished into a passion. His free time would be spent with his nose in a book, typically in one of the corners of the bookshop where Alex worked. As the visits stretched out over the years, Vincent's disdain for Akolai softened somewhat, and he found his curiosity both welcome and refreshing, while Alex found his dedication charming.

Akolai never took for granted the friendship that budded between conversations that revolved around just-read facts or just-completed chapters. He always kept the stained journal on him. The first few pages were sentences he'd written as a clumsy nine-year old, then a smattering of words he didn't know, and eventually an appendix of useful words he could refer to quickly by pointing at them. The journal was a chronology of learning to communicate, but it was only useful to those who could read.

"Akolai? Have you read this one?" Alex held up a leather-bound book with reflective letters that were hard to perceive in the fading light of day. "It's about a man wrongfully imprisoned. He goes through so much to take revenge on the people who imprisoned him." She kept a finger in the book to save her place. "What an idea!"

Akolai shook his head and raised a finger. Over the years, they had developed a code to quickly communicate without having to write everything down or refer to his journal. The raised finger meant *add it to the list of books I should read* and, as he lifted his finger, Alex scrawled something on a paper just out of sight.

"You should get going soon," she added, looking at the clock. "It's getting late and..." She bit her lip.

The last time Akolai had been out late, Evelyn had not been happy. She allowed them a certain amount of leeway, but frustrated at the comings-and-goings of an increasing variety of unsavory guests, she took her emotions out on Akolai and Christian. The belt lashings on his back told a story that still hadn't healed.

Akolai closed the book slowly and set it gently back where it had come from, re-reading the title a few times to ensure he remembered the book, then re-reading the topmost sentence on the page so he could find his place again later. "I should go," Akolai said with his hands in a two-part gesture of pointing to himself, then moving his index and middle finger back and forth.

"Yeah... I'll get ready to close up too... I can walk you to the corner..." Alex said with a wink. It was her code for wanting to talk with him outside the range of her father's hearing.

A minute later the pair walked down the main street, the echo of a bell's clang fading as they made their way forward. It was busier than usual.

"So?" Akolai shrugged at her.

"So..." Alex said, rubbing her arm. In the nine years that had passed since they had met, her round head had lengthened, her figure had filled out, and she stood nearly as tall as him. Her eyes were still wonder-filled orbs, and her blonde hair was as unkempt as ever. Her smile had only ever been soft or completely outlandish, but today, and today only, it was filled with gloom. "Father hasn't told you yet... I'm sure he will... things are tough. The war's ended and we aren't really making any money. It's been good for the Schofields with Lord Ivar commanding the local effort... but..."

Akolai forced his face into a smile. "Things will get better." He drew some shapes and mouthed the words.

"Maybe... but not for us. Not here. We're packing up... and by the end of the summer, we'll be gone."

Akolai shrugged slowly. "Where?"

"Father found someone for me... they come from old money... the Golds. I'll be married off." She raised her head, trying to stand a little taller, a little prouder than she could muster.

Even if Akolai could have spoken, he wouldn't have known what to say. There was nothing he *could* say. The few coppers he had earned wouldn't be enough to sustain the two of them. He reached for her hands, taking them delicately within his. He'd never held a girl's hands like this. They were so small within his. "I'm sorry," he mouthed, squeezing gently.

She had tears in her eyes as she squeezed back, batting them and looking up to try to shake them off. She wanted to pull away, but he drew her into his chest and wrapped her in a hug. She spent longer than she should have in that embrace, long enough to stem the tears, and long enough for a few townspeople to gawk and whisper.

"I should go... they'll think I'm a Weather girl," she joked, turning around and leaving a silent Akolai unable to call for her to come back.

21

"Boy!" Evelyn Webster called to Christian, an older Christian, now seventeen years old. He stood as tall as she and on the cusp of another growth spurt, his eyes deeper blue than ever. "Lord Ivar is set to return tonight. Is the room ready?"

The rags he wore had been cycled from the pile he'd slept on. They had been washed and dried, but compared to the exaggerated servants dresses that Claire and Evelyn wore, it was like they were from two different worlds.

"Yes, Miss Webster. The room was already fairly…"

"Boy!" Her scowl deepened and her eyes squinted. She was in desperate need of glasses, but too proud to admit it. "Is the work done?" She paused for a moment. "Is. It. Cleaned?"

"Yes, Miss Webster," Christian said clearly, standing taller.

"Dismissed," Evelyn sighed against a nearby desk, rubbing her temples.

Christian made his way down the familiar hall of the second floor. His destination was always the same, the room he shared with Akolai in the basement, but on this occasion, a young woman came from the opposite direction. Her green eyes lit up when she saw him, and an ornate black dress with vermilion trim bounced as she walked forward. Antoinette's styled hair curled tightly as it fell.

"My Lady," Christian said with a grin, walking past her.

"Servant." Antoinette met his grin with one herself, turning around as he passed her, changing directions, following him down the spiral staircase at the edge of one of the towers. Halfway down the staircase, Antoinette hopped onto a landing between the floors. "Hey," she added coyly.

"Hey back," he smirked. "Something going on with your father?"

Antoinette's smile faded. "He was supposed to be back last week... then last night... now tonight. Mother isn't pleased at all."

"Neither is Miss Webster."

"Probably for the same reason," she sighed. "Mother's caught wind... battles aren't the only things he's won."

"Oh... What's next?"

"What *can* be? Mother doesn't exactly have talents... and I'm sure I complicate things..."

"Won't he be here more... now that the war's over?"

"If the recent past is any indication, *not*... I don't know if that's a good thing..." she said, continuing down the stairs to the first floor with Christian in tow. The pair made their way down the main hall, towards the opposite corner of the house where a rickety staircase fit for only servants held the entrance to the basement. "Wasn't it the same with *your* father?"

Christian paused nervously. "My father?"

"Claire said he wasn't around much growing up, but he made good money when he was gone?"

"Good... money?" Christian reached into his pocket. Sometimes he still carried the coin Miss Webster had tried to throw away nearly a decade ago. Years of rubbing at it had worn down the face and polished the edges. It was as round as it had ever been, but he'd spent countless nights looking from this copper coin to a few others he'd occasionally been paid with. If he squinted, they looked similar, but upon a further inspection, it was clear that his was different. It was a fake.

"Sorry. I mean..." Antoinette bit her lip. "Good money... for... being poor...?" An awkward smile turned a tactless comment into a joke.

"And what do you reckon good money is for us *poors*?" He met her smile with one all his own. "Ten copper coins a month?"

"I was going to say eight." Their eyes narrowed on each other's as their smiles widened, each fighting the urge to break into a laugh.

"I..."

"Antoinette!" a man bellowed, his voice carrying, preceded by a loud thud that came from the opening of the main door. "Daughter!" the voice boomed again as Christian slipped into the servant's stairwell, watching Antoinette move to the middle of the hall. "Antoinette?"

"Here, father!" she responded in a higher pitch than a moment ago. "I'm here father!"

Christian watched, eyes at ground level as an older man with a chiseled jaw and graying beard towered over her. He wore a heavy green jacket with silver buttons and black trousers. His embrace was rough and fast, and just as quickly as he was done, did he turn, gesturing towards the door. "I've brought a guest."

"Father?"

Christian couldn't see the guest past the corner, but soon enough he would. "Introduce yourself."

Antoinette curtsied. "Pleased to make your acquaintance. I am Antoinette Katherine Schofield, sole daughter of Ivar and Navara Schofield. What is your name, My Lord?"

The voice that came from around the corner made Christian's hairs stand on edge.

"This is her?" he said to Ivar. "Not bad." A singular filthy hand reached forward past the corner and into Christian's view. "I'm Michael, Michael Escoté."

"Child, Michael's father and I fought together, and now that things have settled down... now that you're almost of age you two will be perfect together."

"Father?" Antoinette was too stunned to speak.

"We'll hammer out the details later. Have one of the servants bring us drinks in the parlor. My future son and I have a lot to talk about."

"I'll... I'll go fetch... um..."

Christian emerged from the staircase at her stuttering. "No need!" Ivar said boisterously, spotting him from down the hall. "You there, servant. Fetch us something to drink. Strong and bountiful."

"Right away, My Lord," Christian said calmly as the two men walked away, catching up to Antoinette, her eyes pulsing with uncertainty.

22

"A RE YOU SURE SHE'S A VIRGIN?" MICHAEL ESCOTÉ HELD up his goblet for Christian to fill. Once he'd done so, he took a step back, holding the pitcher of wine close to his chest and staying out of the way. He kept his eyes on the pair. Michael looked to be about their age, slightly taller than Christian, with empty black eyes and mid-length blonde hair. "I've heard they really are the best." He laughed, and Ivar joined him.

The parlor in the Schofield Manor was surrounded by a few sparse offerings of art and an elegant wooden desk. "We'll get assurance beforehand..." Ivar downed his goblet, adjusting himself on one of the lavish armchairs he sat at, his silver-button lined coat snug against his belly. "You there, servant boy, have you any reason to think Antoinette is no longer a virgin?"

"No, My Lord."

"For all we know..." Michael hiccupped, "*he* could be sleeping with her."

Ivar stood up, drawing a short knife from the belt he'd strewn on a lounging chair. He approached Christian quickly, putting the knife to his neck. "Are you sleeping with my daughter, servant?"

As Christian gulped, he felt the tip cut into his skin, back against the wall. The wine in the jug at his chest shook in the space between them. "No, My Lord."

"Tell me the truth and I may spare your life." The tip of the knife was cold against his neck.

"On my life. I have never laid with Lady Antoinette." His eyes avoided Lord Ivar's.

There was a tension in the air that broke suddenly as Ivar removed the blade and clapped Christian on the shoulder. "See Michael," he laughed. "Nothing to worry about. Not like Antoinette would ever share a bed with a servant, right boy?"

"Yes, My Lord..." Christian mumbled nervously, measuring the stains he'd been unable to remove from his shirt against the pristine white one that Michael wore. "Shall I fetch more wine?"

"Michael?"

"Let it flow!" he sang.

"And bring me something stronger!"

"Right away." Christian made his way out of the parlor, pulling the door behind him until it clicked. He headed into the kitchen, reaching for a new wine jug and a glass bottle with an amber liquid. His hands trembled as he held them, a cold chill running up his body that made him sink to the floor. He set the bottles down next to him.

There he trembled, there his breathing hastened, there he felt the spot where the knife's tip had been, a single drop of blood refreshing at each touch, until his sister appeared.

"Christian?" She ran to him, falling to her knees beside him. "Brother, what's wrong?"

He sat paralyzed, the moment inescapable, unable to say anything, unable to do anything.

"Servant!" Ivar yelled from the parlor. "Where has that servant gone?"

Claire reached down and picked up the bottles. "Head downstairs, brother," she whispered earnestly, taking the containers and disappearing down the hall. "I'll handle this."

CHRISTIAN COULDN'T RECALL HOW HE ARRIVED AT HIS ROOM THAT evening. He had never felt such a fear in his life. The tip of the dagger still felt cold against his neck. Even the rare occasion that had warranted a lashing from Evelyn Barett Webster paled in comparison to this fear. He knew Evelyn wouldn't kill him, but he knew no such thing of his Master, Lord Ivar.

Ivar ate, slept, and dreamt violence. It was his cash cow, it was his job, and often it also seemed to be his pastime. Even Lady Navara stayed at an arm's length from Ivar when he got into his fits. Christian found himself wondering about his former roommates, Darius and Chase, and their sudden disappearance. He spent the night looking out the window at the sliver of moon in the sky. At each moment, he wondered when Evelyn would burst through and tell him to get to work, or when Claire might return to check up on him, or when Akolai might sneak down to see if he was awake—but none of these occurred.

Instead, he spent the night in a suspended fear, alone. At some point he drifted off to sleep, and sometime later Akolai returned and slipped into his own bed, deep set eyes measuring his friend, feeling just as helpless as he.

In the morning, when the sun poured into the room, Akolai was already awake, waiting to talk with him. "What happened?" Akolai pointed to the two words in his journal. The phrase was one he frequently used. It had its own spot near other common phrases.

"Nothing..." Christian said distantly.

"What happened?" Akolai tapped the journal with more force.

"Lord Ivar held a dagger to me..." Christian touched at his neck, "but it's nothing. He just took me by surprise. Did you bring me down here last night?"

Akolai nodded.

"Did Claire tell you to get me?"

"Miss Webster." He pointed to her name on another page with common names.

"Did you talk to Claire today?"

Akolai nodded.

"Did she say anything?"

"Antoinette..." He pointed, then looked through his journal to no avail, scribbling on a blank spot, "getting married."

"I..."

Before he could say another word, the door swung open and Claire, with tears in her eyes wrapped her arms around her brother, knocking him onto his back. "Christian..." she cried. "Are you okay now? It's going to be okay."

He took an arm and wrapped it around her weakly. Her hair was a mess, and her clothes weren't up to Miss Webster's pristine standards. He couldn't remember the last time she had held him so tightly. "I'm sorry... I just..."

"I know..." she sniffed while he tried to remember the last time they had both felt so vulnerable. "I know it's because Antoinette is to be married, but you can't freeze like that! You can't give them a reason to suspect if..."

No, Christian wanted to say. *It's not just that... it's also that Lord Ivar put a knife to my throat. It's that I felt like I was going to die, and I was too afraid to do anything about it.* "I know..."

Akolai began to rifle through his pages, but Christian shook his head.

"I can't lose you," she said again, an unshakable terror overtaking her. "It's going to be okay, right?"

"Yeah..." Christian said weakly.

Claire clasped his face between her hands, pressing her face against his, nose-to-nose with her brother. "Say it," she commanded with her glassy blue eyes. "Say it's going to be okay... before I cry any more..." She pulled a strand of her messy hair behind her head and shoved her face against his. "Tell me it's going to be okay."

"It's going to be okay," he lied, letting her head fall against his shoulder. "It's going to be okay, sister."

She cried. For what seemed like an eternity she sobbed, inhaling deeply as she sniffled, the scent of whiskey weak on her dress and heavy on her skin.

"It's going to be okay..." she whispered, unconvinced.

23

Antoinette's mother, Navara Schofield, was the epitome of elegance. She never left her room without making herself proper, and adhered to the rules of formality, even in the face of humiliation. Today was no different, but she found herself angered enough from biting her tongue that she had to let out some frustration.

"Ivar's tendencies flare up in these summer days, don't they?" Every tempered word rang loudly for Evelyn, who knew, as her personal servant, that for every annoyance she grieved, a thousand complaints hid behind the veil of propriety.

Evelyn stood at her back, carefully running a brush down her elegant hair. It was the same shade of black as Antoinette's, though now speckled with gray. The tasks that Claire did for Antoinette, Evelyn performed for Navara. "Yes, Lady Schofield." Evelyn avoided her sharp glances in the reflection of the mirror.

"He rarely joins me at night." She closed her eyes, listening to the brush run through her hair. "It was better when he waged war, at least then he was on his toes and not fattening like a pig to slaughter."

"...Yes, Lady Schofield." Evelyn placed the brush on the dresser.

Navara rose, waiting as she undid the lace backing from her dress, a white so immaculate it could have been fit for a wedding. As Evelyn undressed her, Navara turned, ever so gently, looking at her figure, wrapped tightly in a corset. "Father said elegance begets elegance. Clearly not."

"Yes, Lady Schofield." Evelyn began to undo the corset silently, carefully untying one lace after another until it came off and Navara stood in only her undergarments, waiting as the Head Servant fetched her nightgown and slipped it over her curves and down her body.

"Every conversation since his return three weeks ago has been him praising that boy. *Escoté*. If only he didn't have a name." She turned to let Evelyn button up her nightgown.

"Is that the main issue then, mother?" Antoinette appeared in the doorway, in a nightgown all her own, anger riddling her face. "Not that he drinks like father; not that he sleeps around like father; not that he comes around uninvited now; or even..."

Navara looked up, her expression unchanging as Evelyn held a bonnet. In a gliding motion, almost seamless were it not for the creak of a floorboard, Navara stood toe-to-toe with her daughter, looking into the younger, angrier mirror of her only child. In a measured moment, Navara raised her open hand and struck Antoinette's face with such authority that she fell into the hallway.

Her expression didn't change as she looked down at her daughter. "Mind your manners and get up. A Lady does not kneel." Antoinette did. Mechanically she rose. Terrified, she obeyed. "Servant." Navara snapped, still staring down her daughter. "My bonnet." Evelyn approached, the bonnet carefully placed between her two hands. "Close the door. It seems the walls have ears. And have that creak fixed."

"Yes, Lady Schofield," Evelyn said, striding quickly to close the door, leaving Antoinette in the hallway.

Antoinette remained there for what seemed like an eternity and, as it had been with Christian, it was Claire who found her, and Claire who escorted her back to her room.

Antoinette's cheek was red, but the outline of her mother's hand was fading when Claire dabbed it with warm water. She winced at the pain and

Claire remained quiet. Ever since Michael had appeared, it seemed that the house was falling apart.

Christian wasn't the same.

Claire wasn't the same.

Even Lady Navara was on edge.

"...It all started when father brought him," Antoinette grumbled, pressing her own hand against her face, the warmth of the slap still hot under her skin.

"I can get some cream." Claire inspected her face more carefully.

"No... believe it or not, it's somewhat refreshing... mother's angry too... she just can't show it... and the heat..." she added, noticing Claire was sweating in a maid's dress that had once been too big for her, now snug on her body, "...the heat of the summer makes things so much worse."

Claire dabbed at her face, embarrassed. "Apologies... I haven't been..."

"Don't worry about it... it sounds like the wedding will be in the fall... if that's the case, as long as we have this summer heat... there's hope..." Antoinette exhaled, collapsing onto her bed. "So, did you see him today?"

"Who?" Claire asked abruptly, nervously, adjusting her dress.

"Michael and his parents. They came to introduce themselves and to discuss the date... father was over the moon to see Michael's father, Lord Garrett." She shivered, and Claire smiled weakly as Antoinette tried to make the best of a bad situation.

"You have a date then?"

"Unless it rains... the first day of fall."

"I'll pray for rain," Claire managed to joke, watching as Antoinette's smile broadened. "Where will you live?"

"Michael's father has lands... construction on a house will start soon... I imagine he'll stay here, or I'll go to his family's estate until it's finished."

"But you'll definitely leave?" Claire asked with concern.

"Yes. Would you want to come with me?"

"I will go wherever My Lady commands." Claire said defeated, with an absence of jest.

"But... would you *want* to come with me?"

"I'm in no position to *want*... to say yes... or to say no."

"Claire Bear..." Antoinette said, a little more forcefully, startling her. "You're my friend first, servant second. What do you want?"

"To leave?" Claire said hesitantly. "To leave," she looked down with shame. "I want to leave. I don't want to be in this house with him anymore."

"Unfortunately, he'd join us."

"He would?"

"Of course... we'd be married."

"Ah... Michael... right."

24

"ALEX IS LEAVING AT THE END OF THE SUMMER..." AKOLAI SAID, using his journal as an aid, sitting in the summer sun by the servant's entrance with Christian at his side. His white shirt was closer to tan now, but clean, just like Miss Evelyn wanted it. "I want to go with her."

Christian looked up, taking the sun on his face, looking to a strange set of clouds on the horizon of the warm day. "I know."

"How?" Akolai asked, looking at him closer.

"You visit her every week... and you always come back with a big grin." Akolai blushed. "What about her? Does she want you to come too?"

He nodded sheepishly.

"And Mr. Globaria?"

He looked away.

"Doesn't know?" Christian sat up a little straighter. "Wait, are you talking about running away with her?" Akolai looked to his friend, searching for a response, knowing Christian would interject before he could. "Akolai... you're a servant... you barely have any money... and she doesn't have much either, right?"

"Love," Akolai pressed the word in his journal and Christian buried his head in his hands dramatically.

"Love?"

"You've never loved anyone," Akolai spelled out.

"I love Claire... she's my family... and the only one who'd always stay by my side. Who else would love me back? Who else would protect me like her? Who else wouldn't just abandon me?" Christian stared at a tear at the bottom of his shirt.

"Antoinette?"

"We're not... we're friends... But..." he added, seeing Akolai's sadness, "...but you say you've found love... do what you must, my friend."

Akolai nodded.

"We should get back... it's only midday and there's still work to be done."

"Yeah."

"Miss Webster is going on a trip soon... Lord Ivar and Lady Navara will be gone too. That would be your best chance... no one would notice, for a few days at least."

Akolai's cheeky grin on his face made him beam more than ever. "I'll miss you."

THE CLOUD BEYOND THE HORIZON MOVED SLOWLY, BUT THE SERVANTS within the castle moved quickly. There wasn't much holding Akolai in place. Within the course of a couple of days, he broke the news to Claire, who wished him well and provided a few of her own coins.

A week later, the two male live-in servants stood in the middle of their room. Where once there had been four beds, there were now two. After tonight, there would only be one.

The two shook hands, a shadow of the children they had been present in the men they were becoming. "Look out for the girls," Akolai wrote.

"Look out for Alex too," Christian replied, leaning into the hug that came from the handshake, "and be careful."

"I'm sorry..." Akolai knew that Christian would likely take a lashing from Miss Webster.

"It's okay. Just don't come back... or we'll get double." He smirked, punching him on the shoulder, meeting his grin. "A summer storm's coming... be careful out there."

"Always." Akolai pressed his forehead against Christian's and mouthed something. Unable to say it, his lips moved slowly, and before Christian could ask what he was saying, he was off—through the door to their room, down the basement hallway, and out the servant's entrance, never to set foot again in the Schofield Manor.

With Akolai gone, the room was Christian's. He spent his first night alone, every sound amplified by the emptiness. The noises from the outside world ricocheted into his ears. They streamed through the windows, poured under the doors, and nestled in the cracks of the wall where Christian had once scrawled out the alphabet, behind a loose stone where he kept his coin memento along with the other coppers he'd saved over the years.

It felt surreal to think that the Dusk twins and Miss Webster were the only remaining live-in servants now. When his mind finally settled, he found peace, sleeping like he had never slept before, into the morning light, as the summer storm settled in, and the rain began to fall.

"Christian?" a panicked voice burst through his door. It was one he vaguely recognized, coming from a woman he'd heard talk occasionally, the woman put in charge of the Manor in Miss Webster's absence. "Christian? Lady Antoinette sent me. Hurry. It's Claire. Something's wrong."

25

Claire Sefira Dusk lay sprawled on the floor of Antoinette's bedroom in the early morning hours. Her face was pale, her body drenched in sweat, and her eyelids were heavy on her face when her brother appeared in the doorway. He was out of breath after sprinting from the basement to Antoinette's room on the second floor. The shirt he wore was the same he'd worked in the night before, now glued to his sweaty frame.

"I don't..." Antoinette began, "...we were talking... then she fell..." She retreated a couple of steps in fear.

"Claire?" Christian whispered, rushing over to her, putting a hand on her forehead, feeling a fire well up on his palm. "She has a fever. Rags. We need rags and water."

"Rags!" Antoinette belted at the woman who had fetched Christian, just now emerging into view, equally out of breath, seconds behind the faster twin.

"Yes, My Lady," the woman said in haste, taking off.

Antoinette inched forward. She wore only a nightgown; her dress was on the floor beside her. Claire had just started getting her ready for the day when she had collapsed. Antoinette dropped to her knees slowly beside the twins. "I thought it was the change in weather... she'd been sweating..."

"Brother?" Claire whispered weakly, struggling to prop herself up, and ultimately unable to do so.

"Help me take off her dress." Christian rolled Claire onto her side, beginning to undo the lace backing before Antoinette brushed his hands aside, taking over, undoing the laces more quickly than he could. She pulled the dress away from Claire, leaving her in her own white underdress, so drenched in sweat that parts of it were transparent against her body. "Lay her on her back."

"We can put her on my bed," Antoinette pointed, reaching for Claire's arm, for the first time noticing a frailty she had hid beneath her clothes, eyes scanning her body through the transparent dress—a wave of uncertainty as she made out a large purplish spot on her left side, dark beneath the white fabric.

"No, keep her on the floor. She's burning up." Christian put his hand on her forehead again. "Claire. Hold on, okay?"

"We need a doctor! I'll get Evelyn..." Antoinette said, rising to her feet, looking down at her friend as Christian slowly removed her socks.

"Miss Webster isn't here. She's away until tomorrow..."

"Akolai then... we can send him to fetch the doctor!" Antoinette made a beeline for the door.

"...He's not here either." Christian bit his lip, feeling a tear well up, trying hard to steady Claire's shaking and not add to it. Her hand was weak within his. Her hand was small within his. Her blue eyes tried hard to stay open, their luster fading as she looked up at her brother. "I'll go." Christian brushed away her sweaty hair. "I'll be right back, sister..."

Antoinette knelt beside her. "Hold on, okay? Claire Bear?"

"Brother..." Claire squeezed Christian's hand weakly. "Don't leave me." Her vision grew cloudy as she lay on her back, tears filling her eyes. "Tell me it's going to be okay..."

"Leti... once Leti comes back, we'll send her..." Antoinette looked to the door nervously as the woman reappeared with a bucket and some rags. "Leti... fetch the doctor. Tell him to come quickly."

Leti's face was almost as drenched as Claire's, though nowhere near as pale. She bent over at the waist to catch her breath, gasping when she saw Claire, then turning around and taking off.

Christian remained on his knees, wiping away his sister's sweat, looking away to wipe his own tears, touching her forehead with every passing moment that he could. Antoinette fetched more water when the first bucket was empty, then fetched more rags when the first batch was soaked. "Stay with me Claire," Christian repeated, over and over again. "The doctor is coming." He glanced at the doorway as often as he could. He glanced outside the window as the clouds continued to block out the sun. "It will be okay, sister."

"I won't leave you," Claire whispered, reaching up for Christian's head. She wasn't strong enough to bring it down, but he knew what she wanted. He dropped his head against her chest, keeping her small arm around him, fighting back the tears as he felt her heat radiate through his body, against his face, a fire he couldn't contain, a fire he couldn't steal away from her.

Antoinette's eyes were glued to a bruise on Claire's side, beneath her semi-transparent nightgown.

More than an hour after Leti had left, the main doors to the Schofield Manor finally burst open.

"He's here!" Leti screamed.

"He's here Claire!" Antoinette blurted out on her knees beside her. "He's here. Just hold on." She gently shook her leg.

"Hold on Claire!" Christian said, coming up from her embrace, looking down at his sister, unmoving. "Don't leave me." Antoinette looked at Christian; the same steady stream of tears on her face was mirrored across his. "Don't leave me. Claire. Don't leave me. Sister. Sister? We're family. You said you'd never leave me!"

The doctor appeared in the doorway, an out-of-breath middle-aged man looking into the room, carrying a small leather bag, a light drizzle of rain over his body and a heavy amount of sweat.

"Claire. The doctor's here, okay? Sister. Don't leave me. Sister. Say something!"

"*I won't leave you,*" Claire whispered from the Red World to the brother who couldn't hear her. "*I love you, brother. It's going to be okay.*"

26

Evelyn Barett Webster rolled into the city with a smile spread across her face. After over a decade of service to the Schofield family, she had earned a break. She had taken a vacation, a rarity for servants, but a well-deserved one. Rested and revitalized, the carriage dropped her off in the dead of night, with only a small bag which held her personal belongings.

Though the rain fell, she didn't mind it. She wouldn't let something as trivial as a summer storm ruin the fond memories of her trip. She scurried from the carriage to the servant's entrance and, as she did, she didn't notice a faint sound through the rain.

Slice.

Slice.

Slice.

Evelyn didn't want to make a noise, so she quietly crept past the basement door she knew to belong to Claire, paused for a moment, and, absent a sound, continued walking. As she rounded the main corridor of the basement, she turned to look at the door to Christian and Akolai's room, taking a few steps towards it until it came into sight. The door was ajar and neither boy was in sight. "Diligent, as I raised them," Evelyn whispered to herself with an unusual smile, turning back and ascending to the first floor.

Her room was the one closest to the staircase, and as she opened the door quietly, she realized the house wasn't as silent as it should have been. She could hear Lady Navara's firm voice scolding someone on the second floor and a strange repeating sound, somewhere outside, was more audible now than it had been before.

Slice.

Slice.

Slice.

"It can wait," Evelyn said to herself as her gloved hand caressed the handle to her room. She thought nothing of the voices coming from the second floor until she heard a slap echo through the manor and run down the stairs into her ears. "It can't wait," she sighed, her smile fading as she dropped the small case with her belongings and changed into her maid's dress.

With no haste, Evelyn ascended the stairs to the second floor to find Antoinette staring down her mother boldly. With no knowledge of what was occurring, Evelyn unwittingly entered a battlefield. "My Ladies, I have returned just now."

"Servant." Navara looked past Antoinette's anger. She called her *servant* only at certain times, usually to make a point. "You left us shorthanded. The help in your stead was utterly useless. Assist Antoinette with her morning routine. She needs to look perfect for the breakfast we're hosting."

"My Lady, right away, I'll fetch Claire," Evelyn said quickly, hands folded across her apron in front of her.

"Did I stutter, servant?" Navara glided towards Evelyn. "*You* will assist Antoinette."

"Yes, My Lady," Evelyn said, bowing slightly, avoiding looking at Navara's tensed hand, not knowing if a strike was forthcoming. "Right away."

Antoinette's eyes were hidden in a puff of red and her fists were balled in anger when Evelyn placed a timid hand on her shoulder. "Lady Antoinette?" Her eyes tried to catch Antoinette's, unaware of what had occurred the previous day. "Come, Lady Antoinette."

Navara's firm hand suddenly struck Evelyn who fell to the floor from the shock. "*We* tell *you* what to do. Not the other way around. Now get Antoinette ready, and remember who your Masters are."

Evelyn grabbed at her cheek, but righted herself, looking down apologetically. "Yes, My Lady. My apologies, My Lady. Right away, My Lady." Evelyn steadied her hands from the shaking. "Lady Antoinette, may I accompany you to you room?"

"You might and you will," Navara scoffed, turning around and heading back to her room, closing the door with more force than was required.

When Navara had left, Evelyn took Antoinette by the arm, walking her to her room and closing the door. The room was stuffy, and the slap Evelyn had just felt only added to the heat. She opened the window slightly, just enough to let in a breeze, but not so much that the rain from the summer storm would find a way in.

Slice.

Slice.

Slice.

With the window slightly ajar, the sound was louder now, but Evelyn paid it little mind.

"Lady Antoinette?" She began going through her closet, then pulling out her brushes. "Why are we readying you for breakfast so early? Did something happen with Claire?" Antoinette stayed silent, looking out the window. "If she has failed you, I shall see to it that she is disciplined. If you are displeased..." Evelyn lifted the numb Antoinette's arms out of her nightgown, "...you need only tell me and..."

Antoinette's tears strolled down her face silently. Evelyn pulled out a fine linen handkerchief to wipe them away, but those finely woven threads that in vain attempted to do battle with her emotions could not contain her sadness. As Antoinette looked at the handkerchief, more transparent with her tears, she could only think of her friend. "Claire's gone... she's dead... yesterday morning... she's gone... she's not coming back..."

How? Where? Why? What happened? Evelyn's mind ran amok with so many questions she could have asked, and yet the one that came out of her mouth was a different one: "Where's Christian?"

Slice.

Slice.

Slice.

Evelyn Barett Webster had spared no expense to separate herself as Head Servant from the children of a woman she once detested. Despite the divide in their status, despite the constant orders they were forced to follow, and despite the lashings they would sustain at her hands, she was not the heartless monster many made her out to be. So, when Antoinette answered the question, despite her station, and despite Lady Navara's direct orders, Evelyn raced down the stairs to the first floor and out the doors, heading towards the foreign sounds.

Slice.

Slice.

Slice.

When she arrived at the source, absent an umbrella to stop the rain, she rested her eyes on the silhouette of one of her charges, Christian Nikolai Dusk, spade in hand, backfilling the grave he'd dug beside a tall tree that climbed high into the sky, past his window and past Antoinette's.

He toiled in the same outfit he'd awoken in more than a full day before, drenched from head to toe with sweat and tears and rain. "Christian!" she called to him from the cobblestone path, watching as his arms mechanically continued with the chore. The grave was mostly filled when she called out, and the body of his sister had been laid with care at the bottom. The rain hid his tears, but not his grief.

Evelyn was not a mother by any means. She had no children all her own. She didn't consider Claire or Christian to be one of hers, but fresh off the heels of a delightful vacation with her own sister, with her own nieces, she couldn't imagine being forced to watch them die, let alone bury them by her own hand. "Christian. Go inside, boy. Please," she pleaded.

Christian couldn't see much in the morning darkness, or through the rain, or through his tears, but the tip of his spade knew the earth he'd moved for his sister. His body knew how to work, and his mouth knew how to respond, "I'm almost done Miss Webster. I'll stop when the work is done."

27

THE MORNING AFTER BURYING HIS SISTER, CHRISTIAN'S BODY wanted to rest, still covered in mud, but his mind wouldn't quiet. The events of the day before were fresh, and every time he closed his eyes, he could see his sister laying there on Antoinette's floor: sweating, struggling, or cooling.

The portly man who'd carried the doctor's bag had approached his sister in the middle of Antoinette's room. He'd retrieved a long tube and squatted down, knees creaking like bloated floorboards, pressing one end of the tube to Claire's chest and the other to his ear. Antoinette reached for Christian's hand—clammy and sweaty and trembling, just like hers.

The man placed two fingers over Claire's wrist, then on her neck, then surveyed the rest of her through the thin white fabric of her underdress, eyes resting on a purple discoloration on her left side. "The boy should avert his gaze as I inspect the woman." He looked from Antoinette to Christian, whose eyes didn't abandon his sister as the man shifted her body.

Christian's hand squeezed Antoinette's tighter as the man brought Claire's dress up over her waist, exposing her legs, thighs, and then her entire lower half. Eventually the dress climbed over her naval, revealing a fist-sized bruise against a backdrop of pale flesh that made Antoinette gasp and Christian's lips twitch with fear and anger.

A particular cobblestone on the ceiling of his basement bedroom reminded him of that bruise, and, when he turned his body to another wall, it was the same. Everywhere he looked he saw that tableau of a battered sister beneath a scared façade, and when he closed his eyes, it plagued his mind.

His heart raced now as fast as it did then, threatening to beat out of his chest. There was no Akolai to calm his panic. There was no work left to be done. There was no Evelyn to strike him down to distract him from his thoughts. He didn't want to think that tonight Claire wouldn't sleep in her own bed down the hall, when last night she'd laid there all the same.

"I can help you move the body," the doctor had said as he pulled down Claire's dress, covering her fragile frame. "We can set her somewhere where she won't be disturbed until the mortician arrives." He returned the tube to his leather bag, his portly frame wider and shorter than Claire, the liver spots on his hand showing as he bent backwards, stretching, fanning himself, still slightly out of breath from the jog through the Schofield Manor, but other than that, unnaturally calm.

"Her bed." Christian didn't recall saying these words, but they came from his mouth all the same. The man assented with a weak nod. His two hands reached for Claire's.

"I can take the arms, and you can take the legs."

He began to lift his sister awkwardly before Christian swatted his hands away. "She's not a thing to be carried like that. She's my sister." He couldn't remember saying that either, but he couldn't let her be carried off like that. She'd already lost her life. He wouldn't subject her to losing any more dignity.

Christian dropped to the floor and reached his arms under her neck and knees, lifting her with ease. She weighed nothing, and yet the pain of lifting her up was almost more than he could bear. Her warmth was fading, and he held her close, wanting to share warmth like they had when they were babies, but she wouldn't take it anymore. She wouldn't take it ever again.

His muddy hands quaked. They were cold and wet and impregnated by the smell of the oak from the shovel. The scent of his sister's sweat on his body had already been washed away. Only the indentation on her bed still remembered.

While Akolai had trudged away with Alex in the early storm's arrival, Christian had buried his sister in the hours that followed. Now she rested just outside his bedroom wall, next to the large tree that climbed up to Antoinette's room, behind the wall where he had scrawled out the alphabet when last night she'd been just down the hall.

Antoinette and the doctor were all the procession that followed Christian as he descended into the basement to lay Claire's body on her bed. She slumped as he pulled his arms out from underneath her. He straightened her dress before the doctor took a clean sheet and draped it over her body, escorting Christian and Antoinette into the hallway.

"Will it be a burial or a pyre?" The doctor's eyes looked from Christian to Antoinette. "...So that I can inform the mortician." He scanned them twice over, noticing Christian's clothes, dirty and sweaty, and then measuring Antoinette as she stood before him, nervous and quivering in a nightgown all her own. "Forgive me... are you the Lady of the House?"

"...No. My mother... she'll be arriving in the evening..."

"I'll come back then and sort things out with her."

"Things?" Christian asked.

"Things."

"What things?" Christian's empty eyes stared at the closed door to Claire's room.

"A ceremony? A resting place? Her remains?" He paused. "And the settlement of services."

"Settlement?" Christian asked with confusion as Antoinette reached down for his hand again.

"Cost," she whispered. "Payment."

While Christian tried to remove the mud from his hands and to ignore the features from the cobblestones that reminded him of his sister, two stories above him, Antoinette stared vacantly at the drapes in her room as Evelyn wiped her down, brushed her, and dressed her. Evelyn's hair was still wet from watching over Christian as he'd filled in his sister's grave, returning to ready Antoinette as instructed by Lady Navara.

Without a single word or movement to the contrary, Antoinette stood, a combination of confused, heartbroken, and worried, shedding an intermittent tear that carved through her makeup, glassy eyes the likes of which Evelyn could not ignore. "Some fresh air will do you good," Evelyn whispered as she finished up, looking at a timepiece that she withdrew from under her apron. "Come with me child, before your mother notices."

"A ceremony for a servant?" Navara Schofield's boisterous laugh that evening clanged through the halls of the Schofield Manor as she addressed her daughter, wrapped in a shawl, still smelling of her best friend. *"A pauper's funeral would be a boon in the face of a flame."*

"I can pay... she was my friend."

"You would pay? With what money? She was a servant. She was practically a slave."

Evelyn Barett Webster had never knocked on Christian's door. She had slammed it. She had locked it. She had burst forward through it. She had kicked it. But she had never knocked, and yet, on the morning following Claire's death, only on this morning did her stiff knuckles learn how to be gentle before announcing her presence.

Christian rose from his heap of rags lifelessly, opening the door to his room to find himself face-to-face with Antoinette as Evelyn headed down the hall and around the corner, offering them a moment between themselves.

It could have been a portrait of wealth and poverty as Antoinette stood in a fine dress before him, and Christian in sweaty, dirtied rags. A pair of green eyes caught hold of a pair of blue ones, their vacant expressions melting as the floodgates opened. They wanted to hug each other, they wanted to hold each other, but they couldn't.

Antoinette leaned her head forward, inches from his face, hands on the frame of the doorway to keep herself from falling into him. She'd never been this close to him and yet there was no embarrassment. There was too much sadness to be embarrassed.

"I'm sorry," she whispered so close that he could taste her breath. He gripped the doorframe with his mud-covered hands from inside his room and leaned forward, pressing his forehead against hers. "I'm so sorry."

"I told her it would be okay..." his lip trembled. "I told her it would be okay."

On the far side of the basement, Evelyn Barett Webster leaned against the cobblestone wall across from Claire's room, lips pursed, listening to their whispers, fighting back the urge to join them.

Her eyes watched the timepiece slowly tick, eking out each moment, giving substance to each second before her eyes caught sight of something lodged in the crack under Claire's door. The Head Servant bent down, picking it out of the crack in the cobblestones, stepped over and trampled in the days that had preceded: a distinctive silver button with two engraved swords that shone as her thumb polished it.

28

THE SUMMER STORM THAT SOFTENED THE EARTH FOR CHRISTIAN Nikolai Dusk to bury his sister, was the same one that heralded the return of Antoinette Katherine Schofield's fiancé, Michael Escoté, who arrived with a lecherous gaze that promised to make of her his next conquest. Though Antoinette was in no condition to be up and about on the morning following the death of her closest friend, at the command of her mother and the behest of Evelyn, she was. Her pale lips quaked as they brought a cup of tea to her chapped lips in the parlor of the Schofield Manor, the scent of Christian still upon her brow.

"Three months," Michael's sour face sounded off. "Less than three months and you will be my wife." A raised eyebrow and a wily smirk mirrored those of a soon-to-be-released prisoner set on revenge.

Lord Ivar sat beside his future son-in-law, twice as deep into the wine barrel and half as sober. "Antoinette Escoté." He rubbed his disheveled chin with a smirk and elbowed Michael. "Make me a grandchild and make sure it's a boy! Give me what this one couldn't." He gestured to his wife who sat across from him.

Another man who sat opposite Michael, bearing his same features, let out a boisterous laugh. Garrett Escoté, father of Michael, was as unrefined as the others. "The sooner the better!"

Lady Navara's stoic face didn't crack in the presence of their crudeness. She sat on a lounger opposite the pair, the portrait of elegance, a masterful smile painted on her face, a stark contrast to the expressionless daughter who sat beside her, whose hand she steadied with a caring caricature.

Antoinette sat stifled in that room, stifled from the rain and stifled from the scent of death still wet on her skin, desperate to let go of the mask she poorly clung to and to the false smile held hostage by upturned lips, begging to be let out of that room so she could fall apart beside someone who understood.

"Say something girl!" Garrett balked, spilling wine as he did, raising his glass until a disgusted Evelyn refilled it.

"Pardon her rudeness," Navara said sharply. "One of our servants just died."

Ivar raised a brow, adjusting a forest-green coat, more snug than it had ever been with several eyelets missing their button counterparts around his belly's horizon. "When?"

"Yesterday."

Ivar scratched his chin. "Yesterday? Which one?"

"The servant girl."

"Shame... she was just starting to come into it too." Ivar raised his glass as though toasting an angel and took another sip. "Perhaps something stronger is in order..." A moment of apparent sincerity was swallowed by his next words. "So, what's the problem? We get another."

Evelyn cleared her throat, unaccustomed to joining in their conversations, but too at odds with herself to not speak up. "If I may, My Lords... Claire had been with us for some time and was Lady Antoinette's personal servant."

"Oh." Ivar nodded. "Not a problem! Michael and I will find a suitable replacement. One of the Weather girls perhaps." The two other men nodded eagerly, and Evelyn clenched her jaw and took a step back, resisting the urge to say something that would get her in hot water. Navara's lip turned up, eyes scanning the room, deciding to stay silent. "We can go there this evening in fact..."

"Marvelous!" Garrett added, raising his own glass. "But we should get down to brass tacks and discuss the wedding. Three months is sooner than you think."

"Yes, the midwife will be arriving this afternoon. Let's make the most of the time we have..." Lady Navara began as Antoinette tuned out the rest of the conversation, waiting for the gathering to be over, waiting to be allowed to return to her room.

When the morning had run long and the additional details had been ironed out, Navara, Ivar, and Evelyn left the room, leaving only Michael and Antoinette. "Do you feel honored? You should," Michael said, more alcohol than man, bending over to Antoinette, raising up her chin to force her to look at him.

She struggled to see him, her eyes still watering. She looked past him, eyes out of focus. She looked past him, a seething anger as he held her chin in his hands, his fist balling up.

"Lord Michael?" Evelyn Barett Webster cleared her throat at the threshold. "The midwife is here. Would you leave the room?"

"Perhaps I'll stay," Michael grimaced.

"You will not." Lady Navara stepped through the doorway with a powerful presence. "We'll have the room," she commanded, motioning with her hand until Michael smacked his lips, leaving the room.

When he'd gone, another woman stepped inside, taking a seat across from Antoinette while Lady Navara stood with her back to the door. Evelyn drew the curtains and helped Antoinette out of her dress. "We're just having a peek my dear," the midwife said, an older woman with salt and pepper hair, watching as Antoinette was undressed, then helping her onto her back atop the lounger. "The Lords want their assurances..." she added, placing her hands on Antoinette's knees and spreading her legs.

Antoinette closed her eyes, still watering, shutting out the humiliation of the following moments, trying hard not to feel the old woman survey her, trying not to hear the woman breathe so close to her thighs, focusing only on her own breathing, wishing so much that Claire stood beside her, holding her hand through this shame.

"All done," the midwife said after a few minutes, pressing Antoinette's knees closed as Evelyn quickly began to redress her.

"Well?" Navara asked harshly, placing a hand on a coin purse at her side.

"These things... all things..." the midwife began, putting away the instruments in her bag, "...come with uncertainty... there are ways that the Lords don't understand of *righting* things, but in this case... there is little doubt. The girl is a virgin."

"I see." Navara's hand relaxed from the coin purse at her side.

"If there is nothing else, My Lady?" the midwife asked.

"Relay the information to the Lords." Navara responded. "Evelyn, see to her fee after you escort her out."

"My Lady, might I also escort Lady Antoinette to her room?"

"Fetch one of the servant boys. Let him do it. Clearly my worry was misplaced."

Two hollowed-out husks of humans, Antoinette and Christian, walked in lockstep from the parlor on the first floor of the Schofield Manor, up the stairs to the second, and headed towards Antoinette's room. As the pair approached, they slowed. The last time they had been together in her room was when Claire had died. Now they stood an arms-length from her door, slowly approaching as though the emptiness inside could be worse than the events thus far.

There was no longer any sweat on the floor, and the dress they had peeled from Claire's body had been picked up. Antoinette's bed was neatly made, and her vanity tidied up. Any other person would have just seen a room, but it wasn't what the pair saw.

Christian walked in first, taking Antoinette's hand like he never had, guiding her towards her bed before letting her go. He released her, turning to walk away when she reached out for his hand, catching it and collapsing into his chest, unafraid to dirty herself.

She cried. Silently she cried into his arms, falling to her knees as she did, bringing him with her.

He cried. Silently he cried over her shoulder.

They cried. Silently they cried with the one person they knew understood their pain.

29

THE FIRST FEW DAYS AFTER CLAIRE'S DEATH WERE THE HARDEST. There was a silence between Antoinette and Christian, a heavy and palpable quiet that sometimes caused the other to break out in tears they tried to bat away before anyone would see them, ashamed, and, at the same time, not. Each passing in the hallways was a reminder of what they had witnessed. Their pain was a wound that didn't want to heal, painted with sinister undertones on a canvas of flesh, an incomplete puzzle of events that led to her death with one indomitable purple brushstroke on Claire's left side.

Summer storms were rare, and yet, a week after Claire's death another came, a gentle rain easily confused for a mist that quickened both of their hearts in the dead of night. Antoinette clutched at her chest in her bed, nervous and panicked, tossing and turning for an hour before slinked down from the second floor to the basement, silently turning the handle to Christian's room, expecting to find him lying on his rags, likely asleep, and instead found him wide awake, sitting atop the mound.

Another night of tears. Another night of little sleep. Another night of pain.

Christian sat atop the heap, a serrated knife with a wooden handle in his hands, bone white knuckles holding onto it for dear life, blade pointed towards him, and a steady stream of tears that persisted like the outside mist. The light from his blue eyes was taken in the darkness, and the young Lady of the Manor took a nervous step into his room, unsure if she wanted to stop him or join him.

A seat at his side didn't startle him; a hand upon his own didn't deter him; a reluctant gulp from the woman beside him didn't reassure him. "She wouldn't want this." Antoinette's voice was as quiet as a confession and carried with it the weight of a prayer. "I don't either."

Her hand was soft upon his, but her strength was none. Her hand was no more a deterrent than battling him for control of the knife. She couldn't have stopped him by force if he tried, but it wasn't his arms that needed convincing.

"I should have had enough at least to bury her properly." The doctor had looked to his overflowing hands a week ago, filled with copper coins, dusty, muddy, and unpolished. He didn't need to say a single word to tell him that it was nowhere near enough. "He didn't even try to count the coins..." Christian stared down at the knife in his hands. "I should have protected her!"

"You didn't know." Her eyes looked at the moonlight, reflected in the blade. "I didn't either."

"I think she tried to tell me."

"Me too."

"I couldn't hear it though." His eyes looked up, pooling. "I couldn't hear what she was saying."

"She wouldn't have told us." Another lump in her throat. "She wouldn't have told us even if we suspected."

The edge of the knife in his hands was unremarkable, but the damage it could do didn't need to be pretty.

"...Me or him?" An ominous tone swallowed sadness and spat out anger, the knife in his hands hungry for blood, but not particular about whose. *Me or your father*, he wanted to ask, suspecting but unable to confirm that the man responsible was the only one who'd had access and a propensity for violence.

Antoinette stayed beside Christian in the darkness quietly, mouth unwilling to condemn anyone as the rain continued to fall. "I don't want to lose you too." Her hand reached for the knife more confidently, prying it from his fingers with little struggle and setting it on the floor beside them, reaching her arm around him and bringing him close.

30

WEEKS AFTER CLAIRE'S GRAVE HAD BEEN DUG, THE EARTH LAY flat again; stubborn grass sprouts challenged the summer sun before the coming autumn, and Antoinette and Christian's loss had brought them closer than ever.

Ever since the night she'd caught him holding the knife, when she wasn't taking etiquette lessons in preparation for the wedding, she would follow him around the Manor, keeping an eye on him, trying to make small talk to distract them both from the responsibilities foisted upon them. She'd even arranged Claire's bed to be brought into his room after he turned down the idea of moving into hers.

After the departure of Akolai and the death of his sister, Christian's duties had multiplied. He was busier than ever, but grateful for the distractions and that Antoinette had kept what she'd walked in on a secret. The more time that he spent with her, the more he opened up, and the closer their bond.

A month after his sister's death, the new normal was trending from agonizing to only intolerable. Today he mopped up the bathwater and scrubbed down the clawfoot tub across from her room as she watched mindlessly, unaware that Claire had often times done the same.

"How are things with the Weather girl?" he asked of their newest live-in guest. The one who had arrived a week after Claire's death.

Antoinette rolled her eyes. "Taxing. A little strange. Fancies gardening. What's your opinion?"

Christian stopped and looked back at Antoinette with his sapphire eyes. "Interesting?"

"Interesting because of how she acts?" Antoinette raised a brow, jumping down from the counter and pushing her breasts together, bending over like an awkward duck. "*Oh, My Lady...*" she sounded off in a higher pitch before laughing. "*Right away, My Lady.*"

Christian smiled weakly, watching her impression. "Spot on... She's not mean you know..."

"I know," she pouted.

"But I don't know how Lady Navara tolerates her..."

Antoinette rolled her eyes. "Mother stands on decorum. As long as she is not publicly made a fool of... private matters are another thing entirely... though I do wonder where that line is now. It *has* been strange with father here regularly. He's been going out less."

"I'm aware..." Christian scrubbed the tub harder, bristles bending as he grinded wooden handle against the tub. "Very aware."

"Well, the attraction lives here now..." she mused before biting her lip, ashamed at what she'd said. "I'm sorry... I didn't mean..."

"I know." Ivar Schofield was a sore subject for the both of them that neither knew quite how to navigate. The status quo was tense; some days it was more tolerable than others. Christian stayed out of his sight as much as he could, and Evelyn had quietly taken on any interactions involving him. "Is that the only reason he isn't going out?" Christian asked cautiously.

Antoinette's eyes narrowed. "What else is there?"

"It's... not my place."

"Christian!" Antoinette leaned over the tub opposite him, half of her spilling into the tub. "Tell me."

"I don't..."

"Christian... who's the Lady here?" Antoinette leaned in closer, her face right beside his. Her chest dropped into the cavity of the tub, level with his eyes. She hadn't thought how it would look before leaning over She watched him carefully. "Christian...?" Her eyes measured his lips, and she bit her own, unsure of what would come next.

"...I heard Miss Webster..." Antoinette let out a sigh, leaning in, a little less afraid as he whispered, pressing her cheek against his to hear him better. "She was speaking with one of the kitchen servants about their... settlement."

"What about it?"

"Their... *lack* of settlement. Our lack of pay."

Antoinette's eyes went wide. She turned around and ran out of the bathroom. Christian could hear her dresser drawers opening and closing. She returned a moment later with a concerned look on her face. "Some of my dresses are missing... and some of my jewelry too... Do you think someone...?"

Christian shrugged. "Stole, no. Sold."

"Father was paid very handsomely..." Antoinette felt a realization overtake her. "But... that was when he was working..."

"He does... indulge."

"I'm going to ask mother..." Christian raised a brow. "I'll be discreet!" Antoinette urged as his smile returned. "I can be discreet you know!"

"Yes, My Lady." Christian said, returning to his work.

As he walked through the halls of the Schofield Manor, he wondered if Antoinette had begun to realize the extent of change that he had observed. Where once he had dusted a dozen paintings, now there were only nine. Where once the gardener had tended to the flowers, now the Weather girl fulfilled the role. Where once the smell of meat had wafted down at every meal, now it was only once a day.

The wine was as watered down as it could have been and the finer crystal whiskey bottles long since gone. A summer of indulgence had robbed the Schofield Manor of much, some of it replaceable, some not. Even if there was a begrudged servant taking from the Schofields, there was no way that it would escape Evelyn Barett Webster's all-knowing gaze.

When night fell, Christian trudged down to the subfloor and an excitable Antoinette chased behind him. "It's true," she said, rubbing an arm, feeling the temperature drop as she descended. "Mother admitted as much to me... she's been coordinating the... disappearances," a worried whisper escaped her lips.

Christian nodded, opening the door to his room and Antoinette looked around. It was the first time she'd really focused on what he had, and, upon reflection, it surprised her how sparse it was. Claire had been right about her brother wanting little. Her former bunk bed had been taken apart in the move to his room and the top bunk had been sold before the arrival of the Weather girl.

Aside from the bed, the only other item in the room was a scratched six-drawer dresser that sheltered his clothes from the ground and hid a small stash of copper coins he'd quietly been saving. The heap of rags that had been his bed for so long was gone. There was no single item that said *Christian Nikolai Dusk lives here*—instead only the notion that someone, sometimes, utilized the space.

"Things are fine right now..." she admitted. "But mother is pragmatic. She knows they won't always be." Antoinette leaned against the door with a sigh. "She's preparing... considering father's impulses."

"That's not all that's bothering you, is it?"

She nodded. "But you can't tell anyone."

"Who would I tell?" Christian shrugged. "Who's left to tell?" He looked away quickly.

"Promise. You won't tell anyone?" she said, a little more cautiously.

He nodded. "Mother plans to replace Evelyn with someone more 'cost effective.'" She raised her fingers in air quotes.

"Oh..." Christian looked down, unsure of how to feel towards the woman who'd stood in for his mother for the past decade. "Well... I can do without payment or reward," he said, leaning against his dresser across the room from her. "I'm as cost effective as it gets. So, I'll probably still be here."

Antoinette nodded slowly, looking up at the sky through the window at ground-level, not capturing the essence of his joke. "For how long?"

"What do you mean?"

"Claire is gone... Akolai too... soon Evelyn... then me. How long will you continue serving House Schofield?"

Christian followed her gaze to the sky above. He'd wondered the same thing. "Where would I go?"

"Anywhere. You could go anywhere and be happier... maybe. Everything's changing so quickly."

He folded his arms and took in a deep breath. "Wouldn't you be sad if I left?"

The words came out of his mouth so conversationally. He didn't realize the dread that could come from that innocent question. He didn't know himself why he even asked it, but there the question lingered, in the space between them.

"No, I wouldn't be sad." Antoinette felt a tear in her eye. "I think I would be sad if you stayed, watching the Schofield Manor fall... or watching me turn into my mother... or finally deciding to make him pay..." She walked over to him, leaning against the dresser, then letting her head fall against his shoulder. "Your story only starts out as a servant... that's how mine ends... with someone else taking everything."

He wrapped an arm around her. "You could run... you could do what Akolai did and run." He paused. "You could even command me to go with you..."

She smiled sadly. "'A penniless Lady with no practical skills...' that's what mother calls me sometimes... how many Weather girls started with more before they were sold into a life of opening their legs?"

"But they don't have your acting skills!" Christian strutted around the room the way she had earlier that morning, tossing back his imaginary hair and pressing his imaginary breasts together. "And I have a few coins... more now that I've added Claire's..." His eyes drifted to the alphabet wall behind which Claire lay. "They could be yours."

Antoinette smirked, then grinned, then let out a full-on smile. The sadness was still deep in her eyes, but the joy of the moment battled it and gave her the courage to speak her heart. Her chest pounded and still she beamed, waiting for him to return to her side.

Her eyes twinkled as she took his hand, standing shoulder-to-shoulder with him. "I love you Christian..." she said quietly, looking down, fidgeting with her free hand. "I love you more than him. I love you oceans more than any other man. I love when we talk... and I love that you make me smile..."

"Lady Antoin..." Christian began, pulling his hands away with uncertainty.

"You don't have to love me as anything more than a friend... and I won't blame you if you're not here tomorrow... but... I don't want to be his trophy... I don't want *this* taken by him too..." She teared up, her lips quivering as they reached for his. "Give me a memory they can't take from me. I don't want to go my life not knowing what it feels like to be loved..."

Her lips pressed against his for a moment, feeling the warmth reciprocated as he kissed her back, pulling away for only a second to say, "Neither do I."

31

Evelyn Barett Webster stood at the foot of Antoinette's bed. Her face was contorted as she looked down to the four feet sticking out from under the sheets. She had suspected for a while now. Something had changed since the engagement and Claire's death, but Christian had never confirmed her suspicions and had always managed to return to his room unseen.

On this night, the moon was high in the sky and the tree outside Antoinette's window stood still in suspense. The Head Servant had no reason to be in Lady Antoinette's room, but only days until the wedding and almost two months since their first romantic encounter, she simply had to know.

She exited the room as quietly as she entered, her sneer slowly disappearing. She recalled the countless lashings she had given Christian. He wouldn't have survived the one he would have received for this, but Evelyn Barett Webster was a servant, not a slave, and her services had been terminated.

"You can stay for the wedding, if you wish." Those had been the blunt words of her former Lady after they had told her the news.

She didn't need their charity, and it was clear she hadn't earned their respect, so she exited the Manor, with the same simple case she had used when visiting her sister at the beginning of the summer. Without a goodbye, without a confession, and without a sound. She left in the darkness, and when she was far enough down the road that only the Red World could hear her, she said only two words: "good riddance."

CHRISTIAN WOKE BEFORE ANTOINETTE THAT MORNING. HE DIDN'T have the luxury of sleeping in, but on this morning in particular, he couldn't help but stay back for a moment to take in the sight of the wrinkles he left behind on her bed, and to breathe in the aroma of her perfume, still light upon her sheets.

A smile was spread across his face. A smile he didn't know he had within him, but one he knew could end any day. He treasured the moments he had with her, but when the house stirred, he had to make himself sparse. "See you soon, my love," he whispered quietly so she wouldn't hear as he slipped out of her room.

His footsteps were quick. He glided through the halls, floating above the floor. He didn't make a sound. He knew the false floorboards better than anyone in the Manor, and knew they wouldn't betray his secret; so, when he laid upon his own bed in his room, the glee still upon his face, he knew the footsteps that followed were not those which persecuted him.

The door to his room squeaked open, "Christian?"

Aubrey, the live-in Weather girl, stood at his door looking as ravished as she usually did. A shirt covered most of her body, and the outline of underwear beneath it was all she wore. She was a few years older than Christian, with soft brown eyes that clung to an innocence she'd long since lost. She had been more buxom when she'd arrived a few weeks after Claire's death, but in the two months that followed, she had thinned dramatically.

Lady Navara had made it clear that she wanted Aubrey contained as much as possible. She wasn't allowed on the second floor. She wasn't allowed near her room, or, more importantly, near her bed. Even as she stood before Christian with her shivering feet, she hadn't even been provided shoes. She was Ivar's answer to their money issues and his obsession: a live-in replacement for the exploits he so craved.

"What is it?" Christian sat up.

"Miss Webster isn't here... and I found this letter." She held up a slip of paper. Unlike those written by the Schofield family, it wasn't sealed, only folded over. "I can't read it. What does it say?"

Christian took the parchment hesitantly. "Where did you get it?"

"Here. Under your door. I saw it peeking out when I came down last night." Christian felt his heart quicken in a panic. "The door to Miss Webster's room was open too... and a few things are missing."

Aubrey walked over to Christian's bed and knelt atop it. A passerby would have mistaken it for an advance, but Aubrey was more interested in the warmth the bed promised her cold feet, rather than the man atop it who still smelled of Antoinette.

He looked at the paper, breathing nervously, ignoring Aubrey slipping her hands under his blanket, a deep worry overtaking him as he opened it. "...She was fired," Christian said, reading the letter slowly, "...says she left."

"Is that all?" Aubrey leaned over, squinting at the letters, seeing how they went on and on.

"That's all." Christian lied as she leaned away, pursing his lips, taking a moment to read the rest.

"Oh... okay." Aubrey looked out the window.

"Is that all?" Christian asked.

Aubrey's cracked lips looked down sadly. "Can I sleep here?" He stood up quickly. "When you don't use it... can I sleep here?" He had been by Aubrey's room occasionally. Formerly his sister's, it was more a reflection of what his room used to look like. A mound of clothes was heaped high, and it was where she usually slept. "You don't sleep here much..."

Christian leaned over. "Shh!"

"I won't say anything! And Lord Ivar doesn't come down here much... just when he's drunk. He prefers the parlor... And I can follow your rules. And..." she avoided his gaze and looked down, "...it's starting to get cold..."

Christian sighed. Only a few days until the first day of autumn and she was right, the cold days were approaching. She'd only known the summer and she was already feeling the cold. Almost a decade on a heap of rags and he had never grown accustomed to it, but Aubrey was already suffering in different ways. A black eye and a smattering of bruises were mostly healed, quivering legs had grown accustomed, and the fear had melted into acceptance. Just like him, she was trying to survive.

"You need shoes... you won't survive without them."

Aubrey nodded eagerly. "...And the bed?"

"Fine. But make sure you're as clean as you can be..." Christian looked at her tunic. She'd clearly worn it for days without washing it. It used to be his sister's. It sat snug against Aubrey's body, even now, even as she'd thinned.

"I'll get some night clothes or... I can sleep naked, if you want? The blanket feels so nice." Aubrey's hands had already warmed up under the covers in just the time they spoke. "You can have me too if you want. I think that's a fair trade. You're not rough or anything, right?" Christian stood resolute for a moment, then he grinned, his smile flashed, and he let out an earnest laugh. "What's so funny? I'm a woman. You're a man..."

"I was just remembering... a long time ago there were more of us servant boys..." He tried to compose himself as he spoke next to the half-naked woman on his bed. "...Two of the boys who aren't here got in a lot of trouble for peeping... and the other one wouldn't have been able to tell a girl what he wanted if he wanted to... and me..."

"You?"

"My sister said some people needed a push... said I needed a shove."

"Am I the shove?" she asked quizzically, wiggling her toes under the blanket.

"You could have been, but not anymore..." Christian said, thinking about Antoinette. "If you want a fair trade, just cover for me. It's how Akolai and I got along. If someone ever asks and I'm not here... just cover for me... and if I ever need another favor... I'll let you know."

"And you can be with..." she lowered her voice,"...the little Lady?" Christian was about to ask when Aubrey giggled to herself. "I know what men look like when they have eyes for someone... she looks at you the same you know."

"I know," he admitted. "I know." He smiled.

32

Navara Schofield stood behind her daughter, watching her undress as the maids helped her slide into her wedding dress. With only three days until the wedding, there was little time left for mistakes. Something about Antoinette's sudden joy in the face of a tragedy that had hollowed her out at the beginning of the summer made her uneasy.

Navara watched, with a keener eye than anyone else, noticing a subtlety about her daughter that even she herself hadn't noticed. The dress fit *almost* the same as it had at her first fitting a couple of months ago. There was nothing that really called out to her in particular, but there was something that morning that nagged at her, a rare intuition from a woman who'd rarely been suitable to be called *mother*.

"Clear the room," she commanded, and the three servants, clutching pins between their teeth, midway through fastening knots and holding Antoinette's hair to style, set down their instruments and left the room, closing the door behind them.

Antoinette looked back at her mother, fiddling with the double-stranded pearl necklace she'd chosen to wear with the dress. "Mother?"

"You mustn't be careless," Navara said, taking her position behind her daughter, drawing the laces of the corset tightly, so tightly that Antoinette inhaled sharply by reflex. "Carelessness can take a life all its own."

Antoinette felt her heart begin to race. Her mother had always been careful with her words, and as Antoinette stared at her own unchanged reflection, the delight on her face was washed away. "Do you think...?" she began to ask nervously.

Navara gritted her teeth. The prospect of a question betrayed the confession. "Whatever the case. Don't neglect your charge. Give him what he expects... regardless of what you want. We have our duty." She ran her fingers through Antoinette's hair.

"Mother?" Antoinette tried to stand taller and straighter, letting the unsolicited advice take root, but failing to take hold. It felt odd, she admitted to herself, the idea that her mother would suspect something and not scold her, and, to the contrary, offer advice. Perhaps, Antoinette thought, there was no use in scolding her. Perhaps this one act of compassion was her wedding gift.

The maids were let back in and finished styling Antoinette, leaving the hair pins and jewelry they had opted not to use in a wooden box atop the vanity. Navara's proud reflection looked at her daughter. Ornate red roses climbed up the white dress to her bust while spirals of gold and silver wrapped the train. Lace half-sleeves hung at her elbows beneath her curled hair. She'd never looked more stunning.

The two women looked with pride at her reflection as footsteps hurried towards them. The steps were long and fast, and the corset grew tighter as Antoinette recognized them. They raced up from the first floor and an out-of-breath Christian Nikolai Dusk stood awestruck at the threshold, pausing for a moment to take in Antoinette's beauty, now donning warmer red cheeks which Navara ignored as she turned about face.

"My Ladies..." Christian said, righting himself and standing up straight. "Mi... Lord Michael has just arrived with news. Lord Ivar has had an accident in town... the doctor is on his way..."

Navara took a powerful step forward. "Follow me, servant," she called to

Christian who tried to memorize Antoinette's beauty in the second before he turned to follow her.

"Mother?" Antoinette asked, trying to pick up the train to follow them, stumbling as she dismounted the pedestal on which she stood.

"Stay here child," Navara boomed nervously.

"But..." Antoinette began, before quieting herself. "Yes, mother," she consented as Christian and Navara headed down the hall together.

"What else?" Navara asked, somehow walking as fast as Christian had run without losing her breath.

"Lord Michael and Lord Garrett were with Lord Ivar. Lord Ivar was involved in an altercation. He hit his head and began to bleed."

Navara inhaled deeply. "What else?"

"The doctor was called. Lord Michael ran here and is out of breath near the main door. Lord Garrett remained at Lord Ivar's side at the site of the accident."

"Where?" Silence. "Where?"

"...Outside the Weather House..."

Navara exhaled sharply. "Is that all you know?"

"Yes, My Lady," Christian said, arriving at the first floor.

"Call a carriage to the main door."

"Right away, My Lady."

"...And servant..." Navara called to Christian, "...you'll ride with me."

Christian felt his heart drop. "...Yes, My Lady."

33

CHRISTIAN NIKOLAI DUSK SAT IN THE CARRIAGE ACROSS FROM LADY Navara. He had ridden in one on only a handful of occasions, and never alone with her. As the wheels began to turn, he could see the Schofield Manor disappearing into the background at each turn, a sinking feeling he'd felt only when Evelyn had taken him from his mother over a decade ago.

The trip that would have been forty-five minutes on foot was only ten by carriage. Lady Navara's fingers rubbed against themselves uneasily. It was a habit that Christian had observed as the price for her composure, this twitch that prepared her for the unsavory actions that her station demanded.

"Are you trying to make a fool of me?" she asked as the carriage rolled on.

Lady Navara's sentences, like her questions, also had a point. For Christian to act like he misunderstood them was an insult to them both. "No, My Lady." Christian paused. "I lov..."

"Stop." She raised a hand, and he did. "It's trivial. The beatings you'll take will not replace the ones that she will be forced to endure. She'll pay the price for your selfishness."

"Yes, My Lady."

"Tell me servant... are you stupid, sloppy, or cursed?"

"My Lady...?"

A misunderstanding could have been cleared up if the driver hadn't called back to them. "...Lady Schofield... perhaps we should turn around..." he said as the carriage slowed, coming to the scene of the accident.

"No," she commanded, opening the still-moving carriage door, compelling the driver to stop, and facing the scene head on.

She didn't gasp like other passersby. Her composure didn't waver as she stepped out with Christian in tow, witnessing the concave head of her husband which appeared stricken by a blunt instrument, laying in a pool of its own blood, a smattering of copper coins around his body.

Her eyes measured the bulging wall on the corner then followed it, as though recreating the fall. At the feet of her late husband, a river of water lay spread across the sidewalk. *Did he slip,* she wondered, looking to the direction the water came from. *Did he stumble and hit his head on the wall?* Her eyes looked to the coins on the ground. *A debt that someone finally came to collect?*

Two doors down there was a wooden sign with the symbol of a sun, a cloud, and rain. The fabled Weather House was discreet in its placement, but the gaggle of women that stood outside, scantily clad and completely unashamed, cast discretion to the wind as they looked on, leaving little to the imagination.

Garrett Escoté ran quickly to Navara, shielding her from the scene far too late. "Lady Navara," he exclaimed, "you shouldn't have to..."

She raised a hand to this man, the same as she had to Christian. She thought carefully of what she could say to sound both sincere and proud, instead of angry at her husband for dying in this fashion. "Fetch a cleric... Ivar prayed to the Six Gods... he'd want the sendoff."

"Right away My Lady... and if you need anything, anything at all... you need only say the word." He tucked his hand under his waist for a moment and bent over.

Navara couldn't tell him what she needed, so instead, she turned her attention back to Christian. "Inform Antoinette that her father is dead and that we shall hold a ceremony for him *after* the wedding." Christian stood for a moment, the carriage behind him, unsure of how exactly to proceed. "Go servant. While your legs still work."

"Yes, My Lady."

Christian turned quickly, accidentally kicking a wayward coin scattered near Ivar's body. A sharp tone of metal on stone drew his attention. His eyes dropped down, watching the copper rolling on its side for an impossibly long while before colliding with a wall across the street. With Lady Navara's back turned, he followed the coin and reached down for it, an edge of blood upon its shiny surface. It fit perfectly in his hand, a half-shield on the back of the coin, ridiculously faded, poorly imprinted, instantly recognizable as a fake.

He picked it up, clutching it tightly, hiding a wicked smile as he headed back to the Schofield Manor. He burst out laughing as he ran, ignoring the looks of strangers as he bolted forward, forced to swallow his delight before he returned to his home, arriving face-to-face with Michael Escoté pacing at the entrance, waiting with bated breath to know what had occurred. "Well?"

34

THE DAY OF IVAR'S DEATH WAS A WHIRLWIND. A CONFLICTED Christian marched his way up to the second floor of his home to see Antoinette, still half-pinned up in her wedding dress. The news he had to give her would devastate her, but he selfishly wondered if a part of her would also delight in it.

When the longest remaining live-in servant caught Antoinette's gaze, she knew instantly. The words that followed were merely an echo of what his eyes revealed. "He was dead when we arrived."

The three maids who were dressing her showed more emotion than she did. He didn't know if her love for the man outweighed her apathy or hatred. He'd always cared for her, but the death of Claire was the final nail in the coffin of reciprocity.

"Is that all?" Shades of Navara were accentuated as she returned to her stance. "Continue," she urged the maids whose gazes upon each other betrayed their sentiment.

As Christian made his way down to his room, he wondered if she'd come to him in the night, if he'd find her crying like she had, if she'd fall apart like they had. How much did the death of her father mean compared to the death of his sister. He didn't want her to shed a tear, but she'd felt the loss of a parent nonetheless.

The wedding was days away. Neither Christian nor Antoinette had made peace with it yet and now, a new development added more chaos into the uncertainty.

In the basement of the Schofield Manor, Christian pushed open the door to his room to find it ransacked. His neatly folded clothes had been ripped from his dresser and littered around the room. A lump on his bed gave away the presence of another, and when he pulled up the covers, a naked Aubrey was curled in a ball, bruises over her torso.

"Aubrey?"

The Weather girl's eyes were slow to open. She winced as she righted herself, unashamed and unafraid, using the blanket as a cloak as she sat up, dress and underwear at the foot of her bed. Christian's eyes surveyed her bruises and, rather than cover up her chest, instead the Weather girl blushed and tried to hide the splotches that decorated her body. "It looks worse than it is," she lied. "Last night he was drunk." Shades of bruises, some brighter than others, caused him to grit his teeth in anger as he wrapped the blanket tighter around her body, her auburn hair peeking over the blankets as she looked around, startled by the room in disarray. "I thought I dreamt it." She threw off the blanket quickly, walking around the room and picking up the scattered clothes, leaving him sitting on the edge of the bed. "It wasn't me," she whispered nervously as she began to throw things into the dresser with neither rhyme nor reason.

"I know," he responded, picking up the remaining clothes and laying them on the bed, trying to salvage the slightly-folded ones from the ones that had been completely tossed.

"I think he took your coins." Aubrey bit her lip, on her hunches, timid, waiting for a reproach or a strike. "I didn't tell him you had any. He got mad... I couldn't stop crying... he said he would find someone else and left..." Christian looked to the alphabet wall behind which his sister was buried. Aubrey picked up the remaining clothes, putting them on his bed. "I'm sorry...

if I wasn't here he wouldn't have taken your money..." She wanted to cry, and when he went to offer her his hand, she flinched before taking them, standing shorter, confused and unsure as he wrapped his arms around her.

He was warm.

She didn't imagine he would be so warm.

She didn't imagine how safe and comfortable she could feel in his embrace. When she hugged back, she could feel his tears on her shoulder. "I'm okay," she lied.

"He's gone," he whispered.

"Gone?"

"Dead."

"Dead?"

"Dead."

"He's not coming back?"

"No." Aubrey smiled as she hugged him tighter.

"He won't hurt you again. You're safe..." *sister,* "you're safe."

35

Th e evening after Ivar's death, Garrett returned to the
Schofield Manor to ask Navara if she wished to postpone the wedding
in favor of the funeral. "It would be understandable..." Garrett had said,
while a childish Michael balled up his fist in the background. "Right, son?"

He didn't have a chance to respond or protest before Navara answered.
"The arrangements have already been made." Stoic and true, she turned down
the idea. "Two days from now Michael and Antoinette shall be married... we
can see to Ivar's arrangements afterwards..."

"Many fellow soldiers respected Ivar... it would be most gracious to host a
large..."

Navara's husband was gone and yet, as Garrett prattled on, he didn't realize
that she was more concerned with the aftermath of her husband's death than
the man himself. She hadn't yet decided if it was good or bad, but opportunity
was born from both.

Garrett's proclamation sought more attendees, which meant more mouths
to feed, and more money to spend. Navara would have ordered Christian to

dig a hole beside Claire's grave if it wouldn't have been seen as taboo, but the longer Garrett went on, the grander the opportunity that a shrewd Navara could capitalize on.

"What exactly are you proposing beyond a simple ceremony?"

Garrett struck while the iron was hot. "A festival. A feast. A celebration!"

"A fortune," Navara scoffed coldly, threatening to halt the momentum.

"If you would permit it... it would be an Escoté honor to..."

Decorum dictated she hear him out, the fool who had fallen into her trap. Still, she let him continue long into the night as they worked out the costly details of a celebration he'd be responsible for.

THE NIGHT NAVARA ENTERTAINED GARRETT WAS THE FIRST NIGHT IN a long time that Christian tossed and turned, unable to sleep, another woman by his side. For more than two months, he had slept beside Antoinette, but now her mother knew their secret, now her father was dead, and the following night she would share her bed with another.

The day before the wedding was chaos, with the hired servants working double duty to make arrangements and to update the venue for the newlyweds. For the second night in as many, Aubrey slept while Christian stayed awake.

The wedding day came and went in a flash. The Schofield Manor was mostly empty that day. Neither Christian, Aubrey, nor any of the temporary servants had been invited to attend at the temple, nor the reception that followed.

In the late hours of the night, with only the moon awake to greet them, the newlyweds returned while the festivities wound down. Michael Escoté ambled into the Schofield Manor with Antoinette by his side, steeped in whiskey, excitedly tugging Antoinette across the house, towards her room. He wouldn't remember much of what would transpire behind the closed doors of Antoinette's bedroom, but in the morning, he would wake to find them both naked, and the evidence abundant enough for him to claim a long-awaited victory.

The words of Lady Navara had prompted an added measure of precaution so subtle that only one looking for it would have seen it. The proof that Michael sought was discreetly fabricated upon a white bedsheet. The timeline of events was preserved, and so too was the illusion.

Objectively, she had been a virgin, then they were married, then they had lain together, and now she was pregnant.

In reality, she had been pregnant all along.

36

IT WAS THE MIDDLE OF THE NIGHT WHEN ANTOINETTE STIRRED awake to see Christian under her covers.

Three days of being married and already she was embroiled in a tangled web. She'd been careful to avoid Christian around Michael, it had been part of the agreement that they had made in the summer months leading up to the wedding. She didn't want marriage to change anything more than it needed to—they'd already suffered enough this summer. She loved Christian. At best, she could tolerate her husband.

Michael and Garrett had departed, spreading word of Ivar's funeral to a growing guest list, unknowingly leaving Antoinette's bed empty for another. When she leaned over him, she was careful that her mother wouldn't overhear from her room down the hall. Lady Navara could turn a blind eye to their indiscretions, or she could wake and wreak havoc on them both.

Antoinette placed her lips upon his for a moment. Christian's eyes slowly opened and looked over at her as she feigned being asleep, but a subtle smile and her rosy cheeks fooled no one. His lips were on hers and she shuddered; he always made her shudder at his touch.

When his kisses ran down her body for the second time that night, she took hold of his face between her hands and pulled him close, throwing the covers over them as a shield to the outside world and whispering as though the absent Michael could hear her. "I have to tell you something."

His arm was already wrapped around her, his blue eyes waiting patiently, and Lady Navara's question '*are you stupid, sloppy, or cursed*' echoed within him as she turned suspicion to confirmation: "I'm pregnant."

There was a moment of fear after the confession: the moment before he responded when she wondered if he would behave in any manner other than the one she knew him capable of. There was a moment when she thought of the man holding the knife in the darkness, barely able to tolerate the weight he'd been under.

The moment faded with his smile. "I love you. A family. Our family."

An eager nod overflowed their makeshift tent with excitement as his hand reached for her slender belly. The couple held each other that night, each lost in their own streams of thought, both wondering the exact same thing, but unwilling to break free of the bliss before Antoinette finally spoke up. "Michael can never know..."

"...and neither can the child..." Christian continued, a wave of melancholy settling over them.

"...are you...?"

Christian looked at her with sincerity, and even in the darkness she could sense his light. "No. We're from two different worlds... sometimes by what we do, and sometimes by what we don't... but this..." Christian rubbed her stomach. "...This will unite us forever... even if it's only us who know it."

Antoinette's eyes began to tear up happily, nodding. "Forever."

"A family," Christian whispered with a smile. "Our little secret family."

She locked lips with him and fell back asleep in his arms, hoping to wake in his embrace, unaware of what else the night would have in store for them.

HOURS LATER, THE AUTUMN WIND RACED THROUGH THE TOWN, AND IN the darkness of the early morning, a pair of silver eyes that belonged to a stranger saw an open window on the first floor as an invitation into the Schofield Manor.

If the guest had made its way to the basement, it would have found Aubrey curled up in Christian's bed. If it had continued on the first floor, it would have found a pair of hired servants resting after a long day's work in the parlor, but instead it made its way up the stairs, moving through the rooms until it came to Antoinette's door, a smell in the air that it couldn't ignore.

Despite its height, taller than any guest of the Schofield Manor, it moved quietly in the dark, slowly turning the doorknob and gazing upon the outlines of the couple. As the creature moved to their bedside, hunched over, a weak gust knocked the branches of the tree beside Claire's grave against the window with a thud much louder than it should have been, waking a startled Christian.

He always slept on pins and needles in Antoinette's bed. He was always ready to leave, always prepared to be caught, and though the thud was loud to him, it barely stirred the woman at his side.

There was silence. There was only astounding silence as that creature looked at him with its large silver eyes, flaring four ungodly fangs at Christian beneath a mouth slathered in red. He moved slowly beside Antoinette's body. He knew that this thing was not human. He knew instantly that this creature was a vampire. It scared him, but the thought of Antoinette still peacefully asleep beside him, also in danger, terrified him more.

He found his foot running alongside Antoinette who awoke with a startle. "Christian?"

Antoinette froze to behold the vampire. The pair could make out no more of it save the silver of its eyes, and four long white fangs that protruded from its mouth. It appeared conscious, but at the same time carnal, thin skin stretched tightly over its face and an excited breathing that smelled of iron.

"Run!" Christian hissed, shoving Antoinette off the bed towards the door, lunging at the impending vampire with clenched fists.

There was no time to react before he felt its fangs latch onto him and pierce his neck.

As he pulled away, he felt his skin rip, powerless unto the razor-sharp canines and locked jaw of the beast. The pain sent him to the floor with a gasp.

He tried to stem the bleeding, clutching at his own neck, cupping it tightly, hand holding back the blood that poured out, searching for something to act as a tourniquet.

"...B...!"

"Christian!" Antoinette screamed, drawing the vampire's focus, silver eyes darting from his first prey to his would-be second, a long tongue lapping up Christian's blood, spitting out the chunk of flesh it had torn, ignoring the suffering man at his feet. In one enormous movement, it leapt over the bed to Antoinette.

Christian could feel his teeth shaping, could feel a strength returning to him, and as he held tightly the wound on his neck, could feel the blood loss slowing, his skin struggling to sew itself back together as he Turned.

"...Br...!"

The beast towered over Antoinette, leaning in to make her his meal when Christian charged with his full strength, colliding with it and shoving it against the wall, stones shifting from the force.

It reeled for a moment before a savage rage overtook it and a tantrum-fueled snarl filled the room.

Antoinette let out a yelp, scurrying backwards, retreating against the floor as Christian climbed on top of her, separating her from the beast.

"...St...!"

The vampire loomed; its eyes set on Antoinette, trying to reach at her through the man who'd climbed atop her, shielding her. It lashed at Christian, once, twice, thrice, repeatedly.

"Christian!" Antoinette trembled below him, his body quaking with each strike, his blood spilling onto her as she tried to make herself smaller beneath him.

Its long, sharpened nails slashed at Christian, slicing through his shirt and ripping open his back. A series of blows sought to dismount him from Antoinette, but they were in vain. Christian endured attack after attack until there was a reprieve, until there was a moment to feel his suffering, a moment when he heard the beast wallow in anger.

"*Bite Antoinette!*" a voice said as Antoinette sobbed. "*You have to bite her!*" the voice whispered into Christian's ear. "*If you bite her... maybe he'll stop. Brother!*" Claire's voice resonated. "*Bite her! Save her!*"

"Claire...?" Christian whispered, leaning down to Antoinette's neck, flaring his newly-formed twin fangs as she shuddered, swinging her legs wildly. "We have to trust her... you have to trust me..." His fangs pierced Antoinette's neck and she stopped kicking. As gently as he could, his fangs pierced her.

She shuddered at his touch. Even his bite was warm.

The beast's scream grew louder as Christian bit her, louder as he took in a few drops of her, louder as his body collapsed atop her, leaving them both in a pool of his blood.

It approached Christian's collapsed body, lifting it off Antoinette like a ragdoll before a gust slammed the city. The wind shook the house and snapped the branch from the tree outside, shattering the nearby window and startling the beast. It dropped Christian's body beside Antoinette's on instinct.

Christian couldn't move. He could only watch its bare leg as it towered over them, struggling to keep his eyes open, trying to crawl over to Antoinette again, weak and unable to.

For a moment, for a brief moment, Christian saw another figure, shorter and older, hairless and with red eyes standing beside the vampire, a look of disappointment as it surveyed the carnage. The older man stood beside the beast one moment and in the next, both were gone, fled through the broken second-story window as Christian's heavy eyelids slowly closed.

37

"**A**NTOINETTE!" **CHRISTIAN AWOKE WITH A GASP.**

He was in his bed in only his underwear. His upper half and neck had been bandaged. His eyes focused in the darkness. It was his room, it was his bed, but the window had been covered with something that prevented the light from pouring into the room.

"You're awake," a voice whispered directly into his ear. *"Thank the Gods."*

"Claire?" Christian whispered back, looking around, tongue lapping his parched lips, the taste of iron still in his mouth. "Sister is that you?"

"Brother?" the voice responded. *"Brother! It's me. It's Claire! I'm here!"*

"How is this...?"

"He can hear us?" another voice said.

"Stop!" another screeched.

"I'm not ready..." said a third.

"Goodbye... my love..." said a fourth

"Kill yourself," said a fifth, before the voices began to intermix.

Christian clutched at his head. "I can hear you... I can hear you all...

Antoinette?"

"She's safe brother. She's upstairs." Christian shot out of bed, dropping to one knee from the pain that came from the wounds on his back. *"You can't go. She's with Michael."*

"Michael?"

"You've been asleep for almost a week."

"Is she...?"

"Safe." Claire paused. *"...Safer than you. You're pale, brother... you don't look well..."*

"You... you saved us."

"I didn't know that you'd hear me... no one else has... no other vampire... no other human... I don't even know how you can."

"He can hear us?"

"Stop!"

"I'm not ready..."

"Goodbye... my love..."

"Kill yourself."

"Why... why are they saying the same things...?" Christian held his head, slowing his breathing.

"I don't know... most of them are like that... they just say the same things over and over... a few of us can hold conversations... but that's how it is for some of them."

"What... what happened?"

Before Claire could answer, Aubrey burst forth, opening the door, carrying more bandages in her arms. She teared up to see Christian sitting upright, her lip quivered, and she ran to hug him tightly. "I knew you would wake up!" He winced from the embrace.

"She tended to you when Antoinette couldn't... she kept you safe while you slept," Claire whispered.

"Aubrey..." Christian hugged her back. "Thank you."

She retreated, wiping away the tears from her eyes. "Don't know why I'm crying..." she sniffed, "...but..."

"It's okay," Christian said with a soft smile, his chapped lips tearing. "Can you bring water?" Aubrey nodded, setting down the bandages and skipping out of the room.

"You need blood, brother. Antoinette too... human blood is preferable... I've seen it with other vampires. Deprived of it you age, but not having any at all... you'll suffer."

"Claire... I'm sorry," Christian turned to face towards the alphabet wall behind which her sister lay. "I couldn't..."

"It's done brother. That and this. We're together again. That's more important."

"I..." Aubrey returned with a cup of water. Her maid's dress exposed the majority of her clavicle. He could feel the thirst without Claire needing to say it. His gaze fixated on the throbbing of her neck, the same place the vampire had torn into him. It called to him, and he felt anxious just looking at.

"You can't bite her though... you just need her blood. Do. Not. Bite. Her." Each word that Claire said rung out crisply, despite the other voices in the background.

"Aubrey... I think... I'm a vampire now..."

"You want my blood, right?" She looked back up with a cheery smile. "I'm a Weather girl... I know what men want." She took a seat on the bed beside him. "You can take it, just be gentle..." She felt a blush coming on, remembering their hug from a few days ago. "Not like I need to tell you..."

"You don't have to..."

"I know," she beamed. "You're probably the only man who's ever said that to me..." She tilted her neck to one side.

Christian held up his fingernail, thicker, sharper, stronger than before. "I'm sorry." He sliced at her neck and she winced, but no blood came out. "... It's not deep enough." Aubrey nodded and bit her lip as he sliced again.

His body lurched forward at the sight of blood; his lips wrapped around her neck. At first Aubrey reeled, unsure of how much it would hurt, but once she was over the shock, she relaxed, holding his head against her neck gently. "It's okay," she whispered in his ear, "...drink your fill..."

Aubrey's arms wrapped around his body, holding him like he'd held her. Her cheeks flushed and he didn't flinch as her hands rested on his back; he didn't feel the change taking place as he took in her blood, but even through the bandages on his back, Aubrey did.

Beneath her small fingers, the wounds on his back finally closed; beneath his lips on her neck did his finally un-parch; and beneath the first floor of the Schofield Manor did the vampire known as Christian Nikolai Dusk fully awaken to a cacophony of voices from the Red World, welcoming and cursing their new Listener.

"Kill yourself."

38

Antoinette Katherine Escoté rubbed two fingers against her neck. The bite she had sustained a week ago had healed and her lips were parched. Even without the council of Claire, she knew that she had to feast on blood. As she looked to the naked man beside her, her husband, the blood coursing through his sleeping veins called to her. Her visage was mostly unchanged apart from a light tint of pale that wrapped her body, and two fangs that she hid in her mouth discreetly.

She'd resisted.

For a week, she'd resisted, but suddenly she found herself starved and this man, this unconscious man who'd been making her life miserable surely needed to repay her. He'd laughed at how she'd agonized over her *common servant*; he'd compared her so openly to the other women he'd been with; he'd struck her and then apologized, blaming the liquor. The insult he'd hurled was fresh, the comparison stinging, but in truth, the strike was weak against her hardened skin.

One bite and she would feel relief. One bite and perhaps she might not go crazy. Two fangs felt as sharp as they ever had inside her mouth as she measured him the same way Christian had measured the edge of the knife that summer. A second turned into a minute before she let out a muffled sigh. She couldn't bring herself to do it.

Her door creaked open and her emerald eyes, sharper in the dark than they had ever been, quickly locked onto the face of Aubrey who waved a hand and invited Antoinette down to the basement.

When she walked through the door to Christian's room, to a half-naked Christian without a single scar, basking in the darkness, sapphire eyes more vibrant than ever, she ran to him. Her arms wrapped around him tightly, tackling him onto the bed. Just like Aubrey, she cried, her eyes holding his face closely, trying to erase the memory of the man who swam in a pool of blood in her room, at the base of her bed, in the same place where she'd lost her best friend, forced to face the possibility that she would lose him too.

He drew a fingernail to his wrist and held it up to Antoinette as Aubrey waited in the hallway to give them some privacy. Just like he had, Antoinette's eyes went wide and she latched on, drawing in his blood. "Vampire blood will satiate you, but to heal we need human blood." His familiar voice made her relax for the first time in a week.

"Aubrey's?" Antoinette asked, coming up for air, her parched lips now full, supple, and moist.

Christian nodded. "I don't know how but... I can hear Claire... she's here, with us."

"Hi Ant."

"She says, 'Hi Ant.'"

Antoinette teared up again. "Hi Claire Bear." Her eyes tried to scan the room. "I miss you."

"I miss you too."

"Are you alright?" The dread was heavy as Christian asked, afraid of what a week of abandonment had done to her, afraid of the things he'd missed.

Antoinette nodded. "You might not remember, but before you bit me, you told me to trust you. You... you bit me to save me somehow, right?"

Christian nodded. "I heard Claire's voice... that vampire has been attacking people, and if he bit you like he did me, he might have ripped out your throat."

"He ran once you bit me..."

"It was strange."

"Are you hurt?"

"No," Antoinette lied.

"And the... baby?" Christian kept his voice down.

"I think it's fine... I can't tell yet, it's too early," she said with a smile, placing a hand on her abdomen, her green eyes washing over him pridefully, then shifting away pensively.

"Is something wrong?"

Antoinette bit her lip. "You... look different. You look pale and..." Christian stared back, puzzled.

"You stand out brother. Unnaturally, you stand out."

"Has anyone else seen me?"

"No. Just Aubrey, but if you come back, everyone will know... mother will notice, and Michael will too."

The world of the dead quieted, as if to give him privacy, as if they cared.

"There's something you're still not telling me..." Christian said cautiously, "both of you."

"Brother..."

"...That night... mother saw it... she wasn't bitten, but she isn't well. I've never seen her so panicked. One look at you and she would see that thing again. One look at you and I don't know what she would do."

"I won't leave you... I won't leave you and our child... our little secret family... that was our agreement... we can still run away together. The four of us..."

Antoinette smiled and leaned forward, kissing Christian deeply. He could taste her tears in the kiss as she pulled away. "We're united... remember? No matter where you are, but seeing you almost dead... then watching over you in that bed for a week... praying for you to come back to me... praying that no one would see you and do something to you... I don't want you to risk your life under Michael's temperament... or Garrett's... or my mother's... Nothing good comes of staying in this place."

"She's been covering for you."

"Antoinette... I'm not afraid!" He reached out for her hand.

"Oh Antoinette!" Michael Escoté's waking voice boomed through the

Manor, racing down from the second floor to the basement. "Where are you?"

"I'm afraid for you..." Antoinette whispered, placing her forehead against his, staring deeply into his eyes, ignoring her husband. "I know you don't want to, but for me... when your wounds have healed, leave this house..." A circle of red reflected in each other with her words. "Go to a place we won't find you and save yourself." She kissed him quickly. "And when my mother is better, I'll find you and we'll figure something out, but until then don't come back here. Go far and don't come back to this house, don't come back to this city... just save yourself because I couldn't live..." Her eyes watered. "...I couldn't live if this place took you too."

"No..." Christian rose. Mechanically he rose.

"Take care of him Claire Bear."

"Ohhhhhh wife. Where have you gone off to now?" The voice now echoed from the first floor.

"I love you Christian." She smiled, quickly running up the basement stairs to the first floor.

"Sister, what's happening?" he whispered as he exited the room, passing by Aubrey in the hallway and heading in the opposite direction, eyes set on the servant's entrance that led outside, feet moving of their own accord. "Sister?"

"She commanded you to leave this house brother... you can't fight it."

Christian's tears tried to do battle against the Executive Command, not comprehending what was going on. "I don't want to go," he whispered.

His head tried to turn around, but his legs carried him away, out of the house, down the street, and eventually past the Weather House.

"It's real!" an errant voice from the world of the dead screamed as he ran by. *"It's real!"*

A litany of voices cackled as they watched Christian continue to march forward, eventually making his way out of the city, unable to return to the woman he loved, unable to return to the child in her belly, the voices of the dead ready to keep him company wherever he went.

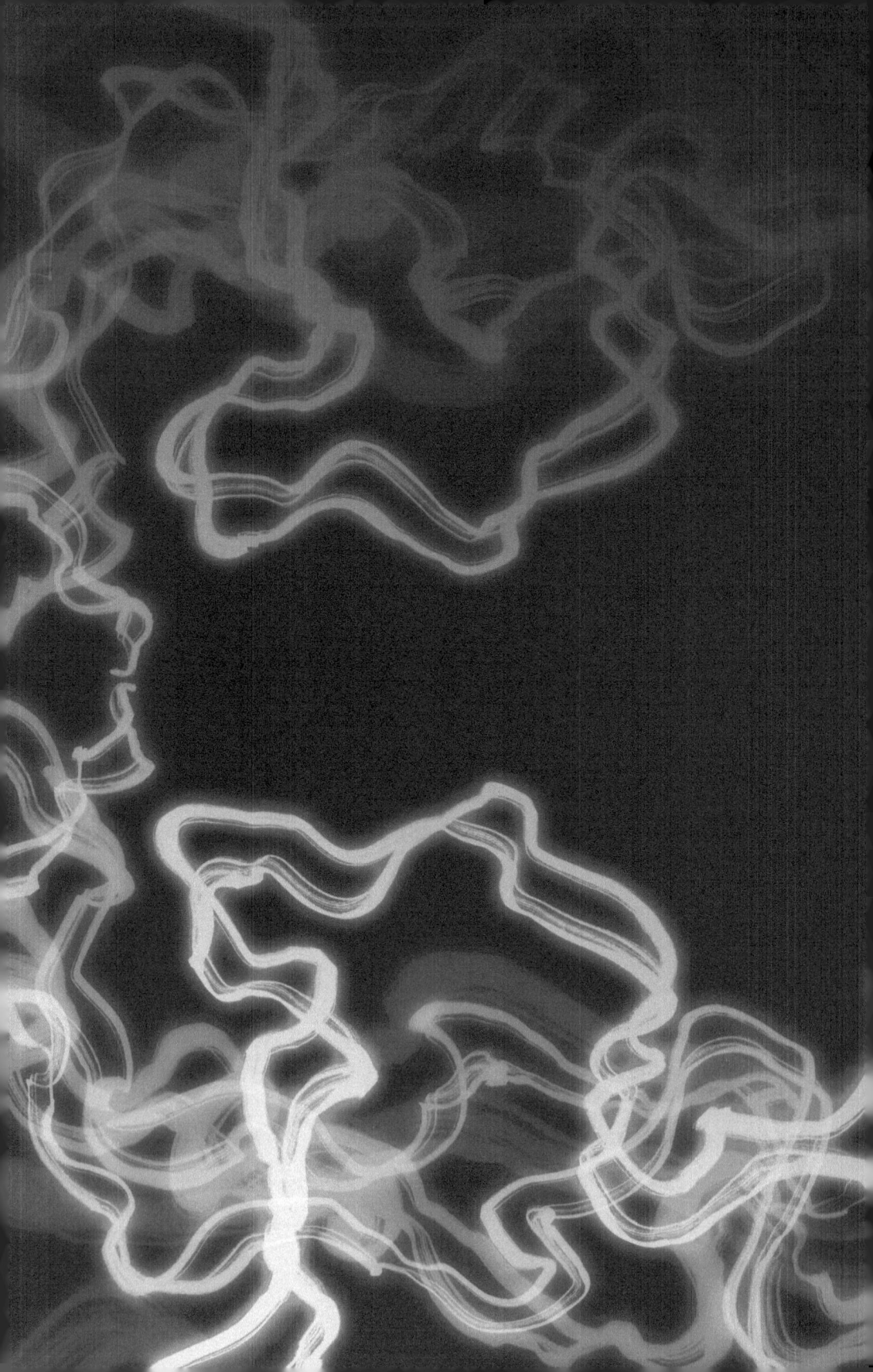

THIRD REGRET

"I should have told you to run."

-ELISE

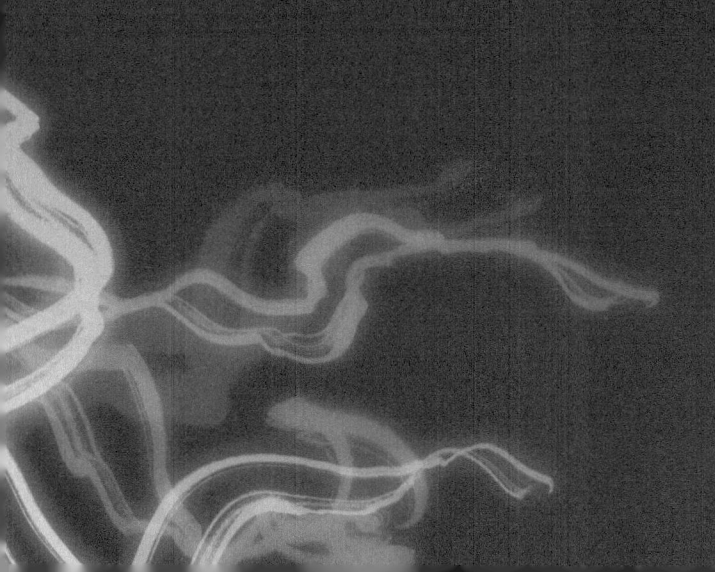

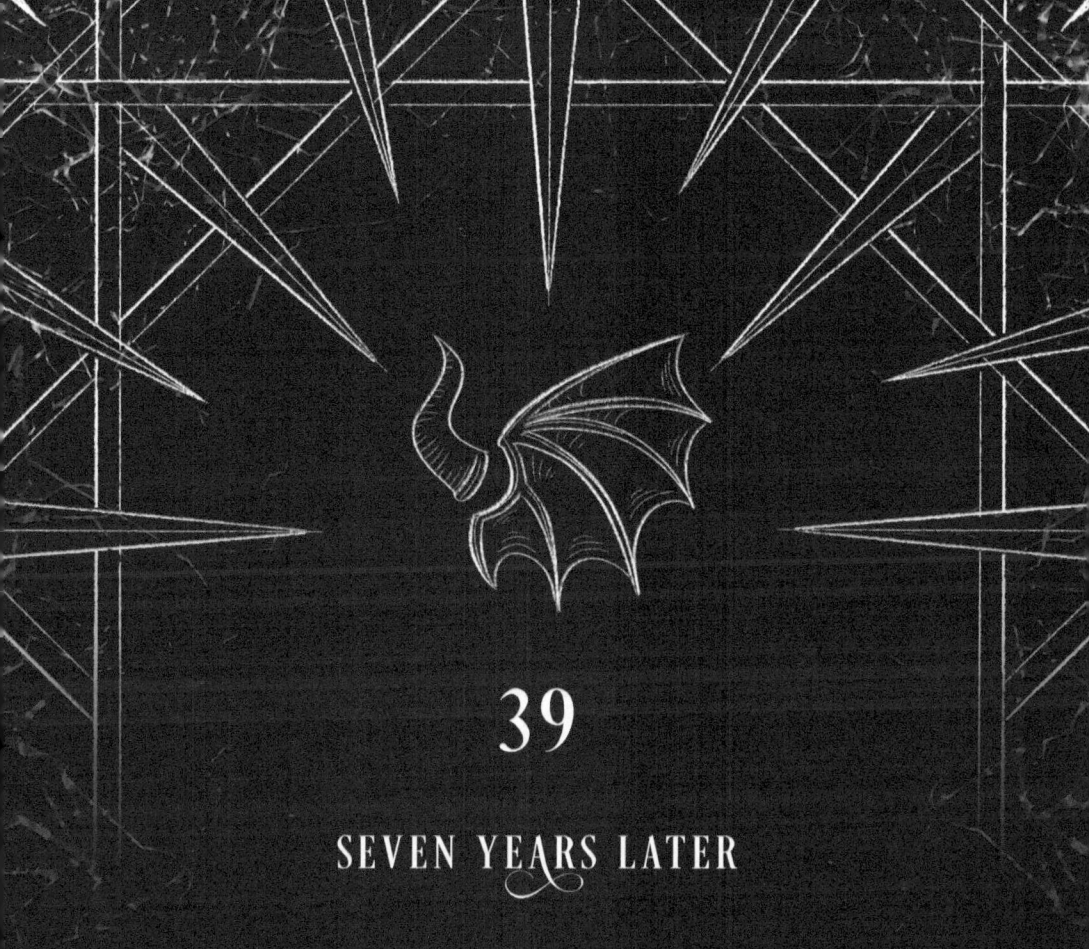

39

SEVEN YEARS LATER

"Christian Nikolai Dusk... the High Listener," a woman whispered to herself in the darkness as footsteps approached. Her hazy gray eyes couldn't see anything, but her keen ears listened for the familiar footsteps. She relaxed, knowing it was him. He was, at the very least, gentle.

Dull sapphire eyes moved about the darkness as Dusk walked through a familiar basement. He couldn't feel the cold anymore, but his human side still remembered what it had felt like. His body still remembered the sensation of a chill in his room at the Schofield Manor some seven years ago.

The whispers from the Red World were louder than the ones from the humans in the basement around him. Some clambered towards the hallway as he marched on, stopped by their wrought iron cell doors and chains; others hid in a corner; still others slept, but one by one they all perceived a presence in the central corridor and the familiar jingle of the keys held by one of their vampire wardens.

Dusk made his way to the end of the hall, to the place where the whispering woman's voice emanated. Most of the humans couldn't see each other very well; the sky was dark, the clouds were heavy, and the moon had a hard time penetrating these depths, but his eyes could see clear as day.

Every cell door was locked. For some it was necessary, but for this woman it was theater. Still, he took the ring of keys, found the one to her door, and wrestled open the iron.

"I could tell it was you." Her words reached him more quietly than she spoke them. They struggled to penetrate his ears, muffled through a mesh of Red World.

"Hello Elise." Dusk stared down at her. She donned a tattered tunic which hadn't been properly washed in ages. Her body was wrapped in a blanket to ward off the cold. She knelt, mounted atop a heap of rags on one side of her cage. The wall behind her held bolted chains which bound her feet. They rattled noisily when she moved, and her leash, like that of the other humans, ran only as long as the cell she occupied. Her state was more savage than any he'd been subjected to. Still, roles reversed, it was now he who had graduated from the bed of rags, but for this woman, in this life at least, there was no prospect of escape from her fate.

"When you're ready," Elise said, needlessly inviting him.

Dusk drew up a singular fingernail and brushed it along her neck. His slice was surgical now. He wasn't clumsy like he had been with Aubrey all those years ago.

Elise didn't wince anymore. Each vampire was different, but each one required a cut. Luckily, Dusk required very little, wasn't relatively rough, and didn't toy with her like others did. She relaxed when his lips wrapped around her neck.

He was the warmest of the vampires who had her.

A timid hand wrapped around his head, inviting a tenderness into the savagery of the situation. He didn't reciprocate, but he didn't pull away either. "Will you tell me more?" she whispered as he drank. "About your life before you came to the Evan Blood Coven?"

"Another time," He responded, wrapping a cloth around her neck like a scarf, taking her hand and putting pressure on the slice.

"The Masters have been coming all night. Is something special happening tonight?"

"The Alastair Coven has fallen... Lord Bruce will determine the fate of those who remain when they are brought in."

"Is that why they cleaned the Silver Cell?" A single cage somewhat removed from the other human cells in the basement shone differently in the moonlight. The cage had silver bars which wrapped it and raw silver spikes that pointed inwards like a macabre iron maiden, rendering any vampire who set foot inside unable to escape. "Are you expecting bloodshed?"

"Never. But we... I always prepare for it." He flexed his hand. Her blood coursed through him, and his strength grew. He felt invincible. Vampire blood rarely made him swell with power, but human blood was another story entirely.

A flurry of footsteps hurried down the hall that Dusk had come from. The humans in the cells before Elise's spoke amongst themselves.

"...Master Ilovo," Elise whispered, recognizing his steps, even in their haste.

The sounds eventually stopped at the door to the cell where Elise was kept. A vampire in gray robes caught his breath, Ilovo. He reminded Dusk of Vincent Globaria, the bookkeeper: short in stature and unassuming. He was often panicked and easily confused, today was no exception.

"Apologies for the disturbance. Our guests have arrived, and Lord Bruce requests your presence in the Great Ballroom immediately."

"Master Dusk..." Elise said quietly, inviting him closer, "...something about tonight feels amiss."

He didn't respond to Elise, but he didn't ignore her warning either. "Ilovo, remember to fetch the carriage when the spectacle is over."

"Yes, Master Dusk."

DUSK WALKED THROUGH THE MASS OF VAMPIRES STANDING IN THE Great Ballroom of the Evan Blood Coven. Most of the Coven had turned out. He climbed the left side of the twin spiral staircase with a landing on the second floor, overlooking the space below. As he ascended, his eyes looked down to the seven men who knelt on the floor below. All but one of their heads were down; only the one who knelt in the center kept it raised; his face was bruised and beaten, but still defiant.

On the second-floor overlook, Dusk stood behind the slotted banister just below his waist. To his left, five other vampires assembled. Together, they formed the six most influential members of the Evan Blood Coven.

On his immediate left stood a tall and proud Daina Erza with a golden-tipped spear that threatened to pierce even the proudest warrior. On the far side, Nier and Saber Levesque, vampire cousins, were nearly indistinguishable from each other with their matching robes adorned with gold lace. Between these individuals and in the center of the six-person group stood the two leaders of the Evan Blood Coven, Bruce Alazar and his bride, Carte Brooks, who, despite not carrying the title of Head, wielded just as much influence as Bruce.

Carte stood as the picture of classic beauty, with platinum hair that curled as it fell over her body and a razor-sharp gaze that calculated everything. Bruce stood as the portrait of power; though not the tallest, his bulging muscles imposed on any onlooker. At face-value, Carte was the brains and Bruce was the brawn, but beneath the surface, things were much more complicated.

With a raised hand, Carte looked down to the floor beneath her. Beside one of the twin staircases, in an area raised only a few steps, a group of five older vampires, the Elders, watched from behind a narrow table, holding goblets filled with blood. As Carte's hand went up, both the vampires at ground level, as well as the Elders, quieted.

"State your names," boomed Bruce from the second-floor balcony to those who knelt, quieting the Coven as his voice echoed.

Only the one in the center spoke. "I am Jason Castille, Head of the Alastair Coven... and these are my brethren."

The defiance that Dusk had seen as he ascended the staircase, he now witnessed from a different vantage point.

"You are mistaken, Jason Castille."

From two knees, Jason looked up at Bruce, clenching his teeth. Despite being outnumbered a hundred-to-one, he did not relent. "I am Jason Castille, the son of Ivan Castille, former Head of the Alastair Coven. *Therefore*, I am the Head of the Alastair Coven."

Silence turned to murmurs. Everyone was waiting for this moment, the moment that Bruce Alazar, Head of the Evan Blood Coven, would humble this man like he had humbled so many before him.

"Jason Castille, rejoice... that I do not strip you of your name or your life." Bruce leapt over the second-floor banister, cracking the tile floor as he landed, then standing tall, towering over a beaten Jason. "You are Head of nothing!"

Jason's pride met Bruce's power. "I am... the..."

Before he could continue, Bruce took his chin in his hand like a small almond, with an enormous hand connected to a thick forearm. "You are mistaken, Jason Castille... but I can understand why..." Bruce shoved his face away with so much force that Jason toppled over. Bruce headed to one of the other kneeling vampires. "Six... these are six vampires who you say serve the Alastair Coven?" Bruce stood behind one of them and placed his hand on the man's shoulder. The man trembled under Bruce's grip. "Pretend..." Bruce began with a wry smile, "...pretend there was a man in this line before you, pretend I asked him if he served the Alastair Coven or the Evan Blood Coven..." A few vampires snickered before Carte's hand quieted them from the second floor balcony. "Pretend he said 'Alastair'... and pretend I punched a hole through his face..." A few vampire spectators began to chuckle and then quieted down. "Now I move onto you and ask: do you serve Alastair or Evan Blood?"

"Evan Blood." The man trembled as Bruce took his hand from his shoulder with a satisfied nod and walked over to the next one.

"Do *you* serve the Alastair Coven or Evan Blood?"

"I serve the most noble of Covens, Alastair!" the man proudly proclaimed, raising his head tall for a moment before Bruce's fist punched through it, shattering his skull, leaving a headless body to collapse on the floor and splattering Jason and a few others, in blood.

The crowd cheered; the Elders roared; and Jason watched as he went down the line, sparing the next man, and then the next, and then punching a hole into the next, before sparing the last.

Bruce held out his hand and Ilovo raced forward with a rag, wiping off the blood before handing Bruce the cloth so he could finish.

"I will say..." Bruce said with a smile, wiping his fist in front of the crowd, speckled with blood. "Rarely..." His eyes looked to the one who he had first spared. "Rarely does the first in line *actually* believe without seeing evidence." He tossed the rag to the floor and Ilovo scrambled to pick it up before disappearing back into the mass of vampires. "You must be a member of the Faith." The trembling man looked down, ashamed. "Jason Castille... a Coven has members... and we have now established that the Alastair Coven has none. A Coven of one is not a Coven. The men who remain on their knees have sworn allegiance to Evan Blood... so I will ask you once, and only once, do you serve Alastair or Evan Blood?"

Bruce flexed his hand. For the second time in as many minutes, pride met power, but only for a second before the former crumbled. "Evan Blood," Jason said, dropping his head in shame.

"That's what I thought," Bruce chuckled heartily.

40

FIVE YEARS AGO, CHRISTIAN NIKOLAI DUSK HAD COME INTO THE service of the Evan Blood Coven. Initially, his reception had been luke-warm, but when the Coven discovered that he was a Listener, their tone quickly changed, particularly Bruce's.

Each Coven had their own thoughts about how best to utilize Listeners, but Listeners were rare. Despite the several hundred members of the Evan Blood Coven, there was only one person at the Coven besides Dusk who could Listen: Ekaterina Leja Vientulis, better known as Katja.

Katja had been with the Evan Blood Coven for almost a hundred years. She had become a member just after Bruce had come into power, absorbed into the Coven after the fall of her own. Despite her tenure as a former member of Bruce's inner circle, in the recent years a partial deafness had grown more severe.

As the celebration for the fall of the Alastair Coven was underway, Dusk whispered something to Carte before moving past the mass of vampires and joining Katja outside the castle that was the Evan Blood Coven.

"Our ride has arrived," she uttered into the cold winter breeze, looking at the horse-drawn carriage.

"Shall we?" Dusk invited her with a hand, opening the door for her.

Katja was paler than most, her skin and her eyes were sunken, and the wrinkles on her neck were many. She could have been his grandmother. Her smile was rare, and her mood was always pensive. There was always exhaustion in the air around her.

The two Listeners took their seats across from one another as the carriage rolled onwards.

"Evan Blood..." Katja said into the carriage, "...continues its rise... and Bruce continues pursuing a fantasy."

Most of the Red World faded in and out as the carriage rolled onwards. When Dusk spoke, Katja struggled to hear him. His words came through in fragments, some lost, and others just above a whisper. Over the years, the Listener's curse had taken firm root with her. She couldn't hear humans anymore. She could barely hear vampires anymore. Soon she would only be able to hear the Red World.

"We need only find it to prove it's not fantasy."

The Evan Blood Coven had traditionally employed Listeners as an espionage tool to learn the secrets of other Covens, but when Dusk had joined, he had weaponized the Red World, using it to spawn preemptive attacks, leading to the swift downfall of many Covens in the last few years, including Alastair.

"Do you, with all your powers, honestly think it exists?" Katja raised a brow nervously. "The power of resurrection?" her voice quieted at the last word.

"At the very least... they existed. Necromancers. That much is clear."

"A hundred years of me trying to find it has come up empty... how many of these errands have we run? Isn't it time we let sleeping dogs lie."

"Is that all we are..." Claire whispered, *"...sleeping dogs?"*

Vampires who couldn't Listen assumed that there were different levels of Listeners, with abilities at different stages. Bruce believed that Dusk, in his prime, was the absolute best. Katja knew better. She had known other Listeners in the hundred years she'd been in service to the Coven, and no matter who they were, each Listener could hear the exact same thing: it was always the last moments of life or a deep regret that reverberated through the

Red World, but never more. Dusk somehow had access to something else. When Dusk was around, not only could he hear those voices, but he could converse with some of them. Some even seemed to retain their sentience around him, like Claire.

Initially, Katja had believed it was only Claire who was special, an anomaly existing in the Red World, but absent Dusk, Katja could only hear Claire's last words. Yet when he was around, she could speak with Claire too, and Claire wasn't the only one. Something about his presence was different. Something about his curse was unique.

"I didn't mean that Claire..." Katja whispered as the driver nursed an emptying flask, the smell of whiskey pungent.

"I know."

"Once you let this go..." Katja said with a wicked smile, "you could be anything... one of the most powerful vampires to ever live."

"Ambition has never been my brother's strong suit."

"On that we agree..."

"...and the one thing my brother wants is out of his reach... for now."

"Antoinette Katherine Schofield." Katja closed her eyes. "You've devised a plan then?"

"An Executive Command cannot be broken. It can be temporarily stunted... but her command... by my will or not, I alone cannot find a way forward..."

"We have a plan though," Claire added.

"You must love her to still toil for her like this," she said with a forlorn remembrance as the carriage rolled on into the night. "How many other women in the Coven would throw themselves at you... yet you pine for the one you cannot have."

"She's my family." Dusk smiled solemnly.

"And she's special."

"Perhaps you simply haven't been around long enough to see how ordinary she is."

41

"**M**aster Dusk, Lady Katja... we've arrived." Ilovo's humbled hand opened the door to the carriage to let them out. As he always did, with a timid bow, he stepped back into the shadows.

Katja emerged first, measuring the night sky. "The sun will be out soon... we'll have to spend the day here and travel back tonight."

Dusk nodded. His gaze looked at the entryway to the former Alastair Coven before him. Once there had been two mahogany doors which stood strong and stoic, keeping out any unwelcome visitors. Now one of the doors was broken in half beside the entryway and the other was gone entirely; only splinters of wood hung on by rusted nails. As the pair crossed the threshold, a crisp breeze rolled through the hallway and the Red World pounded at the heads of the two Listeners.

"Stop!"

"Wait!"

"Run!"

The Red World's voices were panicked and afraid. Some only groaned an eerie and inhuman sound: a last gasp of pain.

"Silence," Dusk's words cut through the emptiness, penetrated the Red World, and hushed the voices. It was temporary, but for a moment, Katja and Dusk could hear their own footsteps as they walked deeper inside.

The structure reminded Dusk of the Schofield Manor, with two above-ground floors and one below, but unlike his former home, an enormous outdoor space was contained within the interior. Katja's face scrunched as she stepped over body after body: sliced, butchered, or brutalized, but still fresh.

"We'll have to be quick..." Katja said as they stepped into the courtyard.

"...or the smell will be worse for you tomorrow," Claire whispered to the pair.

"Sister?" Dusk raised his head up to the sky. "Can you find him?"

"I already have. Follow me..." Dusk and Katja let Claire guide them through the courtyard, through the countless bodies that littered the ground. "This is him."

Dusk leaned down to look at the body. It was an older man, but dressed the same as any corpse, lying face down until Dusk kicked it onto its back. "Tell me your name," Dusk commanded.

"Ivan Castille. Head of the Alastair Coven." The voice, even in death, resonated confidence. Here his body lay, in the Coven he'd ruled over for so long, among the other dead bodies of his fellow vampires.

"The Alastair Coven is no more," Dusk said clearly, the Red World around him erupting in anger. "The last few members are part of Evan Blood now."

"We were... and they attacked. What kind of... strike during a celebration?"

Dusk's eyes had lost their luster. It was evident when he spoke. Their blue was dull and tarnished. Years away from Antoinette had changed him. It may have warranted telling Ivan that it was on Dusk's information that they knew about the celebration, and on Dusk's council that they struck when they did, and because of Dusk that the Coven had Fallen and that he had been killed, but saying so wouldn't change the outcome.

"What do you know about necromancers?" Just like everyone he'd asked before, the answer was always the same variation of *nothing*, but there wasn't any disappointment on the faces of the two Listeners. Even though *nothing* was the expectation, the journey could still yield other fruits. "Tell me where you keep your treasures."

As Ivan Castille divulged the information to Dusk, the pair of Listeners followed his instructions, winding and leading them through the Fallen Coven.

"...Do you ever consider it graverobbing?" Katja asked, stepping over battered bookshelves, scattered instruments, and broken furniture. "This thing we do?"

Dusk pushed a shattered chair out of the way to open a door. "...No other Listener can do what I do. You once said it yourself..." He approached a broken bed in the room. The mattress was tossed and the sheets were stained with blood. A woman's body in a flowing white dress lay dead at the foot of the bed.

"This can't be... not on my wedding day."

"Whether graverobbing or not..." The High Listener tried to tune out the voices, "...what other skill am I suited for that could be so honest?"

"Many vampires hone a craft... you could do the same. Didn't you once say your father was a craftsman?"

"Our father was..." Claire began, but quieted as Dusk ripped off a corner of the four post bed with an inhuman strength.

"Shall we measure the worth of the Alastair Coven..." Dusk spun the top off the bedpost, tilting it over the bed, listening to the rattle as coins, gold, and gems spilled onto the sheets.

"Is that all?" Katja asked, running her fingers through a tiny heap, a little disappointed.

"We still have a hundred bodies to interrogate..." Dusk said, emptying a lavender pillowcase to store the treasures contained within. "It's going to be a long day."

"Let's get to work then."

42

CARTE BROOKS TOSSED IN HER SLEEP. THOUGH SHE DIDN'T ADMIT it, the fall of each Coven brought with it a surreal tension. As her body tossed and turned on the bed, beside the Head of the Evan Blood Coven, her unconscious mind created images of a future where they were on the receiving end of the defeats they doled out.

A man knelt on this very floor, cobblestone turned rubies beneath pools of blood. In the Great Ballroom there were bodies as far as the eye could see. She could see the aftermath of a battle in the Coven, with naught but a few living souls, engrossed in the silence and beholden to the carnage before a thunderous echo shook them...

She awoke in a cold sweat.

Vampires had to push themselves to show exhaustion, but here she was, drenched without doing so much as dreaming. Beside her, Bruce slept, completely unaware, the smell of blood wine still rife on his breath.

She sighed to herself, reaching for the floral robe on the hook near the door and slipping out of the room. As she descended the spiral staircase that climbed up to their room, the only room on the third floor of the west spire, she ran her fingers through platinum hair. When she needed to, she was the epitome of pomp and circumstance, but most of the time she was simply unapproachable.

As she pushed open the thick wooden door at the landing, a cool breeze picked up her robe, settling when it closed. If not for her stubborn beauty, the cross-armed Carte Brooks would have looked out of place, wandering through the halls of the Evan Blood Coven, avoiding the stray beams of sunlight that pierced the halls.

"Armand," she called after she descended a second set of stairs to the ballroom's balcony. A figure shuffled in the space below her, bound for an adjoining hallway, and her call to him made him slow, but she didn't race to catch him, nor did she unfold her arms or unfurrow her brow. "What are you doing up at this hour?"

Armand's nose piqued at the smell of her sweat. He was an old man with a hunched back and his skin was more warts than flesh. He regularly wore an off-putting sneer. On this day, he carried a small leather bag at his side. "Does an Elder need an excuse to be up and about?" His thin eyes peered up at Carte, unable to perceive her face from the angle he looked up from, obstructed by her chest. His back crunched as he righted himself to try to look her in the eyes. "I could *accuse* you of the same." A hint of a jest manifested in the curl of his lips.

Carte's measured gaze showed the same glimmer of humor as Armand, but just as quickly faded, their faces settling into their seriousness. "I couldn't sleep," Carte confessed, continuing in the direction Armand was walking. "What's your excuse?"

"A few Promotions to check on... a few Promotions to conduct... while the opportunity exists."

Carte slowed so that Armand could keep up with her. "I'll join you."

"I'll permit it." Two figures strolled down the hallway of the Evan Blood Coven.

"Is now really the right time for this?" she asked.

Armand hummed to himself for a moment, shooting her a glance. "Some would say it is the best time."

Carte's folded arms flexed, her muscles rippling. "Is that dissent I detect?"

"I wouldn't dream of it."

"And if you did?" Carte looked ahead to the single door at the end of the hall with concern. "What would you say then?"

"We Elders have our role... and the Head of the Coven has his..."

"But?"

"Marcus Diem... Alastair... and soon Red Crescent... we are growing My Lady, and it is becoming unsustainable... and I do not mean the blood slaves." Carte's jaw clenched and her tongue lapped her teeth. She had told Bruce the same, but he was hell-bent on moving forward as quickly as possible. Now they were conquering a Coven every six months, and Evan Blood was growing at the fastest rate that it had since its inception. "My Lady... if I may... why does Lord Bruce send the Listeners to the Coven after the conquest?"

Carte's eyes looked to the doorknob before her. Her empty gaze hid a twitch. The Elders were a lot sharper than they let on. She hadn't been aware that they had been paying attention, but with every word he said, the picture of the future grew clearer and clearer. "Careful Armand..." Her gaze ripped into him "...Treason begins just as innocuously."

Armand forced a chuckle, looking away as he did, pressing against the door. "Then let's move on."

Inside the stone-lined room, ten beds were arranged in an offsetting pattern, five against each wall. Six of the beds were made, and four of them were filled with bodies. Each body was restrained with two pairs of shackles that wrapped around the underside of the beds. The iron frames were bolted down to the floor and as Carte and Armand entered, the bolts shifted, three of the four turning towards the visitors.

Armand, like a doctor, approached the first one, bringing up a lantern beside the man's face. "This one is Kyle..." he said to Carte. "Turned two days ago..." he read from a page in a ledger by the light of the lamp. "Turned instantly... awake and here until the Tide passes..."

"Right," Carte said, leaning down to look at the man who relaxed as she hovered over him. "Fangs," she commanded. He bared his teeth at her. "You served us as a human, didn't you?"

"Yes, Lady Brooks," the man said, watching her with his handsome features, his naked chest rising and falling steadily. "Ten years as a personal blood slave for the Elders."

"Right," Carte said cooly as Armand withdrew a glass vial from his bag, uncorking it. She could feel the fangs behind her lips hunger as she took in the smell of blood.

Kyle's body lurched, his arms and legs shook violently, and the shackles worked hard to keep him in bed. From a dark corner of the room, another set of shackles, much larger, rattled; but in this bed, Kyle savagely reached his mouth towards the vial.

With his free hand, Armand forced Kyle's head down and poured the vial of blood into his mouth, letting every last drop fall, watching as his body relaxed. "There, there, child...

"What's this one's story?" Carte looked to the next bed beside Kyle's where a person lay, completely unconscious, unmoved by the blood at all.

"This one is called... Charles... also Turned two days ago..." Armand flipped the pages in the ledger. "Hasn't woken up since the Turn."

"One more day, right?"

"That is the protocol... three days... if he doesn't wake up by tomorrow, he won't..." Armand pulled out a syringe and stuck it into Charles's arm, pushing the blood directly into his vein. "It's fascinating isn't it...?" He asked, withdrawing the syringe from the unconscious body.

"How some humans reject it?" She watched Armand stow the syringe.

"Indeed... I've overseen hundreds of these transformations and still... it always surprises me when one fails or mutates... as uncommon as it is."

Armand picked up the lantern and headed deeper into the room, to the place where two others lay, taking care to keep an eye on Carte who glided behind him, her eyes looking to an adjoining room with a cell-like door kept closed by a thick chain.

"The last two that will be Turned this cycle." The Elder's body hunched over one of the other two in the bed. "What's your name, boy?"

"Pietro, Pietro Ulma." Carte watched as Armand ran a tape measure over his shirtless body, writing down the measurements of his forearms, chest, thighs, arms, and legs. "Will it... hurt?"

"No more than a few bee stings," Armand said, turning his back to

Pietro and looking at the woman in the bed behind him. "And what is your name, girlie?"

"Cassandra Cross," the woman said nervously.

"Relax girlie," Armand said, measuring her body just like he had done to Pietro. Cassandra blushed when the tape measure wrapped around her. Even though she wore a nightgown, she felt naked all the same. "All... set." Armand closed the ledger. "As Elder, overseer of the Promotion ceremony, do you swear your loyalty to the Coven of Evan Blood?"

"I do."

"I do."

"Then I will now Turn you, in accordance with our tradition..." Armand looked to Carte. "Would you care to assist, Lady Brooks?"

"You Elders have your role..." Carte took a step back, crossing her arms as he walked past her to a dark corner of the Promotion room.

Armand struggled in the darkness for a moment before a sharp tug of iron beat against the floor. Carte watched as the Elder dragged a naked man forward, bound by two chains: one around his neck, the other around his feet. As the man was pulled by the leash, he stumbled. His body was bruised and beaten, his eyes were bandaged with a black cloth, and two sharp spikes stuck out of his ears. As he came into the light of the lantern, Armand pulled on him harder and he collapsed onto his knees at the bed of Cassandra.

Carte's displeasure was palpable, her face twisted in disgust as Armand took a small knife and cut Cassandra's wrist, holding it up to the naked man's mouth like a twisted offering to the Six Gods.

The man's fangs flared; his hands reached for Cassandra's wrist, and, in a swift movement, his fangs sank into her as he began to suck. Cassandra's eyes went wide as he bit. The man groaned in pleasure as he drank.

Carte turned around with disgust. "Put that thing out of its misery after you're done."

Behind her, a sharp blow from Armand forced the naked man to release Cassandra. "If that is your wish Lady Brooks..." the Elder said with an eerie pleasure, "... I can always make another..."

43

CLAIRE SEFIRA DUSK LOOKED OUT FROM THE RED WORLD OVER the Schofield Manor. Powerless to interfere, all that she could do was watch and bear witness to the tragedies that had befallen Antoinette in the seven years following Christian's departure.

One Executive Command and more than a hundred miles away, the man who loved her still forged a path to rescue her, and within the walls of his former home, the woman he had loved was becoming something else under the thumb of her husband.

"Are you there, Claire Bear?" Antoinette sat naked in a corner of her room, looking to the spot where Claire had died at the foot of her bed, calling out to her former servant. She hoped that she was still around, but without being a Listener herself, she could only monologue.

"I'm here," Claire whispered consolingly, pained to see Antoinette's lean figure, stiff like a statue, kneeling in a pool of her own urine.

"Stay." Michael's Executive Command hours earlier had trapped her in this spot.

Antoinette's lips moved, her face moved, but she was otherwise paralyzed. It wasn't the worst punishment he had inflicted on her, but as night turned to day, a lone beam of light crept through the gap between the blinds, walking across the floor, threatening to sear her ankle. Antoinette's tears came steadily. She knew the pain would be nothing compared to the embarrassment and humiliation she felt. She hoped it would be enough to jolt her out of his Command.

"Lady Antoinette!" Aubrey's voice punched through Claire as she ran into the room, toppling Antoinette onto her side, breaking the Executive Command enough for Antoinette to scurry to the bathroom.

Aubrey reached for a towel and threw it on the floor where Antoinette had knelt. Her back ached and she used the bed as a crutch when she leaned down.

"*Thank you,*" Claire whispered.

"Thank you..." Antoinette wept from the bathroom, wiping herself down. "I don't know what I'd do without you."

Aubrey's eyes, stripped of joy, looked up Antoinette's naked body—up her lashings, up her cigar burns, to the red marks still on her neck. Her most prominent features hadn't been touched, but everywhere else had been marred.

"Take some blood." Aubrey offered up her wrist. "Take my blood that you might heal those..."

Antoinette's sad gaze rested on Aubrey's belly. "He did this to me... he should have to see me like this too." She looked away. "Besides... the less hurt I appear... the more he does."

Antoinette offered a hand to help Aubrey from the floor. The former Weather girl rose slowly in her flowing nightgown. There was still some hope left in her, but not much.

"I miss Christian," Antoinette admitted. "I wish I had run away with him then..."

For a moment the room was silent. For a moment the nostalgia of the past kept the darkness at bay, but only for a moment.

A voice called out to them from another part of the house. "Mother?" A child's voice rang out through the halls. "Mother... where are you?" A boy approached the room, passing through Claire.

44

THE CARRIAGE THAT HAD TAKEN DUSK TO THE ALASTAIR COVEN had departed the following night and taken with it Katja and Ilovo. Dusk had told them to inform Bruce and Carte that he would return on his own terms. As long as he was back within a reasonable timeframe, no one made a fuss, but it was when he was gone longer that there were consequences. He and Bruce had an arrangement, and Bruce could be understanding... usually.

"What shall I tell Master Bruce?" Ilovo had asked as he mounted the carriage.

"I'm following up on a lead... I'll need a week." Ilovo nodded humbly.

Katja's eyes peered out at Dusk from the carriage suspiciously. She knew enough to know he was hiding something, but she didn't imagine it was any more dangerous than the key to resurrection that Bruce had them scouring the conquered Covens for, so she let him keep his secrets. His loyalty to the Coven had never been in question.

"...I could accompany you, Master Dusk," Ilovo said, glowing with a tempered excitement from atop the carriage.

"Another time Ilovo," Dusk had said, patting him on the shoulder, *"another time."*

As Dusk watched the carriage depart, his feet began to move, carrying him to another venture all his own, with only his sister to keep him company.

"She still loves you, brother. I think a part of her knows you'll come for her one day," Claire whispered.

"I will... soon."

He walked through the empty fields and sleeping orchards as his sister relayed some of the details of what she had witnessed. She no longer told him the full truth. He couldn't handle it. In times, she admitted, neither could she, a silent specter to Michael's cruelty.

His feet carried him into an abandoned house which would serve as his layover before venturing out at night again, continuing on for another day, then finding refuge in a two-story Victorian house in the height of construction. The floor had been laid, several walls erected, and beams had been put in place to frame the second story.

"Do you hear that, sister?" Dusk closed his eyes and rested his ears, finding a pillar on the would-be porch to lean against. "Not a single voice from the Red World. Absolute quiet. I can hear myself think out here..."

"We're in the middle of nowhere... not another house for miles. No roads... no nothing."

Dusk's eyes looked out. Even in the darkness he could see clearly. The only thing around were trees—a savage and unfolding world untouched by humans or vampires, and unmarred by the violence and death they brought. "It's perfect... and construction is almost done. If we find the key to resurrection... the necromancer blood, we can all be together again."

"That's the promise. You, Antoinette, me... and my nephew."

"That's the plan." Dusk smiled, slipping off into an unusually peaceful sleep while the moon was still out, feeling more human than ever, tucked under the shadows of the partial construction of the future House of Schofield.

"Regardless of whether we find the necromancer blood or not... Six months until we can rescue Antoinette and bring her to a new home away from Michael," she whispered. *"Just six months Ant... you can hold out."*

45

BRUCE'S CLENCHED FISTS RESTED IN THE CENTER OF A LONG TABLE in the conference room that everyone often referred to as the War Room. On one side sat the five other members of his inner circle: Carte Brooks, Nier Levesque, Saber Levesque, Daina Erza, and Christian Nikolai Dusk. Across from them, five Elders, including Armand Hammon, sat. The Elders each donned their hallmark midnight-purple robes.

Each Elder shared the same face of concern. "Lord Bruce... perhaps we should revisit your... our next move. There are some members of Evan Blood who have voiced their concerns at..."

"Six." From the head of the table, Bruce's singular word silenced the Elder who spoke. "For now, six Covens remain within a hundred miles."

"...If we do not strike while the iron is hot... they could unite." Daina folded her arms and leaned forward, the armor she always wore clanging as she did.

"Lady Daina... the growth that Evan Blood has seen these past ten years; the growth we've seen during Lord Bruce's hundred-year reign has been immeasurable..." the Elder closest to Bruce began.

"But?" He leaned forward.

Armand, seated in the middle of the Elders, continued, "...Lord Bruce. Evan Blood has always had favorable relations with Red Crescent. When we Elders came into governance, we settled in three Covens: Evan Blood, Marcus Diem, and Red Crescent. Our paths have never been those of animus."

"...What do we have to gain by conquering Red Crescent?" the Elder closest to Bruce regained his composure.

"What do we have to gain?" Bruce pounded his fist on the table angrily, shattering the wood. "Power. Security. Knowledge. Wealth."

Carte cleared her throat. "Did we not sit in this same room several decades ago, worried about the threats neighboring vampires could pose if left unrestrained?"

"Lady Brooks..." another Elder began, "this was five decades ago, when the threat was real. There is no threat anymore... even Alastair was not a threat. We've stayed quiet, but an attack on Red Crescent is not something we can sit idly by and..."

Bruce was about to rise when Carte put her hand on top of his thigh, speaking up. "The Elders and the Inner Circle have existed, mutually up until now, but this decision, to pursue Red Crescent... is not yours to make... moreover... You will not be allowed to leave the Coven until the siege of Red Crescent is completed..."

"What is the meaning of this?" Armand stammered, rising from his seat, ancient eyes growing wider.

"We were prepared to invite the Elders of Red Crescent to join us, but without your support..." Carte began.

"You will be contained." Bruce rose.

"What he means to say..." Carte continued, standing up, "...is that your dual allegiance is cause for concern."

"Any vampires who survive can pledge their loyalty, Elders included," Bruce added.

"You insult our loyalty, Lord Bruce!"

"We Elders would never!"

"On that we are agreed," he growled. "Shall we finally put to use the Silver Cell you lot are so fond of?" The Elders exhaled in frustration, staying silent.

"Four months from now we will strike down Red Crescent. Since I doubt there are any objections..." The room sat quiet for a moment, "...dismissed." Bruce waved everyone off. As the Elders grumbled, he turned to Dusk. "High Listener, you have your timeline. Make the preparations. Find us an opening."

"Understood," Dusk said with a nod, stepping out into the hallway and heading towards his room.

Before he could make it far, a voice called out to him, "Dusk, hang back a moment."

Nier and Saber Levesque ran towards him in their golden-laced black robes. Both men had their hair pulled back in a ponytail. Nier's face was bushy. He wore an unkempt mustache and a thick salt-and-pepper beard while Saber was clean shaven. Cousins by blood, their brown almond eyes were mirror images.

"We wanted to ask..." Saber began quietly, shuffling Dusk around a corner of the hallway. "Did you know Red Crescent was next?"

"Careful what you say, brother," Claire whispered. *"I've been watching them..."*

"I have been tasked with identifying any potential Covens which could pose a threat to Evan Blood. Red Crescent is one of many that Katja and I surveyed," Dusk said quietly. "I knew it was an option."

"Do they *actually* pose a threat?" Nier asked. "A lot of the ones we've taken down have... but others..."

"...Others we just massacre without an ounce of resistance. Alastair? They were in the middle of a wedding for Gods' sake. Is there actually a reason to pursue Red Crescent?"

"Not a reason you would ever know," Claire scoffed. *"You don't know what Bruce is after."*

"Most spoils don't even cover our transportation. Alastair turned up dry, right? No coin? No gold? Just what we pawn through human brokers."

Dusk's eyes narrowed. "I am the High Listener... my role is to Listen... but few vampires' final thoughts are *I must leave with the gold I hid in the bedpost.*" He smiled weakly. "Think about how rich any Listener could be if I could just ask every vampire who was dead where their gold was?"

"Considering how long Katja's been here... we *would* be flush..." Saber said, returning the smile.

"I can't speak to how real the threat is..." Dusk admitted, "but for Bruce, who wears the crown, a threat always exists. He is the Head. I do as the Head commands."

"Dusk..." Nier said, scratching his beard. "Can I just ask... have you been tasked to research Covens outside of the initial hundred-mile range?" Saber's eyes locked on his coyly.

"Brother, you know what they're after, don't you? They want to know if this will drag on... but they may be asking because they're considering making a move... perhaps out of the picture, or even against Evan Blood. Don't say too much."

"It has come up," Dusk said frankly.

Nier and Saber both let out a heavy exhale. "If it ever comes to fruition..."

"...you'll know when Bruce allows it." He completed their thought, carefully watching them process the conversation.

"The Head..."

"I do as the Head commands," Dusk said slowly, their eyes narrowing on him, then looking to each other with a pensive nod before patting him on the shoulder.

"Well said brother... I'll keep an eye on them..." Claire whispered as her brother headed down another hall, walking towards his room on the second floor.

As he approached a door as average as any other, he withdrew a bronze key and turned the lock, hearing the mechanism click before stepping inside.

The bedroom that belonged to Christian Nikolai Dusk on the second floor of the Evan Blood Coven was unremarkable. A single four-post bed with crimson sheets was the centerpiece of the room. Along another wall was a single dresser, a shoddy manufacturing compared to the fine mahogany vanity that Antoinette had. In front of his floor-to-ceiling window was the only other piece of furniture, a small round table suitable for, at most, two people, pinched between a pair of chairs.

He closed the door behind him slowly, revealing a fist-sized groove in the narrow space behind the door that had been there for a few years, ignoring it before turning the lock and taking a seat in one of the two chairs. As he sat, he unbuttoned the topmost button of his white shirt, slouching, throwing his head back, and closing his eyes.

"Bruce won't stop... will he?" he whispered, leaning across the table to the empty chair where Claire's voice came from.

"When we find the key to rebirth and give it to him... he might. That was the deal we made. We help him get what he wants... and we share in the spoils."

Dusk caressed the edges of the wooden table nervously. "You have your doubts..."

"Katja searched for a hundred years to no end... though she doesn't exactly appear motivated. If we can't find it... I don't expect him to tolerate another Listener for another hundred years. I've seen how he behaves when your trips run long, or have you forgotten what he did to you..."

"That was so long ago..."

"People do not change, brother, and as much as I would love all of us to be a family in the flesh..."

"A part of you wants me to *let sleeping dogs lie?"*

"I don't want this to consume you. The power of a God... in the hands of any man who wants it is dangerous... just as much as this hope... that we can recover what we've lost."

Dusk sat quietly for a moment, breathing slowly. "What do you need me to do?"

"Stay the course. Our priority remains unchanged. We have six months before the house is finished, before we can rescue Antoinette. Stay the course until then and if his obsession becomes insatiable... do what you need to do, for your family."

46

USK STARED UP AT THE CEILING FROM THE CENTER OF HIS four-post bed. With his arms folded across his shirtless torso, he tried to embrace sleep as best he could, to no avail.

The Red World did not sleep. Their voices hammered him night after night, and unlike the future site of the House of Schofield, the dead in the Coven were abundant and unruly. Those who spoke, even the same words on a loop were the easiest to deal with. He could make a metronome of their voices, stitching together their repetition as needed. Those who kept their sentience, like Claire, were also easy to manage. They generally respected him, listened to him, and obeyed him. But the rest—the rest were sheer agony. Voices which screamed from beyond the Divide, voices with words eclipsed by fragments of static, and voices that would relive their death over and over again. They had brought the High Listener to tears more than once. Few Listeners could bear the burden for long, and Katja was the overwhelming exception, the Listener that had lived the longest.

From the Red World, Claire's voice kept the others at bay until they overwhelmed her. She would retreat, regroup, and find her voice again. It was unfair. It was unfair for the twins to suffer from both sides of the Divide, but in this unfair reality they both existed, in unreal circumstances that had never made such a relationship possible.

Dusk needed no clock to know that the day had been spent and the sleep he had craved was another unfulfilled desire. The Coven was beginning to wake and there was too much to do to continue trying, to continue chasing a rest which wouldn't come. "I'm going to have breakfast," Dusk said to the emptiness of his room as he retrieved a folded white shirt, running a hand through his hair, and making his way down to the basement.

"I'll continue watching those two," Claire whispered as he left.

In the basement, every blood slave was awake—a rare anomaly considering the time of day. Dusk stepped onto the cobblestone basement floor and took in a deep inhale. The familiar musk of his former home overtook him, and an unfamiliar pair of footsteps came from the hallway, from the deeper holding cells, near the Silver Cell.

As the footsteps got louder, so too did the Red World.

Dusk recognized the face of the man as he approached, the same who had been forced to kneel before Bruce some weeks ago, the so-called heir to the Alastair Coven, Jason Castille, who looked up at Dusk with disdain for a moment, before slowly lowering his head and slinking around him in the hallway.

As Dusk turned to watch him, Jason took a hurried first step up the stairs before Dusk cleared his voice. "Keys?"

Jason stopped in his tracks, then turned around, holding the ring of keys in front of him and returning to an unmoved Dusk who held out his hand. He set the larger key ring on Dusk's fingertips, avoiding his gaze the entire time. To Jason, the silence was interrupted with human voices and human whimpering; to Dusk, the Red World deafened him.

"I'll be on my..." Jason began, before Dusk interrupted, his eyes focusing on a dagger on Jason's waist.

"Wipe that clean," he commanded, clutching the keys. "You could excite the Coven... walking through the halls with that blade covered in human blood."

Jason looked down at the dagger, running it over his tongue quickly, waiting for Dusk to engage with him again, but he didn't. Instead, Dusk turned his back to him and began to walk towards the darkness of the cells, ignoring Jason as he ran up the stairs.

If the Red World hadn't been so loud, Dusk might have been able to hear the collective sounds of the humans in their cells groaning, but he couldn't. Instead, he only heard the Red World until the metal clang of his key unlocked a cell door and brought him back to this reality.

"Christian Nikolai Dusk..." the woman within the cell whispered weakly, "...the High Listener..."

Christian's eyes shone brightly as he looked down to her. Elise, still shackled, still wrapped in her blanket, tried to hide the slices that Jason's knife had managed on both of her arms—a solitary game of tic-tac-toe upon her flesh, inscribed by a blade, and a rematch to boot. Her soft smile was one to be pitied as she sat up, bringing her hair to one side, tilting her neck to invite his bite.

The Red World quieted, almost as if to return his ears to him, and Christian, who stood in the entryway to Elise's cell, staring at her new brand, began to sense that something was amiss. He walked back the path he had taken. He stopped in front of each cell, his cold blue eyes measuring the humans, each one sharing a series of angry cuts, just like Elise. Some had been sliced on their arms, others on their legs, others on their necks, or face, or chest, or back. Most wounds were shallow, but others were not, and as Dusk made his way back to Elise's door, the quiet anger within him boiled: every blood slave had been cut for sport.

Elise couldn't see the man standing before her, but she could hear his frustration even as he stood still. Her hand reached forward to touch him, but the chains weren't long enough. All the human prisoners were quiet except for a few whimpers; all of the Red World was quiet; the entire world waited on him to make a move. "Elise... you're..."

"It's okay... It's going to be okay," Claire whispered from her cell.

No. It wasn't Claire. It was Elise. It was Elise who called out to him like his sister had, vulnerable, wounded, and afraid. "It's going to be okay..." Dusk clenched his fists. "I'll be right back."

The High Listener did not bolt the cell door as he briskly made his way towards the staircase, ascending to the first floor. His footsteps carried him towards the main hall where an innocuous Ilovo stood, flask in hand, watching over the hallways as though visitors were set to arrive. "Mas..." Ilovo began before Dusk raised a hand.

"Where are Bruce and Carte?"

"Out. They'll return by tomorrow. Shall I pass along a message...?"

"No. Find two vampires. One to man your post and the other to assist us with something, then meet me in the basement." Ilovo watched as Dusk stormed away, quickly moving to fulfill a rare request from a member of the Inner Circle.

Ilovo was a fly on the wall. He blended into the woodwork. He observed and reported his findings plainly. He had never seen Dusk act so forward, but he did as he was told, finding a vampire to watch his post, then headed down to the basement accompanied by another.

"Master Dusk, I've brought..." Ilovo began to introduce the vampire at his side when he stopped, his focus pulled to the humans in their cells. "Master Dusk?" Ilovo peered through the bars at the first human, then at the second, and then at a third, his mouth salivating as he cast his gaze on each one. "What has...?"

"Someone has decided torture an appropriate pastime," Dusk said angrily. "You, fetch some salve," Dusk motioned to the other vampire who nodded quickly and raced back up the stairs. "Only those who are prepared to endure it should dole it out."

"Master Dusk, how can I assist? Do you know who is responsible?"

"Who is responsible? Or who is to blame?"

"Master Dusk?" Ilovo asked quietly, unsure of what he meant.

"You'll guard the cells today, Ilovo. You can do it from here or from the first floor. Today, these humans are off limits."

"To whom, Master Dusk?"

"To everyone." He inhaled deeply, standing taller.

"Perhaps..."

"By order of the High Listener, there will be no more feasting today. Anyone who does not comply can spend some time in the Silver Cell. Are we clear, Ilovo?"

"Perfectly," the man said, taking a nervous bow and reaching for his personal set of cell keys, opening the doors one-by-one in preparation for the other vampire's return.

He could feel the collective humans relax. Even the ones who had held hostility voiced a quiet *thank you* to the High Listener as he walked past them, back to the cell where Elise knelt, hands on her knees, feeling a wave of relief as he returned.

"Thank you," She said crisply, with a sad smile on her face, covering the child's game etched upon her arm.

"Elise." He paused, waiting for his sister to interject before continuing. "Would you accompany me?"

Fear.

Excitement.

Panic.

Hope.

"...To where, Master Dusk?"

Pain.

Dread.

Hope.

Longing.

"To safety..."

Concern.

Hope.

Possibility.

Uncertainty.

"...Yes."

47

ELISE'S HANDS GRIPPED THE COLD STEEL OF THE UNKNOWN DEVICE in the darkness before her. Though the room was lit, her graying eyes had long since lost the ability to perceive any light.

"Just lift when you're ready," Christian's voice echoed within her. She knew what would happen. He had told her what would happen. But she didn't believe that it actually would.

Her naked silhouette in the center of the room shivered and the silence strangled her. Every day for years she had heard someone talk or snore or whisper or breathe. She hadn't known a silence like this. It disturbed her to be in such a silence. It disturbed her that people could experience such a quiet, while others could be robbed of it.

She lifted the handle carefully.

At first, nothing happened, but as the steel lifted higher, a strange hiss filled the space around her. She turned the device as far as it would go, and a cold rain poured over her. The rain took her by surprise, and she let out a small squeak, not unlike the unexpected cut of a new vampire. The rain was cold, but she was used to the cold. It wasn't the temperature change that startled her, but the suddenness.

From her cell she had heard wind whistle and thunder roar. From her cell under the Evan Blood Coven she often waited for storms to come, and had even felt a wayward rain strike sideways and take her by surprise. She had learned to listen for the signs, but this device offered no such warning, and yet, the rain washed over her all the same.

It was pleasant.

Her face tilted up towards the darkness, towards the source. Her arms stretched upwards as far as they could, running over a series of pips from where the water fell. Her hands traced the metal body of the device producing the rainfall, running the length of the machine from the lever she had turned.

"Return it once you're done," he had said.

Elise gripped the handle again, slowly lowering it, letting the pressure die down and trickle. "Incredible." Her voice was a whisper in the room, knowable only to her. With a smile on her face that she didn't know she could make, she turned the handle again, restoring the rainfall.

As the water fell, her hands ran over her face and unmatted her hair. They traversed her body, over the countless slices that dominated her flesh, concentrated on her neck and shoulders. Her hands glided over her arms, atop the tic-tac-toe games that Jason Castille had just etched on her body. Her nails pried away the grime that saturated her, unaware that the water began to run clean at her feet. Her arms found her body a warm consolation, absent the weight of the chains that had bound her for so long, impregnated with her scent.

As she considered it further, she realized the water was warmer now, not hot, but not as cold as it had been when she had started. She could have lived under that waterfall forever, but she knew he was waiting outside. She took another minute. Selfishly, she waited another minute before slowly pulling back on the lever, returning it to its resting position, waiting for the stream of drops above her head to dissipate into a few droplets. Once it had stopped altogether, she mustered the courage to speak. "I'm... done."

Christian pushed the door open to step inside the shower room, then shut it behind him.

Elise stood naked before him. Her arms rested at her sides like a porcelain statue under the winding contraption of a shower that the room had been assembled around. Her gray eyes stared forward at him, unable to see him, as her chest rose and fell nervously.

He was staring at her, and she knew it. He was staring and she didn't need to see to confirm it; she was used to it. She'd been blind for almost as long as she could remember. "Thank you, Master Dusk," Elise said quietly, "for this... opportunity."

She followed his footsteps with her ears until he stood a foot from her. She stood nervous in a foreign territory—unsure of the size of the room, the obstacles within, or even where the nearest corner was. The room was unfamiliar. The situation was unfamiliar. She yearned for her cell, standing naked before the High Listener, but oddly enough, she wasn't scared.

His eyes surveyed her body, but where she assumed lust, it was pity he felt. She wrongly assumed that it was her breasts that drew his gaze, and though they were part of the journey, they were not the destination. The scars over her body were plentiful, and the latest addition of two incised games were just another in a long line of her suffering. His eyes climbed up her body, measuring each scar, noticing even those he himself had inflicted on her: small, but very real. He was complicit in her pain. He couldn't forget that. He didn't want to forget that.

"I..." Elise began, unnerved by the silence, unsure of what she would even say.

"Before I was the High Listener..." he began, taking her hand in his and placing a towel upon it, a towel which she took quickly, covering up rather than drying herself. "...I was a servant. I took my fair share of lashings... lived with scars like you do..." He took a step back, turning away from her, his voice bouncing off the cobblestone wall.

"You once said as much..." Elise said skeptically, drying herself as quickly as she could while she knew he wasn't watching.

"...When I was Turned, my scars faded... and when I had human blood for the first time... they disappeared entirely."

"That must have been nice," Elise said with a tinge of sadness and longing, dabbing her sliced body dry.

"It wasn't..." Dusk said, folding his arms, looking at Elise's scars out of the corner of his eye. "Becoming a vampire robbed that part of me..."

"Stole... your scars?"

"Stole my suffering..." He closed his eyes.

"I don't..."

"If I still had them, I could take your hand and press it against them. You could travel their lines and feel the depth of my pain. Instead, I can only tell you about them... and you have the option of believing whether or not it's true. You might be surprised to know, given our roles... but becoming a vampire was the beginning of a miserable reality for me..."

Elise felt her breathing return to normal as she listened to him talk. "I believe you... if that helps." She held the towel nervously against her front. "Could I be so forward as to ask you something... Master Dusk?" She bit her lip nervously. "If you are to take me... as others have... would you be so kind as to warn me? I wouldn't resist... and it would be..." she blushed, "...in both our interests..."

Dusk smiled warmly. "You remind me of someone..."

"Someone you loved?"

"Someone I love." Dusk inhaled deeply.

"Is that why you're doing this? You see her in me?"

"No," Dusk said sadly, turning to look at her. "I see who I used to be."

48

"..." **S**OMETHING HAS TO CHANGE." DUSK STOOD ACROSS FROM Carte Brooks and the Head of the Evan Blood Coven. Bruce sat at his usual spot, at the head of a long table in the War Room. On one side of the table, four of the five Elders also listened to Dusk's account of the treatment of the blood slaves. All the while, Bruce yawned and Carte's attention appeared torn, otherwise distracted by the meeting that was to follow.

"...You can oversee them how you see fit, and we'll settle on a punishment later. You can even keep the girl exclusively. As long as we have our fill—do what you will."

"I find it refreshing..." Carte said with a vacant smile. "That you'd stand up for something. You always were too..."

"Agreeable," Bruce said out loud, forgetting that they were in the company of the Elders. He cleared his throat. "Is that all then? When the guard told us it was urgent... we thought..."

"...but it's fine!" Carte interjected with a tinge of annoyance that Bruce might have been about to say something he shouldn't have. "If there's nothing else, see yourself out. We have other business to tend to."

Dusk gave the group a quick nod before exiting, pulling the doors closed and heading down the hall, leaving Carte and Bruce in the room with the Elders. The pair had just returned from one of their many secret trips. The Elders didn't know where they had gone off to and, if not for the Red World, then Dusk wouldn't have known either. The Elders were growing weary of the leadership, and Dusk knew the meeting about to take place would be one of contention.

The halls of the Evan Blood Coven were livelier than they had been in a while, and, amidst the familiar faces that roamed the hall and acknowledged the High Listener, newer additions appeared to have little idea who he was.

"*Did you think it wise to put yourself in a line of fire for her, brother?*" Claire's voice scolded him from the Red World. Each major decision the twins had encountered they had faced together, but Elise was a product of Dusk alone. "*She is no one.*"

Dusk surveyed his surroundings, waiting for the vampires to move about the castle, waiting to make sure no one was in earshot when he whispered back to his sister. "Did you hate it that much... being no one?"

Claire let out a sigh of exasperation. "*Brother...*" she continued in a calmer tone, "*our goal...*"

"Remains unchanged."

"*You expect me to believe that?*"

"Have I done anything to suggest otherwise?" Claire scoffed at his question. "If you have something to say sister, say it."

"*Very well...*" Claire inhaled calmly. "*Before you delude yourself anymore— listen clearly, brother. Elise is our age. She has let you see her naked. She has embraced you. She is upstairs asleep in your room... presumably where you plan to let her live. Oh! And she reminds me of Ant. At a minimum anyone would assume this is an elaborate ploy to lie with her. Myself included. Her included.*" Dusk was about to interject. "*We're going to save Ant within six months...*"

"Yes."

"*So where does Elise fit into this? Why introduce an unknown element? You won't be satisfied with leaving her behind once you get to know her. You can still undo this, brother,"* she pleaded. *"Return her to her cell... give her another day or two if needed and implement your conditions for better human treatment. Take your frustration on Jason if needed. It's not your job to save her."*

"The world isn't fair," Dusk whispered. "Living brings misery enough by itself. How many nights did I sleep on a pile of rags? How many nights did you shiver awake because of the cold? We would have been more comfortable on the ground of the first floor... but that was no place for a servant."

"It was our station then. Our station has changed now."

"Our duty has not... I'd forgotten that... you have too, sister. The world is unfair enough without such a handicap. We both lived it... and now we have an opportunity, not just for petty revenge... but for justice... to change the rules."

Claire sighed loudly. *"Fine,"* she conceded. *"You're right,"* she acknowledged, her tone softening. *"But you make things more complicated than they need to be."*

"I will find my way back to Antoinette... but living is complicated, sister."

She laughed. *"I suppose it is."*

"Is that it then?" Dusk asked.

"I suppose it is," she repeated, flustered.

Dusk's eyes looked ahead as his sister quieted, noticing the sunken cheeks of the former Listener, Katja, approaching from the far end of the hall with a journal in hand.

"If you're going to see Bruce or Carte... they're otherwise occupied," Dusk spoke, and Claire repeated his words; her echo cutting away the static that Katja heard daily.

"I was coming to find you... I went to your room and found one of the slaves making herself at home."

"Yes..." Dusk said, as Claire repeated things with a matter-of-fact tone. "That's a story for another time."

"Bruce wanted us to begin strategizing. With our next target so far away and..."

"...his obsession with necromancers," Claire added.

"Indeed." Katja inhaled sharply. "This will involve more than just the two of us. We'll need others who can be trusted to trade places with discreetly. I have some names we can go over... but considering how large the Coven is and that our target is almost a hundred miles away... we'll need to plan carefully."

"Four months?"

"Three."

Dusk clenched his teeth. "So be it... we'll discuss it in your room."

Katja nodded slowly, leading Dusk down the hall.

Just around the corner, a defiant Jason Castille quietly hugged the cobblestone wall. He had arrived just in time to catch the tail end of their conversation. "Three months... large Coven... a hundred miles away..." he repeated to himself.

As the Listeners walked away, Jason emerged from the shadows, his eyes locked on the small journal that Katja carried. The fall of his Coven still weighed heavy on his shoulders, and though the bruises on his face had healed, the humiliation had not; it wouldn't heal until Bruce Alazar was dead. No sooner had he thought this than the doors to the War Room burst open. One door flew off its hinges and landed near the corner where Jason stood. Bruce stormed forward angrily down the hall, making eye contact with Jason for an instant, thoroughly enraged.

Carte called out to him, appearing in the doorway. "Bruce!"

The Head of the Evan Blood Coven stopped just before Jason, his foot resting on the downed door. He turned around to look at Carte who tried to maintain her composure.

The couple yelled at each other, but Jason didn't hear what they said, instead his focus was elsewhere. Bruce stood with his back to him in a narrow hallway. He stood two feet away from him, and the dagger at his hip was heavy and hungry for more blood. He stood with his back to him like he did not know who Jason Castille was or what a threat he could be. He stood with his back to him, but one day he would regret underestimating him.

49

"**C**AN I TRUST YOU?" CHRISTIAN NIKOLAI DUSK HAD HELD AN ENVE-
lope closed with a wax seal. His eyes bore into Ilovo. It was neither his
usual look of detachment, nor the stern command of the High Listener.
This look carried with it risk, and Ilovo felt honored to accept it.

As he listened to Dusk's instructions, the man nodded, occasionally repeating
back the information as if to confirm. When the instructions grew lengthier, he
reached for a journal at his side to write on, but Dusk lowered his hand carefully.
There could be no record of this request.

Ilovo took pride in being a confidant; for too long he had been underestimated. There was a chance now, an opportunity to prove himself, and taking that
envelope, held meekly by a crimson seal that could be undone with a single swipe
of his long nails, was proof enough.

In the early morning hours, while the Evan Blood Coven slept, Ilovo
ventured out. He took a single horse this time, not the carriage that he was
normally the driver for. His body was hidden beneath a dark listless piece of
fabric that was more bedsheet than clothes.

Few vampires traveled during the day. None preferred it. Ilovo, however, had been the errand boy for the Evan Blood Coven for many decades. He knew the comical sight of a dark figure atop a dark horse would have made some people burst at the seams, but decades of traveling told him that this singular unexceptional article of clothing was best for these types of outings.

In the afternoon hours, he stopped to rest under the shade of a wall that might once have belonged to a house. The long journey was more taxing because it occurred during the day rather than the distance. His horse, with thick bushy legs and a majestic silver mane, cared not for the time of day, so long as it came with a promise of rewards. Today these were apples, which Ilovo cut in half with a small knife he carried in his pocket. They gushed under the steed's mighty jaw.

He ran his hand over the horse's mane as he offered the apples, taking a bite of each one himself, his tender brown eyes reflected in the horse's. He had grown used to being on his own. He had grown used to being ordered around. But as he patted his inside pocket, his fingers running over the edges of the letter, he tried to recall the last time he had been *asked* to do something. It was as refreshing as the fruit was to the horse.

"Just a few hours to go, Cres," Ilovo said to the horse as he filled a nearby bucket with water, soothing the horse that neighed at his name. "The journey back will be rough... we have to return before anyone gets suspicious..." His hand dug around in the saddle bag, pulling out a small flask and taking a long drink, an amber liquid running down his mouth. "But I'll make sure you have a few days to rest before our next outing. He doesn't look down on us, you know... even though we're pathetic." He pulled one final red apple out of his bag, offering it to the horse. The red of the apple was reflected in Ilovo's brown eyes as Cres crunched down on it, spraying him with the juice, prompting a laugh.

After a short rest, Ilovo and Cres set back out, riding until the sun was low in the sky. He'd hoped to arrive before it had set, and as Cres navigated off the dirt road and onto cobblestone, the vampire messenger breathed a sigh of relief. *Right on time.*

His eyes looked one way and another as the horse moved down the street. The sun had set, and the man, small in stature, led the horse until he was able to tie it to a post beside a water trough. With an easy smile, he handed a coin to a man who leaned against the post. "Will you be long?" the man asked, running his hands over the horse's face as it drank.

"An hour or two. Just delivering something."

The man nodded, securing the rope that Ilovo had tied. "I'll be here for another three... after that, it's at your risk that you leave 'im here." He nodded and continued up the road on foot.

As Ilovo walked, his head swiveled back and forth. He'd never come by this city, but he'd ridden past the place enough times on longer trips. He didn't recognize the run-down bookstore that the Globarias had owned; he'd never seen the Weather House sign before, nor the woman just outside who looked him up and down disappointedly before turning her back; and though he'd never seen the Schofield Manor, the description that Dusk had given him fit it to a tee.

As Ilovo rounded the squared structure of Dusk's former home, he noticed the disrepair that was about the house. The servant's entrance was covered with fallen leaves, the cobbles were mossy, and the ground was uneven. In fact, as Ilovo stopped, there was only one place where there was a semblance of beauty. Beside a window there was a small rosebush surrounded by a few wildflowers and a tall tree. Ilovo was unaware that it was where Claire was buried. He paused for a moment to consider the spot, then shook his head and carried on.

When Ilovo approached the front door, the caution that Dusk had offered him rang out. *"Only give the letter to Lady Antoinette. No one else can see it. No one else can know about it."* He raised a hand to the door, chipped and scratched, but before he could knock, it swung open brutishly.

"What do you want?" A man stood a head taller than Ilovo, his greasy blonde hair fell into the spike traps of his stubble, and his white shirt was stained by alcohol, sweat, or both: Michael Escoté.

With four words to his breath, Ilovo caught sight of his two fangs, and the man's head tilted forward. "I..." Ilovo kept his lips pursed as much as he could. Decades of dealing with outsiders had trained him to be discreet, though it certainly made him appear more inept than he was.

"You're here for Aubrey?" Michael Escoté's pallid presence kept one muscular arm on the door. As Ilovo looked at the bulging arm, he knew that Michael didn't practice restraint. He drank blood often and plentifully. He'd seen enough vampires burn out consuming blood in excess. A couple of the Elders had experienced it firsthand. Ilovo couldn't take him now, but with a little preparation, it wouldn't have been difficult.

"Yes... it's my..."

Michael raised a hand. "Don't care. Payment first."

He took a step back, reaching into both of his pockets, pulling a small coin purse out of one. No sooner did he pull it out than Michael swiped it from him, dumping the coins into his hand, tossing the empty purse back to Ilovo, counting the dozen coins.

"Isn't that a bit..."

"Consider it a future payment. The next time, she's free. And don't get her pregnant like the last one." Michael chuckled, throwing open the door. "She's in the basement. Take a left, down the stairs. She'll find you..." With these words, Michael forced Ilovo inside while he sauntered down the street.

Ilovo peered out the front window, making sure he was gone before breathing a sigh of relief. His other hand, still in his pocket, released its grip from the small knife. He was glad he didn't have to use it, he didn't even know if he'd be capable.

As he stood in the main hall, he looked at the three possible directions before him. To his left, a hallway dead-ended in what appeared to be an opening to a spiral staircase; to his right, the path appeared to wrap around the wall; and straight ahead, the hall opened up into a large room.

Before he had a chance to make a decision, he heard a voice whispering. He cautiously stepped forward, finding a woman standing in the center of a large room. She was the picture of elegance. Her dark hair was styled atop her head, and an ornate silver dress was accented by a three-strand chain that clasped onto a choker. An amethyst stone from the necklace rested against her chest.

The woman stood still like a statue, facing Ilovo as he stepped into the room. Her eyes were a distinctive green, and the corners were heavy, falling into the shadow of her bags. She bore no smile, but rather a look of wonton despair as he approached her. "Lady Antoinette, I presume?" Ilovo moved slowly, making sure no one else was around.

His caution was undone as he looked around. The space was nearly empty. The mantle of the fireplace was barren, and two raggedy chairs sat around a table that wobbled at his gaze. There wasn't anything to look at in the room except the statue of the woman who stood before him. "Lady Antoinette?" he asked again, watching her eyes look forward, even as he approached her from the side. "Ah," Ilovo said, recognizing the situation. "Bear with me a moment, My Lady." He took her open fist and quickly sliced the palm of her hand.

Antoinette reeled, letting out a gasp as she clenched her hand, her body relaxing as she stepped back. "Thank you," she said quietly. "May I ask your name, My Lord?" She watched as the wound on her palm closed, then turned her eyes to take in the unremarkable man who wiped her blood on his shirt.

"I am no Lord," Ilovo chuckled. "Forgive the intrusion... but I suspected a shock might be needed to break the Command."

"You're a vampire too?" Antoinette asked cautiously.

"Indeed, My Lady." He reached into his coat pocket and withdrew the letter. He took a step forward, expecting Antoinette to take a step back, but she didn't; instead, she reached out her hand and took the letter, running a finger over the crest on the wax seal.

It appeared hastily affixed, half was pronounced and the rest invisible through the thinness of the wax, but she could make out a small bat's wing. "What is this?"

"Master Dusk has entrusted me to bring this to you, and only to you."

"Christian?" Antoinette asked hopefully, her finger running over the seal again, her figure relaxing even more, green eyes lighting up. "He's... well?"

"Indeed, My Lady," Ilovo said with the common parlance of a good friend. "He provided me with explicit instructions to deliver this to you. He said that I should wait until you have read it, then destroy it."

"I see..." Antoinette tore open the letter, the wax seal falling to the floor as she did. Her eyes instantly recognized Dusk's clumsy writing. Unlike Claire's pristine lettering, Dusk's was jagged. Sometimes he held the quill wrong; sometimes the ink clotted; but there was no mistaking that this was indeed his writing.

As Antoinette read the letter, her eyes grew more and more hopeful. When she got to the end, she pursed her lips, looking away and pressing the letter against her chest, then bringing it up to her nose. After she was done, she read it over once more, then folded it neatly back, taking a step forward to hand Ilovo the letter. "Can you give him a message... from me?"

"Yes, My Lady."

"I'm not the only one who misses you."

"Will he... know what that means?"

"Dusk knows everything," Antoinette said with a cheeky smile.

"Lord Dusk is indeed a knowledgeable man."

No, Antoinette thought, looking to the table with the wobbly chairs. *Not Christian. Claire. She'll know what I mean.*

Antoinette escorted Ilovo out the servant's entrance with an iron pot. The pair watched as the letter burned, standing in an awkward silence until the flames went out.

"...Thank you, again," Antoinette said gently, "...for earlier."

"If I could offer a suggestion... though it is not my place."

Antoinette smiled, her beauty more pronounced now than it had ever been. "Please, My Lord."

"I once knew a man cursed with a similar predicament..." Ilovo said carefully. "Though not always possible... he had a pair of shoes tailored for him. He walked on the tips, for the sole was weak. It could support him, but not for long."

"My Lord?" Antoinette asked, confused.

"After extended periods of immobility, the weak sole would cause the shoe to buckle. A hidden spike would impale his foot and he would self-actualize from the Command." Her eyes lit up. "...It was rather barbaric... but he is pathetic... he couldn't raise a hand to stop him. It worked until he was found out."

"Then what happened...?"

"He ran... one day he mustered the courage to run away... at a great cost."

50

Elise's body sat up on the bed. Though her eyes faced forward, she could see nothing. Still, she could perceive a man sitting on one of the two chairs that wrapped around a single table. His breaths were shallow and calm. He slept in the darkness before her.

Her hands stretched over the satin sheets of the bed. It was so large that her fingers could barely touch the edges if she stretched out her arms. Her body stiffened as she did so, slowly laying back in the middle. She couldn't recall a time when her body had hurt so little.

Why was she so uneasy then?

She bit her lip gently, lost in thought. It had been a week now and the High Listener hadn't said much to her. He hadn't touched her any more than the occasional feeding. The most unsafe she had felt was when she was naked before him in the shower, but the second time she'd thought nothing of it.

Why had he been so concerned with her in the dungeon then? Why was he so unconcerned with her now?

Surely, he must have realized how much he had changed her life by simply removing the chains she'd been saddled with, or provided clothes which were not tattered, or even given a reprieve from the noise of the dungeon! Surely, he must have known that giving her a shower, or a bed, or even a bite of a meal that was not scraps was more than she could have ever hoped for.

What was he thinking?

During the nights, he would leave her alone. The first night, she'd wandered around the room, feeling everything from the bed to the table to a small notebook. She'd reached up the walls to try to touch artwork, but found none; her hands had dug through the drawers of the nightstand searching for anything other than clothes, and only found a few small boxes with some children's toys; she'd even run her hands around and under the mattress and came to the same sparse realization of his room. The only curiosity she noticed was a fist-sized depression behind the door, but besides that, the room was barren.

Elise had touched almost everything that she could, mapping out the room she was in, as well as the adjacent bathroom in the High Listener's second-floor room. There was only one thing left to check. She contemplated the place she knew the door was for a long time before her curiosity got the better of her. She gripped the brass of the doorknob and turned while he was away. Quietly she rotated the doorknob, not knowing if it would yield until the latch clicked. The door opened slowly into the hallway before she caught it and pulled it closed, her heart racing as it did.

Was she not caged?

The weight of the absence of the chains was liberating, and though the door remained unlocked, Elise remained inside, finding herself humming throughout the day, spinning around in place, and tidying up those things she made a mess of until his early return.

His footsteps were light. He was the lightest vampire on the floor by leaps and bounds. Anyone else might have said that he crept, but they didn't realize he'd been disciplined for being too loud on more than one occasion. As the days went on, Elise recognized the truth of his words about being a servant. His behavior, his caution, and even his humility were so engrained into his being that he didn't know how to turn them off. He was one of the six most influential vampires in the Evan Blood Coven, and yet he treaded so carefully that it appeared a farce.

But he was aware of his power.

Elise recalled how Dusk had acted when he'd learned that the humans in the dungeon had been tortured. He was powerful, but he was so tempered that no one saw it. By spending time with him and seeing his encounters with other members of the Coven, Elise knew that Christian Nikolai Dusk was the ultimate actor. He had everyone in the Coven fooled.

But to what end?

She thought it curious, she confessed, as he slept in the same room as her, with his legs propped up on one chair while he sat in the other, that while everyone else schemed for power, it was the one thing that he very clearly did not want—at least, not in the way that everyone else did. It was a means for him, but she didn't know to what end.

A deep inhale was the telltale sign that he awoke, and Elise's face of concern turned to a smile. "Good evening, Master Dusk," she said sweetly, sitting up again in the bed, wearing a white, lace nightgown that sheathed most of her body.

"Elise," Dusk said calmly, looking her way for a moment, "good evening."

He was on his feet quickly. She could hear the shuffle of clothes as he changed. He would be gone the full night, like he normally was, and though there was no substitution for every amenity that she had, the one thing she desperately wanted was purpose. "Master..." Elise began, swinging her legs over the side of the bed, "...this may be out of place..."

Dusk was buttoning up his shirt when he looked back at her. It felt strange to wake to this woman, but not unpleasant. It was odd, he thought, that just having someone nearby made him feel much more at ease. "Yes?"

"Is there perhaps some way I might be of service to the Coven in my new... role?"

"*Oh?*" Claire asked teasingly from the Red World. "*Didn't I tell you, brother?*"

"You have something in mind?" Dusk asked, ignoring Claire's teasing. She hadn't made a move with him so far; he had no reason to doubt that in the early hours of this evening it would be any different.

She could feel a blush coming on that she tried to shake away. She didn't know why, but something about the way he handled his conversations with her, however brief, made her feel far more empowered than she was used to.

That was it. He made her feel like she was a Lady, and not merely a slave of the Coven. For someone who had had so many decisions made on their behalf already, the idea of a suggestion becoming reality felt strange, but the High Listener himself was a bit absurd. "I am grateful for everything... but I wonder if I could assist with the maintenance of the other humans?"

Dusk's sapphire eyes measured her. She sat straight on the bed, with her gray eyes staring forward. It was an earnest request to do more in service of an institution that had only ever treated her like the slave she was. It didn't seem right, but Dusk himself still felt the impact of his upbringing. His Master was in another house, yet still he served her. His station was higher than hers in this Coven, but he would always be at her beck and call.

"Go on." The High Listener said very little, and because of that, every word that Elise said felt more important than it should have. *That was his true power: letting others live out their fantasies under the guise that he had no hand in achieving them.* The most notable example that Elise knew of was the Evan Blood Coven's conquests as of late, which everyone accredited to Bruce, though she knew the success had been guided by Dusk's hand.

"Now that the Coven has given control of the humans to you..."

"Careful brother... this is the phrasing of someone set out to manipulate you."

"...Master Ilovo... or one of the other newly Turned vampires are responsible for providing us with our food, clothing, bedding, or necessities... I would like to liberate the vampires from chores that we humans can do ourselves." Elise finished her thought, waiting to hear what reply would come. *You're blind. You can't do any of that. You'd only get in the way. Why ask for this? To escape? To aid the other humans? To begin an uprising? What would you offer me if I said yes?*

Dusk raised a hand to the Red World as his sister was about to protest, eyes narrowing. "You know the feeding schedule. We'll have you responsible for the first meal. I'll have Ilovo walk the route with you... but..."

Here it was. The trade-off. The slight.

Her thighs tightened nervously. From the darkness, his hand took hers. She jolted at his touch as he held her hand, unsure of what would come next, unsure of what he was doing until he placed something in her palm, closing her fingers around it. She rubbed the object between her hands. It was fabric, that much was clear. The fabric was emblazoned with something. Her fingers ran over the elevated stitching.

"...this is the crest of the High Listener," he said. "When you go out, you will wear this crest. It symbolizes that you are under my protection... protected from humans, vampires, or whatever else lurks in these halls."

"Master Dusk...?" Elise asked, quite confused. "Is... that... all? I need only wear this...?" *That was it? No painful bloodletting? No forcible relations? No punishment for her request?* All she needed to do was ask and wear this piece of fabric? It made no sense. This benefited him in no way, and yet not only did he casually allow it, but he also encouraged it. Her thighs untensed and she felt hot under the collar of her nightgown. "Why..." she began. "Why say yes, when you could have easily said no?"

Dusk paused. "That way of thinking reminds me of my sister... she too found it hard to accept a gift without any strings."

"You paint me in such a light," Claire scoffed.

"...perhaps because so few *actually* came without strings," Dusk said, taking a step towards the door. "Something has to change, and what better time than now?" He opened the door and looked back at her. She sat on the far side of the bed, her hands balled into fists that rested on her legs, waiting. "I'll provide Ilovo with instructions and see that he fetches you when it's convenient."

"Thank you... Master Dusk," Elise whispered as the door closed.

51

J ASON CASTILLE'S SNEER WAS PLASTERED ON ANOTHER FACE THAT
roamed the halls of the Evan Blood Coven. A former member of Alastair,
Henry Beltran stood of medium stature, brown hair, and brown eyes—a
look so subtle that he could easily blend into a crowd.

Henry's pace was deliberate, his movement slow, and his caution high.
Anyone who would have taken a glance at the figure would have known that he
was up to something, and though prior days had yielded nothing of substance,
he suspected that today would be different.

As he walked through the main corridor, he quickly homed in on the
human who walked carefully beside the Coven's errand boy. Ilovo's voice was
earnest as he spoke to the girl who bore the crest of the High Listener upon
her chest, not paying any mind as Henry walked past them, tuning out any
more of their small talk.

As the former Alastair member headed for the main entrance to the
Coven, he watched as the Listeners exited the grounds. Like a seasoned
reporter, he made some scrawls on a piece of paper, returning it to the

pocket he'd drawn it from.

The next few hours of wandering brought nothing notable. He stopped to watch another vampire who he didn't recognize repair the door that Bruce had destroyed; he found Nier and Saber playing a board game near the common area; he even spotted Daina practicing her spearplay in a training area that was normally closed off.

With a heavy sigh, Henry looked down at the scribbles he'd made throughout the night. They weren't letters or words, but rather sketches. He couldn't read, so he tried hard to remember what they all meant. In a moment of frustration, he crumpled the paper and hurled it down a hall, then looked at the lone ball before letting out a sigh of desperation, going to retrieve it.

As he went to pick it up, he heard the familiar voice of Bruce towards the end of the hall. The voice was quiet and, as Henry spun around, he found that it came from above, from a small grate that connected to an unknown area. He put his back to the wall, sitting in the spot with his head down, feigning the appearance of being asleep, as he eavesdropped.

"...once I find it..." Bruce's words came through quiet, but slurred. "...I'm getting rid of them..."

"Bruce..." Carte Brook's voice came through quiet and clear, "...it's been a century..."

"A century wasted relying on Katja."

"She tried."

"Did she? She led us along and the Elders... I tire of their *counsel*." He spat. "They talk about knowing their role and use it to get under my skin. I could kill them all right now and wouldn't lose any sleep."

"You know why we can't."

"Once I get the blood... we can. I can. I will."

"And then what? We can't exactly raise a newborn around... this?"

There was a pause. There was a lengthy and calculated pause. "We'll make some cuts."

Jason Castille's elbows rested on the table in the War Room as he listened intently to what Henry had overheard. He didn't know exactly what Bruce was after, nor why he and Carte were discussing a newborn when everyone knew that a vampire could not bear children, but there were a couple of key points about the discussion that were both relevant and concerning: Bruce planned to eliminate the Elders in due time, and eventually, perhaps even members of Evan Blood.

He could use this information—the real question was *how?*

A day went by, and still Jason bit his tongue. If he presented it incorrectly, he could become a target himself. He needed to know where the Elders' loyalties were, and to that end, he reached out to the only Elder who appeared somewhat approachable: Armand Hammon.

52

IN A DIMLY LIT CORNER OF THE EVAN BLOOD COVEN, IN THE SMALL library accessible only through the Promotion room, two men sat in silence. Jason Castille, after a week of contemplating, sat across from the Elder he had decided to confide in, his thumb nervously spinning a ring on his finger. Across the circular table with a sigil containing six circles, Armand tried to right his back to sit up straight. His fingers were interlocked on the table before him, and the crimson lining of his purple robe was the most pronounced color in the room.

"...is that all, then?" Armand asked, after Jason relayed the entire story, just as Henry had told him.

"Surely this concerns you," Jason added.

"Indeed it does..." *but not the part you're thinking of,* Armand failed to add. Of course he was concerned about the notion of Bruce deciding to excise the Elders; and granted, the notion of killing off members of the Coven also carried a certain sense of egotism; but as Jason exited the room, unable to get a read on Armand's thoughts, it was the parts of the conversation that Jason was too young to understand that resonated with him the most.

Hours later, when he sat around the same table with the other four Elders, they too fixated on these parts, just like Armand.

"But did he say the word?"

"No," Armand said lowly.

"No? Or did the Castille boy keep it from you?"

"No," Armand repeated. "If Bruce had said it... he would have brought it up."

"Could there be another explanation?" another asked.

"For a vampire having a child?"

"No," Armand said with a sigh. "Not unless they plan to Turn a pregnant human... and they would need to consult with us for that. We can collectively count on one hand how many times such a child has been successfully carried to term."

"What is the probability that he's unraveling the key to necromancy?"

"Few know of that sordid history... fewer believe it... but you think he does? And you think he will find it?" With each *and* the skepticism grew. "One does not simply become a necromancer."

"It does explain a lot," chimed in another. "It explains his little... excursions..."

"If necromancer blood were easy to find, someone would have done it already." Armand said curtly. "If it were possible, they wouldn't be extinct, but recall... one day they *didn't* exist... then they *did*... and then they *didn't* again. Only our Master knows how they were created... but it begs the question of what if a vampire, what if Bruce, could become one?"

The Elders mumbled amongst themselves.

"We cannot forget... he may be targeting us too. Is that really something we should let idly fester?"

"Would *you* challenge him?"

"Not openly!" Everyone nodded in agreement. "The problem is those he surrounds himself with. They will not easily fall..."

"That Daina is a fine specimen."

"Agreed."

"But fine or not, they must be dismantled."

"By who?"

"The Castille boy is clearly up to something..."

"We cannot go against the Head of Evan Blood..."

"...but we could stand aside or offer temporary support."

"The possible outcomes?"

"Bruce falls... Carte succeeds him. Her desire is more... manageable. Her tongue... controllable."

"Or Bruce and Carte perish... the line of succession falls to the High Listener... as it is written."

"Dusk?"

"His position would be a proxy. He doesn't have what it takes to lead a Coven... but it could yield a reprieve, and a rare opportunity to install someone ourselves."

"Is there a scenario where an outsider ascends?"

"The Castille boy?"

"There are others vying for the title that are infinitely more qualified..."

"Though less motivated."

"I think we can all agree..." Armand interrupted the dialogue. "The priority has shifted. As long as his ambition remains what it is... Bruce Alazar cannot stay in power." He paused, waiting to see if another Elder would interject, and when none did, he continued. "We have our directive to maintain. I'll prepare a correspondence to our Master. She must be made aware, and we'll need to speak with Katja... her allegiance has always been cautious."

"We should also have a contingency in place."

"A contingency?"

"...in case we're openly challenged."

"In case the Coven is ever in jeopardy."

53

ELISE HUMMED TO HERSELF AS SHE CAREFULLY WALKED DOWN THE steps to the basement, counting them as she went, carrying a small burlap sack in one hand and running her other along the wall. *Twenty-five, twenty-six, twenty-seven, twenty-eight... twenty-nine.*

"Elise!" a voice called out from one of the cells, waking others who called out to her too. She felt a small sense of pride as they did; she puffed out her chest when they said her name; she stood taller as she walked, reaching into the burlap sack at every few steps, and holding out a roll of bread that the caged humans took.

"What's the main course today?" One of the humans asked, his arms resting on the bars as he gnawed at the stale piece of bread. "Steak? I'll have mine medium."

"Stew," Elise said. The humans let out a collective groan.

"It's always stew!"

Elise turned her face to the one who had requested the steak. "Would you prefer the scraps you got before I took over, Port?" Her scrunched-up face cracked a smile as the man before her rolled his eyes.

"Fine... I'll close my eyes and pretend."

Elise continued making her way down the line until was before the cell that was formerly hers. It was still empty but even standing before it felt odd.

"You going to ignore me all day, or are you going to feed me too?" a gruff man snapped at her from a cell she hadn't gotten to yet.

She took a few steps towards the voice, withdrew a piece of bread, and tossed it towards the cell. A scrawny arm poked through the bars, reaching for the roll as the other humans erupted in laughter.

Elise still recalled the first day she'd come by to hand out food, in the company of Ilovo. This man, a newly acquired blood slave, had grabbed her arm and brutishly pulled her towards the cell, sending her body colliding into it before Ilovo had stepped in. The human's temper was still high, and now Elise used a neighboring human to hand him most of his food.

"Your time here will be short..." she mustered the courage to say. "Those of us who have been here for years know... those who are always angry don't survive long."

"I would rather rot..." the man said, hurling the roll of bread at Elise's face, causing her to reel from the shock more so than the impact, "...than continue to be a meal to these monsters."

There was silence for but a moment before one of the other humans spoke up. "Elise... I'll take that bread. By your left foot. Can't let it go to waste." The human who had groaned, Port, said with a chuckle as everyone else began to clamor for the projectile bread. She bent down, feeling around, finally picking it up. "Over here!" Port continued as Elise tossed the bread in his direction, then finished up with the remaining humans.

Before she began the ascent to the first floor, she turned her head back. "You won't rot..." she said somberly, bringing a hush over the humans, "...they'll kill you before you do... and they'll throw a celebration with the buckets of blood they'll drain you of."

One. Two. Three. Elise began to ascend the stairs, *...twenty-seven, twenty-eight, twenty-nine.*

When she finally reached the landing of the first floor, empty burlap sack in hand, she let out an exhale, stretching the sack between her hands. For six weeks she had fed the other humans, taking at least two trips for each meal to ensure she didn't drop anything. As she walked back to her room, she had memorized every crack in the floor, every groove in the wall, and every loose stone that shifted under her feet.

Most of the other humans had lived with Elise for months; some had lived in a cell beside hers for years; but the newer ones, the ones that didn't realize how much better it was now, irritated her. Granted, even amongst those who had spent a long time in the dungeon, there were days when they were short, but an apology would follow, or some self-inflicted penance.

The spot on her face where the loaf had struck her didn't hurt, but the humiliation of the moment made it throb. She just wanted to go to her room for a moment, to sit on her bed, to catch a second wind before supper, but as she reached for her door, she found it already ajar and was reminded that neither the bed, nor the room, nor the door belonged to her.

"Master Dusk?" she called into the emptiness, hearing light breathing as she took a hesitant step forward.

"You sound disappointed," he replied distantly from one of the chairs in his room.

"Apologies... I was merely lost in thought. I didn't know when to expect your return from your scouting trip..."

"I didn't know myself..." He watched as Elise confidently closed the door behind her, then made her way to the other chair, feeling around for its back.

"May I join you?"

"By all means."

She wrapped her hands around the chair before taking a seat. "Is anything the matter?"

She heard a distinctive *thud* on the table in front of her. Her hand reached forward, a finger running around the base of the object, which she instantly recognized as a crystal goblet. "You'll find out soon enough... but Katja is dead. She and a few others didn't survive the scouting of Red Crescent."

"Didn't survive?" Katja asked. *"You sacrificed ... to save yourself!"*

"We all would have died if we didn't."

"Ah," Elise said quietly. "Would you prefer that I leave you alone?"

"No..." Dusk said quietly. "Keep talking. The Red World is loud... and she won't let me mourn her."

"We? You *knew ... were coming!* You *... have warned us! He could ... warned us!"*

Elise was quiet for a moment, thinking how best to proceed, but rather than pry any more, she did as she was told. "Since you've been gone six weeks..." she began, "...a lot has happened..."

Dusk closed his eyes, focusing on her voice, despite Katja's echoing from beyond the Divide.

"Why?" Katja asked. *"Why with all your ... didn't you warn us so we ... all ... escaped."*

"And what?" Claire snapped. *"And have them chase us here? Or strike us here? A few losses ensured our success."*

"...Master Ilovo gave me a tour of the Coven and..."

"I only ... helped you! You fed me to ...!"

"...started with breakfast only. That was for about the first week... something you might find interesting..."

"That's enough!" Claire barked.

Dusk drew the glass goblet to his lips, the intoxicating smell of blood mixed in with the alcohol.

"...Master Dusk...?" Elise couldn't see the state that he was in, couldn't see the defeat on his face, but as she reached forward, her hand slid over his. She steadied his quiver as best she could.

"Please... continue..." he said, conflicted, looking across the room to the space behind the door where a second depression, as large as his fist, accompanied the first one.

54

THE NIGHT AFTER DUSK'S RETURN, A *GRAND CELEBRATION* WAS underway. By order of the Head of the Evan Blood Coven, every single person was required to attend. The courtyard behind the ballroom was as packed as it had ever been, and barrels of blood wine were carted out. While most drank and smiled, those that knew of Katja and the others who had died mourned their losses, occasionally recounting a story of deeds from a time long before Dusk.

Bruce had even ordered the humans out of their cells. For most, this was the first time in years that they had seen the unobstructed view of the night sky, and while the taste of blood wine was revolting to them, they happily held onto their glass chalices and made small talk, intimately aware of the awkwardness of the situation. By midnight, some were chatting with their Masters as though they were friends.

"A decade of living here..." Elise said, holding her own goblet. "I never imagined it could be so lively."

Dusk looked down at his half-filled goblet, his bloodshot eyes scanning the room, glossing over the fact that Jason Castille's cup was still full, and that he was deeply engrossed in a conversation with Nier and Saber.

"You shouldn't beat yourself up, brother," Claire's council rang empty.

"It wasn't right... Perhaps we could have done it another way."

"You weren't sent with warriors. You were on their land. A trap was the only way to survive."

Elise raised a brow. Dusk was talking quietly, but he didn't seem to be mumbling to himself. It wasn't the first time she had heard as much. She turned her head away, but her ears couldn't help but focus on his voice.

"We can't change the past," Claire said sadly.

"I suppose not," he whispered.

Hours after the celebration had begun, the Coven watched as a large pyre lit up the world. The members of Evan Blood continued to drink and speak as it died down, and it was a drunk Ilovo who finally mustered up the courage to step out of the shadowy corner he'd been in.

"Master Dusk..." he said as he approached. "Elise," he added, seeing her nearby. "My condolences. I know that you and Katja were close..." Dusk nodded. "If I'm not out of line... I could lend additional assistance... should you require it."

"I..." Before Dusk could say another word, he heard glass shatter somewhere near the pyre, a string of curse words, then laughter. "I appreciate it... but I think I'll take my leave now..."

"...I'll join you," Elise said quickly, offering her glass to Ilovo, who took it, looking down at the nearly full goblet, devouring it in one fell swoop.

The pair walked in silence through the main halls, up the stairs to Dusk's room, and eventually stood in the quiet, with the raging celebration as nothing more than a backdrop.

Elise's clothes still kept the ashes, and without an ounce of shame, she undressed by the side of the bed and slipped on her nightgown, reaching down for the bed before she sat. Unsure of whether or not Dusk was watching her, she nervously spoke. "I'm sure the bed is more comfortable than the chairs..." Her heartbeat raced. "I wouldn't mind if we slept in the same bed."

She didn't mean it in any way other than literal, but she felt her face flush as the words came out of her mouth. She leaned into the silence, hearing the familiar sound of clothes hitting the floor, then a soft creak as the bed gave way, and another as Dusk lay his body on the bed.

She slowly let herself fall, and a moment later, she lay awkwardly next to the High Listener, uneasy again. He was awake. She could tell that he was awake, and his stillness unnerved her.

"What is it like? Listening?"

"...A curse," he whispered, "subject to a constant agony you cannot escape from."

"So, I'm your agony now, brother?"

"Like not being able to see," she whispered up at the ceiling. "An ordinary existence would be your ultimate reward... and we wouldn't take it for granted."

"Katja lived for a hundred years with this curse... but it's different for me..."

"How so?"

"Don't tell her."

"...It's complicated," he sighed.

She reached for Dusk, finding his hand lying in the space between them, nestling her small hand in his.

He didn't hear her next words over the maelstrom of the Red World, all he heard was Katja's repeated condemnation. *"I ... still be alive if it weren't ... you,"* Katja spat.

"Or my brother would be dead."

"I'm sorry..." Dusk whispered.

"Why do ... let her have ... much power over your life when you ... to live with the consequences?" Katja ignored Claire.

"I..."

"She could have ... you from this pain. She could have ... you. She ... have saved me, but instead she let me ... and made ... an accomplice. Does that sit well with you ..." With each phrase that Katja spoke, a few words were lost.

"Ignore her brother... You know all too well that the Red World can lie."

"I know," he whispered, closing his hand around Elise's. "I know."

55

"LEAVE HER, MY BOY." MICHAEL ESCOTÉ'S VOICE ECHOED through the main hall as he departed the Schofield Manor, leaving a child of six to stare at the woman before him. The boy stood with his hands in his pockets. A white long-sleeved shirt under his seven-button vest was tightly closed around his neck by a black bow tie. His black curly hair was parted above his left eye.

Antoinette Katherine Schofield reached her shaky hands up to her head. Her fingers caught the rough cuts in her hair, and her eyes looked down the mess of hair that she had been relieved of. She avoided the eyes of the boy who stood before her with a morbid curiosity, watching the woman spread her arms forward on the stone floor and sweep the clumps of hair towards her body.

"It will grow back," the boy's voice interrupted the mourning, and Antoinette's gaze looked up at him weakly as he jumped on the bed behind her.

Her green eyes had lost their luster. She couldn't think of a way to respond that wouldn't make her angry, so she bit her tongue, like her mother had taught her, listening to the bed lurch as the boy bounced up and down.

A minute later, Aubrey stood in the entry way. She couldn't contain her gasp as she witnessed the butchering that had occurred this time. "Lady..."

Antoinette rose to her feet quickly, letting her dress flow and attempting to iron out the folds that had come from kneeling. "I'm okay... it will grow back," she said, a bit hollow.

"Dram... go play outside..." Aubrey said to the boy, who, slow to respond, finally stopped bouncing on the bed and ran out of the bedroom.

Aubrey leaned against the doorway and let out a deep exhale. Her arm wrapped around her swollen belly. Antoinette's eyes looked to her, angry for a moment, then filled with compassion. "I didn't want to ask for your assistance given your state..."

Aubrey nodded. "Not to worry, My Lady. Now tell me, what do you need?"

Antoinette closed the door gently behind Aubrey, turning the brass key on the inside of the room so that the door locked. She made her way over to the dresser on the far side, avoiding her own butchered reflection as she did. She pulled out a drawer with its neatly folded clothes still inside, carrying it over and setting it on the bed with an inhuman strength that always impressed Aubrey.

With a delicate hand, Antoinette reached to the back of the dresser, to the space which the drawer's presence would have made inaccessible. She retrieved a folded piece of paper, pursing her lips for a moment before handing it to Aubrey who carefully opened it, finding a small red wax seal contained within the folds. The seal bore a small bat's wing and something on the opposite side which was less pronounced. "What is this... My Lady?" Aubrey asked, looking down at it.

"I don't know myself..." Antoinette said, returning the drawer to its spot in the dresser. "But I need you to find out who it belongs to, and, if you can... where they live."

56

ELISE WAS ALWAYS FIRST TO WAKE. HER DUTIES HAD EXPANDED from helping the humans with their daily meals, to providing their washcloths, to now, assisting with the communal blood harvests. Her responsibilities had grown and so too did her pride in them. So, even on the days when she awoke with bags under her eyes, the notion of a task to do, and a comfortable place to start her day from made her glow. Her routine was generally the same, but the banter with the humans, and even the occasional banter with some of the vampires, made her days go by quickly.

"... You know Elise..." a human by the name of Port, who had been in the dungeons with her for a few years now, began, "...I could help Master Dusk too. You and I could finish in half the time, and we could find other ways to be useful too."

Other humans were quick to jump into the conversation.

Elise stifled a laugh. "It's not a bad idea Port." She handed him a stale roll of bread from her satchel. "It would be nice to get you all out, but..."

"Well just think about it!" he said abruptly, interrupting the gentle letdown that Elise was going to offer, juggling the single roll.

"...Wouldn't you run?" From the end of the row of cells, the same man that had hurled a piece of bread at Elise spoke. "Wouldn't you get away the moment you could? You're not blind like her."

Port continued tossing the bread up and down. "Nah. If I get Elise's deal, why would I? An occasional shower. A warm bed. A good-looking partner to share it with." Port's childish grin watched as he made Elise's face flush. "What more do I need, Vega?"

A few of the other humans mumbled in assent.

"What more do you need?!" the man growled. "Vampires not to feast on you. Vampires not to treat you like an object. Respect! They have no sympathy. Even your golden example takes a cripple and turns her into a tool—complete with a brand of ownership. I've seen rats treated better than us." He rattled his bars.

Port's face was serious for a moment, then it cracked in a smile, and finally he blew a raspberry as he laughed. "Yeah, and I've been treated better by rats than you." Some of the other humans began to laugh, then even Elise giggled to herself.

"I don't get it..." Vega said frustratedly. "You're all delusional..."

"We're not," Elise said. "Watch... Port..." She turned to him. "Are you a slave?"

"The best looking one here!"

"Freya?" She turned to another cell. "Are you a slave?"

"Every day."

"Hecate?" Elise turned to the cell next to Freya's. "What about you?"

"Mhmm..." she said.

"Vega?" she finally asked.

"Are *you* a slave?"

"I'm not..." His face turned red. "This is temporary. Only until I get out." His grip tightened on the bars and he shook them. "I was taken! And I'm supposed to be fine with that?!"

"Some of us are... some of us were even sold without a surname." Elise balled her fist. "You were taken and people once called you *Master* or *Lord*. We've never been Masters or Ladies or Lords... and we never will be, but..."

"That life is behind you," Port added with a raised brow. "You've got two choices now: be an ongoing meal for a vampire or two, or be a final meal for a small celebration... and the funny thing is... it's only *half* your choice."

Elise walked proudly back to her room that evening. Rarely had she felt so steeled in her resolve that the thought of asking for more didn't frighten her, but as she stood at the foot of her bed, recognizing that the High Listener was only stirring because she had burst forth so confidently, her sureness faded.

"Master Dusk..." Elise cleared her throat nervously, listening to him sit up on the bed. "I have taken care of the humans now for several weeks and..." With each word, she felt herself deflating. "I have a concern that I would like to raise... if it wouldn't be too much to humor me..."

He watched Elise's confidence turn on itself, then be reignited with two words. "Go on."

"The humans have some concerns... valid ones which I believe we can satisfy at no risk to the Coven."

"Go on..."

"Some of the more..." Elise tried to think of an appropriate word to use, but came up short. "Some humans..." Her delivery became less rigid. "Some humans would ask that they also be allowed to use the bathing facilities."

"Some humans?"

"Those I trust. Those I know that will neither flee nor cause commotion."

Dusk thought for a minute. It was a minute that made Elise's knees feel weak. Just as she was about to recant her idea, Dusk spoke. "What would you say to this request, if you were I?"

"Master Dusk, I would never presume to..."

"Elise."

"I..." She stared at the floor shamefully. "I wouldn't entertain it, Master." She nodded to herself slowly, as though accepting her own defeat, fighting back a rare tear.

"At least she's realistic," Claire added.

"...When I was a servant... my Master thought so much of my sister, that she entrusted her to run errands for her; and my sister thought so much of myself and another that she too asked that we be extended the same courtesy." Elise listened intently. He was so often a man of few words, but in his moments of clarity, he made up for it. "That freedom made me never want to leave."

"Brother..."

"Master Dusk... why did you leave?"

Claire was silent. For the first time in a long time, she decided not to intervene.

"Seven years ago, my Master... Lady Antoinette..." It had been so long since he'd referred to her like that. "...The love of my life, pregnant with my son, wed to a man of status who she despised, issued an Executive Command that I leave... to protect me from his hand... because she knew he would kill me without hesitation... because she knew I lacked the conviction to fight back."

"...You Turned her?"

"She could have died if I hadn't." Dusk blinked away the excess moisture from his eyes, recalling the vampire that had attacked the both of them that night, some seven years ago.

"We're going to save her, brother... don't forget..."

Elise walked around to Dusk's side of the bed, sitting beside him and placing her hand on top of his. "I'm so sorry, Master Dusk." She jostled slightly when he leaned his head against her shoulder, keeping quiet until the moment passed, unsure of how to reignite the conversation.

"It never bothered me..." Dusk said, standing up and dusting himself off, "... being a servant never bothered me until the moment I realized that it meant she couldn't be with me. Even then I tried to shake it off..."

"Being a servant..." Claire thought, *"...it seems like so long ago."*

Elise remained quiet, unsure of what she could say. "Maste..."

"Get me a list of the humans you trust. I will vet them, and, if I agree, you may accompany them, one at a time, to the bathing facilities. *You* have my confidence... but even those you confide in do not."

That was it? Elise thought. *Why were his conditions always so... just?*

57

ILOVO COULDN'T RECALL A TIME WHEN THE EVAN BLOOD COVEN had been as busy as it was in the weeks leading up to the attack on Red Crescent. His trips around the grounds had never been so lively, and it seemed that everyone, himself included, found themselves hurried by the tasks that they had been assigned.

Daina, the esteemed spear user and single greatest technical fighter of the Evan Blood Coven, found herself recruiting her trusted allies, seeking any new talent that may have been overlooked since the last raid, and training those who would join her ranks. Ilovo knew, despite never partici-pating himself, that Daina always led the so-called *Swift Offensive:* the first strike on every Coven, dangerous and risky, but meant to quickly thin the ranks. She was agile, she was sharp, and to all but those who knew her, she was ruthless.

"Ilovo!" Daina's voice boomed from the training hall, stopping him in his tracks. She was the only vampire who regularly trained hard enough to sweat, and today her muscles bulged as she looked past the mess of hair that fell over her face. "You'll join me for our usual drink once we've bested this one?" Ilovo nodded excitedly. "First though... we'll need some more weapons."

Ilovo felt small and weak beside her, unable to muster the courage to stand tall. "Yes, Lady Daina."

"Three longswords, two spears, a short sword, and two daggers."

"I'll fetch them."

Daina ran the back of her hand over her forehead. She was stunning, Ilovo admitted to himself, but he was too terrified to say anything. She clapped her hands in his face. "What are you waiting for?"

"Yes!" Ilovo said quickly, turning to head to the armory.

As he raced across the courtyard, his eyes caught sight of Nier, Saber, and one of the former Alastair Coven members speaking. While he couldn't hear what they were talking about, it did strike him a bit strange that, despite everyone else running around, the three of them seemed to be taking their time. He didn't think anything of it in the moment and, in his distraction, turned a corner and collided with Carte Brooks.

Carte watched as he stumbled and began apologizing profusely. At her side, the High Listener, Christian Nikolai Dusk, stopped to acknowledge him for a moment, snapping closed a notebook in one hand and offering the other to Ilovo.

Carte's sublime beauty was out of place in the chaos. With her back to Dusk and Ilovo, she scanned the area, ignoring his prattle, silenced by a question: "Was there anything else?"

As Ilovo stood back up, Dusk uttered a simple *no* and offered her the leather-bound book.

Carte's eyes narrowed, her left fang slipping out of her mouth and resting on her lower lip. As she surveyed the room, she caught sight of Daina swinging her spear tactically through the small opening of the door across the way. If she had surveyed the room from the opposite side, she too would have caught sight of Nier and Saber conspiring with the Alastair man; instead, the trio dispersed, and she saw only the men moving about in the same vicinity. "I'll fill in Bruce." Carte took a sideways step, receiving the notebook from Dusk, and heading towards the courtyard, leaving the two men behind.

"I do apologize, Master Dusk," Ilovo said quietly. "It was not my intenti..."

"It wasn't me you struck," Dusk said with a hollow smile. "Why were you in such a rush?"

"Lady Daina requested armaments; I'm on my way to fetch them."

"I'll join you."

The pair walked in silence. Ilovo stayed a half-step behind Dusk as he guided the pair to the secluded area that climbed into the rarely used storage room of the Coven. The staircase and storage room, similar to Carte and Bruce's quarters, were completely separated from the rest of the Coven, despite also being on the third story.

Ilovo fidgeted with his key ring as he cast open the door to the armory, revealing hundreds of weapons with various levels of rust. "Three longswords, two spears, a short sword, and two daggers." Ilovo repeated the request out loud more for himself than for Dusk, making his way over to the swords as Dusk followed him into the room.

The armory was poorly maintained. The weapons had been gathered after each Coven had been raided, but with so many raids and so many conquests, many had only been transferred, but never cleaned or used.

Dusk picked up the nearest short sword and an equally unremarkable dagger. "Master Dusk, have you a need for weapons too?"

"Perhaps just a small knife," he said cautiously, setting down the weapons and picking up a small knife.

"I'll catalogue it later..." Ilovo said, placing the weapons that Daina had asked for in a central location. "It's a shame, isn't it, Master Dusk? That these tools sit here unused."

Dusk picked up a shining longsword, looking at its warped blade. "The alternative isn't much better, is it?"

He paused for a moment as Dusk pocketed the small knife. "...Perhaps you are right."

"Still..." Dusk added, bending the blade back to reduce some of its warp. "It shouldn't be an excuse to keep them in these conditions. It reminds me of my father's workshop..."

"Your father, Master Dusk? Was he a blacksmith?"

"No..." Dusk said, setting down the sword neatly, "a tinsmith. He could shape any piece of metal well enough, but the details... they always bogged him down. The sheen would be uneven or the thickness irregular... if function was what you were after, my father could provide it. But if it was perfection that you sought... you were better off finding someone else."

Ilovo wrapped a piece of twine around the requested weapons, holding them tightly against his chest as he exited the room, making sure to lock the door behind him before descending the stairs with Dusk. The steel of the weapons clanged against each other and, when they reached the bottom, Dusk went one way and Ilovo continued on. He returned to Daina, who he found in the same training room, surrounded by the groans of vampires who lay on the floor, thoroughly trounced.

She took the weapons and threw them into the middle of the training ground, turning her back to Ilovo, "Will you join the raid this time?"

"Oh no My Lady..." Ilovo said quietly. "I could never keep up."

Daina smirked, punching Ilovo's shoulder playfully, unaware of a sharp cracking sound. "Neither can they!"

Ilovo smiled weakly as he turned around, clutching at the spot that she had stricken. He descended the nearby stairs to the slave's cells. He descended more quickly than usual, though not so fast that he was running. He quickly caught up with Elise who had just finished closing Port's cell.

"Smell that?" Port asked, taking in a deep inhale. "It's not me for once." His body thumped on the heap of straw that made up his bed as other humans chuckled to themselves. Elise offered a small giggle as Ilovo arrived, the basement quieting as he did.

"Master Ilovo," Elise said with a bow. "I've just returned from accompanying Port to the bath..."

Ilovo walked past Elise briskly. "Yes, yes..." he said, opening the door to one of the slaves across from Port, closer to the staircase. "Just popping in for a quick snack..." Ilovo made his way into the cell to a red-headed slave, who held out her hand. "I'll be quick, Freya." He made a quick slice on her upper arm, flaring his fangs and closing his lips around the wound. A moment later, he let out an unbridled moan of pleasure as he drank.

"Master Ilovo?" the slave named Freya whispered in the tense quiet, interrupted only by his breathing.

"Ah..." Ilovo said happily, pulling away, flexing his hand and rolling his shoulder.

"Is everything alright?" she asked nervously, not knowing Ilovo to be so abrupt.

"I..." Ilovo cleared his throat. "My shoulder was broken..." he admitted, not disclosing the cause was Daina's *playful* punch. "It's healed now."

Everyone let out a sigh of relief and Ilovo suddenly became aware of the silence.

"You shouldn't worry us, Master Ilovo..." Freya said softly as he closed the door to her cell.

58

"DO THE NERVES EVER GET TO YOU, MASTER DUSK?" ELISE walked alongside him in the early evening hours. "...Now that the raid is almost upon us?" She stood tall and proud next to the High Listener, occasionally, inadvertently taking the lead.

"Before I Turned... before I knew of the Red World... I feared death. It paralyzed me." He touched his neck, remembering the feeling of Ivar's knife at his throat in the Schofield Manor.

"You no longer fear it?"

"Not for the reason you might think. I still have work to do."

"Rescuing Lady Antoinette? Rebuilding your family?" she asked nervously, not wanting to know where she would fit in in the aftermath of his success.

"Yes." He opened the door to his room, stepping through and waiting for Elise to join him as he made his way to the small table.

She took a seat at the edge of the bed, facing him. "Speaking with you... sometimes it feels like it isn't a life you're living for yourself... almost like it's a chore." She paused, pursing her lips for a moment. "You don't laugh... you don't spoil yourself... you don't indulge..."

"He's always been like that."

"It's strange, Master..." Elise padded, often worrying about the casual way that she sometimes let herself behave. "It's those things you deprive yourself of, that I believe garner your respect, not just as a Master, but as a person. I wonder if Lady Antoinette admired that about you too."

"That's not quite right... he was less guarded before he came here. He had that luxury, at least."

"I don't know what she saw in me. Before Claire died, we weren't particularly close, but Claire was important to both of us. We needed each other in those fragile times, and from that need something else grew."

"Strange to hear you admit that."

"Is she in the Red World too, Claire?"

"She is."

"Do you ever Listen to her?"

"Don't..." A pause. *"Say what you want."*

"Sometimes I talk to her."

She smiled cheerfully. "What a wonder it would be if she could talk back... From what you've told me, she strikes me as the kind of older sister that would take care of you, even from the Red World."

"Maybe this Elise isn't so bad... but she's no Ant."

"I had a sister too... a twin..." Elise added, "but she died a long time ago. We were both babies. My mother told me about her before she sold me off, but I don't remember her at all... there was a fire... I lost my eyes... she lost her life. Her name was..." Elise's thoughts were interrupted by a pounding on the door. "Master Ilovo?" Elise whispered before the man announced himself.

"She's right."

Dusk walked across the room to open the door. Ilovo stood outside, gave Dusk a quick nod, then headed down the hall, to another door which Saber opened.

"It seems that it's time to iron out the details for the strike on Red Crescent." He pulled the door closed behind him, making his way down to the first floor.

"Once we have a timeline, I'll work out the plan for Antoinette. The house will

be finished by month's end. We still need an ally. Ilovo has proven himself..."

"Dusk!" Bruce's voice thundered from the repaired War Room. He sat at the head of the table, like he usually did, and his voice enveloped the room. The five Elders were already seated on one side and Dusk took his spot on the other with Daina, Carte, and Nier. A minute behind, Saber arrived last and waved his hand to Ilovo, instructing him to close the door. "It's time." As Ilovo stood guard inside, the individuals discussed the final plan of attack.

With Dusk's reconnaissance delivered to Carte, Bruce relayed the information, with Carte occasionally filling in the necessary details that his excitement made him omit.

"Daina's Swift Offensive will consist of..."

"Myself and nine others," Diana responded. Carte's otherwise imposing figure appeared scrawny by comparison as Daina flexed her muscles.

"Only nine this time?"

"Be grateful it's not less."

"Very well," Bruce grunted. "The Elders felt it unwise to leave the Coven unattended considering the distant journey... Saber and Nier have volunteered to stay back."

The cousins nodded. "We'll hold down the fort."

"They're planning something with Jason Castille... I don't know what yet... but I'll find out ahead of the journey."

59

"Take a seat..." Antoinette offered a chair to a pregnant Aubrey who took it gratefully. "You're progressing quickly..." Aubrey nodded as she sat down in Antoinette's room, watching as she closed the door, quieting the sounds of the boy who ran around in the halls. "Did you learn anything about the wax seal?" Antoinette asked eagerly, her hair trimmed much shorter than it had ever been so that the haircut-gone-awry would not show as prominently.

"Yes..." Aubrey said uncertainly, "...I asked Vincent..."

"Globaria?" She nodded. "I thought him gone?"

"He returned under interesting circumstances..."

"Ah." She nodded. "And?"

"He said..." Aubrey pulled out a slip of paper and handed it to Antoinette, who took it quickly and began unfolding it. "The wax crest is old... and it belongs to..."

"...The Evan Blood Coven?" Antoinette opened the paper, the seal from Dusk's letter suspended against the parchment for a moment, then falling onto the floor.

"There's no address... just a general reference to where it is..." Aubrey gulped nervously. "Will you... go?"

"I can't wait any longer."

"...will you take Dram...?"

"I..." She folded the letter nervously. "...I can send for him, for you both... once I find Christian..."

"Are you awake brother?"

Christian Nikolai Dusk opened his eyes lazily. The sapphire brilliance was gone; in its place an unpolished azure. Elise was always first to wake, but today was a different story. There was a heatwave that had been steadily approaching. A half-naked Elise had her arms atop the High Listener, sprawled out atop the covers, clutching to the cool he emanated as he slept. He gently took her arm, holding it up so that he could slip out of bed.

"The house is complete. The furniture will be installed by the time the raid ends... but we still don't have an exit strategy... and we still have to discuss what to do with Elise."

Dusk stepped into the adjoining bathroom, closing the door behind him quietly. "She'll have a choice."

"...There's also a plot afoot. Jason Castille is mounting an offensive. He's been communicating with Red Crescent regularly. They'll be expecting you. Stay cautious. I'll be by your side."

"Who do I have to worry about?"

"Nier and Saber may be compromised... though it's hard to be sure to what extent. The Elders want Bruce gone. His search for necromancer blood has them acting very strange."

"Do we know why?"

"Whatever the case, we can fool him... if need be."

"And Antoinette?"

"I checked on her a few days ago, no change."

"If only you could be everywhere at once," Dusk said cautiously.

"Luckily I travel much faster than you." She paused. *"...Tell Elise to stay alert. If Bruce returns, there will likely be an ambush. Will you warn him?"*

"No. I am to help him find the key to resurrection, the necromancer blood, not to protect him or the Coven. We all have our roles."

"Nier and Saber trust you... whatever the outcome, you have a place in either future. We're almost there, brother..."

"I know..." he whispered with a wishful smile. "I know."

When he opened the door, Elise stirred. "Master Dusk?" She reached around the side of the bed, but didn't find him.

"I'll be going soon." He took a seat beside her as she sat up.

"Did you want to drink before you go?" Elise craned her neck sideways, feeling the cold steel of a small blade slice her at her collarbone, then the familiar feel of Dusk's lips as he latched onto her. She used one arm to prop herself up and slowly reached the other around his back. The heat was something else, but it wasn't the only reason she felt so hot. "I've been thinking..." Elise began as he drank, "as a form of repayment for your hospitality..."

"They're gathering brother. Make haste."

Dusk pulled back quickly. "Before I go..." he interrupted, taking her hand and placing the small knife he had taken from the armory in it. "Take this... and keep it close while I'm away..."

"You... can't tell me why, can you?" she asked slowly.

"Months ago... in the dungeon you warned me that something felt off..." He stood up, throwing on his shirt. "It's the same for me."

"Be safe, Master Dusk..." she said as he left. "...And return to us safely..." she whispered when he was gone.

60

A HUNDRED VAMPIRES DEPARTED THE EVAN BLOOD COVEN IN THE early hours of the summer night. After half a day's ride, the eleven carriages split into three groups. Daina's, who would launch the initial offensive, took the most direct route. Carte and Bruce, who would launch the second strike took a less direct path. The High Listener, accompanied by the other sweepers, took the longest and most roundabout.

Three cautious and direct nights after traveling, Daina's single carriage landed at the designated location, on the outskirts of a castle nearly the same size as Evan Blood. Her gold-wire wrapped spear glistened in the moonlight. She could hardly wait to strike as her team performed its final reconnaissance.

The following night, Bruce and Carte arrived, confirming the information that Dusk had gathered, obtaining the new information that Daina's team had learned, and wasting no further time.

No sooner had the horses been tied up than Daina began her assault. Opting to go the direct route, rather than attempt to break through the wine cellar maze that ran underneath the structure, Daina and four others assaulted the front entrance, while the rest of her team went in through windows and back doors. With all the commotion that Daina made up front, few suspected the pincer attack until it was too late.

As Daina's golden-tipped spear and razor-sharp fangs thinned out the herd, she made her way up to the roof of the Red Crescent Coven. A handful of dried grass was all she needed in the summer heat, and as she wrapped the kindling she'd collected the night before with a small piece of twine, she set it on the apex of the roof, rotated her spear around, and struck with the back.

Sparks shot out from the flint concealed at the end of the handle, but the grass did not ignite. She went to strike a second time, but the commotion in the Red Crescent Coven had escalated, and the greatest spearman in Evan Blood found herself alone and surrounded as the dried grass slipped down the roof and onto the stone-covered ground below.

She'd trained for this kind of challenge.

Under a sliver of moonlight, Daina battled six members of Red Crescent for control over the apex of the roof. One by one she defeated them—the unarmed nobodies that challenged the great warrior, but no sooner had six fallen, than another six risen. With no fire atop the castle, the reinforcements from Evan Blood continued waiting for her signal. Another three fell before the first managed a decisive blow against her.

She'd lived for this kind of challenge.

Daina felt a sword carve into her shoulder; a sword turned into a cleaver as it sliced her arm clean off. Without a chance to mourn for her lost limb, she caught the falling spear with her other hand and drove its blade into the jaw of the one who'd cut her so foul, delighting with a bloodied expression of joy as she did. In her moment of ecstasy, the strength of the multitude was obvious. They attacked in an unavoidable manner, skewering her and kicking her down the slope.

She'd die for this kind of challenge.

Daina straddled the Red World as her body slid down the roof. Her remaining hand clutched the spear with what might endured as her ragdoll body painted the slate tiles. She gripped the spear tightly, rotating it as she fell, the flint-end taking the two-story impact first. Sparks exploded a moment before her body collided with the ground below, finally catching the kindling.

When Carte and Bruce saw the smoke rising from the low ground, they knew there was a problem, and before they had a chance to make a move on Red Crescent, they heard the sounds of vampires surrounding them from where they watched. Were it not for the faint smoke in the distance, the Evan Blood Coven would have been sitting ducks.

They had a chance.

Atop the Coven, the Head of the Red Crescent dropped to his knees. The spear tip that had pierced his jaw and severed his tongue had been removed, but the blood wouldn't stop. His surviving allies offered their blood to no avail. He was too far gone to do anything other than preserve his life for a moment.

In that moment, the Coven was in chaos.

Within the walls, the members of Red Crescent managed to defeat Daina's remaining allies at a heavy loss. Outside, a weak defensive position was being taken by those who still had their wits about them. Further off, the majority of the Coven attempted to catch Bruce and Carte's team off guard, and quickly learned why Bruce Alazar had been so feared. He decimated those in his way and approached mightily.

A bloodied Bruce, now absent a single eye, wielded an oversized ax and cut through the remaining forces. With Carte at his side, he secured the rest of the Coven, coming to the initial site of the smoke and seeing Daina's body shattered by a stone she'd fallen atop. Upon seeing this, Bruce felt a rage well up inside him and changed his conquest strategy for the first time in a dozen raids: this time there would be no survivors.

Bruce would deliver an executioner's blow on any member who remained. "They're not worthy enough to submit to Evan Blood," he told Carte as he took a seat on a piano bench in the ballroom, slamming the ax into the ground and surveying the carnage of some fifty bodies and dozens of pieces of broken furniture.

"What about the Elders?" a bloodied Carte whispered in his ear, seeing three old men in recognizable robes huddle against a wall nervously.

"They knew we were coming. Find out who betrayed us. Then kill them. For Daina."

"For Daina."

THE FOLLOWING NIGHT DUSK ARRIVED TO THE SLAUGHTER. THE RED World had never been so loud. It screamed and cried as he approached to find Bruce with a bandaged eye holding a goblet of blood in one hand, with Carte beside him holding one all her own. Several members of the Evan Blood Coven quieted as the sweepers arrived.

Daina's golden-tipped spear, handle still drenched in blood, leaned against the piano and glistened in the candlelight. A sinister scowl was upon Bruce's impending face as he narrowed his gaze. "High Listener... your work is light today. We rest only long enough to ensure any scattered roaches are put down. Tomorrow, we make haste to my Coven. There are traitors in our midst, and we will rip them out, root... and... stem."

61

ELEVEN CARRIAGES HAD DEPARTED THE EVAN BLOOD COVEN LESS than a week ago, now only seven returned. Though the sun blazed atop their heads, the hooded drivers steered the covered wagons onwards while the vampires inside hid from the light. In the leading carriage, Carte and Bruce rode, faster than the others, eager to see what hell awaited them on their triumphant return.

"*I can stay back to investigate,*" Dusk had offered his opinion at the Red Crescent Coven, but Bruce had refused. There was too much betrayal in the air already, but just like he had on the way to the raid, he rode with the sweepers in the last carriage, filled with the spoils of the conquest, the scent of blood rich on the treasures.

A mere hour separated Bruce's carriage from the sweepers. Too many vampires surrounding Dusk made it so that he could not communicate freely with Claire.

"*Jason's put the plan in motion. Bruce and Carte will be ambushed as soon as they arrive. Nier and Saber have allied with him. The Elders are lending their support them... but the Coven is rebelling. There's no telling what will happen. Be careful, brother."*

Before Ilovo had a chance to stop the leading carriage, Bruce had already exited, mighty ax in hand, throwing the front doors off their hinges as he powered down the would-be Hall of Houses until he came to his own Great Ballroom. With Carte at his side, he looked forward at Nier and Saber, each with a sword in hand.

His gaze surveyed the room around him as the vampires took a side. Before anyone could offer an explanation, Bruce was already attacking, his powerful ax swinging with abandon, ignoring the skirmishes breaking out around him. With Carte at his back, defending him from any rogue attacks, Bruce charged forward, challenging the cousins with his mighty blows.

From the sidelines, Jason looked for an opening, doing his best to stay out of the conflicts that were surging, sinking into the walls like the Elders attempted to do, aptly aware that his involvement was second to the cousins' betrayal.

"They're breaking Carte and Bruce apart now... Bruce is challenging Nier and Saber, but they've realized he has a blind spot. He's being struck. Carte is being pushed back."

Dusk closed his eyes as his carriage rolled forward, trying to ignore the other voices.

"The second carriage arrived... they're supporting Bruce, but Jason is commanding others to be on the lookout. The main hall is a trap now. Anyone else who comes through will be stopped immediately... the third carriage didn't stand a chance."

"Driver..." Dusk called out. "Go around the back of the Coven."

"The fourth carriage is lost too... Bruce is weathered... Carte too... they appear..."

Suddenly, Claire grew quiet. So suddenly did she grow quiet, that even Dusk grew nervous.

"Claire?" he whispered, ignoring the glances of the vampires in his carriage.

"Some fled to the basement early to get away from the fighting, but they were killed. A human escaped his cell. He's made his way up to your room... he's threatening Elise."

"Driver!" Dusk called out again. "Faster!"

"Elise is trying to reason with him... the fifth carriage broke through... Bruce's leg has been sliced... he's losing blood... oh no!" Claire was coming through choppier now, a fresh batch of dead voices muffling her words. *"She's been stabbed. Elise has been stabbed."*

Dusk recognized the dip in the road that the carriage went over and opened the door, staring into the night. He had never run so fast. He ran around the side of the Coven, leaping to the second-floor window of his room, not quite making the jump, using his arms to pull himself through, disregarding the glass he impaled himself with as he did so. The cuts on his arms and hands began healing after he pulled himself inside to find Elise in her white nightgown, clutching at the red pool on her chest.

In the light of the moon, Dusk could see a crystal stem from a goblet sticking out of Elise's chest as a man scurried out. "Elise." He tried to catch her as she fell onto the floor, breathing slowly, clutching at the spot where she'd been stabbed, just below the High Listener's patch that he had made her wear.

"She's dying brother."

"M..." Elise couldn't manage a single word. Her free hand dropped the knife Dusk had given her, stained in red, but not with her own blood. His rage was stronger than the bloodlust, but any other vampire would have gone wild at the sight of so much fresh blood.

"...You can save her... maybe. If you bite her... maybe you can save her."

Elise let out a gasp, feeling the High Listener's fangs puncture her shoulder. Her lip showed the faintest of smiles as tears streamed down her cheeks. *She'd never experienced it, but she knew his bite all the same. Just like him, it was gentle.*

"Your blood brother. There's no time get any other."

The darkness of the room was clearing up as the High Listener put his bleeding hand against her mouth, forcing her to drink. Her hazy gray eyes were adjusting, beginning to see the High Listener who trembled as he held her.

"More blood brother! She needs more!"

Dusk re-opened the wound on his hand. *Who said that?* Elise wondered as her eyes unclouded. For the first time since she had been a child, she could see something. She wanted to embrace him, the figure who cried over her, but she could barely move.

"Breathe brother... your wounds were just as severe when Ant saved you. We stabilize her now... we get her human blood later."

"C...Claire?" As he spilled his blood into her, the Red World opened up to Elise, flooding her ears.

"You can hear me?" Elise's breaths were slow and shallow. Her eyes were restoring, but the pain in her chest was not subsiding. She was losing blood faster than she could heal.

"Master... Dusk..." Elise mustered what strength she could to touch his cheek. *Why was he so quiet? Why was he always so quiet?*

His blue eyes were buried behind a wall of tears, and she couldn't see them. All the humans had talked about them. He had the brightest eyes of any other vampire in the Coven, but she couldn't see them because he wept. She didn't imagine them like this. She didn't imagine him like this.

"I won't lose you. I can't lose you too," he whispered as quiet as a prayer, remembering how hot his sister had felt in his arms.

"We're trying to save you Elise... relax... we're going to save you."

You can't. Elise knew pain. She knew suffering. Even as a vampire, even in this brief moment, she knew the reason that Dusk's eyes were so painted. She could have bathed in an ocean of blood and it would have been for naught. There were some wounds that even vampires couldn't heal from.

Elise's gray eyes, now with a tinge of green looked to the man who wept for her. She took in a deep inhale, using what remaining strength she had to speak. "Don't let the sadness consume you..." Her eyes flashed red, as did his. "I want to see you smile when you find what brings you joy..." A single hand wrapped around his head, pulling him down into a kiss.

It was warm. How did she know it would be warm?

"...That's my Executive Command to you, High Listener." She whispered from the Red World, watching from beside Claire as Dusk pulled away from the kiss, trembling as he held her body close to his.

The taste of her lips was on his for the first time.

The taste of her lips was on his for the last time.

"Sister..." He held her close, so close that Elise could feel his passion on the other side of the Divide, as close as he had held Claire when she'd died in his arms, trying to filter out the voices that plagued him. "Tell me who did this."

62

A MOMENT OF CHAOS ON BOTH SIDES OF THE RED WORLD SAW THE High Listener at last resonate with his feelings. An ear pressed against the Red World told him of Elise's killer's position in the Coven, and an ear pressed against the other distinguished a crack just slight enough to buckle.

His body wasn't built like Bruce's—he wasn't raw strength.

His body wasn't as honed as Daina's—he wasn't refined muscle.

But he was a vampire all the same, and his title as High Listener was not just for show.

When Dusk's foot slammed down on the second-floor hallway outside of his room, the ground collapsed, spilling down with an impact so strong that it also caved in the floor below, sending Dusk straight down to the hallway in the basement, just outside the slave's cells.

He wasn't alone.

Just below the second-floor hallway, the murderer had tried to flee; and when his ceiling collapsed atop him, he tried to evade; but when the floor beneath him collapsed too, he had nowhere to go. He fell a distance of twenty-nine steps that Elise had walked up and down countless times, in service not only to the humans as a whole, but to him as well: Vega. The humans retreated against their cell walls when they saw their roof cave in.

The High Listener stood atop a pile of rubble, paying no regard to the bone that splintered out of his leg. The man who had fallen through the floor, Elise's killer, Vega, was a half-covered bloody pulp that clung to life.

The humans were quiet as Dusk took the few steps necessary to stand over him. Vega's lips moved, but no sound came out. His left leg was pinned under a stone. His right arm was broken in two. His face was a fractured menagerie of skin and blood and bone, and even still Dusk reached down and took him by the throat, paying no mind to the leg that ripped off as he separated man from member.

"All she wanted..." Dusk said, holding up the dying man. "...was purpose." His breaths were slower than Vega's as he fought back his own tears. "You took that from her. You escaped these cells... and you could have fled into the night... but you chose to climb those stairs... you chose to seek her out... and you chose to kill Elise *before* fleeing."

"I'm s..."

Another human, Port, who had been looking away, clutched at the bars with white knuckles. Freya, in the cell across from him, cried. Hecate, in the cell beside Freya's, reached her arms through to comfort her, anger written across her face as other humans reached for pieces of rubble and hurled them at the dangling Vega.

"She wanted purpose—you stole that from her. You wanted revenge—you took that on her." His grip tightened around his throat as he looked up through the hole, past the first floor, ignoring the chaotic fighting of the power struggle that went on around him. "You don't deserve to join her in the Red World, but since I can't prevent that... I'll take you there myself."

Freya looked away in her cell as Dusk squeezed Vega's neck and dropped his body onto the heap of rocks. The pain in Dusk's leg was like nothing he had ever felt. He stumbled to descend over the pile of rubble, falling against Hecate's cell.

The humans were silent.

The Red World was silent.

How long had he waited for such glorious silence?

"Master Dusk..." Hecate took a rock and sliced her arm, fighting back her own tears. She slid her arm through the bars, reaching it across him. "...You can take my blood to heal. That filth isn't suited to be your meal."

He nodded, his tears spilling onto Hecate's arm as he drank her blood, his back sliding against the cell as his broken leg slowly healed.

"Brother... Bruce is dead... Nier and Saber too... and... Carte fled."

Minutes later, unfamiliar footsteps made their way down twenty-nine worn steps. The pointed face of a once-defiant man now ebbed with confidence. "I had wondered..." Jason Castille emerged as Dusk pulled himself to his feet, a sliver of bone inching its way back into his leg, "...where *you* had gotten off to. I thought that surely you would have heard their screams and ran away... but perhaps I overestimated your abilities, because here you are... the last member of Bruce Alazar's inner circle, the fabled High Listener, Christian Nikolai Dusk."

63

BRUCE ALAZAR FORBADE THE USE OF THE SILVER CELL IN THE basement because he did not believe in keeping vampires as prisoners of war. *"Bend the knee or die."* The former Head of the Evan Blood Coven was not one to mince words, but the new Head had a decision to make with regards to the singular member of the old regime who hadn't raised a finger to him.

Forty-eight silver-dipped bars enclosed the High Listener in a prison all his own, constructed down the way from Elise's former cell, leaving Dusk to wait until a judgment would be passed on him. The silver spikes pointed inwards, confining his space, rendering him barely able to move without cutting himself on their jagged edges.

"You made this bed... you die..." Katja's voice whispered from the Red World.

The humans tried to keep his spirits up, and if their voices weren't so drowned out by the Red World or so defeated themselves, perhaps they could have. Instead, they merely kept him company in his misery, mourning their own loss as he mourned his.

A day went by. The rubble was cleared out and the humans were hungry. No Elise came to feed them, and Ilovo was stretched too thin to assist.

Another day passed. Wooden planks covered the hole on the first floor, darkening the basement cells. Ilovo came by with a singular meal for the humans, but nothing for Dusk. His leg had healed, but Jason wanted him weak for when he was to face his judgment.

A week went by. The humans were fed twice daily now, but their condition had relapsed. They fed on the scraps that reminded them of a time before Elise had taken over. A new batch of slaves were thrown in with the rest. Some killed themselves and others lunged out at the vampires, submitting themselves to death at their own hands. "Recruiting good slaves," Port remarked ironically, "wasn't as easy as it seemed."

"How we felt... you betrayed us..." Katja's voice kept him company.

A month went by. The lack of blood had a strange effect on Dusk—it quieted the Red World a little—he could sleep through the night better. The Elders would occasionally come by to check on the humans or to look at him. They weren't on his side, but they didn't want him dead. Considering the circumstances, it was the best he could hope for.

"It's time." Claire's voice came down like a verdict and it was Armand, accompanied by two other vampires he didn't recognize, who came, keys in hand, to bring Dusk to the first floor where the inaugural gathering under Jason Castille's leadership would occur. He was taken up the stairs by the two vampires, past an assembly of others who stood near or around the courtyard. There, before his former members, he was shackled to a ring of metal that had been staked in the ground.

Armand took his place in the Great Ballroom beside the other four Elders, who stood behind three men, at the center of which was Jason Castille.

"Bruce Alazar is dead. Carte Brooks has fled. In their stead, I, Jason Castille, heir to the Alastair Coven, have assumed control over Evan Blood." The remaining vampires nodded, some in glorious assent, others with an angry reluctance. A month after everything had transpired, it felt like the monologue was more for Dusk than for anyone else who had witnessed the changes unfold firsthand.

"Many of our brothers and sisters were lost... but we will rebuild. A Coven of law and order will emerge from the ashes. Those of you who are here, mark my words, we will see a Coven that will reach new heights... and you will reap new rewards!"

The Elders clapped enthusiastically, as did those vampires loyal to Jason. The rest, those who had been forced to accept his rule, clapped listlessly.

Dusk was silent in the middle of the room, on his knees before Jason Castille, with a front-row seat to the charade. He knew that Jason would call him out too.

The vampires around the room were already wondering why it was he, and he alone, who knelt in the center of the room. There was only one reason he wasn't dead yet: Jason wanted to make a spectacle of him too.

As Jason rambled on, he declared the advent of a new doctrine, the *Castille Addendum to the Evan Blood Charter*, a mechanism to extend the reign of the Coven outside the walls, by allowing the creation of *Houses* for long-standing members. He wasn't as ruthless as Bruce, but just like him, he wanted his power to be vast and measured.

Dusk already knew the details of the new Addendum. Claire had told him about it while he had waited for his sentencing in the Silver Cell. His eyes scanned around the room lazily.

"Be discreet, brother."

Antoinette Katherine Schofield stood in the Evan Blood Coven, surrounded by other vampires, her eyes filled with concern and love. Nervously she fixated on him, wanting so desperately to go to him, wanting so desperately to save him. Dusk needed no second glance to recognize the stark green eyes of the woman he loved, finally close enough to touch, but still out of reach.

64

ONE WEEK AGO

"**M**aster Dusk..." Ilovo had come to him in his Silver Cell before the sentencing. "Lady Antoinette has arrived..."

Antoinette's tired eyes finally settled on the Coven in the distance. She clutched at her chest nervously. She was filthy, covered in grime and in need of a bath; her clothes were dirtier than they had ever been, and her hair was a mess, but looking towards the Evan Blood Coven, she was filled with a strange sense of hope and possibility.

A covered wagon on the main road slowly rolled forward. Its non-descript features were no cause for concern as she continued walking down the road. The driver looked back at her for a moment as he passed, then stopped just ahead of her.

"Lady Antoinette?" Ilovo had asked with surprise. "Why are you here?"

The High Listener sat caged in his cell as he had for three weeks, several dozen silver spikes pointed at him like spears. He couldn't escape if he wanted to. *Why, when he had all the access to the Red World, did these surprises keep him on edge!* "How?" A simple question from the caged Listener rang hoarse, raked over a parched mouth. "How did she find me, Ilovo?"

Antoinette held up the wax seal from the letter that Ilovo had delivered. "He said he would come for me... but I couldn't wait any longer."

Ilovo dismounted the wagon and opened the door to let her in. "Something's happened." He moved aside some paintings in the carriage to make room for her to sit. "Stay quiet... I'll fill you in."

She had made her way to the Evan Blood Coven after he didn't come for her. With no idea about the turmoil that the Coven was in, she had shown up, and by luck had been greeted by Ilovo, who recognized her. He had filled her in on the relevant details about the Coven, and about Dusk's recent incarceration.

"Master Dusk... what would you have me do?" Ilovo stood nervously before him in the Silver Cell.

"Jason is casting a wide net to find more vampires... say that she was sought out as part of the new initiative. He can't know she's related to me."

Ilovo nodded. "Shall I bring her?"

"No," Dusk and Claire said in unison.

"Not yet at least. Keep her away from me, away from the slaves. Keep her away until it's safe."

"Did he say anything about me?" Antoinette had asked Ilovo as she was shuffled into a bedroom in the Coven.

"He said to keep you safe... you can't see him yet. It's too dangerous, but he did ask that I give you this." Ilovo handed Antoinette a slip of paper which she opened.

"What is it?" Antoinette asked.

"Directions to a house he built for you both... for when the time is right..."

She held the paper close to her chest and nodded happily.

TODAY

JASON CONTINUED HIS MONOLOGUE BEFORE THE COVEN, A SINGLE man on his knees, bound by chains, in the center of his spectacle, ironically forced to endure the lecture of a man keen to rule by doctrine. He covered the broad strokes of the Castille Addendum before discussing his efforts to recruit new vampires from the neighboring regions. With the assistance of those vampires who remained, as well as the information gathering network that the Elders had cultivated, they had been able to bring in solitary vampires, and would continue seeking out more to rebuild their diminished ranks.

The Elders clapped as all eyes, Dusk included, turned to look at the seven new vampires, Antoinette among them, standing nervously near the entrance to the Coven.

With his back to Jason, Dusk turned to admire her. She was just as he remembered her. He wanted so desperately to run to her, to hold her again, but he couldn't. She had commanded him to leave to save him from Michael Escoté, and he knew that inciting any emotion now would draw Jason's eye. His fate might well be sealed, but he couldn't risk any scrutiny falling to her.

"We have but one final order of business before we close the chapter that was Bruce Alazar's reign over Evan Blood—the High Listener who allied himself with the former Head—we will now decide his fate. Christian Nikolai Dusk..." Jason said pridefully, playing with a ring on his finger, "do you still serve Evan Blood?"

65

BRUCE ALAZAR'S ROBES WERE TOO LARGE FOR JASON CASTILLE TO fill. It had taken many hours for Ilovo to tailor them to his lanky figure. To Jason, the robes, like the crown of a king, represented power. Once stripped of it, now he clung to it. He needed to display it for all to see.

After Ilovo had tailored the robes, he'd been sent to the former Alastair Coven to bring back the portraits of the Alastair Heads who had come before him. One by one, Ilovo had been tasked with cleaning and hanging the portraits on one side of the great hall. Every person who walked through the main doors would be forced to walk past them, to pay homage to the origins of the new Evan Blood Coven.

Now, equipped with the heavy garments that once belonged to Bruce, Jason's gangly figure seemed fuller of itself as he waited for an answer. He didn't emanate power, but at the same time he demanded recognition: this usurper who had kept his hands relatively clean as Nier and Saber had fought against Bruce, finding an opportunity to eliminate all three of them in the chaos of the battle.

"Give me your answer."

"He plans to kill you regardless," Claire's voice coached her brother.

The High Listener's throat was dry, and his voice was raspy as he turned his back to Antoinette and faced Jason. A month without blood made him appear more weathered than he was. Jason needed to believe that he held all the cards. "The Evan Blood I served is gone." Dusk looked up to Jason, measuring his sinister gaze. "I was High Listener for Bruce Alazar, but it is not my place to assume I would have such a luxury under your rule. I humbly ask for your grace, to serve Evan Blood under your leadership, and to help rebuild the Coven under the doctrine of the Castille Addendum."

Armand smiled mysteriously as Jason's lower lip twitched at his blatantly rehearsed plea. "...Go on."

"I, Christian Nikolai Dusk, who has never raised a hand against you, and who took no part in the struggle, ask to be the first vampire granted the privilege of creating a House under your Addendum, to grow the Coven from afar, and to use my abilities as a Listener to bring wealth to *your* Coven. I submit this request to you, Jason Castille, Head of Evan Blood."

"Well said brother."

"He'll be reluctant to let you go." Elise added, *"he'll interpret this as a ploy to flee."*

"You do see how this sounds?" Jason said, stepping forward with his arms behind his back. "This sounds strangely enough like you're planning on running away." Several other vampires nodded in assent. "Perhaps to join Carte Brooks and launch a rebellion?"

"As expected."

Dusk lowered his head. "If My Lord can provide a more suitable way for me to serve the Coven and help with rebuilding under your leadership, you need only say the word. I am at your command."

"He's not good at thinking on the spot. He's a schemer..."

"Play on his ego."

"He didn't expect you to submit to him... make it clear that killing you goes against his desire to grow the Coven."

In the silence of the moment, as Jason Castille contemplated a way to kill Dusk while not appearing like a hypocrite, Elder Armand stepped forward.

"Christian Nikolai Dusk, you have indeed served the Evan Blood Coven faithfully for nearly a decade. You, who has never raised a hand against another vampire, would have the blessing of the Elders to go forth... with some additional conditions."

Jason nodded quickly. "Yes." He perked up, lips curling skyward. "You'll have to abide by more rules *in addition* to the Castille Addendum." He didn't notice the wave of relief on the face of one of the new recruits, the fear that subsided as Antoinette's bated breath finally escaped her chest.

"*This is an opportunity.*"

"*Remember: Jason must believe he holds all the cards. Give him a chance to humble you some more.*"

Armand closed his eyes. "You will take up residence in the Red Crescent Coven—far enough away to grow Evan Blood, but not so close as to jeopardize the primary rebuilding effort." Armand rubbed his chin. "You will be responsible for the care of the Manor and be subject to unscheduled visits by Evan Blood. If your whereabouts are *ever* in jeopardy during these visits, you will be considered a rogue agent and deserter." The Elder's eyes surveyed the room. "And... to ensure that nothing is amiss, Ilovo will accompany you and be required to periodically update Evan Blood."

"In person!" Jason added pointedly. "He'll deliver his reports in person."

"Yes, My Lords." Dusk nodded as Ilovo's face twisted up nervously, unsure of how he had been roped into the arrangement, his legs trembling.

"*If things go awry with Jason, the Elders may use Ilovo as a tool to communicate with you.*"

"*They're betting on both horses... you are the rightful heir, after all.*"

"*An assurance... but one Jason isn't aware of.*"

"And!" Jason added quickly. "You'll be held to a higher standard of success. It should be no problem for a member of the former Coven's Inner Circle... let's see... you will be required to maintain a House of at least seven additional *unaffiliated* vampires."

The room began to stir. Unaffiliated vampires were scarce. Practically, this meant finding humans, Turning them, and keeping them as well. Most humans who got a taste of being a vampire didn't want to be under the confines of a Coven. It was the reason that the Elders made humans serve so long before Turning them, slowly indoctrinating them into the Coven life so they would be less likely to take the gift of vampirism and flee.

"My Lord, the task you set before me is difficult. To achieve this in a decade would be difficult," Dusk attested humbly.

"He'll counter."

"Five!" Jason proclaimed proudly. "You'll have five years to prove how capable you are! If you have not done so, you will face consequences... to be determined."

"Nicely done, brother."

"Master Dusk... would you be willing to advocate for my friends, for me?" Elise's whisper rang scared in his ear. *"Please?"*

"...My Lord... to assist with this effort, I would ask to take some of the human slaves with me..."

"*My* humans?" Jason balked. "I..."

"Three..." Armand said, scratching his chin. "In recognition of your service, and an offer only extended to you, High Listener, you may buy three of our slaves for twice the going rate and take them with you. We will expect payment within a year, otherwise you will return them to us."

"Yes, My Lord." Dusk lowered himself closer to the floor. "Thank you for the honor..."

Jason inhaled deeply, booming over Dusk's quiet voice and clapping his hands together once. "An auspicious day!" He clapped a second time. "On the day the Castille Addendum is enacted, the first house, the House of Dusk is also inaugurated. We look forward to your service, *Christian*."

66

CHRISTIAN NIKOLAI DUSK STOOD AT THE THRESHOLD TO HIS room. His bed had been shifted, the mattress torn, and the drawers from his desk had been thrown. In the month he'd been in the dungeons, they had turned his room upside down looking for anything incriminating, but had found nothing. He hadn't been so reckless.

A few articles of clothing had been thrown around the room, his few personal belongings taken, and, atop the spot where Elise had bled out, one of the gowns she had once worn poorly attempted to hide the stain of her blood.

"You did what you could..." Elise whispered. *"Now do what you need to."*

From the adjacent bathroom, as Ilovo waited outside, a pair of green eyes beckoned for him, reaching for him, pulling him in. Antoinette Katherine Schofield wrapped her arms around him and rested her head against his chest, sobbing quietly, leaning over to kiss him, then holding him closer.

Seven years of emotions and seven years of love lost, pain, and suffering spilled out.

Dusk held her tightly, knowing the moment couldn't last, knowing that any longer could draw speculation.

"I'm sorry." An apology for an endless amount of suffering. "I'm sorry I told you to go... I didn't know."

"I'm sorry too." An apology for an endless amount of impotence. When at last he had an out, when at last he had an opportunity to save her, here he was, cursed to be without her again. "I can't stay."

She nodded, holding his face. "Here..." She pierced her lip and kissed him, letting him take in her blood. "We'll be together again..." She pressed her forehead against his, smiling weakly. "I love you."

"I love you." He put his arms around Antoinette, breathing in her scent, rubbing her back, memorizing her body with his hands, struggling to keep the tears away as he did.

"When the time is right... will you come back to me?" She asked with a hope that rode the edge of despair.

"Always," Dusk said sweetly.

"Master Dusk." Ilovo hissed from the hall. "Please, make haste."

"Break the command you issued..." Dusk said, more seriously. "Let me return to the Schofield Manor when the time is right..."

Antoinette looked away sadly, knowing exactly why he was asking. She nodded, her eyes flashing red as she rescinded her former command before looking away again. "But be safe Christian... I don't want to put you at risk..."

"You won't... but he needs to pay. He needs to suffer for killing our son... he needs to pay, so that we can move on."

THREE YEARS AGO

"*...BROTHER...*" CLAIRE SEFIRA DUSK'S VOICE WAS QUIET FROM THE SMALL table in her brother's room at the Evan Blood Coven. If she'd had lips, they would have been pursed, and if she'd had eyes, they would be watering. She surveyed the windowsill in his room, lined with small wooden boxes. Each box was a different size and marked with a different number.

Christian smiled broadly as he fidgeted with a rounded portion of a metal rocking horse that sat atop his table, watching it teeter back and forth. "He'll probably be too old for this when he gets it..." His bright blue eyes waited for the hand-sized toy to stop rocking before placing it into an open box. Once the toy sat carefully inside, he slipped a wooden lid atop it and carved the number *4* on the outside with his nail. "...But I think he'll like it. I know we would have."

Claire watched as he set the box neatly on the windowsill beside the other three, squaring the edges as he did. He took a seat at the table across from her voice, posture relaxed. "Is Antoinette doing anything special for his birthday?"

"...*brother... I...*" Claire tried to tune out a babbling that only she could hear, too far away for even the great High Listener to catch wind of.

"I wouldn't be surprised if he has to share the day with Aubrey's boy again... that Dram. Though I suppose you and I always shared our day, and it only brought us closer." He chuckled, and his brilliant blue eyes looked out his window. "This was a good idea you had, sister... I won't show up empty-handed when the time finally..."

"...*brother, stop.*" Her breathing was heavy, so heavy he could almost feel it from the other side of the Divide. Her eyes would have been puffy if she sat before him. "*He...*"

"Sister?"

"*I'm sorry, brother,*" she whimpered. "*I'm so sorry... he's gone.*"

"...gone?" He smiled meekly. "On an excursion you mean?"

"*No,*" her whispers cracked and the Red World was quiet, greedily watching her confession as a child babbled in a distant part. "*He's dead brother...*"

"No..." He shook his head. "No... What happened?"

"*Michael... Michael, he...*"

"No..." Dusk could feel his chest tighten as his fists clenched. "No..." He could feel his eyes water as he began to pace. "No!" He screamed, sending his fist against the cobblestone wall, shattering his hand, leaving a concave crack as the only marker as he fell to his knees in pain. "Why...?" He shook his head.

"..."

"He'll pay." Dusk looked to the four boxes on his windowsill, lower lip quivering. "He'll pay for what he did." He flared his fangs angrily. "I'll make him pay." He paused, voice hoarse as he struggled to talk. "I'll make him pay... but it won't bring him back."

"Br..." Her brother raised his eyes to the ether, a shell of the man he had been minutes ago, his broken hand dangling at his side, battling between a crippling sadness and a burning anger. *"Bruce has been searching for something with Katja... a way to bring people back from the dead... I don't know if it's even possible... but if it is, we might be able to bring him back... I'll do everything I can to help you bring him back... and to rescue Ant."* She paused. *"We'll make him pay, brother. We'll make him pay for what he's done."*

TODAY

WITH A FINAL KISS, DUSK WAS OFF, FOLLOWING BEHIND ILOVO AS THE pair was greeted by the three human slaves at the main entrance of the Evan Blood Coven, leaving Antoinette behind.

"Oh, Claire Bear..." Antoinette whispered nervously as she approached the window, unknowingly crushing a metal horse that had been tossed under one of the shirts in his room. As she pulled back the curtain, she watched them exit the Evan Blood Coven from the second floor. "...What did you tell him?"

"Only what he needed to know," she whispered back to a woman who couldn't hear her, turning to see the fist sized-hole in the wall behind his door. *"Only what I knew he could handle."*

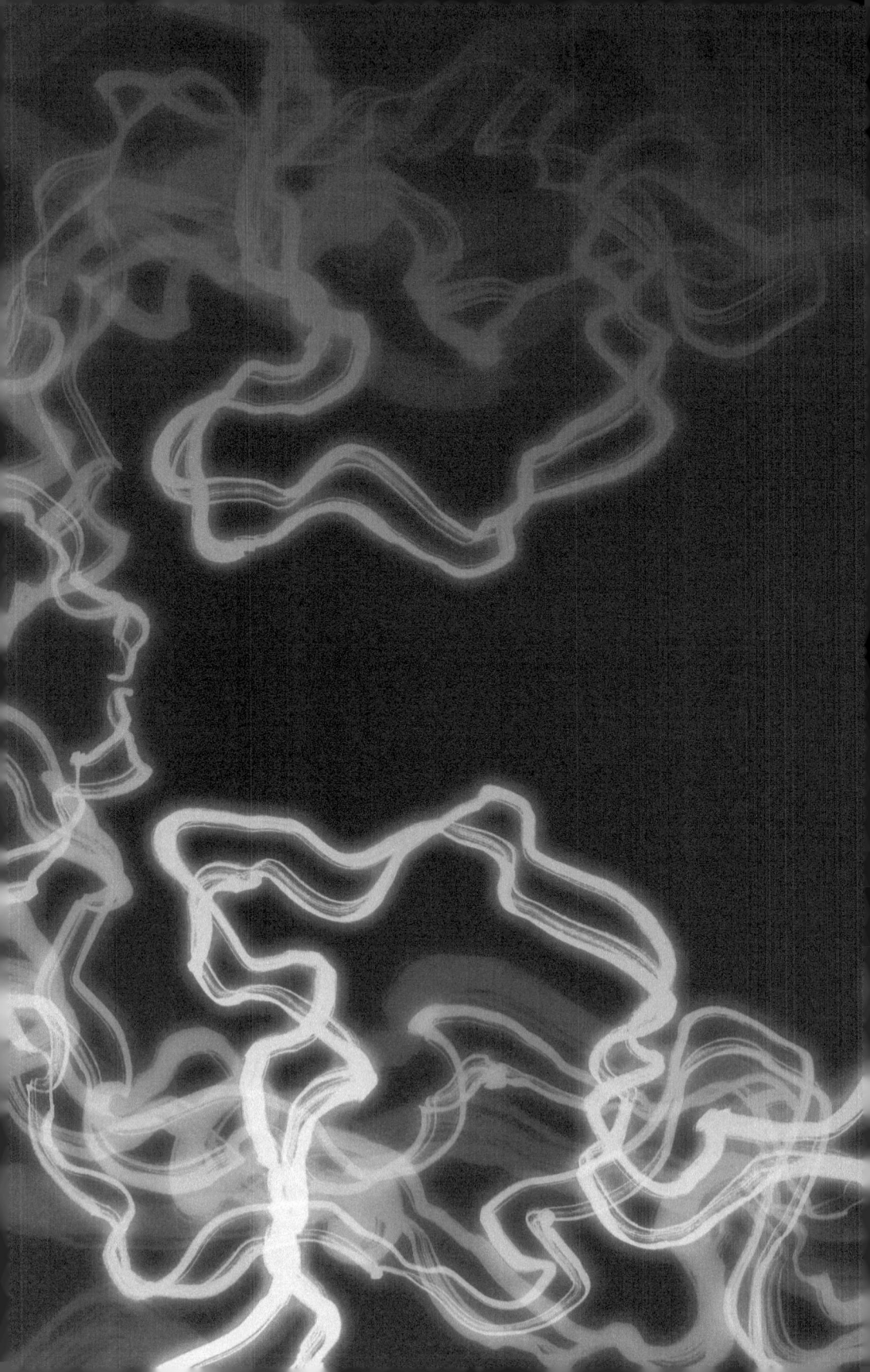

FOURTH REGRET

"I should have said 'I love you.'"

-HECATE SERINA

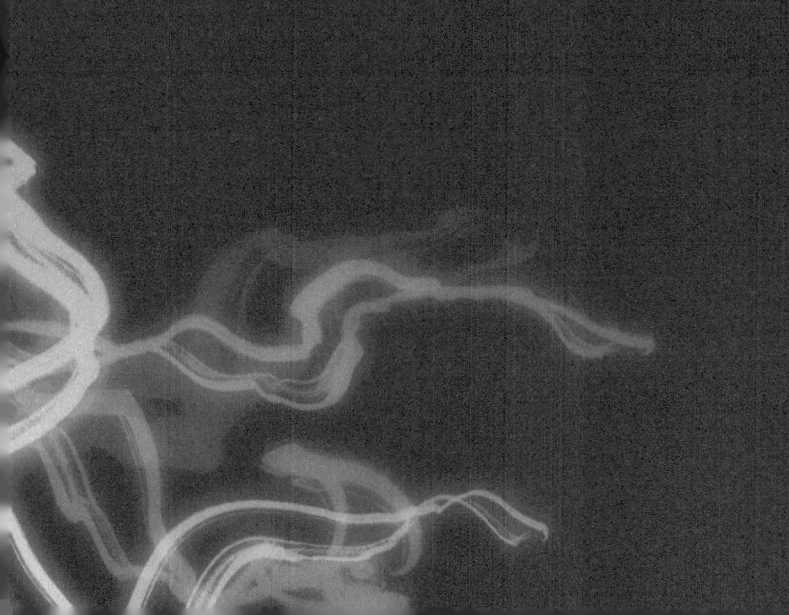

67

FIVE YEARS LATER

"**H**OW LONG HAS IT BEEN THIS TIME?" MICHAEL ESCOTÉ'S black eyes slowly opened, blending into the darkness of the room. The metal collar around his neck kept him pinned against a cobblestone wall. His body would have buckled long ago if a series of metal binds didn't keep him suspended in place. His legs were trapped by three rings, his arms were held by three more, and the coup de grâce, the one at his neck, ensured he couldn't move at all. "How long have you forced me to sleep this time?"

"Not long enough." Dusk's cold blue eyes bore into Michael's. With a firm strike, his fist fractured one of his incisors, body reeling and collar jostling, but unable to collapse from his suspended state.

"Kill me if you're going to kill me!" Michael snarled, trying in vain to flex against the steel restraints.

"Not yet..." Dusk took Michael's chin in his hand. "I don't want you polluting my Red World. Port?"

A pair of earthen eyes in the darkness lit up. "Go to sleep Michael... the next time you wake will be when you hear one of our voices say your name."

"No... not again!" Michael's eyes flashed red, as did Port's.

He tried to resist. In vain, he tried to resist the Executive Command to no avail. His eyes slowly closed, returning to the darkness as the two men exited the storm cellar, slamming the hatch to his personal cell closed, emerging in a field under a star-filled sky.

As Port padded the lock to Michael's cell, a bulky Christian Nikolai Dusk approached the walls of the place he had called home for the past five years. His cool blue eyes were the only remnant of the man he had once been. His figure was sharply defined now, muscles bulging as he swung his arms, and an air of dominance that he commanded. The scrawny High Listener who had served under Bruce was gone.

At his back, one of the human slaves he had left the Evan Blood Coven with some five years ago, Port Chinda, donned a casual smile. A rogue fang slipped from behind his pale skin as he raced to catch up to Dusk. "So, now we just wait to see if Mikey's fangs Turn Marie and Jeremiah?"

"...You look like you have something to add." His quiet way of extracting information hadn't changed since he'd been dispatched.

Port followed him into the former Red Crescent Coven, now called the House of Dusk. "Last time we went through a recruitment, only Ausch survived..."

"Only Ausch complied," Claire whispered to her brother.

"...was going with a smaller number the right call?"

"We're smarter now."

"I've been Listening." His powerful strides took him into the single-level ballroom of the former Red Crescent Coven. A stunning grand piano stood in the middle, surrounded by ornately decorated tables, each with a crimson centerpiece to match the drapes, highlighted by the silver accents from the moon which spilled in through the skylights. "I know their lives, inside and out. I know what the weather was like when they were born. I know who they first confessed to. I know what they had for breakfast yesterday. We're not so improperly prepared this time." Dusk turned around, folding his arms across his broad chest, drawing attention to the elegantly-trimmed vest struggling to contain his chiseled body. "I'm confident they'll both survive."

"A lot has changed... you've learned how to weaponize us."

Port stopped, slipping one hand into his trousers, his other hand resting on his pinstriped top, admiring Dusk where he stood, a goofy smile across his face. "A lot *has* changed... you know... I still remember the first time we set foot in this room..."

FIVE YEARS AGO

THE CRIMSON DRAPES THAT SHIELDED THE RED CRESCENT COVEN'S ballroom from the light of day matched the smears of blood that varnished the floors. Between sprawled bodies from the recent raid by Evan Blood and fractured furniture destroyed in the struggle, Dusk's slow stroll through the room magnified his insignificance as the Red World's symphony deafened him. Starting a House all his own without Antoinette had never been part of the plan, but Jason Castille hadn't given him much of an option.

"You did what you had to brother... to survive."

From the back of the room, one of the human slaves who had accompanied him, Port Chinda, spoke with an innocent candor unbecoming of a slave. "At least the chandeliers are still intact." His brown eyes, the same color as his tattered tunic, looked towards the ceiling, fixed in the middle of his pale face as his strawberry blonde locks wrapped around his forehead. He marveled at the majesty of the room, slowly looking down to see the death and destruction that Evan Blood had left behind.

Dusk took a seat on a torn piano bench near the middle of the room. He ignored the tri-colored ivory keys at his back as he surveyed the hundred dead bodies in the room, barely able to hear himself think through their screams. He had rarely been so overwhelmed by the Red World, but then again, the slaughter was still relatively fresh and the magnitude was tenfold what it was when they'd conquered Alastair.

"Silence!"

At a glance, Dusk could tell that some of the bodies had been humans. The vampire corpses were easy to tell apart. They dressed nicer and their features were sharper. The human bodies were simple and soft, scattered at the edges of the room with their plain clothes and formerly white aprons, slaves or servants, just like the ones he'd brought along, just like the one he'd once been.

"It is by Elise's will that you three are here..."

Port hopped over one of the vampire bodies as he made his way to Dusk, slowing as he approached the new Master he'd been sold off to.

Hecate and Freya Serina followed behind him in their muted crème tunics, with Freya leaping over the body in their path, while Hecate chose to walk around it. Hecate stood tall and serious, her cheekbones high and her features defined. Her short hair hung over one side of her face. Opposite her, Freya's big grin stood as a stark contrast, with a smile warmer than most, and a playful innocence he'd long since lost, long red hair landing on the same side as Hecate's.

"It is by Elise's will that you are here... but you don't need to be." He inhaled as the three humans stood before him, with Ilovo bringing up the rear, nervously taking a sip from a flask he tucked in his inside pocket. "A choice for you all... and one I wasn't offered. You can go. You can be free... or you can stay and help me build this cursed House of Dusk."

Port raised his shoulders, looking up at the moon through the skylights. "When Vega killed Elise... you made things right. I've never been able to choose a Master... but I trusted Elise... and she trusted you, Master Dusk."

Hecate crossed her arms. "I already put my faith in you. I've seen firsthand what kind of man you are."

"Me too!" Freya added, steadying herself against her sister, Hecate. "Does that mean we wouldn't be slaves anymore? We would be...?"

"The founding members of the House of Dusk." Ilovo's gaunt figure said, nervously approaching the group.

68

"L ORD DUSK." FIVE YEARS AFTER ARRIVING, HECATE SERINA'S slender figure approached from the far side of the ballroom. Her slim-fit ensemble of black and gray against white dulled her hazel eyes. Her stride was brisk and determined, but as she approached, she forced a smile, pinching her lips together and raising her eyebrows to soften the moment before they reset. "Ausch is watching over Saya and the other prospects..." She rested one of her pale hands on the piano, her black-painted fingernails blending into the stain. "Lord Dusk?"

"We were reminiscing..." Port said, taking a seat on the bench, ready to strike a note when Dusk lowered the fallboard, preventing him from pressing any of the keys and prompting an expression of exaggerated betrayal for a moment.

"Is this really the time?" Hecate folded her arms across her vest, watching as Dusk only paid half attention to them, clearly lost in Listening.

"If not now, then when?" Port attempted to lift the fallboard, deciding against it when he encountered resistance, this time from Hecate. "Who knows what will change once the House of Dusk's newest additions settle in."

"Ausch hardly changed anything when he joined."

"True... but do we honestly expect to find another person like him? He's so..."

"Rigid?"

"Yes!" Port threw his hands up emphatically, standing a head taller than Hecate, putting an arm around her shoulder, hanging off it dramatically. "Can you imagine if he had been with us those first few months? He would have worked us to death!" Hecate managed a small smile before Port noticed, pinching her cheek with a grin. She pushed him away, regaining her composure.

"Perhaps," Hecate declared, entertaining the idea, "but I still remember how much work it was clearing out this room... and another set of hands would have made it so much easier."

FIVE YEARS AGO

"When they're all naked..." Freya said, pulling the trousers off one of the bodies, "...it's hard to tell which ones are vampires." She tossed the pair of pants into a heap with another dozen, wiping the sweat off her brow as she looked at the former Red Crescent Coven up the hill, a castle almost as large as Evan Blood.

"I can tell," Hecate said as she pulled the shirt off one of the bodies, leaving it stark naked and dragging it slowly towards the mound of fully naked ones, away from the partially clothed ones. She tossed the shirt in the pile of shirts. "It's like they still look down on us." She swung her foot against the pale vampire's body beneath her.

"You're awfully grouchy today." Freya unbuttoned the dress of another, slowly pulling the stiff arms through the sleeve holes and maneuvering it around until the dress came off fully. Her eyes danced as they looked at the dress. The vampire wearing it had been pierced through the neck, and the garment was only stained with blood, but not torn at all.

"This is exhausting... and it seems like a waste of time..." Hecate turned over a body with the shirt sliced completely down the middle, buttons and eyelets on the same side. "It feels like we should be doing more."

"We need clothes... don't we?" Freya held up the eccentric dress: orange lined with black lace and a pleated white underskirt sewn in. She held it against her figure, tossing her long red hair atop the bust and pulling the sides against her body. "And it would be a waste to burn these too. We could have them tailored to us... or maybe we could do it ourselves?"

"You've never even held a needle," Hecate said, blowing the loose strands of her short hair out of her face.

"Well..." Freya said excitedly, stripping down quickly and trying on the dress. "A minute ago, I had never worn a piece like this either." Hecate stopped and looked up at her sister, spinning around in the ornate dress, surrounded by the bodies. "Well?" Freya asked, posing nervously. "How's it look?"

Hecate's frustration faded, her frown softened beneath her sweaty face, and eventually she rested her eyes as she looked at Freya. "It suits you quite well," she admitted with a nod.

Freya let out a squeal of joy as she ran to look at the pile of dresses. "You need one too!" Hecate took a nervous step back in her simple tunic as Freya bounced around. "He-ca-te!" Freya pouted, enunciating her name. "You will wear one too, won't you?" Her batting eyes wore down her sister.

"I..." she sighed. "Fine... but not like that one. We're not built the same."

"I'll say!" Port slowly made his way towards the sisters with another body on his shoulder, bending over to roll it off at the base of the heap. When he rose, he turned to look at Freya and let out a low whistle. "Lady Freya!" He took a knee before her and reached for her hand, kissing it dramatically, prompting Freya to giggle and snort. "This humble slave is without words!"

Hecate pushed Port from the knee he was on, causing him to fall over dramatically. "Is that the last one?"

Port stayed on the ground, crossing his legs casually, watching the unabashed Freya who changed out of her ornate dress and back into her simply stitched tunic beside him. "For today. The entire first floor is cleared out. Kitchen, ballroom, the entry way, and parlor... we even took care of the few that were in the wine cellar." He rested on his arms as he looked at the mountain of bodies. "Did you count them?"

"Ninety-three," Hecate responded. "Including that one..." She looked at him as his breaths slowed. "You alright?"

"It's the walk..." Port said, rubbing his legs between deep breaths. "Up and down that hill."

"What do you expect? We never really got to be up and around much in the basement of Evan Blood."

"Yeah..." Port said devilishly. "I miss my little slice of paradise."

Hecate pursed her lips and shook her head, bending over to undress the newest addition when Port craned his head slightly, lifting his leg to raise her tunic over her ankle.

She pulled away quickly, kicking his arm. "Hey!" Port winced.

"A few days out of your cell and you're comfortable enough to be a pervert again?"

Port's face went wide with shock. "Hecate—I have seen you naked more times than I can count, and I can close my eyes and see it again, just like in the dungeon. Same for your sweet sister... but pray tell..." He raised an eyebrow. "Why do you have trousers on below that intoxicatingly earthy tunic."

Hecate's face flushed as Freya came over, squatting down to lift Hecate's plain tunic slightly. "Sister?" Freya teased. "Why *are* you wearing trousers?"

Hecate sighed. "If I must be clothed... and if you two must know... there is some... appeal I feel wearing them, strange as it may be." Each word made her cheeks a little redder.

"First of all..." Port said, standing up, dusting himself off. "No one said you had to be clothed." Freya hid her smile by turning away as Hecate rolled her eyes. "But..."

"But?"

"Freya! Hold her down!" As quickly as he said it, Freya pounced on top of her sister, pinning her against the grass. Port tugged at Hecate's simple tunic as Freya restrained her. She squirmed at first, but gradually stopped resisting, letting the two of them tear away her tunic. She covered her chest as Port dug through the clothes piles, handing her a black and white lace shirt, turning around while she buttoned it up. "How's that?" He turned to look back at her proudly.

"I don't..." Hecate ran her hands over her sides. The shirt fit her well enough and, though the trousers were a little large, when she stood up, she felt taller, prouder even. "Freya? Does it look... bad?"

Freya shook her head happily with a squeal. "It suits you sister! It suits you quite well."

"Port?"

"In the absence of being naked... which I fully condone for either of you..." His cheeky grin turned into a sincere smile. "You've never looked more stunning." Hecate punched him playfully, looking away, but not before Port caught her gaze. "Sweet Freya! Are those tears of joy I detect on your sister's face? A rare smile from little miss serious? Could it be? Is this a cry for a hug?"

"It must be!" Freya squealed excitedly, throwing her arms around the both of them and squeezing tightly. Port wrapped his arms around them too and, though Hecate stood there limply for a moment, she quickly hugged the both of them before pulling away.

"How will Master Dusk react?" Hecate asked as she stretched in the new clothes, adjusting the lace ends. "Perhaps he prefers his women in dresses." Her face flushed as the words came out of her mouth. "Not *prefers*, but... if we are to live together, perhaps there is a standard of life..." Port and Freya couldn't contain their grimaces with each word she said, "...that he wishes... to keep?"

"Master Dusk doesn't strike me as a man concerned by..."

"...much?" Port asked.

"...anything?" Freya corrected with a shrug. "He doesn't say much... even the month he was down in the Silver Cell near us."

"No." Hecate adjusted her collar. "His concerns are different. We will be living with him, but from what Elise told us... it's almost like he won't be living with us."

Freya nodded sadly. "Master Ilovo did say we're bringing the bodies this far just so he can hear himself think... being a Listener and all that..."

"He didn't want a House, but he did choose to save us," Port added genuinely. "He could have left us behind."

"We meant something to Elise, and she meant something to him."

"...Had he ever killed anyone before Vega?" Hecate's question brought about an eerie silence.

Port's cheery smile faded as he bent over one of the naked bodies. "Maybe I'll just move these a bit further away from the castle."

"I'll help."

"Me too."

69

Antoinette Katherine Schofield's elegance was unchanged as her emerald eyes stared at the stack of letters neatly arranged on her desk. Once every few months for the past five years she had written Christian a letter, and each time his response felt less and less like him. It wasn't hard for her to tell what her faithful servant was feeling when he wrote: anger, betrayal, frustration, and disillusionment.

In the years since her arrival at the Evan Blood Coven, she had unraveled his life as the High Listener and, though she had never served under Bruce directly, she took note of the changing of the guard and the growing pains that came with it. The longer she lived in the Evan Blood Coven, the more she realized why he had been so keen on not reaching out to her when she had arrived: he wanted to protect her.

More often than she liked to admit, she found herself staring at the portrait of him that now hung in the main hallway. One side of the hallway was lined with former members of the Alastair Coven that Jason had come from, and the other half was mostly bare, with just a handful of portraits belonging to the few vampires who had managed to start their own Houses.

"Today's the day..." Antoinette whispered, placing a hand on his frame. "Today is the day that I find out if I can start my own House... wish me luck."

"Good luck."

Jason Castille's tailored purple robes glided into the War Room on the first floor of the Evan Blood Coven. The chiseled features of his anger from years past had settled into a confident façade. A pair of followers, one on either side, made up his entourage as his eyes scoured the individuals standing around the table, waiting for him to take his seat at the head.

On impulse, Ilovo went to close the doors, recalling the time that Bruce had sent them flying down the hallway in anger, but before he could reach them, another person had closed him. *That's right,* he thought to himself nervously, *this is no longer my role.* With a smile of pride, he took his seat, as did everyone else, including Antoinette, whose hands rested on her orchid dress, quietly smiling despite the nerves that consumed her.

"We are here..." Jason began, flipping open the pages of a ledger that one of the vampires had handed him, "...to discuss the state of Evan Blood, the progress of the Houses, and..." He flipped the page, scrunching his face. "That appears to be all." He handed the book back to another vampire who took out a quill. "Armand... let's start with you... Coven finances."

As Antoinette nervously paid half-attention to the finances, the vampire recruitment, the notable lack of reconstruction going on in the Coven, and the priorities for the next few months, she was oddly reminded of a time when she was younger, sitting in on events where her mother or father were the center of attention, trying hard to stay attentive while remaining perfectly still.

"My Lord..." The Elder continued, emptying the goblet of blood wine in front of him and making a face of disgust, jolting Antoinette out of her thoughts. "...We also have another prospect for a new High Listener. He will be visiting in a week's time."

Jason groaned. "Let's hope he's not as demanding as the last one... If there's nothing else, onto the state of the Houses now that we have... six?" He looked around the table. "Provide your reports."

Antoinette listened intently as one-by-one, the first five vampires gave accounts of their Houses, the progress, and the difficulties they were facing. Each vampire's struggle seemed to be different, but they all had one problem in common: money. One vampire's House was in such dire straits that they could not conduct repairs on their manor. Another had been forced to pay off some locals to avert their curious gazes. Each member of their respective House insinuated, in one way or another, that they needed money to stay afloat, progressively making Jason's face contort more and more.

"Ilovo?" Jason interjected, cutting off the rambling man. "Your accounts typically end on a high note. Regale us. How goes the House of Christian?"

Ilovo's meek figure scrambled, setting down his own empty goblet and rising to his feet. He stood taller than he had many years ago. He was only half-afraid to look Jason in the eyes and, for the first time in a long time, the many looking expectantly upon him did not make him cower. Five years in the House of Dusk had done more for this man than a century in Evan Blood.

"Our number of vampires is expanding as we speak. We are at the cusp of having three more vampires join our ranks by month's end. Our finances are under control. As usual, the House of Dusk provides a modest donation to Evan Blood." Ilovo heaved a burlap sack of coins onto the table that made Jason's eyes light up.

As Jason motioned to the coins, they made their way around the table, through the hands of Antoinette, Armand, and finally found a home nicely in front of Jason. Like a prized pot around a card table, he kept his hands at the base of the bag, mentally guessing the amount contained within.

"Despite the donation..." Jason cleared his throat, "...Christian should be reminded of the timeline he was prescribed. Only one new vampire in the past two years... time is ticking, and there is a clock on his particular House, regardless of his financial efforts."

Ilovo nodded. "Yes, Lord Jason. We don't foresee any issues with our newest members."

"Optimism before a Turn is a dangerous thing... It's always a gamble."

"Not this time, not for us... for us it's almost a certainty."

"If there's no new business..." Jason looked around the room.

Antoinette raised her sweaty palm and, acknowledged by Jason's nod, rose to her feet. "My Lords, Lord Jason. I would like to humbly request to create my own House, the House of Schofield, under the Castille Addendum."

"Oh?" Jason raised an eyebrow. "Do go on."

"My Lord." Antoinette held up a sheet of paper, trembling nervously. "I would like to create my own House, the House of Schofield. I have secured a property. I will be selling a family estate to secure finances. I have been in discussion with two other members of the Evan Blood Coven who would be willing to join me. I would like to obtain permission to proceed."

Jason leaned back in his chair, his thumb playing with a ring on his finger. All eyes bounced between Antoinette and Jason. "Antoinette..." he said soothingly. "...A House is a challenging endeavor, and not all are suited to run one." Five faces fell flat with those few words. "Until we evaluate the success of more Houses, another House is out of the..."

Ilovo raised a hand, waiting until Jason acknowledged it to speak up, still not daring interrupt him. "My Lord..." Ilovo began nervously, a move he would never have made before. "At the risk of being too direct, I believe the humble House of Dusk can not only provide financial support for Evan Blood, but also mentorship. We would ask My Lord to consider allowing Lady Antoinette, and anyone else who might benefit, an opportunity to see how Lord Dusk has made our House so successful."

"Beyond being a Listener, gifted slaves, and a great Coven as a residence?" one of the Heads of Houses asked with disgust.

"Go on," Jason added with intrigue, quieting the other man.

Ilovo ignored the failing Head's remarks, speaking only to Jason. "With your permission... would you allow Lady Antoinette, or anyone else who might find value, to accompany me back to the House of Dusk for a short period, that they may see firsthand *how* we are successful, so that their Houses, if allowed, can also flourish."

Antoinette could feel her heart beating out of her chest as she tried to stay calm. All eyes gravitated back to Jason. A few of the vampires representing other Houses also leaned in curiously, some desperate for an olive branch.

"Truth be told..." Jason said with a grin. "I too find myself curious... given that Christian has yet to return in the five years since he left."

"Since you all but banished him."

"I do wonder..." He pawed at his chin devilishly. "Would the *humble* House of Christian be able to accommodate us? Who knows who else might want to accompany us once word got out. You did say 'anyone who might find value,' but if it's too much..."

"My Lord..." Ilovo placed his hand across his chest. "I will discuss this with Lord Dusk, but I see no reason that we cannot prepare a reception to welcome those interested and provide accommodations."

"A prestigious gala to showcase the most successful House would surely bolster the Coven's spirits..."

"...That's not what he suggested."

Jason rose, prompting Ilovo and Antoinette to take a seat. "I suppose if you could be ready within... a month... those of us in power could show our faces... and this could be the perfect venue to prove that the House of Christian has met the requisite number of vampires. You sounded confident that you would have them by the end of the month, isn't that right, Ilovo?"

"Yes..." Ilovo felt his throat dry up as he cleared it, nervously looking at the empty goblet before him as Antoinette slid him hers, his eyes watching Jason as he made his way around the table. Ilovo's suggestion had spiraled into a *prestigious gala* and, although it was also an opportunity to prove the House had met the required number of vampires, it was far more than he had bargained for when he'd decided to speak up.

"Wonderful!"

"Perhaps those who might benefit from mentorship could come a day or two early?" Ilovo added quickly.

"A rare instance of a good idea." Jason clapped his shoulders, leaning down to whisper. "The only question then: will the House of Christian disappoint?"

Antoinette hung onto each and every word of the exchange. He was advocating for her on behalf of Dusk and, though the situation was evolving, his tact was to ensure that they might reunite again, with as little cloak and dagger as possible.

"We will schedule a date upon my return, My Lord, and I will see to it that the invitations are mailed by week's end."

70

CHRISTIAN NIKOLAI DUSK SAT AT A CHAIR IN HIS ROOM IN THE House of Dusk. Before him sat a deep well of ink and a thick journal filled with his writings, drawings, and scribbles. A history before his time, recited through the echoes of the Red World, was at his fingertips. A thousand voices reciting a thousand fragments created one cohesive record of the world as they knew it, piecing together a history that few had lived, fewer knew about, and even fewer still remembered.

Now, the relevant history of the world had been distilled into a few pages, serving as a prelude for the legacy that Bruce had failed to unravel: the origin of the so-called necromancers, and more specifically, their progenitor, Baralai Odin, who had been able to resurrect the dead.

Those who knew of Odin, even in the Red World, were angry with him. Those who he had brought back to life had pleaded with him to also resurrect their loved ones, but their pleas had fallen on deaf ears. Odin had not obliged their requests. He had long since perished, disappearing into the sands of history. Like those who couldn't hold on, he was neither in the world of the living, nor in the Red World.

Dusk couldn't ask Odin directly how he had done it, but with each passing day he was getting closer to unraveling the mystery of resurrection and, with it, the notion of bringing back his dead son, his sister, and Elise. The newest batch of recruits promised to hold the final pieces he needed to put the puzzle together.

"You have a visitor."

Dusk set down the quill, leaving the book open to breathe before a childish knock on his door interrupted the silence of the living world. As he rose from his chair, the back knocked against the desk, tipping the inkwell over. "Come in."

Dusk pulled a rag out of a drawer in the desk, attempting to corral the ink as it tried to penetrate the wood, memories of Antoinette flooding him as he recalled a similar incident years ago.

Behind him, Freya Serina bobbed and smiled, making her way across the room in a pristine white dress lined with a pastel blue shade of lace. Her head bent down to inspect the ink river, putting her hand down on the desk so the ink wouldn't travel to the journal. "It's rare to see something out of order in your room..." He wiped off as much ink as he could before taking Freya's hand with a fresh rag. "Did you call for me?"

"I did." Freya's curious gaze looked down at the journal. Her eyes followed the lines and squiggles, then looked over to some symbols drawn on the pages. "You could learn too," Dusk said, reassuringly. "Hecate and Port did."

Freya smiled. "Sometimes I like not knowing..." She ran a finger across the ink to make sure it was dry before flipping through the pages. "This could say anything. This could be..." she came to a page with a spider-web like drawing, "...a pattern for a dress." She flipped the pages to one with words. "This could be a love letter to Lady Antoinette." She flipped some more, "A recipe for a steak dinner..." She turned back to where he had left off, "And just now... you were writing about my stunning smile... weren't you?" Her grin lit up the room as she spun around, a wide smile that showcased her twin fangs, taking a seat on the edge of Dusk's bed, softening him with each wild notion.

"We've had this conversation before, haven't we?" He took a seat next to her.

"Maybe." She batted her eyes, looking out the window. "But you didn't call me here to reminisce."

Dusk nodded, seriousness returning. "Ilovo... is making some promises."

"He's back?" Freya perked up.

"No."

"Oh." Her head dropped. "...Bad promises?"

Dusk paused for a moment. "With good intentions." Freya's glee faded. "He's promised that we would have more members, and that we would host a celebration for the Evan Blood Coven within a month."

"A party?" Freya's thoughts began to race, ignoring the first promise. "We're hosting... a party?"

"Yes, but..." Dusk took her hand, grounding her in the conversation. "We will need you to help organize it."

"*I'm* hosting a party?" Freya was about to stand up when Dusk put his hand on her leg, keeping her seated.

"Freya." He turned her head to face him. "I'm trusting you with this. It needs to be..."

"*Tame,*" *Claire whispered.*

"*Ordinary,*" *Elise added.*

"*Formal.*"

"*Elegant.*"

"...over the top!" Freya pushed Dusk's hand aside and leapt to her feet, her legs outstretched, her arms up, and stars in her eyes. "Food. Vampire food and human food. If humans will attend? How many people? Oh." She gasped. "The ballroom! Dancing? A ball! Port can play. Do you think Hecate will wear a dress? I can convince her. What will *I* wear? What will *you* wear? People. Conversations! Gossip?"

"Freya!" Dusk stood up, taking her arms, holding her like a man trying to contain a hurricane. "We have to get through the recruitment first." She nodded with a cheesy smile. "Say it."

"Saya's already set... and Marie and Jeremiah..." She shook with excitement. "...then we throw the most amazing party man or vampire has ever seen!"

"But first?" Dusk looked at her, ignoring the footsteps that were approaching. "Freya. But first?"

Freya took in a deep breath, lifting her arms and putting her hands on Dusk's cheeks. "But first Marie and Jeremiah need to survive the Turn." She nodded Dusk's head as his grip on her loosened before she planted a huge kiss on his lips, an emphatic smooching sound as she pulled away. "Then a celebration!" Freya bounced towards the exit where her sister, Hecate, stood, watching the last seconds of the scene unfold. A moment later, the stunned Hecate felt Freya plant a huge kiss on her lips too, exiting the room in a flash, leaving Dusk and Hecate in a daze.

"Lord Dusk?" Hecate asked, wiping her lips with a confused smile. "Did my sister say celebration? Are you planning something for the new recruits?"

Dusk wiped his own lips. "We have a new development with Ilovo... take a seat."

Hecate's smile faded as soon as Dusk said the name, settling into a chair beside him. "Go on."

71

As Hecate listened to Dusk, her face grew sterner. Although Ilovo's actions came from a place of love, reuniting Antoinette with Dusk did not warrant the risk of inviting the Evan Blood Coven to the House of Dusk. As Dusk finished, she waited angrily for her new orders. "He shouldn't have made such a promise... Honestly the favor he's curried with Freya goes overboard sometimes..." She inhaled deeply, interrupting her own rant. "What do you need from me?"

When Dusk stood up, Hecate felt herself shrink a little. When he got close to her, she felt a little uneasy. Years of teasing by Port and Freya had made her realize that the admiration for Dusk was more likened to an infatuation, and, though a part of her wanted to act on it, the constant mention of Antoinette as such a driving force for his actions made it clear to her that only rejection awaited. Instead, she resolved herself to serve him as best she could, but occasionally her body overpowered her brain, and now she struggled to take her eyes off his lips, wondering if Freya's kiss had transferred his taste.

She admired the man who stood in front of her, in part out of respect for how he had brought them up with neither care nor want, and in part out of loyalty for the man Elise had trusted to her bitter end.

"Michael." Dusk's single declaration of the name made Hecate's face sour again, just like the mention of Ilovo. "We need to find another place for him... There's a risk that someone from Evan Blood will use the festivities as an excuse to snoop." Dusk placed a hand on her shoulder. "Can I count on you?"

"Of course you can. She'd jump off a cliff for you. Honestly, brother, you keep surrounding yourself with..."

"Careful Claire... some of us might take offense."

"Always."

"Good, follow me." Hecate followed Dusk from the deepest room on the second floor of the former Red Crescent Coven to the wheat-covered field out back. As they walked, Dusk picked up a pair of shovels, handing one to Hecate who took it suspiciously, leading her down the hill behind the Coven, stopping at the bottom, her eyes surveying the area with a stern determination. "The snakes are gone Hecate, you saw to it yourself."

"They could come back," she said, pounding the shovel on the ground, looking for any movement in the tall grass, but seeing none.

"And they wouldn't stand a chance." Dusk removed his coat, then his shirt, revealing a chiseled figure that the former Christian could have nestled into. Five years of resolve had allowed him to carve out this body. Hecate felt her normally stoic face flush as the moonlight struck him, cascading over his muscles, unmarred by the injustices of the human life he'd lived.

"I take it we're not out here to burn him?" She recalled the mounds of bodies she'd undressed during the first few days she'd been in his service as she twirled the shovel in her hand, trying not to stare.

"Not yet at least. We'll be putting him in a hole for the foreseeable future... at least until after the new recruits Turn... at least until after the celebration." Dusk swung the shovel like a scythe, clearing out a small swatch of dried grass.

Hecate's lips tightened in delight, as did her grip on the shovel. "How deep are we digging?"

"I'll tell you when to stop."

As the two vampires worked through the night, each slice from the spade hollowed out a pound of the earth's flesh, slung with ease. Working tirelessly and in unison, the pair dug until they stood in a comfortable hole, their heads beneath the level ground they had started at, resting against the edges of the hole, propped up by the wooden handles of their spades.

Dusk closed his eyes. The Red World seemed quieter in this abyss, and a rare feeling of content washed over him.

"Lord Dusk?" Hecate's hazel eyes stared at him from across the six-foot hole.

"I was just enjoying how rewarding this type of work can be."

She shoved the spade into the side of the hole, carving out a seat, watching as Dusk did the same. "Do you miss it? Your former life?"

"A rare question... coming from you."

Hecate turned away ashamedly. It was true. It was the type of outburst her sister might say, but the silence also made her feel at peace. "Port says he misses his cell sometimes. I think it's a joke... but maybe..."

"Life was straightforward then." He looked into her shining eyes. "It was harder too, but there was no hiding bodies. There was no being ousted by a Coven. There were schemes... but I was too small to be a part of them. I suspect that may be what Port misses is the simplicity of it all. It's why my role is what it is."

"...I can't say I hated it." Hecate wiped the sweat from her brow, undoing the top button of her shirt and fanning herself with the bottom, revealing her midriff as she did so, not catching the stolen glance of the man she fawned over. "There were moments I hated... but ironic as it may be, it was only the last month that was truly difficult—after Elise showed us possibility, after Elise died and we lost it... after they caged you too." She wiped the sweat above her breast, suddenly realizing what she was doing, changing how she fanned herself in an attempt to play it off, hoping the heat she felt on her cheeks wasn't visible in the scarce light of the would-be grave.

"*Sorry.*"

"She's sorry." Hecate smiled earnestly, forgetting her shame, her eyes twinkling as she looked up at the stars through the opening of the hole. "She never wanted you to suffer on her behalf."

"She changed everything for us... I only wish she could benefit from this afterlife too."

"*You can trust her, you know. She wouldn't betray what you've been planning.*"

"*Reluctant as I am to admit it... I agree.*"

Dusk nodded, standing up. "One more request. See to it that he's delivered to his new resting place. I'll finish cleaning up the land around here and we'll scatter some clover seeds."

Hecate nodded. "Consider it done. Perhaps I'll command him to jump into the hole himself." She smiled wryly, enjoying the rare grin that Dusk flashed back at her. "Perhaps I'll drive another knife into his chest like the night we captured him..."

THREE YEARS AGO

THE SERVANT'S ENTRANCE TO THE SCHOFIELD MANOR NEVER LOOKED as small as it did to Dusk. Each stride down the cobblestone slope propelled the former High Listener and his loyal servant towards a reality that he had waited years to fulfill.

"Take him alive if possible." He handed Hecate a knife and a hank of rope. "If we can't, do what you need to do." Her determined eyes nodded. She had waited two years to finally prove herself as something other than simply his housemate. She would not let this opportunity pass her by.

As the pair made their way through the servant's doors in the basement of the Schofield Manor, Christian paused to peer into his former room.

The mattress he had used so long ago still remained. The bed was barely held together by spider webs; the dresser had lost most of its drawers; and the window that had seemed so far away was smaller and dustier than it had ever been. "My former cell."

"*Kill yourself,*" an errant voice whispered.

"A suite compared to mine," she quietly responded.

Each step felt like a memory he'd long since forgotten, of a past he couldn't erase until the final loose end was handled. Up the stairs, on the first floor of the Schofield Manor, the parlor where Christian had been threatened by Ivar Schofield had its doors wide open. The room had been hollowed out. The chaise was gone. The vases and bookshelves had been picked clean, but the memory of the terror still remained.

"Steady yourself, brother. I'm still here. You're not alone."

"This is where Ivar set his eyes on you... this is where my weakness became your undoing..."

"You're not here to avenge me."

The quiet climb up the stairs to the second floor was the most daunting. A thousand memories flooded the younger Dusk twin as he ascended. He had met his Masters on this floor. He had lost his sister on this floor. He had found a lover on this floor. It felt surreal to approach so calmly with a knife in his hand, ready to kill a man if he could not contain him, but the reflection of a mighty Dusk in the window at the end of the hall steadied his resolve. He wasn't just a servant anymore.

A pair of black eyes at waist-height watched the two individuals creep through his household. A nine-year old boy, Dram, was about to make a sound when Aubrey quietly emerged from the master bedroom that had once belonged to Navara and Ivar Schofield. Her black eyes took in the two individuals who stood before her.

A man larger and sturdier than any she'd seen measured her as she stepped forward in the light of a lantern. Dressed in a white nightgown, donning more gray hairs than she had a decade ago, and less cheery than she had ever been, with one look into the pools of his eyes, the once-Weather girl recognized the former servant. "She said you'd come," Aubrey whispered, holding out an arm for the boy who ran to her, wrapping his arms around her nervously, unsure of what to do in the silence of the standoff. "This is Dram... my son."

Hecate's stance shifted as Dusk softened. His son would have been about the same age if he were still alive. "Go to my room," he said. "I'll find you when it's done."

Aubrey nodded. "I also have a daughter... she's asleep..."

"Go. I'll fetch you when it's done."

Aubrey hurried Dram along, his head spinning backwards, wanting to see what the strange woman and the large man were doing heading into his father's room.

"Hecate. Stay here. Intervene if needed."

"Be careful brother."

Dusk pushed the door open to Lady Navara's room to find Michael Escoté sprawled out on the bed. His breathing was slow, but as Dusk approached, the floor creaked under his massive frame, startling him awake.

Michael leaped out of bed, clenching his fists. He didn't recognize the stranger in his room, but as his gaze measured him, and the knife in his hand, his instinct took over. He launched a fist towards Dusk, which Dusk caught with ease.

"Who are you?" Michael had seemed so much more imposing a decade ago, but he was the same as he had been then: wild and daring, flaring his fangs and striking hard, surprised that Dusk did not go flying from the impact. "You're a vampire too?"

Hecate leaned against the hallway, clutching the knife in her hand, holding it up to her chest, her heart racing like it never had before, trying to steady it, waiting to strike if needed.

"You don't remember me." Dusk's clenched fist collided with Michael's ribs, sending him falling onto his knees. A splatter of blood coated his dark cloak as Michael gasped for air before another blow fractured his ribs. "I've been watching you."

"What do you want?" Michael scrambled over the bed, then towards the wall, leaning against the bed post. "Money? I have money. I can get you money." Michael grabbed at his side.

"You killed my son... you tortured the woman I love. You cost me my family. I want you to suffer." Dusk leapt over the bed quickly, arm outstretched, unaware that Michael had gripped the corner post of the bed, ripping it off and swinging it like a bat, striking him before scurrying out of the room.

"Dram!" Michael Escoté called in the darkness of the hallway, unaware that Aubrey restrained him on the first floor. "Boy! I need blood!"

Dusk reeled, flaring his own fangs as he raced out of the room to find Hecate atop Michael with a knife impaled in his chest. "Master Dusk!" Hecate cried out, struggling to pin him down despite the broken ribs.

"Dusk?" Michael Escoté's eyes went wide in a moment of realization. "Wait! Wait!" Hecate rolled off him, extracting the knife as she did, his hand flailing and slapping it so hard it flew across the room, crashing against the stone wall. He clutched at the wound before Dusk put his hands around his neck. "Wait..." Michael struggled to breathe as he spit up blood. Dusk's grip tightened, squeezing until Michael's body went limp, letting it crumple on the floor.

Hecate's heart was still racing when she began to wrap the rope around him, tying up and securing his arms against his body.

"You could have killed him," Dusk said callously, picking up the knife, blade broken in three pieces.

Hecate pulled tightly on the rope, brushing the blood from her trousers and fixing her shirt as she rose to her feet. "I practiced on enough corpses to know where the heart is." Her smile faded as a pair of black eyes looked at her in the darkness, measuring her angrily before turning around and running down the stairs. "Should I...?"

"Don't bother." Dusk pocketed the knife shards, picking up Michael by the knots in the rope, carrying his body down the first flight of stairs, then into the basement, paying no mind to the trail of blood streaming from Michael's mouth. When he arrived at the basement, Aubrey's eyes watched Dusk as he dropped the body in the hallway. "It's done."

"Christian..." her sorrowful voice filled the emptiness. "He's not a good man, but..."

"I know." Dusk held out an envelope, which she took. "Money... and directions to a house. Antoinette's... one day. Until then, yours, should you so choose."

His eyes looked past her as she opened it up. He took a measured step inside his old room, looking at the dresser absent most of its drawers, wrapped in the same cobwebs as the rest of the room.

Aubrey looked at Michael's limp body in the hallway. "Is Lady Antoinette...?"

"Surviving. Like we all are."

Dusk dropped to one knee inside his room, lifting the dresser from a corner and slowly unscrewing the leg, revealing a cavity inside. He tipped it over onto the floor, all eyes watching as seven copper coins rolled out. After he replaced the leg, his eyes surveyed the coins, picking up only one of them. The coin was tiny in his hand, a half-shield on the back was tarnished, dull, and poorly imprinted. At a glance anyone could tell that it was a fake.

"Will you come back?" Aubrey wrapped her arms around her son as he fiddled with the coins that had been in the envelope.

"No Aubrey." He looked around his former room one last time, slipping the singular coin in his pocket. "My work here is done."

72

"Lord Dusk..." Ilovo approached the Head of the House of Dusk at his desk with a messenger bag slung across his body and his head bowed. His tan trousers, off-white shirt, and slow movements almost camouflaged him against the room. As he approached, Dusk rose, shielding the journal he was working on from the once-humble servant. "I have returned with some news..."

"I've heard." Two words added to the tension as Ilovo waited with bated breath to learn if his actions had been a mistake or not. "What's done is done."

"My Lord, I only..." Dusk raised a hand, quieting him for a moment before he worked up his courage to continue. "All these years you have searched for an opportunity to reunite with Lady Antoinette. I saw such an opportunity and I took it, for you."

Dusk couldn't help but grin. Five years ago, this man would not have challenged a fly, and yet now, despite the consequences he knew could befall him, despite his station, and despite his own fear, he had grown. His confidence wavered, but five years ago there had been none. The former Ilovo would have approached with excuses and apologies, cowering before anyone who had a modicum of control over him. He had evolved.

Dusk sighed, shaking his head slowly. "You're not wrong, but as usual Ilovo... your timing is atrocious. On the coattails of new recruits, we now have to deal with planning a celebration as well, risking our secrets, inviting others into our home... have you forgotten how the first round of recruiting went?"

"No... and I'll do everything within my power to ensure a smooth transition, but My Lord... are you not proud of what the House of Dusk has become? We could very well be in the early stages of a Coven all our own. The other Houses are failing, and they wrongly believe our success, your success, My Lord, is only because you are a Listener. They should be so lucky to witness our greatness."

The former messenger rarely spoke with such passion; and rarely did his trembling subside into such an impassioned plea. Ilovo, sent on a fools-errand to oversee the formation of the House of Dusk, had found his place within these walls. He had served a key role in building something tremendous and, just like the humans-turned-vampires, had risen higher than he ever could have at the Evan Blood Coven.

"You know very well my ambition, Ilovo, but if it would further your pride for them to see how you live, let them come." Ilovo's chest deflated in an exhale as he received Dusk's reluctant approval. "I've already assigned Freya to spearhead the preparations, but we'll need your assistance as well."

"I procured the blood wine for Master Bruce regularly. I will see to any preparations that Freya is not familiar with. I'll also see to it that the invitations are sent."

"Hecate can assist as well, if needed." Ilovo looked away for a moment, nodding gingerly. "Before we get ahead of ourselves, the priority today is the new recruits. Marie and Jeremiah have yet to wake. I've already tended to their rooms on the wing opposite ours. Ausch is likely in need of some relief."

"Understood." He reached into his bag, brushing a golden flask aside and pulling out the journal he always traveled with, flipping to the bookmarked page and scribbling something in the margins. "Also... My Lord... if I may say..."

"Have you all conspired to warn me about the number of recruits? Freya is the only one who hasn't raised the topic."

"No, My Lord..." His shame carried his eyes to the floor, "...your actions simply affect..."

"You should not need reassurance, but I've taken precautions. I've studied these humans extensively. I've Listened to the Red World to better understand why other vampires have failed to Turn. I will take the risk. Are we clear?"

"Yes, My Lord."

"Is there anything else?"

"No."

"Then you can go."

73

"R ISE AND MOON!" PORT'S SMILING FACE CALLED OUT ON THE
second floor of the House of Dusk, drumming on the doors rhythmically
as he made his way down the hallway. His brown eyes were happily
inset against his pale face and his strawberry blonde locks were splayed over
his head. "Much to do, much to do!" With a pep in his step, he thumped at
each door a few times until he came to the one at the end of the hall. His smile
shifted to the side as he contemplated whether or not to beat the same rhythm
he had on each of the previous doors. "Eh, why not?" he mumbled, slapping
against the wooden frame then turning back down the hall with a skip.

"You know..." Hecate said, emerging from the closest door to the end of
the hall, buttoning up her vest over her white shirt, tucked into her trousers,
"...it's awfully early to be so annoying." Port's smile was not discouraged by the
admonishment.

A door further down the hall opened. "Come now sister," Freya said,
emerging in a black and green ballgown, brushing her long red hair over her
shoulder. "Let Port have his day." His grin broadened, standing beside Freya

Hecate folded her arms across her chest. "Very well, but only because after the new members get to know you... they'll think just as *highly* of you as I do."

His eyes narrowed. "You..." His retort was interrupted by the door at the end of the hall.

Dusk stood on the threshold of his room, donning an elaborate crimson tailcoat lined with silver buttons. The man he had been would have been invisible if he'd stood behind the man he was now. "Does everyone have their assignments?"

Hecate's eyes admired the Head of the House of Dusk, a welcome change from the rags he usually wore. He walked with the powerful stride of a modern member of the nobility. "Quite the change... for the good, My Lord," Port said, measuring him as well.

Freya nodded happily. "Thank you, sweet Port." Her eyes admired Dusk as he passed in front of her.

"One of your designs?" Port whispered.

"A dalliance." Freya admired her handiwork. "But we'll need something even grander for the ball."

"I'll be in the parlor with Saya."

"Yes." Port and Freya saluted in unison, heading down to the first floor.

THE HOUSE OF DUSK'S PARLOR WAS JUST OFF THE MAIN HALL, THE closest room off the entrance of the former Red Crescent Coven, boasting the same luxurious crimson drapes that adorned the ballroom. The room was adorned with the same trimmings and a crackling fireplace that kept the night at bay while candlestick torches lined the room and surrounded the upholstered seating.

A midnight-colored silk cravat stretched around the neck of Ausch Enimor who waited for his Lord to arrive. The collar held high the sharp features of his face. A shadow of a beard and mustache climbed into his short wavy hair. His unnecessary rounded glasses made his gaze even more piercing, and each button of his waistcoat sat neatly pressed against his body. With his arms behind his back and shoulders slanted low, Ausch tilted his head in acknowledgement as Dusk arrived, nodding gently to the woman who sat on the lounge at his side.

Saya Prederia Basque watched as Ausch departed, leaving her alone with Dusk. Her face was thin and her chin rounded. Her dark hair waved as it cascaded down her back. She wore a blue-gray dress with a matching corset and several rings on both her hands. Her twinkling red eyes waited for the Head of the House of Dusk to take his seat across from her.

"Good evening Saya."

"Good evening, My Lord..." she began carefully. "Before we begin... I want to confirm our arrangement... Once I've helped you with your task, I'm free to go?"

"You're free to do as you wish. Free to go... free to stay... free to live somewhere else, in another house, in another place. Our alliance need only be on paper... but I've searched for you for years. Others have searched for a century."

Her smile was hollow. "I've met other Listeners, but I've never seen anyone like you," she said nervously. "You're something else entirely."

He leaned in closer. "Tell me, Seer of the Red World, what do I look like?"

Her eyes twinkled with red as she looked around the room. "Humans do not usually exist in the Red World until they die. Occasionally, fragments of an important human exist in both realms, kings or queens or the like. I saw one from afar once... existing in both planes, influencing both realms. But we are vampires, our existence has already been shifted. Yet there is something unique about you, especially you." Her eyes scanned the space around him. "The Red World is stagnant most of the time. We move through it, but we don't affect it. Somehow, you're different—even sitting there, the Red World wavers around you, ebbing and flowing, merging and separating. It's unnatural."

"Does she know that some of us can see the Red World at times? That we catch glimpses of..."

"There..." Saya pointed into the nothingness. "Something... someone flocks to you."

"What about..." Claire fled. *"...this?"* she whispered more quietly.

"Now they retreat."

"Is that so unusual?"

"It is almost as though you can openly communicate with them... when it has only ever been the case that the Red World repeats the echoes of the dead." Saya watched something that no one else could see, the strands of red from the world beyond interact with the essence of red she knew to be Dusk. "What are they telling you?"

"Anything. Everything."

"It's absurd..." She tilted her head. "The essence of the Red World is the essence of death. To retain more than a fleeting thought is rare, but those that move around you almost appear like that of a vampire. Almost whole. If I couldn't see that there was no physical presence here, I would be convinced you stand beside two others."

"My mentor, Katja, another Listener, said something similar."

"It's disgusting... wouldn't you agree? Bearing the weight of the Red World." She closed her eyes and took in a breath. "But at least I can close my eyes. You can't close your ears, can you? You have it worse in that regard." His calm gaze measured her eyes, twinkles of red interspersed in her pupils. "It did surprise me that you can still hear the humans... you must be newly Turned yourself... a decade? Two?"

"Less. Though sometimes I struggle to hear them clearly."

"It will get worse. Eventually you won't hear them at all. Did your mentor tell you that? Did they tell you of the curse that would befall you? One day you'll hear only the Red World, and I suspect one day I'll see only the Red World." She paused. "Many have searched for me over these past centuries. None have come close until your Ausch, in the dead of night, in the middle of a forest, in an unextraordinary piece of landscape, came directly to my front door and knocked. At your instructions, I assume? Or perhaps, at theirs?"

"Claire and Elise."

"Claire, Elise, Lord Dusk—tell me, why have you dragged me from my hollow? Why do you need my eyes?"

"To see something we cannot... To find a power removed from this earth."

"Necromancers?"

"So, you know of them."

Saya's eyes shifted to the area behind Dusk. "If you want this to be private, perhaps we should wait." Her gaze traveled beyond the wall, adjacent to a hallway which ran deep down the House of Dusk. As her eyes twinkled, she watched as a strand of red moved through another realm, eventually stopping before the closed door to the parlor, opened by Hecate a moment later.

"My Lord, Saya, we have news..."

"Marie..."

"Marie has awoken."

"We'll continue this discussion later."

"I wish I could have observed it..." Saya whispered quietly to herself. *Seeing how a human becomes part of the Red World.*

74

WHEN THE LORD OF THE HOUSE ARRIVED IN THE RESPITE ON THE first floor, he overlooked the cleric, Jeremiah Ethan Andor, still lying unconscious in a bed, a vermilion sash and silver robes folded neatly at his side. He turned his gaze to Ilovo, who stood beside Marie Elzunaga, wide awake, a shade paler than she had been the day before, sitting up on the small bed.

"Lord Dusk?" She asked, confused but cogent. "Am I a vampire now?"

Yesterday a young bespectacled girl had stood before the members of the House of Dusk. Her features were muted, hair brought in a neat bun, and bearing thick rimmed glasses which magnified her eyes. She fidgeted with a light coat over a pilled lace dress. "My name is Marie Elzunaga. P... pleased to make your acquaintances." She had attempted to curtsy, but had staggered and lost her balance as she did, overtaken by a bright shade of red as she stood up.

"Will you join us?" she had been asked. "Will you become a vampire and serve the House of Dusk?"

"Vampire..." she whispered audibly to herself, nodding excitedly, needing no convincing. "Yes!"

"Remarkable..." Ilovo commented, taking her hands and flipping them over, seeing that the two pricks from Michael's fangs were completely gone. "A transformation this fast is seldom observed."

"How do you feel?" Dusk asked as she blinked, slowly at first, then more rapidly, eventually removing her glasses and opening her eyes widely.

"Well?" She squinted for a moment. "I can definitely see clearer..."

"Ilovo, blood?"

"Right away." Ilovo retrieved a vial of blood from a nightstand and handed it to her. As Marie removed the top she was overcome with desire, tilting the vial back and taking in the blood. Her eyes fixated on the drawer, hungrily reaching for it before Ilovo pinned her hand down firmly. "Calm. Calm yourself Marie."

She nodded, fighting the urge, looking away until the want subsided, taking a deep breath to steady herself and opening her eyes wider. "I..." She looked around, touching her face. "I can see clearly. Even clearer than a minute ago?" A broad smile spread upon her face. "I don't need glasses anymore?"

"You were right to select her Claire... and your prediction was spot on," Elise whispered.

"If we're right Jeremiah will take days to Turn. It hasn't ever been measured like this, but..."

"We need to know. If he brings us back... we need to know how Turning works, so we don't squander the opportunity... so we don't die again in the process."

"We'll administer blood in rations for the first few days," Ilovo added. "Newly Turned vampires who don't engage in moderation can become addicted to blood. It can overwhelm your impulse control and render you savage. Around vampires, it's not a problem, but in the presence of humans, you could feast and kill indiscriminately. Some vampires become unrecognizable as vicious beasts... driven by a singular purpose."

"And Jeremiah?" Marie stared at the unconscious man on the bed beside hers.

"Give him time... hopefully the transformation will take and he'll come around."

75

SAYA PREDERIA BASQUE SAT BESIDE JEREMIAH'S BED. TWO DAYS had passed since Marie had Turned, and Saya had chosen not to leave Jeremiah's side. She didn't want to miss a rare opportunity presented to her, glittering eyes peering into a Red World no one else could see, waiting to see if it would accept Jeremiah.

On the outskirts of the former Red Crescent Coven, Michael Escoté's unconscious body found itself at the bottom of the hole that Dusk and Hecate had dug. A sturdy table kept the dirt from piling on him directly while an Executive Command dictated that he sleep. Twenty feet below the earth, only a rough patch of dirt marked his living grave as Freya peppered seeds over the tilled soil.

In the furthest room of the second floor of the House of Dusk, its founder sat at a desk, acting as a scribe for the words of the Red World, confident that the road that Bruce had started down so many years ago might finally be within his grasp, confident that he might one day be able to resurrect those he'd lost.

Port and Hecate made their way into the House through the main door. They'd been gone two days, preparing for the upcoming celebration at the behest of Freya and Ilovo.

Port's cheery smile carried him jauntily down the main hall as Hecate marched onwards. "Ah, the refreshing feel of home." He tossed open the doors to the ballroom as Hecate followed.

"And the prospect of peace and quiet."

"Oh, come now. I often accompany you to town. You've been extra snippy lately."

"No." Hecate raised a finger. "You *and* Freya often accompany me. Together you entertain each other, but you by yourself..." She sighed, running a hand through her short hair. "You ramble on and on like you're at one of your shows."

Port covered his mouth dramatically. "You noticed! You've been? When? Which one? What was your favorite...?"

"Port." Hecate pinched both cheeks with one hand, stretching her pinky and middle finger across his mouth, causing it to shut.

"Yesh?" Port slurred.

"Fetch Ilovo and have him meet me at Lord Dusk's room."

"Confident he's there?"

"If his routine is any indication... he should be done with his self-imposed chores and writing..."

"What do you suppose he writes about?" Port mused as he leaned against the piano that sat in the middle of a polished and ornate ballroom.

"I was under the impression he had told you too," she teased.

"You know?" Port crossed his hands, overtly offended. "Wait... do you?" he asked nervously. "Hecate?"

"Fetch Ilovo." She smiled wryly.

"Lady Hecate?" Ilovo walked into the ballroom with his head held high, Marie trailing behind him happily. "Did I hear my name?"

Her eyes narrowed, looking from Ilovo to the newly Turned Marie who stopped in her tracks nervously. "Come. We'll update Lord Dusk."

"Ah... yes," Ilovo nodded, turning to Marie. "We'll finish the tour when I'm done. Until then..."

"...I can keep her entertained," Port interjected, taking a seat at the piano and patting the bench beside him happily. "A front row seat for our newest member."

Marie looked to Ilovo for approval, then met Port's wide smile with one that tried to hide its uncertainty as she sat beside him. While Hecate and Ilovo made their way to Dusk's room, a jolly medley of ivory keys echoed through the halls.

"Lady Hecate..." Ilovo began as they reached the second floor, setting eyes on the door at the end of the hall, "...if I might be so bold..."

Hecate stopped, turning around quickly. "No Ilovo, you might not. Though you don't exactly need my permission to be, do you?"

"I..." He looked at the floor. "I apologize for..."

"You overstep. We all have our roles here and yet how many problems have arisen because you've overstepped? George? This celebration?" Ilovo pursed his lips as Hecate balled up her fist, resisting the urge to strike him. He flinched, his back curving on instinct. "Ilovo, your apparent good deeds, Freya withstanding, become our punishment. From now until this celebration is over, I have but one demand of you."

His eyes opened hesitantly. "Lady Hecate?"

"Don't."

"Don't...?"

"Anything that is outside of the norm. Don't. Don't think about it. Don't act on it. Don't volunteer it. My patience for cleaning up your messes is wearing thin, and the goodwill you've curried is running dry."

"I just..."

"I don't need an explanation, Ilovo. I need you to do better. If you can't, I need you to stay out of the way." Hecate knocked on the door at the end of the hall, turning away from the shadow of Ilovo she'd left behind. The man who had stood up and defended the House of Dusk in front of Jason crumbled into the shell of a man he had been so many years ago and his leg began to throb, but as Dusk opened the door, he tried to right himself, tried to fix his hair, and tried to hide the pain on his face behind a plastered-on smile.

Ilovo followed Hecate into Dusk's room as she spoke. "Port and I have secured audiences with the requested agencies. We've vetted all but one of them to ensure discretion." Ilovo's eyes took in Hecate's confidence. He attempted to stand as tall as she did, slipping his hand into a pocket like she did, but no matter how he tried, his face couldn't exhume confidence like hers. "An event attendant service has been contracted for the day of the celebration. We'll have eleven staff on hand to serve and tend to the needs of our guests. A steward will arrive three days prior, to decorate the ballroom and adjacent hallways. They'll perform nominal work on the outdoor spaces as well. Approximately a week before, a household staffing agency can attend to clean the grounds, top to bottom."

"*Can* attend?" Ilovo asked quietly, watching Hecate pierce him with a sideways glance.

"The proprietor will be sending one of his domestic helpers to assess. He'll arrive within the next few days. Most agencies balked at the idea of performing a one-time service on a castle this large. Still—it seems unnecessary considering your daily efforts. We can manage, if needed."

"Ilovo?" Dusk's callout reminded him that he was in the conversation as well.

Unlike Hecate, Ilovo withdrew the trusty journal he never traveled without. "Y... yes." He thumbed towards the final pages that weren't blank. "Let's see... I've been showing Marie around the grounds, but specific to the celebration... Freya's been hard at work preparing new ensembles for us... let's see... I've secured four barrels of human blood which will arrive by week's end. The alcohol is also in route and Lord Ausch will pick it up." Ilovo paused for a moment, looking from Hecate to Dusk. "I do agree with Lady Hecate... considering our reserves in the cellar, we should have sufficient blood wine already. These preparations seem... excessive."

"We're leaving Jason no opportunity to refuse to acknowledge us. In this case, excess is the standard and perfection a necessity. Lady Antoinette will also be attending..." Dusk's blue eyes twinkled for a moment as Hecate's stern face fell, her shoulders slouching a fraction more. "Ilovo, what of the transportation?"

Ilovo cleared his throat, unaware of Hecate's crestfallen posture. "I've arranged transport for the House Heads a day before the celebration. This will include Lady Antoinette as well. They will be expecting to meet with us individually so that we may educate them on the House itself."

Dusk nodded. "Are there any news on Jeremiah?"

"Lady Saya remains at his side... he has yet to complete his transformation. It's already been two days. Perhaps..." Ilovo looked to Hecate, "...never mind. We will continue to monitor him."

"Good. Carry on then," Dusk affirmed. "Hecate, can you stay behind for a moment?"

"Yes, My Lord." Hecate crossed an arm over her chest as Ilovo stepped out of the room, closing the door behind him, letting out a tremendous exhale as he did.

"Is anything the matter?" She asked cautiously.

"When Jason visits... when everyone visits... the House of Dusk must show unity."

"Always, My Lord."

"Your problems with Ilovo run deep. I won't take a side. You've made mistakes, and I've supported you. He's made mistakes, and I've supported him. You've both done well to serve the House. I won't ask you something as impossible as forgiving him or letting him move on, but from now until after this ordeal is over, we need peace."

"I..."

"Hecate."

She sighed. "Understood, My Lord."

76

Evelyn Barett Webster's elegant brown hair was no more. In its place, a luxurious mane of white sat neatly pressed against her head. Her signature thin lips showed no emotion, but her eyes danced behind large spectacles as she approached the former Red Crescent Coven. "My word."

A well-loved copper and black dress lined with brass buttons down the front hid her figure. Her steps were short and calculated and, as she rang the knocker of the main door, she straightened her neck, giving pause to her sharp jaw as Ausch Enimor opened the main door. A head taller and every bit as straight as he could stand, on this night, a black silk cravat paired with the frame of his circular glasses.

"My Lord." A modest curtsy interrupted the silence. "I am Evelyn Barett Webster. I come at the behest of the Reginald Staffing Agency." As she straightened, her eyes looked over his grace and elegance. She could tell at a glance that he was born from nobility, but it struck her odd that he opened the door to such a grand estate personally. "I have come to bid on the services requested."

"Very well." Ausch opened the door fully, allowing her to step through, his eyes measuring each movement she made, watching the small leather bag she carried in front of her, holding the handles with both hands. *It doesn't look very heavy*, he concluded, *the bottom is not caved out. It is merely an appearance. It's always an appearance.* Ausch's tongue lapped his teeth as he shut the door behind her. "I'll show you to the parlor."

"My Lord..." Evelyn began, looking around as she walked down the entry hall. "Forgive my imprudence, but has the previous housekeeper been long?"

Ausch pushed open the double doors to the parlor. "Why do you ask?"

"With all due respect, when our services were requested, my patron, Abel Reginald, was under the impression that the cleaning would be extensive, considering the budget." Evelyn ran a finger over the fireplace mantle. "However, the care undertaken suggests otherwise."

"The Lord oversees the grounds personally. In the upcoming weeks he will be preoccupied with an event. His standards are high."

"Forgive me, are you not the Lord of this House?"

"Not of this house." Ausch pressed the raised fabric in the spaces between the buttons of his waistcoat.

"And your Lord sees to the work himself?" Her eyes looked around the room nervously. Apart from a thin layer of dust, by all appearances, the castle was regularly and meticulously cleaned.

"'*Dust doesn't take a day off*,'" Ausch said, moving a vase over the fireplace slightly, rotating it to match the adjacent one on the other side of the mantle. "This is what My Lord says."

"...I... I couldn't agree more," Evelyn said with an awkward smile, slightly taken aback.

"My Lord will meet with you momentarily. He is a man of few words, but great expectations. He will give you a tour of the grounds and return you to me. We can discuss timelines and payment... as well as a few other details, thereafter. Did your patron communicate our need for privacy and discretion?"

"He did. I am *fully* aware of the circumstances."

"Oh?" Ausch said, watching Evelyn's hands nervously clutch at the bag. "It appears you may be. In any case, we operate with discretion. As long as you do the same, your safety is guaranteed."

"I served a great House for many years, rest assured, I understand discretion."

"Then I shall fetch the Lord." Ausch took large strides to exit the room, leaving Evelyn alone for a moment, unaware that she buckled when he did, using the lounge to right herself, unclenching the bag and patting her knuckles to restore their color.

Several minutes later, a pair of footsteps preceded Ausch's return. As Evelyn stood up and plastered on a smile, another set of feet emerged.

Christian Nikolai Dusk stood at the threshold to the parlor, his murky blue eyes looking unto the woman who he had spent a decade living under. Though her hair was now white, at first glance he saw only the woman who had been: with brown hair, a sharp tongue, and the occasional wooden stick in her hand. The maid's outfit that she had worn day in and day out was gone now, replaced by the everyday-elegant dress that she nervously wore in his parlor.

Evelyn Barett Webster rose from her curtsy, standing tall in the presence of the unknown stranger. His figure was large and built. The clothes he wore were bespoke and sophisticated, and it wasn't until she met his eyes that she realized who he was. The shadow of the boy she'd had a hand in raising lived somewhere inside the bulky body of the man who now stood before her.

"Chr... My Lord," Evelyn said humbly, unsure of why a wave of nostalgia came over her.

"Miss Webster." Christian felt smaller than he had in a long time standing before her. It took a moment before he realized the change in their stations and the reversal of their roles: he was no longer required to take her orders. He was no longer there at her behest.

"Evelyn, might be more appropriate now, My Lord." For a moment she considered that it might have been an absurd joke that she was summoned to this castle, in the presence of this man, to be humiliated. But in the space of the silence, it became clear to her that this was just another twist of fate in her long and winding road. "I..."

"I'll give you the tour, please follow me, Miss Webster."

Evelyn withdrew a small ledger as Christian took her on a tour of the castle. She would note the details around the dwelling as they walked. Occasionally, she would sketch the outline of rooms, or point to taller spaces, or run her finger over walls or under stones. The longer they walked, the more and more writing filled the pages of her book. When she had walked through almost each hall and every room on the first floor, the tour finally ended in the ballroom.

As Christian pushed open the doors and stepped inside, Evelyn's jaw dropped. She quickly regained her composure, jotting down more notes before finally slipping the ledger back into her bag, standing in the quiet of the ballroom with uncertainty.

"I must confess... never did I imagine I would see you again... and certainly not like this." She looked through the windows in the ceiling to the sky outside. "Things turned out well for you..." She swallowed nervously, "...and I feel as though an apology is in order."

"It isn't Miss Webster," Christian said, turning to look up with her. "Nothing you ever did to me was so terrible that it warrants apologizing for."

Evelyn's eyes glossed over. "Twenty years ago... I would have hated this for you. I would have hated this for anyone besides me." A deep inhale gave her pause. "I hated your mother. Watching her smile in spite of everything frustrated me to no end. Even when I took the Head Servant position at the Schofield Manor, she congratulated me. Strangely enough that made me angrier."

Christian's ears strained to listen to Evelyn Barett Webster's confession. It was not dissimilar to the revelations so many clung to before they crossed over to the Red World. Few had the opportunity to make amends; few were able to leave their regrets on this side of the Divide.

The two people who stood in the room were not the same as they had been over a decade ago, but like he was taught to do, Christian listened until she was done. "Mother has always been that way, hasn't she?"

"The only day Franchesca wasn't was when she handed you and your sister off to me. It brought me joy then... her suffering. I thought she deserved to be as miserable as I was. I thought you and your sister deserved more. I wish I could have followed her example, instead of trying to bring her down to my level." Evelyn's voice cracked as she said the next few words. "Congratulations Christian... on your achievement." A rare smile, almost unbecoming on a woman who regularly wielded a wicked grin, brought a strange calm into the room.

"My mother..." Christian said, closing his eyes and pressing his ear against the Red World, "...chose you for a reason, Miss Webster."

"After the collectors came for your father and didn't find him... they made an example of her. She knew it wasn't safe for you both... she knew I lived far away. I was the only one she knew... there was no choice."

"That was part of the reason," Christian said with a bittersweet smile. "You were chosen, Miss Webster, not to love us, nor to praise us—you were chosen because my mother knew that we would be safe under your care." He flashed a rare goofy smile, like that of a child playing with Claire or Akolai in the space behind the Schofield Manor. "She knew you would take us to a place where my father's ghosts would not reach us... but she also knew you would not let us slide like he did, or share his same fate. A hard life... but an honest one."

"I..." Evelyn cleared her throat looking away.

"You were an unstoppable force, Miss Webster. My mother knew, if only to show us the heights we didn't deserve, that you would keep us close. I have no doubt you made her proud."

"Your sister... Claire... when she..."

"While you were gone, Miss Webster. Our true suffering was only when you were absent... when your back was turned... when we weren't under your wings." He pursed his lips. "I never did thank you for the letter you left me... I know writing it wasn't easy."

Evelyn struggled to not tear up, her voice breaking, "I think about it every day... I couldn't stop him... but you deserved to know that it was Ivar who was responsible for her death. I'm sorry Christian. If your sister were here... I would tell her the same."

"*I know.*"

"He died shortly after..."

"I learned about it at Lady Navara's funeral a few years later..."

"*Does she know how?*"

"Do you know how he died?"

Evelyn looked into Christian's childish eyes. "An accident. It was an accident... as I understand it?"

"*Tell her, brother.*"

Christian shook his head, trying to contain a grin. "He got into an argument because he didn't have enough money to settle a debt. He tried to use a counterfeit coin... my father's coin. He was caught, slipped, hit his head on a wall, and died outside the Weather House... where Lady Navara found him." Evelyn measured the eyes of the man before her as she listened to the story. Her forehead relaxed and her lips parted, revealing her crooked teeth. She drew a gloved hand to her face to cover her mouth, trying to hide the smile as the man before her grinned.

There, in the center of the ballroom of the House of Dusk, the former servants of the Schofield Manor each shared a singular smirk in a moment that very well could have turned into a morbid laughter if not for Hecate interrupting their quiet glee. "Lord Dusk," Hecate's voice carried across the ballroom. "Jeremiah's awake... would you?"

"If you'll excuse me... Hecate will see you back to Ausch, Miss Webster."

"Until next time... My Lord." She dropped into a happy curtsy and turned away.

"Lady Webster, I'll accompany you back to the parlor." Evelyn paused, taking in Christian's figure once more before walking in lockstep with Hecate, a gentle smile plastered on her face. "He's a great man, isn't he?" Hecate asked, seeing how she eyed him.

"And a good one too," Evelyn said as she headed into the parlor. "If I had a son, I'd want him to grow up to be like that man..."

77

THREE DAYS AGO

"Jeremiah Ethan Andor." The human had stated his name confidently, wearing a gentle smile and a long silver robe. His hands rested below his waist, near the tips of his cleric's sash which wrapped around his neck, a shade of red darker than his hair. He listened intently to the proposal of becoming a vampire, waiting until the silence settled in the air before speaking. "Hmm... As a disciple of the Old Religion... I serve Lords already. If you would ask me to turn my back on them, I must kindly..."

"Jeremiah," Dusk's voice rang crisp. "The Old Religion has all but faded from this world. You are one of a handful who remain faithful. Your house of worship has been burned. When you die, you will not be replaced." The man's face remained calm as he listened, unoffended. "As a vampire your life would be lengthened, your teachings could persist, and, more to the point, I would neither ask you to give up, nor turn your back to your faith, only to bring glory to this House, as long as it does not conflict with your teachings."

"You are a man of fortune, are you not?" The cleric paused, looking around the parlor. "Though this may appear greedy... Once I confirm the ramifications of becoming a vampire... if you would procure a space for me in town that I may further my cause, where I might reside, I may have no reason to decline."

"That can be arranged. As far as the ramifications... Ausch?"

"Turning carries with it a few risks," Ausch Enimor began. "First, if a Turn fails, the human will likely die. Second, in rare instances, a vampire may develop extraordinary abilities, at a cost to themselves. Third, a vampire is intolerant of the light of day—bothered by it in short bursts and poisoned by it after long exposures. The same is true of silver. Finally, a vampire cannot bear children."

Jeremiah hung onto each word intently, nodding along as though he knew this already. "The ancillary account of Erik's scripture purports that those bestowed a gift by the Six Gods trade the children they could have sired, for the essence those would have had."

"...In exchange," Ausch continued, "...a vampire obtains the possibility of a lifespan ten times that of a human. Their strength and speed are multiplied. Human blood also provides restorative benefits which can all but revive a dying vampire."

"What say you, Jeremiah?"

"The scripture is the only child I need, and if I should fail in the Turn, it is by the will of the Gods. I would be honored to join you, Mister Dusk."

TODAY

JEREMIAH'S EYES SLOWLY OPENED. ALREADY QUITE PALE BEFORE THE transformation, his features were only marginally sharper, but as he sat up in the bed, he could feel the power welling within him. He flexed his fist, looking at Saya who sat in a corner watching with astonishment as he got to his feet, reaching for the pressed robes by his bedside and slipping his body through them.

"How do you feel?" Dusk asked, stepping into the room with Ilovo and Marie behind him.

"Chosen," Jeremiah said with a serene smile. "Reinvigorated. How long has it been?"

"Almost three nights," Marie said, slipping around Dusk. "Saya stayed by your side the whole time."

Jeremiah looked at Saya, seated and awestruck, her star-speckled eyes relaxing above her bags, shutting them tightly for the first time in days. "Is it done then?" he asked, looking around unsurely. "Have I said goodbye to being a human?"

"We'll provide you with some human blood to ease you in... but yes..." Ilovo said excitedly, "it's done. Welcome to the House of Dusk."

78

A WEEK AFTER JEREMIAH HAD BEEN TURNED, FREYA SERINA closed an eye and tilted her head, standing in her humble bedroom on the second floor of the House of Dusk. Before her, an arrangement of mannequins with elegant dresses lined with pins stood proudly, waiting to be finished. Folded, balled, and tossed, a variety of fabrics made an appearance on her bed while her eyes darted back and forth from mannequin to swatch.

Her cheery glee was replaced by a rare irritation when Ilovo appeared at the threshold to her room. "Something wrong?"

Freya took a frustrated seat on the bed, paying no mind to the fabric she sat atop. "Not enough," she said, falling back on the bed. "Not enough time. Not enough fabric. Not enough grandeur. It all falls short."

Ilovo chuckled as he joined her on the bed. "They look fine to me, and rest assured, Jason Castille is a man of many talents, but discerning style is not one of them."

Freya sat up, running her hands through her hair and crossing one leg over another. "Lord Dusk hasn't asked much from me... ever." She shrugged.

"Hecate does so much for him, you and Ausch as well... but Port and I... we're just along for the ride... but this is a chance!" A twinkle in her eye restored her beauty. "A chance to do something for him that will speak volumes about us. Port is composing something special and so am I..." She looked at the mannequins, "...but they all fall short."

"I'm sure he would praise anything you give him. Lord Dusk has never been..."

Freya blew a raspberry. "You don't understand. You don't owe him like we do. You've proven yourself already, and I love you for it... but nothing we do can ever repay him. He made Lords and Ladies of us, of slaves."

"He changed me too."

"I wish he could just tell me what he wanted." She stood up and looked at the outfits. "But that's the problem with him. He wants not." She scoffed hearing herself say those words. "Or rather, he wants what we cannot provide... a life with Lady Antoinette... a child... a family."

"He treats us like family. Some would say that means we are..."

"You know what I mean."

"You could ask him?" Ilovo mused hesitantly. "He's likely working in the armory at this hour." He pulled out a pocket watch, checking the time. "Actually, he'd be just down the hall... either listening to Jeremiah's preachings or Listening to the Red World."

"What?"

"What?"

"What did you say?" Freya looked at Ilovo quickly, excitement washing over her face. "Say it again!"

She began digging through the piles of fabric as Ilovo spoke. "Actually, he'd be just down the hall... either listening to Jeremiah's preachings or Listening to the Red World." He paused for a moment, watching her rummage through the clothes, then watching her drape a swatch of black fabric over a mannequin that she stripped. "Freya?"

"The Red World!" She said looking at the mannequin. "The Red World..." she repeated again with a smile. "That's it!"

Freya pressed her lips against Ilovo's, not giving him a chance to lean in, then patted him on the head excitedly before running out of her room in her semi-transparent nightgown. "Freya, clothes!" Ilovo called into the hallway.

"You've all seen me in less!" she called back excitedly, running barefoot as fast as she could to the opposite wing of the House, taking a moment to compose herself as she stood in front of a door, knocking on it gently, adjusting her nightgown nervously.

"Come in," Saya responded from the opposite side of the room, standing up as Freya entered.

"Saya," Freya said excitedly. "I'm making something for Lord Dusk... I need your help. I need you to tell me what the Red World looks like."

79

"I T IS A WONDERFUL THING..." JEREMIAH ETHAN ANDOR BEGAN,
seated across from Dusk, "...to turn religion into fact." He stared down
at his skin, only a shade paler than it had been before becoming a
vampire, running his tongue over his twin fangs as a weathered book sat atop
his lap. "Shall we continue with the teachings of the Old Religion?"

"Before we do..." Dusk leaned forward, interlocking his fingers. "I'd like to
deviate slightly." The cleric looked up from his tattered tome curiously. "Does
the Old Religion speak about other races besides vampires?"

Jeremiah slipped a finger into his book, closing it and stroking the cover,
looking up and thinking. "Not directly... not in those terms. As a theologian
though, I have read some fascinating accounts of multiple races from *other*
religious texts. The Old Religion is clear that there exists only man, those
blessed by the Gods, and the Gods themselves. As a vampire here before you, I
would safely interpret the second as vampires."

"And there are no other races?"

"Only the one who stands above them all, but why do you ask?"

"Is rebirth possible? Either by your Gods or by the so-called blessed?"

"The creation of all life is not directly credited to Gods, but rather his inheritance. Rebirth as you might interpret it, as a physical reformation, is not a consideration. The Old Religion claims the memories live on in the Akashic Record... which some can access, but rebirth is not strictly possible... at least there aren't any accounts of it."

"The Red World?"

"Tell me more about the Akashic Record..."

Jeremiah scratched his chin, closing his eyes. "It exists as the compendium of knowledge. A world unseen, in a place mostly inaccessible, existing here, but at the same time, not. It's the abstract term for the afterlife, where souls without a body go."

"Don't press this yet. We have time now that we have all the pieces."

"Ask him when the Old Religion was last amended."

"Why?"

"When was the Old Religion last amended... when were the final texts or accounts added to your bible?"

"It was codified about a thousand years ago with prophets bearing witness to our Gods. The final revisions, called ancillary doctrines, were added in the hundred years that followed. This tome that exists..." He ran his hand over a tan book with a crème-colored ribbon spilling from the spine, "...is one of only a few left. I would venture to say there are less than a dozen complete bibles... this is why I would like your help—to reprint and redistribute the word. To grow the Faith in..."

"Jeremiah." Dusk raised a tired hand, halting his words, pressing his ear to the Red World.

"What did that tell us?"

"A thousand years ago, the Old Religion didn't acknowledge rebirth, but we know it occurred with necromancers. We also know that Bruce searched for it for a hundred years. It's broad..."

"...but it's a timeline. Do you think Saya can use this information to narrow things down?"

"If not, perhaps we can."

"We've never been this close."

"Mister Dusk?" Jeremiah stared onwards, unaware of the conversation around him.

"Perhaps Marie could accompany you into town tomorrow to help you find a location suitable enough to become a church."

"That's a splendid idea!" Jeremiah's face lit up. "She could have an eye for something inviting, and I could search for something worthy. Shall we resume the teachings?"

"Another day Jeremiah... I suddenly find myself otherwise preoccupied."

He stood up and adjusted his sash. "Then I shall leave you to your thoughts."

80

"Y ou're quite knowledgeable, My Lord." Marie Elzunaga followed Ilovo closely through the halls of the House of Dusk. For the past week, she had regularly tailed him, asking all manner of questions relating to Houses, Covens, vampires, blood, the Executive Command, and every which question in between. When she would overhear anyone speaking about any topic that could even be tangentially related to vampires, her eyes would light up and an inquisition would follow.

As Ilovo went about the House, performing his administrative duties, Marie followed, gradually learning his routine, assisting with the cooking, or laundry, or the occasional cleaning that Dusk was too busy to perform. "I have been a vampire longer than anyone here," Ilovo declared proudly. "I served under Bruce Castille as primary administrator for the Evan Blood Coven for many years."

"I'd like to accompany you next time you go... if that's permitted," Marie added, unsurely, fluffing one of the lounge cushions.

"We'll have to ask Lord Dusk... since it will be before the celebration."

She nodded excitedly. "Incidentally, does the Evan Blood Coven have a library?"

"We had one for the longest time. It was lost when two of the spires came crashing down in the..." Ilovo paused for a moment. "...There was a lack of management. There are only a few books left, most of them under the watchful eyes of the Council of Elders... under lock and key."

Marie nodded excitedly. "Speaking of locked doors, do we have a library here? I didn't know if perhaps..." She trailed off, moving to fluff another pillow.

"Lord Dusk requisitioned the majority of books prior to the first recruitment." Ilovo cleared his throat nervously, looking at Marie's dancing eyes. "The majority of books, that is, are either in Lord Dusk's room or in the armory. He works there some mornings... you could ask him when the room is open... you'll hear the strike of a hammer on steel... just follow the sound. There was little need for books early on..." He paused again. "When Hecate, Freya, and Port arrived, none were literate. Lord Dusk taught them to read. Well... Hecate and Port at least."

"You've done a lot for them... haven't you? I see how Freya looks at you." She giggled.

He smiled and nodded. "Freya and I do enjoy each other's company... though Lady Hecate sometimes complicates things." He cleared his throat. "About the books... is there something in particular you are looking for?"

"Anything. Everything?" She bit her lip as she watched the flickering light of a candle. "I want to help, but I don't know with what."

His smile relaxed. "Freya still struggles with that to this day. For now, you can just be. Lord Dusk sought everyone out specifically... so I'm sure you have a role to fill, but for now, relax." A wave of reassurance washed over her. "If you are curious... after Lord Ausch arrived, he read through the library, top to bottom. If you have specific questions, he is much better informed than I."

Marie shook her head. "Speaking with him doesn't come as easily as it does with you. He's rather..."

"I'm rather?" Ausch appeared silently in the doorway to the parlor. With two words, he made Marie leap back nervously, knocking into the curtains, a ray of light slipping in and catching her hand which made her squeal and fall back further. She shuffled to her feet, standing behind Ilovo.

"I... I didn't..."

"Did you need something, Lord Ausch?" Ilovo interjected calmly.

"The housekeepers will be working throughout the castle today." Ausch looked at Marie for a moment. His stare was empty as he slipped one of his hands into a trouser pocket. "Is she done with those pillows?"

"Yes," Marie said quickly. "I was just..."

"Follow me." Ausch said, turning around and walking down the hall.

"Go," Ilovo whispered, ushering a nervous Marie towards the man.

Ausch was halfway down the hall when Marie finally caught up to him. "I apologize if I offended you, My Lord." For each long stride he took, Marie had to take two. "Where are we going, exactly?" she asked as Ausch turned down the hallway, walking towards the direction she knew descended into the basement.

"Ilovo has procured the blood to make more blood wine—the preferred choice of the uncouth vampires that roam the halls of Evan Blood, and the previous inhabitants of this castle. You and I shall mix the ingredients. It will be a good opportunity to observe your personal control in the face of vast amounts of human blood. We want to make sure you don't get overwhelmed if one of the help happens to bleed. A newly-Turned vampire's intuition might take over, and neither of us want to deal with the consequences of that."

She gulped as she descended into the basement, looking at the rows and rows of bottled alcohol. "Did Ilovo procure all this... for the ball?" she asked, reaching for a dusty label.

"No. The former proprietors of this estate liked to indulge. The basement runs under the entire Coven... even after selling off a sizable amount, the collection remains fairly extensive."

Ausch approached a small assortment of wooden barrels in the middle of the room and pried the lid off one. As soon as the crowbar came up, Marie could feel her senses dulling, her eyes drooping, and a gnawing hunger tugging at her. It took all her willpower to stay put while Ausch's eyes measured her resolve. "I... I think I'm fine."

"Vampires call it the Tide. The rushing sensation that strips down your humanity and reduces you to an animal. In times gone by, the humans would weaponize it." He handed Marie a leather apron and put on another. "They would fill containers with blood and hurl them like explosives, using that moment of impact to strike us down. When you're prepared, it's easy to hold back, but when it comes from nowhere, for a moment, you aren't yourself. A moment is all you need to be killed." Marie felt a cold wave of fear wash over her as Ausch spoke so calmly about death. "Bring those larger barrels so we can get to work."

As Ausch and Marie began mixing the blood with the other ingredients, her eyes would occasionally stare at him. A roll of equipment used to measure, including ladles, spoons, scales, and cups were methodically chosen as each batch of blood wine was mixed. The process was meticulous, and between each batch, after sealing the barrels, Ausch took time to wipe down the instruments he'd been using.

"Is there a reason you're so precise, My Lord? Would it not be essentially the same if the measurements were slightly off?"

He folded over a washcloth and laid it on the table before him. "It would," He conceded, before moving onto the next barrel.

"...Perhaps," Marie said nervously, holding up one of the wooden containers filled with small white crystals, "...it would be faster? And if the taste is nearly the same... would it matter?"

Ausch inhaled deeply. "You're a vampire now Marie. You have a dozen human lifetimes ahead of you. If you cannot concern yourself with doing things the correct way now, what hope do you have of living out those lives?"

"I only thought..." she looked down, ashamed, "...you called it uncouth... My Lord."

"The drink *is* pedestrian, but that is no reason that it should also be inconsistent." He paused for a moment, his eyes gleaming behind his spectacles. "You're a purveyor of literature, are you not? A book would be essentially the same absent all the 'a's and 'and's. It would lose no meaning, but that's just not how books are. Any writer who cut such corners could hardly be called an author, wouldn't you agree?"

"Perhaps you're right, My Lord..."

"I know I am," he responded, taking a wooden mallet and hammering down the lid of the barrel.

81

THE KNOCK LAID BARE AT DUSK'S DOOR WAS FIRM AND PRECISE, but the woman outside his door was anxious. She wasn't quite sure how Freya had managed to convince her to stand here, with a crystal bottle of red liquid and two goblets, but here she was, oddly nervous over something so mundane.

Dusk usually called out 'come in,' but this time, he opened the door himself to see Hecate holding up the crystal bottle with a wry smile. Her slim legs wrapped in form-fitting trousers carried her over to the desk where he had sat at, night in and night out, for years. She took the spare seat beside the window as he came over, closing the journal he'd been working on.

"What's the occasion?"

Their eyes watered as Hecate poured the liquid. "In all the panic... we never got to toast. The House of Dusk is complete."

Dusk took the goblet by the stem, his murky blue eyes staring into the pool of red as the woman in front of him clinked her chalice against his, downing the blood wine, her straight back relaxing for a moment as she did watching as Dusk took a measured amount for himself. "We're not out of the woods yet."

Hecate's eyes followed Dusk's, looking over to his journal. "We're getting there, but the question..." she said as she poured herself another glass, "...is what happens next?"

Dusk didn't interrupt Hecate as she topped him off. "I need you to accompany Saya on an errand."

"Into town?"

"Further. You'll be gone a few days." She nodded, setting down the empty glass.

"This errand..." He paused, letting the wave of voices from the Red World quiet, "...is important. For you to understand I need to share something with you... the whole story, and the future of the House of Dusk." Her face grew stern, but her eyes shone excitedly. "You cannot tell anyone about what is in this journal... Not Ilovo, not Port, not even Freya. Saya knows only on the condition of her unique skill." With each word, Hecate nodded along.

Finally, she thought, *a chance to actually prove herself.*

"What would you have us do?"

"Kill yourself."

"Quiet!" Claire hissed.

Dusk ignored the voices, picking up the journal carefully, placing it in front of Hecate with a rolled-up piece of parchment. "Take this map... and take this journal... see for yourself what I'm planning... the future Head of the House of Dusk should know." Hecate toppled the empty glass, flabbergasted by his nonchalant delivery of the news. "You'll accompany Saya to find the secret to resurrection, necromancer blood, and when I have it..." He paused. His eyes glistened as he righted the glass. "I'll introduce you to my sister and you'll meet my son."

It was the early hours of the morning when Hecate finally left Dusk's room. Her coat had been taken off, two of her blouse buttons had been undone, and the look on her face was glee personified. The wine was still red on her cheeks. Her usual ferocious gaze was an optimistic edge as she closed the door to his room and turned around.

Freya Serina watched as her sister emerged around making a face she'd never seen, bliss personified and down two buttons. As Hecate caught her gaze, she watched Freya's eyes grow to twice the size they had been, jolting down the hall to her, covering her grinning mouth.

Freya mumbled excitedly under her sister's hand, bouncing in place as Hecate dragged her to her room. "Did it finally happen?" Freya mumbled as Hecate let her go.

"Better!" Hecate said to a Freya who plastered on a confused expression. "Well... just as good," she corrected. "Lord Dusk let me read his journal and... when he leaves... he'll entrust *me* as the heir to the House of Dusk."

Freya's spirit tanked. For the first time in a long time, the smile that occupied her face was completely gone. "When... he leaves?" A stunned Freya struggled to find the words for her disappointment despite her sister's enthusiasm. "Congratulations?" she finally decided on. "I'm so happy for you."

Hecate took Freya's shoulders as she tried to walk away. "Sister... we all know it's coming... he's made his plans clear and believe me, I would adore it if he stayed, or if he chose me over Lady Antoinette, but..." Hecate's eyes deviated from Freya to a mannequin beside her bed. A stunning black coat, with moonlight highlights, and decisive red threads embroidered throughout spilled out of the coat with a deliberate precision. "Sister, what is that?" She approached the coat with a cautious amazement.

"Do you like it?" Freya tried to smile weakly.

Hecate reached out. Her black tipped fingernails graced the lapel of the coat. Her fingers traced the red of the threads, interwoven throughout the entire outfit. "This is stunning."

Freya clapped her hands together excitedly, her smile returning. "It *is* your color palette... with a little red mixed in."

"It's so..."

"It's the Red World, on fabric," Freya said proudly. "A piece made especially for Lord Dusk. Do you think he'll like it?"

"If he doesn't... perhaps you could even sway *me* to wear it."

82

IN THE BALLROOM OF THE HOUSE OF DUSK, A FOCUSED PORT stared at the ivory rectangles before him. His eyes consumed the entire eighty-eight keys, darting from one to the next as his right heel tapped the floor nervously. A blank sheet of parchment was upright on the piano stand, waiting to be filled with notes, waiting to become something more, but a disavowed look of frustration upon the usually cheery Port made it clear that today the inspiration was absent.

"Lord Port?" Marie called from across the room as she hurried forward with a grin on her face.

Port wiped the desperation away and turned to smile at her, lowering the fallboard. "Little Marie. Where have you been?"

She smiled awkwardly, scratching her head as she approached. "Here and there... My Lord," she said nervously. "Lord Ausch assigned me some work and... I'm just trying to be useful."

"Is my need for help so apparent?" Port hung his head.

"No. I didn't mean... I..."

He smiled wryly. "I know. Truth be told, I find myself in the same position. Waiting for inspiration to strike. So, talk to me, entertain me, ask me questions that I might shake this nasty block. Tell me—do you love music too?"

"Oh... okay..." Marie wrapped a finger through her hair, trying to figure out which question to answer first. "I had a harp when I was little... I always loved strings but I uh..."

"You...?" he peered at her with wide eyes.

"I actually have a question... I haven't really spoken to Lord Dusk since... well ever?"

"You get used to it." He deflated slightly. "Don't worry. It's not you. He's... preoccupied."

"It's just... he spends a lot of time in his room... talking," she whispered nervously.

"He has a lot on his mind. Once things blow over, he'll return to his ways and you'll see him in the halls keeping the dust at bay or righting swords... but Lord Dusk is a Listener... a vampire who can hear the Red World, the voices of the dead. They keep him company. They tell him stories. Perhaps they even tell him jokes and entertain him. Lord Dusk is never truly alone."

"Lord Ilovo said something similar... it's not something he can just stop, is it? It's ongoing?" Port nodded. "Who does he talk to? What do they tell him?" Her eyes lit up.

Port pursed his lips. "Did Freya tell you where we came from? That we were slaves to the Evan Blood Coven?" Marie took a seat beside Port, looking forward. "He took us in, because one of our dear friends, Elise, convinced him to, before she died. A slave's job is to obey. In our own ways, we all do. We ask little of him, but we move on his command. Ausch... in his own way, shares that obedience. You're a member of our House now, and though it will be uncharacteristically un-Port for me to say, you simply cannot ask these questions. Don't ask what he knows. Don't ask who he hears. Don't ask me, and don't ask the others. In time... he may share some things with you."

"I didn't mean..."

Port's lips came together, the frustration of the piano bleeding into his spirits. "What you might see as curiosity, is his torture. What you might wonder innocently, is at the expense of the dead. What you may want to investigate, he endures."

"It sounds like he is a slave too... a slave to the Red World." Marie lifted the fallboard. "I won't ask, thank you Lord Port. But is it a crime to wonder what they sound like? What the Red World sounds like..."

"Hmm?"

"The Red World." She struck a low note. "Does it sound more like this?" She tapped a high note. "Or maybe more like this?"

Port's eyes grew as the note echoed. "That's it!" He threw his head back. "Oh! And it pairs so well with Freya's cloak. The Song of the Red World... title may need some work." Port wrapped an arm around Marie excitedly before scooting to the middle of the bench, forcing her to stand as he wiggled his fingers. "Go on now." He shooed. "You can hear it when it's done."

Marie nodded excitedly, skipping towards the exit, stopping before Hecate just outside the ballroom, hearing the piano's keys echo throughout. "L... Lady Hecate..." Marie's head dropped low. Every interaction she had had with Hecate thus far had been curt. "L... Lord Port and I..."

"I heard," she mumbled through folded arms, peering through the crack between the double doors.

"C... can I go?"

"You can." She continued watching Port as he played, a gentle smile spreading upon her face.

83

LESS THAN A WEEK BEFORE THE BALL, BEFORE JASON CASTILLE AND the Evan Blood Coven would arrive in the House of Dusk, Freya's jaw closed deliberately on an unsuspecting carrot that, a moment prior, had been sitting on a platter atop the grand piano in the ballroom. The following day, the decorators would come and breathe life into the ballroom again, but as Ilovo, Freya, Port, and Hecate circled the instrument, a collective moment of silence overtook them before the decisive footsteps of Dusk approached.

"Look who's out of his room!" Freya clapped with a half-eaten carrot in her mouth.

"Finish your food before talking," Hecate scolded as she pushed the vegetable platter away from her sister's greedy hands, watching as Port picked up the remaining carrots and tossed them into the air, catching them one-by-one with his mouth.

Ilovo coughed slightly, finishing the small, pickled cucumber he'd been eating before hiding his mouth as he refilled his goblet, downing the contents in one fell swoop, tongue lapping his teeth. "Lord Dusk."

"This brings back memories." Dusk said, standing at the edge of the piano, looking around the room, now truly spotless, like it had been so many years ago. "This used to be our table, didn't it?" Dusk ran his hand over the piano's top.

"Ate here everyday." Freya leaned on the piano, supporting her head with both hands as her elbows waxed the surface.

"It felt impossible to make headway," Ilovo added. "But we did."

"My back still hurts thinking about moving those bodies," Port added, slipping onto the bench, watching Freya and Hecate nod. "Say, why did we stop eating here?"

"I know!" Freya raised her hand, opening her mouth for only a moment before Hecate shoved a cucumber inside, keeping Freya's mouth shut, despite her struggling.

Ilovo smirked for a moment before Hecate's death gaze wiped the smile from his face too.

"Oh!" Port said quickly. "We stopped after Hecate decided to try to cook for us."

Hecate's face had never turned the shade of red that it did in that moment, as all eyes fell to her. "I... it was my first time!"

Dusk pursed his lips before smiling broadly, unable to contain himself.

Freya leapt away, swallowing the cucumber. "That..." she caught her breath, "that was the first time I remember seeing you smile Lord Dusk," she said with a cheeky grin, pinching one of his cheeks sweetly. "That was when I saw what Elise saw in you... after months of living in near silence with a stranger... that's when I first felt that you would keep us safe."

The others nodded in unison. "I'm... sorry," Dusk found himself saying. "I didn't know how to be anything other than myself..."

"None of us did." Port shrugged.

"Though I will say..." Dusk put an arm around Freya, letting her nestle into his arm. "As someone who has been a longtime servant and, temporarily, a slave... that was by far the worst meal I have ever seen."

Port and Freya erupted in laughter as Hecate turned beet red again. "It... it brought us all closer! It served a greater purpose." She nodded, comfortable with her justification.

Port slid out of his seat and walked over to her. "My beautiful Hecate... I wake up grateful every day that you did not attempt a redemption." He planted a kiss on her forehead, dodging a weak punch she threw.

"You know... I *can* cook now." Hecate straightened up. "And as far as comedies go, I'm not alone. Port. You banged on this piano for years before anything not resembling death was produced. I thought *I* was beginning to hear the Red World!" Freya slapped Port on his back, letting out a thunderous laugh as everyone but Port snickered.

"Hey... I... the keys weren't tuned!" he protested.

"And sweet sister..." Hecate continued, "do you not recall that we had to have you work in the separate wing of the House because every other stitch was a pinprick on your finger?" Freya's giggles subsided as Port began mocking her, imitating her finger being pricked by a needle repeatedly.

"And Ilovo... you could hardly decide which way to walk without Lord Dusk's instructions. 'Oh, he's the Master,' 'I'll ask the Master,' 'Do you think the Master would mind?' Honestly, it was pathetic." She hunched her back, making nervous hand motions as she did, wiping the smile from Ilovo's face as he stared down into the blood wine, the red of the liquid reflect in his eyes for a moment before Port slapped his back and everyone, Hecate included, giggled, smiled, and laughed.

"We've all grown..." Dusk said, turning somber. "No matter what happens... I thank you all for everything. I never imagined I could be so blessed." He raised a glass, waiting for everyone to do the same. "To family."

"To family." They all raised their glasses.

"If I may say..." Ilovo found himself interjecting nervously as he ran his finger over the lip of his goblet, his leg twitching. "That is... we all grew here together... because you allowed it so... but you have grown too My Lord... and you have supported us in turn. From the High Listener who never uttered a word against the Evan Blood Coven, to a man capable of anything, running the only successful House, more successful even than Evan Blood. We too are grateful to serve under the man you have become."

"Hear, hear!" Port said, his goblet empty, reaching for and raising a carrot as everyone smiled. "But I must add... before this topic becomes taboo, before you leave us and Hecate outlaws it... Hecate, how on earth did you confuse the briquettes for the actual meat?" He asked, pointing the carrot at Hecate before her fist propelled him across the room and into an early sleep.

84

Saya Prederia Basque sat opposite Hecate in the carriage on the first day of their journey. Her red eyes witnessed the web of red flow through the world around her as the wheels ambled on. The self-proclaimed High Seer sat in silence for hours on end, only speaking up when a change in direction was needed. It wasn't until half a day had elapsed that the hired driver paused to rest the horses, disembarking and leaving the two members of the House of Dusk alone.

Saya released her grip on the seat as they slowed to a stop. "You make good company," she finally said, looking out the window, letting the light of the falling sun separate the two women for a moment before the curtains blotted it out again.

"Is that supposed to be a joke?" Hecate sat upright, withdrawing a pocket watch to look at the time, then staring forward at Saya.

A simple dress hugged Saya's body and a tight bodice seduced any onlooker's gaze. Her long hair cascaded over her body in smooth waves and, her face, like usual, was absent any expression, looking past Hecate like a porcelain doll. "Not at all." A simple smile made her appear more approachable than she actually was. "When I finally decided to live alone, I rarely went into town, by choice. I'm grateful for the silence."

"We have that in common."

MARIE ELZUNAGA DONNED AN EARTHEN DRESS AND AN OVERLY EAGER smile as she bounced up and down, waving to Freya and Port as she entered a different carriage bound for Evan Blood. Ilovo managed a determined wave to Freya as well, catching a blown kiss and bidding her a soft smile as he did, ignoring Port's goofy grin as he waved the couple off.

As the carriage rolled past the wheat fields that surrounded the House of Dusk, Marie found herself unable to sit still. She fidgeted with the curtain's drawstrings as Ilovo took his comfortable driver's seat behind the horses, urging them forward.

"I still can't believe Lord Dusk let me accompany you!" Marie called from inside the carriage, opening a small window so that she could talk to him from inside. "He must trust you a great deal."

"That is my hope..." Ilovo said as he rolled up his sleeves to his elbows. "We *have* been in each other's company over a decade."

"You said once the House of Dusk is recognized, it will no longer be subject to a special punishment that Lord Jason could impose, right?" Ilovo nodded, his twin black horses continuing down the familiar path, slowly leaving behind the House of Dusk at the top of the hill. "Does that mean members could start their own Houses without jeopardizing Lord Dusk?"

Ilovo chuckled. "Less than a month here and already thinking of starting your own House? You're a bit..."

"Not me, *you*. I overheard Hecate say she would inherit the House after Lord Dusk departs. Did I misinterpret that?"

Ilovo turned his face to look back at her. It was still the same gaunt face of the man who had been dragged into this ordeal five years ago; his cheeks were still sunken. "Our affairs are not to be shared with Evan Blood..." His eyes were the same dull shade of brown, but even as his lips moved, his profile was surer, and he did not immediately discount the notion that Marie presented. "The House of Ilovo..." he whispered quietly.

"It has a nice ring to it." Marie admitted, kneeling on the bench to be able to slip her head through the window to look up at the stars.

"I couldn't possibly... not someone as pathetic as me..." His leg began to twitch nervously.

"You seem more than capable to me."

The carriage rolled over a hole, startling them both and Ilovo cleared his throat, sitting up taller, a gentle smile on his face, "...I don't even know if that's allowed."

"Well," Marie yawned, "wake me when we're almost there... I don't want to miss a minute."

85

Two days after the carriage carrying Saya and Hecate had departed, Hecate interrupted the quiet from inside the stagecoach. "Is it true that you have no intention of staying on once Evan Blood releases their hold on us?"

"Once the celebration is over, once this charade is done with, I don't plan to stay. As soon as you and I find the origin of necromancers... or discredit the notion altogether... my contract will be fulfilled." A map lay open on her lap.

"And you'll be a member on paper only?"

Saya's legs swung under the bench she sat atop, clutching the seat below her as the carriage moved on. "This is a rare opportunity for me to make an ally. I believe it's a fool's errand, but a future ally is a certainty. Today he needs me. Tomorrow perhaps our roles are reversed. And a vampire who has lived as long as I learns to take things in stride... surely you can understand that?"

Hecate folded her arms across her chest. "How so?"

"You wear a dress as you accompany me. Clearly it bothers you. I hear you fidget with the fabric. I see you bring up the bust. You press it against you to make it something it isn't. I've known you for only a few weeks and I know this bothers you... so why pretend?"

Hecate adjusted the string of pearls around her neck nervously, trying to sit still like Saya in her own dress, sliding down on her bench seat slightly as she did. "The outside world isn't as tolerant as the House of Dusk, and I am a reflection of My Lord."

"You love him, don't you?" she grinned, a sliver of humanity peeking out.

"His heart belongs to someone else already... standing by his side is an honor."

"And that doesn't bother you?"

Hecate's glare pierced her. "You were never a slave, were you, Lady Saya?"

Antoinette Katherine Schofield hadn't been able to fall asleep the night prior to Ilovo's arrival. While the Heads of Houses spent the night drinking and badmouthing others for their failures, Antoinette had weighed each outfit she owned, twice.

Five years ago, she had managed to steal a kiss before Christian's expulsion from Evan Blood; more than a decade ago he had managed to steal her heart. Now, with each dress she tried on, she was one step closer to being beside the man that she had spent so many years thinking about, and so many years regretting the command she'd issued.

The jewelry she had been able to take with her had been pawned or sold; the elaborate dresses that her mother, Navara, had managed to keep, had been sold or burned by Michael; but, as she ran a shade of red over her lips, she hoped that despite everything that had changed, they hadn't. It was the only thing that she had looked forward to besides the occasional letter that Ilovo had been able to slip her way.

"My my my..." A female vampire stood at the doorway to Antoinette's small room in the Evan Blood Coven. The four-post bed she once owned had been reduced to one half the size on a weak base; the elegant drapes of the Schofield Manor were now tattered rags, layered upon one another to ensure the sun wouldn't bleed through tears from both layers at once; and the elaborate vanity she had owned had been reduced to a single mirror within a cameo frame. "If I didn't know any better, I'd think you were about to seduce someone."

Antoinette rolled her eyes. "Who would I seduce Orpha?"

A young Orpha deReville smirked, her fangs slipping out of her smile. Her petite figure eyed the taller and more elegant Antoinette, bobbing her head back and forth contemplatively as she sized her up. "Looking like that... someone who likes proper ladies... but..." Orpha rubbed her finger across Antoinette's lips, smudging her lipstick, "... you could seduce a lot more now." She looked at the mirrored reflection of the two of them. "Men like to feel powerful... we need to look weak. That's how I plan on catching Jason's eye once he's done mourning his wife."

Antoinette shook her head with disgust, wiping away the lipstick several times over, reaching for the cannister to reapply. "I've had a lifetime of men feeling powerful at my expense. I'll look the way *I* want."

"And you require lipstick for that?" Antoinette felt a blush come on before Orpha sighed. "If that's the look you're hellbent on," she said in a calmer tone, "go with a darker shade."

"I..." Antoinette looked down at the remnants of lipstick in the golden tube.

"Come by my room. I have some." Orpha smiled. "But you'll owe me one." Antoinette nodded excitedly, following her out, leaving an elegant black and white dress neatly laid out on her bed.

While the two women waded through shades of red on the second floor, a starry-eyed Marie had just arrived and tried to devour the main hallway of the Evan Blood Coven with her eyes. As she walked down the Hall of Houses, she stopped at the front, staring at the innermost portrait of Christian Nikolai Dusk.

"Is this...?" Marie pointed as Ilovo caught up to her. "Is this what he used to look like?" She measured the man in the oversized portrait. He looked nothing like the Lord Dusk that she knew. This man was unsure and wavering, thin and pale, almost comically so. His eyes were the same. His cheekbones were the same. His hair looked the same, but the portrait of Christian Nikolai Dusk was indistinguishable from the man who'd welcomed her into the House.

"Perhaps when he first arrived... more than a decade ago." Ilovo scratched his chin before the portrait. "The painting certainly doesn't do him justice as he is now... but it was not so long ago that he looked like this. He changed quite a bit after starting the House of Dusk..."

"...and I am quite eager to see for myself..." The familiar voice of Jason Castille heralded his arrival, appearing on the threshold of the Hall of Houses, staring at Ilovo with a tight grimace. "That is... unless the ball is canceled?" His intonation rose as his eyes fell to Marie, who took a nervous step behind Ilovo.

"Lord Jason." Ilovo straightened himself before a small bow, noticing Marie attempt a poor curtsy from his peripheral gaze as Jason raised a hand to them, blessing their return to a standing position. "In fact, our preparations are nearly finished. We await your arrival, but have come to escort any of the prospective Heads for a pre-ball welcome."

"I see... and who is your slave?"

"M... My Lord Jason Castille!" Marie squeaked nervously. "My name is Marie Elzunaga, one of the newest members of the House of Dusk. Pleased to make your acquaintance."

Jason looked Marie up and down, from her brown dress, to her out-of-place hair, to the crooked smile she tried to muster, the smell of sweat upon her. "Yes... well..." Jason put his hand out, inviting Ilovo into the Great Ballroom, walking in stride with him as Marie fell back. "Tell me Ilovo... is the entire House of Dusk so pedestrian." Marie kept her toothy smile present, ignoring the slight as she looked around the room with curiosity. "This one looks like she came off the streets..."

"That's mostly correct, My Lord Jason," Marie said from a step behind. "I was between homes when Lord Dusk invited me into his graces."

"Between homes?" Jason repeated, clearly confused by how easily she discounted his criticism. "As in... a vagabond?"

"Not technically, My Lord Jason," Marie said, her head pivoting from one side to the other, trying to get a feel for where each door along the edges of the Great Ballroom went, eventually tossing her head upwards to look at the overlook on the second floor. "My family owned two homes adjacent to one another. An earthquake caused both to be destroyed, but the walls from one house fell upon the other and created a type of third shelter... which is where I was living at the time."

"Marie... perhaps..." Ilovo began.

"No no..." Jason raised his hand, now invested in her story, wanting to get the full scope of details so that he could retell it later. "Just to be perfectly clear... an earthquake caused two walls from nearby houses to fall onto each other... and you lived in that space before Christian offered you a room in the former Red Crescent Coven?"

"Yes, My Lord Jason. Not on the streets."

"Marie... I think..."

"And one last question." Jason stopped in the middle of the Great Ballroom, paying no attention to the other vampires who caught snippets of the story, trying as hard as he could to refrain from overtly displaying the glee the story gave him. "How long were you between homes?"

Marie's cheeks inflated as she blew out some air. With one hand on her hip, she looked up, thinking. "I couldn't tell you the date exactly..."

"An estimate is fine."

"Four or five years ago."

"F...f...f..."

"Lord Jason!" Elder Armand called from across the room. "And is that Ilovo?"

Jason put a fist up to his mouth. "A House of slaves and urchins..." he mumbled to himself, shaking his head as he walked away. "Slaves... and urchins..." he repeated with a giggle as Armand made his way over to Ilovo, giving Jason a quizzical look as he took his leave.

"Marie..." Ilovo said nervously, "... in the future... leave the talking to me."

"Did I say something wrong?" she asked, looking at the old man approaching with his purple robe.

"You..."

"Ilovo!" Armand said with a smile. "Come to reprise your old role?" The Elder clapped him on the shoulder despite standing a full foot shorter than him.

"No, My Lord," Ilovo said happily.

"A shame. Things ran more smoothly with you here... the latest messengers decided on vampire blood to make the blood wine... tasted like death."

"Who would voluntarily...?"

"Them. It was *their* blood."

"Oh..." Ilovo gritted his teeth in disgust. "How did Lord Jason take it?"

"As a eulogy," the Elder chuckled as Marie got eerily still. "You must be a new one." Armand pressed his nose against her arm and inhaled deeply. "Still detect a bit of human on you. Just Turned...?"

Marie looked to Ilovo, who shook his head. "She's new to this world is all... My Lord."

"Hmm..." the Elder added suspiciously. "In any case, you wanted me to give this one a tour, I presume?" Marie felt a wave of cold wash over her. "Oh come now... I don't bite... oh wait..."

"Lord Armand will give you a tour of Evan Blood while I seek out those who will be accompanying us back. Once the horses are rested, we'll be on our way before night's end."

"Lord Ilovo..." Marie began nervously, "I could accompany you as well."

"Nonsense!" Armand said, taking her by her wrist, overpowering her small frame and ushering her along.

86

SAYA OPENED THE CURTAINS ON THE THIRD DAY OF THEIR JOURNEY, watching the line of sunlight on the floor of the carriage slowly fade away as night fell. "I do wonder..." she began, looking at Hecate curiously, "... if any of you understand how dangerous the idea of resurrection truly is. The stories say that even the father of necromancers couldn't control his power... and Christian is still just a boy... even if it is possible... what hope does he have of wielding such a power?"

Hecate crossed one leg over the other, pulling down her dress to cover her ankles. "Lord Dusk is a capable man."

"Your infatuation with him blinds you from the stakes." In an instant, Hecate bridged the gap in the carriage, her hand at Saya's throat. Saya remained still, leaning her chin up, allowing Hecate's grip to tighten. "It's not an insult." She raised her own hand slowly, putting it on Hecate's wrist. "It's a warning from a woman who's lived a similar life..." She pushed Hecate's hand away weakly. "He's a man who has invested years in this endeavor, to bring back those he's loved and lost. Where do you fit in if he succeeds? Where do you fit in if he fails?"

Hecate shoved Saya's hand away, taking her seat with a scowl. "Do not delude yourself into thinking that I am so naïve. Not once have I claimed that I could replace the sister he lost, or the woman who died in his arms. I am his slave, and Lord Dusk has a place for me. I could be by his side or jailed in a cell under his command. That is enough for me."

Saya's lips curled solemnly, shaking her head. "It shouldn't be." She steadied herself on the seat before standing up and casting open the door, stepping out into the darkness. "You could be so much more..."

A STONE-LINED ROOM IN THE FARTHEST CORNER OF THE EVAN BLOOD Coven was home to a wrought iron door, usually kept shut by a padlock and chain. Beyond the room the Elders had used to oversee countless Promotions was a small library where Marie Elzunaga happily sat, at a circular table in the center of the room bearing a weathered sigil made of six circles on the table-top, surrounded by a dozen bookshelves stacked high with books.

"Marie... we're leaving soon." Ilovo found her nose buried in a book.

Her glistening eyes peered up, her lips smacked together, and her cheeks puffed. "Do we really have to?"

Ilovo nodded, running his finger over one of the bookshelves, blowing off the dust that had accumulated on the ledge. "I used to come here regularly... the dust settles in this room more so than others." He tilted his head over the table, looking at the book that was open. "This is...?"

"The Evan Blood Charter!" Marie said happily. "It was on the book stand when Armand let me in."

Ilovo looked to the lectern, noting the silver chain that bound the book to it. "That book is the only one that can't leave this room. Notice how it's the only one chained."

Marie nodded excitedly. "It's fascinating... parts of it are like a book, other parts like a diary... others like a ledger. Rules of the Coven, the history, the formation, the humans who were successfully Turned... and those who didn't make it." Ilovo nodded, tidying up some of the books on the shelves as he made his rounds. "I wish I could finish it, maybe next time?" she pleaded. "And... maybe we could borrow some of the other books?"

Ilovo chuckled. "Let's ask Lord Dusk to let you into the library once we return... the carriage will be full on the way back."

Marie frowned, but stood up, stretching her back as she did. "You know, I read the House Charter... there's nothing in there preventing a member from starting their own House. They only need the approval of the Head of their House, and, of course, the Head of Evan Blood."

Ilovo leaned over, flipping to the last few pages curiously. "Is that so?" He skimmed the charter's dozen pages quickly, nodding along as he did. "Perhaps it's a consideration for another time." He shut the book, picking it up and holding it against his chest. "Can you find your way out? We'll be departing soon."

"Absolutely. I'll just find my way to a restroom first and meet you there."

Ilovo nodded as Marie left, taking the book back to the lectern, tugging at the chain which had coiled upon itself, caught on a slit at the edge of the table. As Ilovo tugged on the chain, the round table in the center of the room rotated clockwise until he wrestled it free, chain jolting towards him and catching his palm, causing him to stumble, tipping over the lectern and the book as he fell. With a grunt and a sigh, Ilovo looked at his bleeding hand, wrapping it up in the handkerchief he carried in his back pocket, gently nudging the table slightly so it returned to the outline of where it had been in the center of the room.

He lifted the ornate lectern with ease and reset it, then bent over to pick up the open Charter. As he picked up the book, the chain dragging on the floor, his eyes skimmed over the open pages which read *Evan Blood Charter: Line of Succession*. His eyes went wide as he read through the two pages, simply written.

This couldn't be right. Ilovo scoured the pages from the last few years, searching for an addendum to the Line of Succession, but there was none. *This means... Lord Dusk is the rightful heir to Evan Blood?*

As he returned the book nervously, he padlocked the door and added another chain for good measure. He encountered one of the other Elders in the hallway and handed them the key. "My Lord..." Ilovo began nervously, "...

Has Lord Jason secured another High Listener? At the gathering last month, I believe there was mention..."

The Elder scrunched his nose until it turned as purple as his robe. "He did not in fact." The man said angrily. "He questioned a Listener who would charge for his services—said that it should be an honor to be a High Listener and that anyone who expected payment for such an honor could die. Why?"

"I just..."

"Do you know of one?" the Elder asked excitedly. "Or might Dusk return?"

"I encountered one," Ilovo lied, scratching at the back of his head. "Or so I thought. He turned out to be a ruse. I just wondered how you were faring."

The Elder shook his head angrily. "If Lord Bruce had not killed so many vampires perhaps there would not be such a scarcity... and if Lord Jason could unclench his purse perhaps we could fill the void... alas... at least we have a ball to look forward to tomorrow. Tell me Ilovo, will there be blood wine?" He raised a depraved eyebrow.

"Of course, My Lord."

"Made with *human* blood?"

"Is there any other way?" he joked nervously.

87

O**N THE THIRD DAY OF** H**ECATE AND** S**AYA'S JOURNEY,** S**AYA'S OPEN** hand slammed against the inside of the carriage suddenly, startling Hecate awake. "Stop! Stop now!" The pounding of her hand against the wooden frame continued, Saya's eyes remaining wide open, her chest rising and falling excitedly.

"Have we arrived?" Hecate asked, pulling open the curtain, retreating at the midday light as she did.

"No," Saya said shakily, blinking slowly. "No... but... there's something..."

Hecate didn't have time to ask any more questions before Saya threw open the door, stumbling out of the carriage. As she made her way forward, she clutched at a small purse that hung in front of her, boldly heading down the road, guided only by the Red World, a world that only she could see.

Two minutes later, Hecate stepped into the light, donning a dark dress, a black veil, and a wide brimmed black sunhat. She moved quickly to catch up to Saya, making her way down a paved road that led to a stone gate which marked the entrance to a town.

"Why isn't the sun affecting you?" Hecate asked as she hurried forward, noting how Saya walked completely uncovered, her arms and face in direct sunlight while Hecate could feel the warmth singe her skin even through the clothes.

"I can't perceive it... the sun," Saya answered quickly, racing forward.

"...Where are we going?" Hecate stepped lively behind her, craning up to see the stone gate, trying to make out the name of the town they were walking into, avoiding the awkward gazes of the humans who watched the two women strangely make their way down the main road.

Saya stopped in the middle of the street abruptly, craning her head upwards for a moment in awe.

"Saya!" Hecate hissed, grabbing her wrist and spinning her around.

As Saya turned, her ankle twisted on itself and she tumbled over. The small purse that she held fell from her hand and a dozen coins spilled on the street around her, drawing gazes from some humans that were walking by, pointing and laughing.

Hecate inhaled with frustration as the two of them bent down to pick up the coins. They both reached for the same coin when Saya looked at Hecate, her nose almost pressed against her when she whispered, "Listen closely. Someone stands behind me. A hundred yards. Discreetly look at them. Tell me about them."

"What?" Hecate attempted to pick up the coin that Saya pressed deeper into the ground.

"Discreetly," Saya repeated.

"The woman?" Hecate asked, looking across the street in the distance to an area with vendors and stands.

"A woman? Describe her."

"Short. Dark curly hair." Hecate squinted, measuring the figure that walked across the street from one vendor to another. For a moment the woman looked towards Hecate. She wore a curious gaze, measuring the two women for only a moment before continuing on her way. "Looks a little like you. Dresses a little like you. Plain. Average. I don't know. What do you want?"

"Is her face covered?"

"She's not wearing a hat if that's what you mean. Why?"

"What's she doing?"

"Saya!" Hecate got to her feet angrily. "What is this about?"

"Hecate. Please. Trust me." Saya began slipping the coins in her purse, straightening up slowly.

"Just turn around. Look for yourself."

"I can't see her. I can only see her reflection in the Red World."

"She's..." Hecate crossed her arms angrily. "Buying something. Flowers? Maybe roses?"

"From who?" Saya turned to face the woman. "A human?"

"Yes. A human buying flowers from a human. Saya, what is this about?"

"Memorize that face Hecate. Once you have done so... we can go, and I will tell you." Hecate watched the woman from afar, purchasing her flowers, exchanging her coins, then continuing down the street in a direction opposite them until she was out of sight. When she was firmly gone, Saya locked her arm with Hecate's, turning to walk back down the street in the same direction they had come from, her heart racing.

"Now are you going to tell me what that was about?" Hecate asked as they headed back to the carriage.

"The Red World is essentially a reflection of this world. A tapestry of lives horizontally sewn across the world. In mountains, the tapestry runs taller, but in valleys it descends. In cities and plains, it's flat. The Red World is a reflection of lives and deaths—at various altitudes, connected to others who have lived and died, but that woman... even from here..." Saya turned around at the carriage, looking into the distance of the town that they had returned from, craning her head up, "... I have never seen anything like her. A bundle of threads thicker than any I've seen... almost like a collection of people inhabiting one space, but stranger than that... a single thread that stands on its end, rising from her and ascending into the sky."

Hecate looked up at the sky for a moment before they retreated into the shadow of their carriage, clutching at her dress, desperate to scratch at her skin. "Ascending into the sky? How is that possible?"

"It isn't," Saya said nervously. "A soul cannot be bound to the sky... and yet..." she quieted down, "she connects to something up there."

"Which is?"

"I wonder..." Saya smiled wryly. "I wonder if this means we're getting closer to the origin of necromancers." Her cheeks lifted. "Oh Hecate... I thought it all a ruse but perhaps..." Her eyes followed the red streak that climbed into the sky in the distance. "Perhaps we're about to uncover something truly amazing."

"It may have to wait... Lord Dusk will be expecting our return."

88

AUSCH ENIMOR DELICATELY BROUGHT A STEAMING CUP OF TEA to his lips. A single button from his silver vest was undone when he set the teacup back in the middle of the saucer. The parlor at the front of the House of Dusk was silent in the early evening. Port wouldn't be banging on the piano for at least another hour, and Freya was too busy with her work to leave her room for very long. Saya and Hecate had yet to return, and Jeremiah quietly observed prayers in his room. Ausch felt his shoulders drop with a relaxed exhale as he finished his tea, knowing this would be the last moment of peace he would have for the next few days.

An hour after he was done with his tea, forty-five minutes after the cup and saucer had been returned to the kitchen, and thirty minutes since he'd begun going over the schedule he'd made up, did the first of two planned carriages begin to roll up the hill.

As Ausch rose, he buttoned up his vest, closed the schedule with a satisfying thud, and consulted his reflection in a shining vase before making his way to the front of the House, standing with his arms behind his back as Ilovo brought twin black horses to a halt.

Before the carriage had come to a complete stop, Marie swung the door open with the enthusiasm of a performer, skipping out excitedly. "Lord Ausch! We've returned."

"I see that..." He pressed his frames against his face, doing his best to up-curl his naturally downward-facing lips, not quite rising so high that they were parallel with the ground. "And who have you brought to us?"

"Let's see..." Marie put her hands together, interlocking all but her index fingers which she used to gesture to the carriage as it stopped. "We have four Heads of Houses, Lord Magnus, Lord Jamesson, Lord Cande, and Lord Rezin... and we have a prospective Head of House, Lady Schofield."

Saya beamed as the four men made their way out of the carriage, ignoring Ausch altogether as they marveled at the grandeur of the castle. Ausch stood unmoved as Antoinette disembarked, ignoring the castle altogether, meeting his eyes with her own emerald gaze, feigning a smile, and taking the edges of her dress in her hands, dropping into a low curtsy. "Good afternoon, My Lord."

Antoinette persisted in this frozen state as the Heads of Houses around her pointed from the fields, back to the road, then to the walls of the House of Dusk. Marie took care petting the manes of the horses while Ilovo unloaded the few bags that had been brought, setting them at the entryway, glancing at Ausch's unmoved figure for a moment before escorting the carriage to a building on the side of the house.

Ausch swung his gloved hand in front of his body dramatically, bending over in a deep bow. "Pleasure to make your acquaintance, Lady Schofield." As he righted himself, he reached his gloved hand for hers, taking it and bringing her up as he did.

Antoinette breathed a sigh of relief and smiled warmly as she reached for her small brown suitcase. Before she could take it, the handle was in Ausch's hand and his back was to her, ascending the stairs as the other men scrambled for their own belongings and clambered up the steps.

Marie watched curiously as Antoinette followed them, noticing how Ausch carefully set her small brown suitcase inside the hall as he waited for the entire party to file in. With two claps of his hands, the men began to quiet, attempting to look past Ausch to the hall behind him or attempting to round him to see the state of the parlor on his right. With each uninvited movement, Ausch's hands twitched behind his back, faintly hearing another carriage pulling into the space where Ilovo had just dropped everyone off.

"The House of Dusk bids you welcome. I am Lord Ausch Enimor, though I have forsaken my surname. You may refer to me as Lord Ausch or My Lord." He looked ahead to the carriage rolling in, catching sight of Hecate stretching as she descended.

"I'm..."

Ausch snapped his finger beside the man's face, silencing him and startling the others whose grins turned sour as Antoinette remained still and looked on. "There will be time for introductions later." Ausch adjusted his vest slightly, pulling it taught. "Lord Dusk has proposed a tour before the ball tomorrow. You will all have an opportunity to meet with the older members of the House in the hopes that our wisdom will allow you to correct your shortcomings." He looked to Antoinette as one of the men balled up his fists. "Or in your case, Lady Schofield, prevent you from diving into their pitfalls." One of the men turned to glare at Antoinette who mustered an embarrassed smile, listening to the sound of movement behind her.

"Due in part to Ilovo's tardiness," Ausch continued, "time is somewhat limited today, but we shall make do. This evening we'll show you to your rooms, tour the grounds, and you shall have the opportunity to meet with Port and Freya. Port is our resident entertainer who, despite his appearance, fetches a fair price for his services. Freya is our resident clothier who has, most notably, secured recent commitments with the prestigious Gold Family. Tomorrow..."

One of the men cleared his throat and raised his hand. "My Lord?"

Ausch exhaled, blinking slowly. "Yes?"

"These are the human slaves, isn't that right?"

"That we are." Hecate Serina brushed past the group and stood beside Ausch, donning a matching silver vest and trousers, standing almost as tall as him with one hand in her pocket. Her eyes glossed over the four men, instead landing on Antoinette, measuring everything about her: from the elegant black and white dress, to her figure, to the dark red lipstick that contrasted her green eyes. Antoinette measured the woman with an equal curiosity.

"Does that bother you?" Hecate returned the question to the man who'd asked it, a look of disgust on his face as he took in her appearance.

"This is Hecate," Ausch interjected before the man had a chance to answer. "Another former slave, in case that needed clarification. Hecate oversees transactions and mercantile. She secured the Gold Family relationship and routinely secures work for Port and distributes some of our other... assets." Ausch cleared his throat. "You'll all have an opportunity to learn from her as well."

"Looking forward to it," Hecate said brutishly, turning around and heading down the hall.

"As for myself, I primarily manage the House finances, investments, and real estate holdings."

"Lord Ausch." The same man raised his hand again, this time not waiting for a sign to continue. "That's all well and good, but we're here to be Heads of Houses, like Dusk, not..."

"...workers." The other men nodded.

Antoinette pursed her lips and looked away. She needed no further indication based on the events thus far to know this was both the wrong time to ask a question and the wrong question to ask. So, when Ausch's eyebrow twitched behind his spectacles, though subtle, she took a measured step back.

"It's refreshing..." Ausch said with a wicked smile, his voice deepening as Saya made her way past the group and into the House, avoiding all eyes, "... to think yourselves entitled to such a luxury, absent an inheritance. Perhaps you've come under false pretenses... but to be a successful Head of House you have to contribute. So, listen carefully so you can reflect on what Lord Dusk does as you consider how you manage your own Houses. The castle you set foot upon is cleaned daily, by Lord Dusk. The fields and food you will see on our tour is cultivated by his hand. The carriage you rode upon and the horses that led you here were both tended to by him. If that should be insufficient, an armory on the second floor is where he restores weapons to be resold. You will find however, that there is no throne for a Head in this House, because if there were, we servants and slaves would not stay to follow a man who believed it was our duty to serve him."

"Lord Ausch, I meant no..."

"When next you see Hecate or Freya or Port... ask them. If you seek a life where all is brought to you, where those around you are consigned to feed you, where you can believe yourself to be the master of your own world, I would venture that they would say a House is not the thing for you. You might ask yourself if you're better suited to be a slave. They can assure you, no one will challenge you for your cell."

Ilovo arrived behind the five visitors, shaking his head, his mouth slightly open, eyes gawking nervously at Ausch. When Ausch caught sight of him, he quickly flashed an abrupt smile that made everyone uncomfortable as he checked his pocket watch. "Ilovo, take Lady Schofield's things... we're already running behind."

89

HOURS AFTER THE ARRIVAL OF ANTOINETTE AND THE FOUR Heads, the group sat around a table in the ballroom, clapping excitedly as Port struck the last note of a melody and made his way over to them. The three rectangular crystal carafes that had been filled with blood wine had been emptied as the men each finished their third gobletful, while Antoinette nursed her first. At each sound she found herself quickly turning, hoping to see the man she loved, but in the hours since their arrival, he was nowhere to be seen. Her ring and middle finger pinned the wine glass to the table, surveying the stray humans who put the finishing touches on the already-lavish ballroom around her.

A dozen tables, each with a dozen seats framed the two sides of the ballroom. Each table, with the exception of the one they stood at, had a full fourteen-piece place setting and a clean white linen. Even Antoinette had only accompanied her mother, Lady Navara, to a single event with such formality and decorum.

In the center of the room, a grand piano was displayed with its top propped open, sitting on a large open floor that had been buffed to a near mirror finish. Around the room, the drawstrings of each crimson curtain had been drawn into tidy bows, and the overhead window was so clean that it appeared there was no ceiling at all. Each candle on the wall boasted an unburnt wick. To say the opulence was excessive was both necessary and appropriate.

"Too kind, too kind," Port said with a bow, bringing his own goblet back from the piano and standing around the men.

"I must say..." one of the men hiccupped drunkenly, "I worried you lot wouldn't know how to have a good time after those few hours with Lord Ausch." He slammed down the goblet. "But this wine is superb!"

Port chuckled, unrolling his long sleeves. "I'll pass the complements to the chefs." He buttoned his pinstriped shirt at the wrists, running a hand through his wild hair. "Once you're finished here... Lady Freya will be your next host."

"The seamstress?"

"*Clothier*," another corrected sarcastically.

"Clothier," Port repeated, his large grin shrinking slightly. "Her techniques are winning quite the acclaim, and even though *we* don't wear dresses..." he caught Antoinette's gaze, "...Lady Antoinette withstanding... it is a thing of beauty. An art, as it were."

One of the men groaned. "Do you honestly think she could teach us anything?"

Antoinette smiled politely, releasing the wine glass and rubbing her index finger against her thumb below the table.

Port scratched his chin coyly. "If nothing else, perhaps she could teach Lady Antoinette something while we fetch another crystal of wine?" He raised an eyebrow to their greedily nodding heads. "Lady Antoinette... how would you fair with a bit of time away from *these* men?"

Antoinette felt her heart skip a beat as she swallowed, steadying her hand. "If the Lords don't mind... I've actually been very curious about dressmaking. Is it quite... intricate, My Lord?" Antoinette asked slowly as Port called over one of the human maids.

"Indeed." He looked to the maid. "Another two crystals of wine, if you please." His gaze turned back to Antoinette. "Lady Freya could bore you to sleep with the details if you let her."

"And My Lords do not wish to join?" Antoinette queried the table once more, the men collectively eyeing the serving cart across the room from where the maid fetched the wine.

"Have at it," one of them said. "Port... I do say, our indulgence won't deprive the Coven, will it?"

"Nonsense!" another hiccupped. "They must still have rows of this in the cellar!"

"Indeed we do," Port said gleefully. "Drink your fill. You're our guests, after all." He observed how the men removed the crystal corks, staining the white linen of the table. "Madam..." He stopped the human maid. "Lady Freya's room is on the second story of the east wing, first door on the right as you ascend the stairs. If you would be so kind as to fetch her, could you inform her how excited Lady Antoinette would be to discuss dresses." He grinned broadly as she nodded.

Minutes later, Freya Serina bounced down the stairs and into the ball-room with a wide smile. Her arms swung in front of her happily as she waved at Antoinette from across the room, beckoning for her. Antoinette gripped her dress, dropping into a quick curtsy, leaving half the glass of wine as she hurriedly made her way over.

"Lady Antoinette, I presume?" Freya said, appearing in a blue gown with sewn-on crystals. A pair of matching earrings swung as she came to a stop. Her flame-colored hair flowed as it cascaded down one of her exposed shoulders.

"Lady Freya," Antoinette said nervously. "It is a pleasure."

"The pleasure is all mine," Freya spun on one heel to turn back around, walking away from the ballroom and towards the hall that led up to the second floor. "Port's message said you were very excited to discuss dresses."

"...Yes," Antoinette said hesitantly, following Freya up the stairs.

"My room is just up here. It's quite a mess but you'll be able to see every-thing I've been working on." She paused at the top landing. "Some of the work is what's called Avant-garde. That means experimental, so no laughing," she warned with a smile and a wagging finger.

"I would never..." Antoinette said sadly, reaching the landing.

"Like I said, this is my room..." Freya began, putting her arms across the doorway, blocking the majority of her dresses from view, "...and if you really want to talk dresses we can... but there's a door just over there," she pointed to the one at the end of the hall, "...to Lord Dusk's room... and he hasn't stopped talking about you since we moved in. So maybe you should pay him a visit, and we can talk dresses afterwards... if time permits."

Freya bit her lower lip, watching as the light came back into Antoinette's eyes as she approached the door, nervously turning the handle and pushing it open.

90

CHRISTIAN NIKOLAI DUSK STOOD FACE-TO-FACE WITH ANTOI-nette Katherine Schofield, an entire world of voices knocking on his ears and somehow remaining speechless as she slipped into his room, shutting the door behind her.

Her arms quivered as they slipped under his, a mild hesitation as she pressed her chest against him, then nestled her face under his, batting away her tear-filled eyes until his arms wrapped around her body, until he made her feel safe again.

"Christian." A single word was uttered, almost like a prayer to a God she thought had long since abandoned her, returned once more.

She paid no mind to his refined frame, to his chiseled face, to his longer hair. Everything about him was different on the outside, but he still radiated the same warmth he'd given her when Claire had died, the same comfortable and endearing sensation that made her knees weak as the embrace slipped onto the floor.

"I've missed you so much." His voice rang different now, different than that of the boy she'd loved, and different from the Lord who commanded the House. She couldn't have compelled him to love her any more than he did. His arms ware careful not to crush her, but to make sure that she knew she was protected in this place, in this room, in his familiar arms.

The passionate nights they had shared in the Schofield Manor over a decade ago were behind them now, but as Antoinette pulled back to take in his face, the memories came flooding back. Her arms reached for his cheeks, holding him steady like he might disappear again, like he might leave her for another five years. She leaned into his hand, pressing her own cheek against it before meeting his lips, boldly sharing the vibrant shade of crimson she had agonized over.

He was warm. Even as a vampire, he was always so warm.

She rose to her feet to share the color of the undergarments she'd picked out just for him. The flicker of the newborn candles that lined the walls breathed life into every moment of ecstasy as they rekindled a flame that circumstance had resigned them to abandon. While those four Heads of Houses below drank their fill, these lovers did the same, two sets of fangs and two pairs of lips delighting in everything the other had to offer.

They took a familiar position under the sheets, staring up at the same ceiling once again. "I could stay here forever." Her hand reached for Christian's, her fingers finding a place between his, her head finding a spot atop his chest. "I could love you forever."

"Tomorrow I should be free of my duty..." The light returned to his crystal eyes, "...and once you start your own House..."

"You'll come?" she sighed excitedly. "And we can put this mess behind us and live each night like tonight. Live in the same house. Eat meals at the same table. Sleep in the same bed. Pick up where we left off."

"Be a family," he whispered. "Get married?" He wondered out loud for the first time, not catching how her eyes lit up and her cheeks flushed. "Though I would settle for being your servant again... to be under your command."

"I will never command you again." She bit her lip, legs moving under the silken covers.

"It's strange..." he smiled stroking her head, calming her feet. "What being vampires robbed us of... perhaps being vampires can pay tenfold."

"Time?"

"Time."

"But that's not all... is it?" She looked up at him hopefully. "Your letters were cryptic... there's something more, isn't there?" She traced a circle on his bare chest.

"Being a vampire... being a Listener... it might be able to return to us the things we've lost."

"You mean Claire?"

"Not just Claire." His lips kissed the top of her head. "A goal I've been working for day in and day out which nears completion... to also return the child Michael stole from us... to bring back our son from the Red World... a second chance for all of us to be a family... while we still have time."

"Kill yourself."

"Quiet!"

Antoinette turned her head away from him, making her way across the room to the journal on his desk, unashamed that his eyes were upon her naked body, but unwilling to let him see her cry. "Oh Christian." Tears ran down her face, falling onto the journal sadly before she leaped into bed again, sliding under the covers, taking his arms and wrapping them tightly around her as she closed her eyes.

91

ANTOINETTE IRONED OUT THE WRINKLES IN HER DRESS AS BEST she could, not recognizing the blissful gaze that stared back at her from the mirror in Christian's room. Her hair was a mess, her skin was aglow, but a quiet fear loomed in the back of her mind, dismantling the joy she felt.

A knock at the door made her jump back and she stood in quiet paralysis in his room. Christian had left to speak with the other Heads of Houses who were drinking the night away in the ballroom.

"Lady Antoinette?" The somewhat familiar voice of Hecate pierced the doorway. "May I come in?"

Antoinette unlocked the door, taking a nervous step back, standing tall, a few hairs still out of place atop her head, doing her best to warmly smile with her green eyes as her hands clutched at her dress.

Hecate opened the door to Dusk's room, slipping inside quickly and returning the door to its closed state. Her nose winced at the smell of the room, eyes surveying the untidy bed and the woman who stood silently in the middle, attempting the same mannerisms as Saya.

"Lady Hecate..." A deep curtsy, mirroring the one she offered Ausch was interrupted.

"I'm a slave Lady Antoinette. Both formality and honorifics are wasted on me."

Antoinette stood up slowly, taken aback. Her eyes washed over Hecate, donning the fine silks that any Lord would be happy to wear. Her short dark hair was indistinguishable from many suitors who had pursued her before Michael. Her physique was betrayed, not by the atypical trousers and vest, but by the way her clavicle hugged her bodice, protruding in a delicately unabashed manner. "Mother would have agreed with you, but I am a visitor in your home."

"Right..." She slipped a hand in her pocket, looking at the woman who stood before her. Her long dark hair framed her soft-featured face. Two stark green eyes looked both calmly and curiously towards her as her flowing dress hugged her features, accentuating an elegant necklace that she wore. Dainty bare feet were barely visible and her arms, absent any muscles, meekly carried the same grace and presence. "Lord Dusk is keeping the other guests entertained, and Freya is finishing her work. I would be pleased to show you to your room for the night... we can avoid the ballroom."

"Oh..." Antoinette looked sadly to the bed, "I thought perhaps..."

Hecate reached her free hand over her own hair, scratching the back of her head awkwardly. "I can convey this to Lord Dusk, but he..."

Antoinette nodded, sitting on the edge of the bed and slipping on her shoes, ignoring Hecate's gaze as she watched, unaware that she puffed out her chest.

"He's usually careful, you know?" Antoinette said softly.

"He *is* overly cautious," she agreed, opening the door and leading Antoinette down the hall, walking slower than usual so that her visitor could keep up.

"Our Head Servant had a low tolerance for mistakes. Christian learned quickly... some of the other boys did not."

"Did Lord Dusk have many friends growing up?"

"Not particularly." Antoinette paused briefly, "Does he now?"

She grinned. "Not particularly..."

"Was Elise your friend?" Antoinette blurted out nervously.

"A fellow slave... and yes, a close friend."

Antoinette paused again. "He loved her, didn't he?"

"Perhaps this is better a conversation for you and..."

"He must have loved her to risk the future we were planning." Hecate stopped a few steps ahead of her. "He almost got himself killed avenging her... that's what others who were there said. Is that not what happened?"

"In Lord Dusk's defense... he almost got himself killed avenging you too," Hecate retorted.

"How... what do you mean?"

Hecate scratched the back of her head, posture tensing up. "Again, perhaps this is a better..."

Antoinette reached for and took Hecate's free hand. "Please, Lady Hecate. He would tell me if I asked him... but in these matters he often confuses his intentions with their perceptions."

"Lord Dusk... is a good man." She inhaled with a sigh. "...But the man you see now is not the same who left Evan Blood five years ago. He is not the same man who brought me and my sister to this place... That man was a man determined to exact revenge on the one who hurt you, at any cost. It fueled his transformation... it consumed him... but not at our expense. Never at our expense. He would have died in the pursuit of his revenge, or yours... or your child's... but he succeeded." Hecate smiled. "He's always loved you... even in the company of Elise... even as others could have offered him the same." She looked away nervously. "He is a man capable of much affection... sometimes it's easy to mistake it for more. It's not his intention to confuse... but he raises us up when our destiny was to stay down. Would you blame us if we tried to offer what little we have as repayment?"

Antoinette swallowed nervously. Her eyes looked Hecate up and down, her feminine sensibilities truer the more they spoke, and a nervous question she could no longer repress began to spill out of her mouth. "If I could ask one more question, have you and Chri..."

A steady metronome of footsteps interrupted the conversation and heralded Ausch's arrival around the corner, causing both Hecate and Antoinette to jolt. "Forgive the intrusion," he said as he approached. "If you don't mind Hecate, I can accompany Lady Schofield to her room." She raised a curious eyebrow, looking back at Antoinette who nodded hesitantly. "We have some estate finances to discuss. You *are* welcome to join." He bent his elbow, standing beside Antoinette who locked her arm with his.

"I think I'll pass," she said as they made their way down the hall.

Antoinette turned to her, catching her gaze once more with a timid smile before continuing along with Ausch. "Forgive the haste, but Lord Dusk has asked me to draw up the deeds to do away with the Schofield Manor. I need only a few signatures and a few moments of your time."

"Don't you need," Antoinette hesitated nervously, "Michael's signature?"

"It was already obtained," Ausch said curtly, walking in lockstep with Antoinette at his side, losing a half step as Antoinette froze for a moment. "Your signature is merely a formality. Occasionally, when it comes to middle-class estates, having all parties, even those not directly responsible for the estate sign away their rights, makes the process airtight."

"Middle-class..." Antoinette could hear her mother hiss in her mind. It was an insult to everything Navara Schofield had worked for, to everything she had sacrificed for under the thumb of Ivar Schofield and yet, as she recalled the sparse furnishing of the house, the lack of servants, and the diminished state she'd fled from five years ago, perhaps a middle-class skeleton of a home was more than she deserved.

"This way." Ausch ushered Antoinette towards a staircase that climbed to the third floor with a single room. In the center, a small table with neatly arranged stacks of papers was surrounded by a wall lined with books. The room unfolded into a large space with a variety of weapons, hammers, anvils, and other smithing tools beside a cobblestone fireplace. "If you'll take a seat, I'll guide you through the relevant portions..."

Antoinette sat with her back to the books, looking at the workspace before her. "Is this where he comes to work?"

Ausch looked up from the documents to the other half of the room where the smithing equipment was. "Indeed it is..." He paused for a moment. "Did he tell you that?"

She shook her head. "It feels like him. Calm. Deliberate. Functional." She smiled. "Apologies, My Lord, but before we begin... what do you plan to do with the Schofield Manor?"

"My preference would have been to sell it," Ausch said, re-organizing the documents on the table. "However, Lord Dusk instructed me not to. The Schofield Manor as you knew it will be demolished."

"I see..." Antoinette said sadly, taking the quill in her hand, signing the first document, a tear in her eye.

"...In its place, Lord Dusk has commissioned a school to be built which will offer literacy free of charge." Antoinette's tear of sadness landed as a tear of joy as she signed the next document. "We have commissioned instructors for the foreseeable future..." He picked up another document, adjusting his glasses and skimming the paperwork. "Alexandria and Akolai Globaria."

"Akolai and Alex..." Antoinette took the employment offer with a big smile. "Christian really does raise everyone higher, doesn't he? He's always been like that, even when Cla..." Antoinette stopped suddenly. "What about...?" Ausch looked at her curiously through his round frames. "The construction...?" Antoinette said cautiously. "Will it... disturb the land?"

"Ah," Ausch adjusted his glasses. "Lady Dusk's grave may be disturbed, but she will be returned. Our construction administrator is intimately aware of the significance. We plan to build over the basement and her adjoining resting place. I shall personally oversee the foundation to ensure Lord Dusk's orders are carried out to a tee."

"Lady Dusk..." Antoinette said with a nostalgic smile, "...what a beautiful name."

92

FOR THE FIRST TIME IN OVER A DECADE, ANTOINETTE KATHERINE Schofield spent the morning talking, loving, and reminiscing with her former servant turned Head of House, almost as though no time had passed. But through the hours of the morning and into the early evening when the whole of the House was set to wake, it was not Christian who fled before Evelyn Barett Webster could catch him, but instead Antoinette who quietly ran barefoot through the castle, shades of the girl she used to be in her smile, down the path that Hecate had shown her hours before, to the quiet room that would keep her secrets. With a grin almost as wide as her face as the voices from the other Heads of Houses buzzed in the corridor outside, Antoinette feigned a groggy yawn, pressing her dress before nonchalantly emerging into the hall she had just come from.

"We hope your night was pleasant." Jeremiah Ethan Andor, resident cleric and newest member of the House of Dusk appeared in the hallway, arms tucked in the sleeves of his silver robes, absent his vermilion sash.

"You're the cleric?" one of the heads said, adjusting his trousers and forcing a wrinkled shirt into his pants.

"A proud devotee of the Old Religion." Jeremiah's eyes closed slowly, his bright red hair giving his face a more human skin tone. "We always seek oth..."

"Let me stop you right there." One of them raised his open-fisted hand in front of him. "The four of us have been together a long time, and we don't worship but one God. He's golden. He's round. He's valuable." The three other men nodded and chuckled.

"I always appreciate being in the presence of true believers."

"How's that?" the man asked.

"Just like me, you worship a God who does not reveal himself to you." Antoinette hid her smile through pursed lips. Like a slow-moving beacon of light, the realization washed over the other men whose faces collectively soured. "In any case..." Jeremiah said, turning to Antoinette before they could retort, "...we're finalizing the arrangements for the guests who should arrive momentarily. Ilovo will make the announcement once the first carriage arrives. We do hope you'll be timely."

As the sun began to set, the first of a dozen carriages arrived at the House of Dusk. It was Freya Serina's glowing face and eccentric blood-red dress that greeted the guests and chaperoned them from the main hallway to the ballroom, delighting in watching their faces drop in adoration of the magnificent splendor. Ilovo, Jeremiah, Ausch, Marie, and Port greeted the guests as they arrived in the ballroom, taking their coats, offering them wine, and inviting them to mingle. Without exception, each of the first few carriages elevated the mood as the vampires from the Evan Blood Coven swayed to Port's lively piano-playing.

"It's already quite a turnout," Ilovo said with a grin, following Freya back to the main entrance. "I could see to the rest of the carriages..."

"Nonsense!" Freya said proudly, adjusting a rogue strand of her red hair. "I love seeing their faces. It's quite a delight... being a thing of marvel."

"You were always a thing of marvel," Ilovo said earnestly, watching as the next carriage came up the road, squeezing her hand.

"And you were always sweet to me…" Freya beamed, kissing him quickly, then pulling away. "But no time for that today!" She clapped her white gloved hands excitedly. "Do you think this one will be Lord Jason's carriage?"

"Not unless this is the last one." Ilovo crossed his arms, shifting awkwardly in his red-accented suit. "He'll be last." He squirmed. "He likes to make an entrance."

"Ilovo!" Freya smacked his elbow. "The fit is fine. Stand up straighter and you wouldn't be so fidgety." Her cute scowl made him stand up a little taller. "See? Better, right?" Ilovo nodded, a faint blush invisible under the moonlight. "This next carriage looks a bit fancier." She held her hand over her brow, squinting to see further. "It could be Lord Jason?"

"That will be the Elders' carriage. Did you ever meet them?"

Freya put a finger to her lips. "Only when they brought Hecate and I in. They have their own special blood brought in… so they didn't come down much, if at all… I can't remember them coming down but maybe once or twice when we were little… and once or twice when Lord Dusk was locked in the Silver Cell."

"Mind your words around them…" Ilovo straightened up, standing taller. "They'll turn on you in a heartbeat… and they can hold a grudge."

The carriage slowed to a stop, elegant purple accents shining brightly under the moonlight as the driver opened the door to five purple-robed old men. They followed the pair down the hall without so much as a raised brow or word of adoration. Even as the doors swung open to the ballroom, the Elders didn't say much, moving like one collective unit towards a vacant table.

Freya and Ilovo took their leave in opposite directions, unaware that Ausch, as he had done so with every guest who took a table, approached the group. His suit, an elevated version of Ilovo's, with distinguished cufflinks and a pointed tailcoat made him appear as a noble.

"Boy!" one of the Elders barked at a human servant who stood only a few feet away as Ausch watched on. "Fetch us some wine!"

Ausch's hand clenched behind his back as he took in the sight of the five men and the human that had been secured for the ball. With a quick step, he whispered in the human's ear, sending him hurrying out of the room as he approached the table. "Gentlemen, Lord Dusk has requested we prepare a special reserve for the Elders of Evan Blood."

"Ho?" One of the Elders raised a brow.

"I was informed..." Ausch began, bending over the table, his voice above a whisper, hard to hear through the other conversations around him, "...that the Elders would appreciate a *younger* vintner." Their eyes greedily grew wider as the helper returned with a wooden cask which he set on the table, handing a small prybar to Ausch who opened it, retrieving the wide-based crystal decanter inside. "Regrettably..." Ausch said as he pulled the stopper from the top of the glass, "...we could only manage to procure one bottle's worth."

As Ausch split the wine between the five glasses, four of the Elders inhaled the aroma, salivating from behind their cracked lips. "If I might inquire... Lord...?"

"Ausch. Ausch Enimor." He bowed.

"Lord Enimor... precisely how aged is this particular variety?"

"There are no words to describe how aged it is," Ausch said cryptically as the Elder's eyes grew wider with anticipation, ignoring his departing bow as Ausch turned around, a look of absolute disgust that he had been able to keep at bay now ravaging his face.

"Lord Ausch?" Antoinette approached him quickly as he walked away from the Elders' table. "Will Lord Dusk be joining us soon?" A dark green dress made her eager green eyes stand out all the more. Most other vampires in the room wore an outfit, but only Ausch and Antoinette knew how to command it. Everything from the way their hair fell, to their stance, to the way they carried their arms. It was clear that they were the only ones not pretending.

"Freya just went to call the remaining members of the House. I expect they will join us momentarily."

93

Hecate Serina stood nervous in the presence of the reflection that stared back at her in her room. An ornate black dress with a crimson trim and large train much better suited for her sister fit her body oddly well, though her face was sterile to the beauty. As she spun around in her room, catching herself at different angles, she resolved that while the clothes she wore on a regular basis—her trousers, vest, and button-down shirt—arguably revealed more about her figure than this dress did, the illusion of who the dress made her appear to be unnerved her. So, when Freya burst through the door to her room as she often did, Hecate was startled.

"Sister!" Freya squealed with delight, wearing a dress with an inverted color scheme: red with black accents, instead of Hecate's black with red. "You look amazing!" Freya wrapped an arm around her sister's waist, squeezing into the oval mirror in front of them.

"It's a beautiful dress..." Hecate admitted, her lips twisting up in a smile that didn't climb any higher up her face, despite her sister's open-mouthed gawk, "...but it doesn't feel like me." She tossed the ruffles of the dress and she ran a hand over her exposed collarbone.

"I know," Freya pouted. "But it looks so good!" She bounced up and down next to her sister.

"She's right." Dusk appeared with a soft smile at the doorway to Hecate's room in a white button-down shirt, looking at the sisters, a small wooden box in his hand as Hecate turned around, her shoulders dropped, her face flushed, a shy smile that matched the dress more so than the woman.

"See!" Freya beamed. "Even Lord Dusk agrees with me."

"I..." Hecate looked down.

"Actually Freya... I was agreeing with your sister." Freya's face fell, her lips plumped, and her eyes went wide and starry as her sister's expression changed, cheering up some.

Hecate's arms wrapped across her covered chest nervously as she turned away from him. "Perhaps I'll change?"

"Freya, can we have the room?"

Freya nodded, walking past Dusk as methodically as she could, shooting a nervous glance at Hecate as Dusk kicked the door closed.

"Lord Dusk?"

"I brought something for you..." He held out a small wooden box which Hecate took nervously. "An accessory to wear... if you wish."

Hecate's fingers ran along the corners of the box, shifting from one side to another, trying to find an angle where her shoulders wouldn't feel so exposed beside him. "Freya wouldn't be happy..." Hecate joked, "...about not wearing this dress she made... or even about you choosing now of all times to accessorize."

"She's outside."

"I wouldn't be happy about Freya eavesdropping either. It might even want to make me not wear the coat she's worked so hard on." Dusk said loudly, causing her to squeal on the other side of the door, then innocently whistle and scramble in the hallway. Hecate laughed, leaning against her vanity, silently staring at the box. *"A House of slaves and urchins,"* Dusk said with a grin, looking at Hecate's unwavering face. "That's what Jason called us the other day."

"Does that offend you, Lord Dusk?"

"The truth is difficult and we often take offense to it. It's hard to swallow, but easy to digest. A lie is the opposite... isn't it the same with that dress?"

"I want to make you proud. I want to make Freya proud. I want to make the House of Dusk proud... especially since you said you'd be entrusting me with it... when the time comes." She bit her lip nervously. "It would be best if you just told me." She nodded affirmatively. "Simply tell me to wear the dress. I do better at following orders."

Dusk laughed, taking a step closer to her, rolling up his crisp white sleeves over his forearms, angling the mirror towards the two of them. "I could tell you... to put the box down." Hecate did. "I could tell you to... stand up straight." She did. "I could tell you to... stand by my side." She did, nervously brushing shoulders with him. "I could tell you to..." He thought for a moment, "...to tell me that you would be comfortable in that dress."

She looked herself up and down in the mirror, then looked away, reaching for the box again, desperate to have something to hold onto. "I... can't."

"That's the part of you ready to lead, telling you your answer." His warm smile lit up the room.

"I'm sorry." She extended the closed box to Dusk, which he pushed away.

"Fortunately, this particular accessory was meant to go with whichever outfit you chose."

Hecate nodded, batting away a tear from her eyes as she slowly lifted the hinged box. Her eyes squinted as she turned around, setting the box down under the falling light of the moon through her window. "Is this...?" She pursed her lips as she turned to face Dusk, a broad smile that finally climbed from her lips to her eyes as she gave him a tight hug. "Thank you, Lord Dusk... it's..."

"You." "Perfect." They said in unison.

94

JASON CASTILLE'S EYES SQUINTED AS THE HOUSE OF DUSK CAME into focus. He had been to the castle only twice: once as heir to the Alastair Coven, and once in the immediate days after his coup, hunting for anything of value. Now, as the former Red Crescent Coven came into frame in the middle of the night, the moon high overhead and a sea of torches lighting the way, his mind measured how magnificent it was compared to Evan Blood.

"Ilovo!" Jason appeared in a silken, all-black coat with a dozen rings spread across his fingers. He rode in a carriage all his own.

"Lord Jason, welcome to the House of Dusk. Right this way."

As Jason made his way down the long hall, his eyes darted between pristine artwork, elegant fixtures, and an inviting hallway that widened as it headed towards the ballroom. "Christian certainly has made himself at home in the house I've permitted him to use."

"Yes, My Lord," Ilovo said with a humble smile, his arching back betraying him as he led his former Master down the hall.

"I do wonder if the space could be better used. Surely a meager House doesn't need all this space, does it Ilovo?"

"Perhaps..."

"Perhaps I'm right?" Jason continued heading down the hall.

"Perhaps multiple houses could coexist here?"

"Multiple Houses?" Jason paused in the hallway for a moment, looking at Ilovo's grin. "What a marvelous idea. Perhaps we could have each of the slaves start their own House." Ilovo's grin began to fade as his sarcasm grew. "And to top it off, why not have *you* start a House too? The House of... is Ilovo your surname?"

"...is that such a ridiculous idea?" Ilovo asked nervously. "That other members of the House of Dusk... or even I myself... could start our own Houses?"

"Ilovo... my boy..." Jason clapped his ring-laden hand on his shoulder. "Leave the aspiring to the adults. We carry both the ambition and the sentence." He looked around the hall. "Too much opulence may be skewing your perspective. The strong and smart are born to lead, the pathetic rest are born to follow..." He listened to the sounds of voices and laughter growing as they approached, disregarding Ilovo's pained expression. "...And occasionally one slips through the cracks... but let's see exactly how much pomp and circumstance a common follower can bleed from a stone."

"...Yes... My Lord..." Ilovo rubbed his twitching leg, tossing open the doors, staring forward as the crimson landscape of the ballroom unfolded before his eyes.

A dozen tables filled with vampires from Evan Blood laughed, ate, and drank, paying no mind to Jason Castille as he walked through the doors. His eyes scanned the room, counting more than a dozen waiters scurrying back and forth, refilling wine, taking dishes, and bringing out more food in a chaotic and precise waltz.

As Jason made his way to the Elders, his eyes counted the silverware at each place setting, feeling oddly uncomfortable with the number of knives, forks, and spoons surrounding each of the small stacks of plates. When he arrived at the Elders' table, he noticed the elegant decanter, now emptied of its contents, replaced by a common square one, just like the rest of the tables.

A man in the middle of the room played the piano with an elegant precision that made many of his fellow vampires swoon as they witnessed the feat, clapping between indulgent sips of wine.

The black-on-black outfit that Jason wore muted him against the backdrop of other vampires wearing their fancy dresses and brightly colored ensembles. He played with one of the rings on his hand as the Elders tried to make small talk with him, his eyes still surveying the room, looking for the 'slaves and urchins,' unable to find anyone who fit the description. Even as he angrily took the gobletful of wine and drank it, his neck collapsed in delight: a thousand times better than the swill they had recently had, and ten times better than anything he had had at Evan Blood in a long time.

"Where is Christian?" Jason asked angrily, raising his glass for one of the servants to fill.

One of the Elders shrugged.

"Who cares?" another asked, tearing into a thick cut of steak.

"If his arrival means an end to this amenity..."

"...let him never show his face!" another cackled, joining in another drink.

"Ilovo!" Jason snapped his fingers, pulling him away from his glass of wine. "Where is Christian?"

Ilovo took another glass from in front of Freya and looked towards the doors on the far side as they were thrown open with a loud bang. "Here he comes now."

95

Port's piano playing stopped. All eyes turned and all conversations quieted. Everyone looked towards the main entrance. Christian Nikolai Dusk stood in the center of the doorway, a black form-fitting coat with a deliberate and chaotic web of crimson threads adorned his body. As he moved, the stitched threads swayed beneath the hems, freely flowing in the air like the ends of a spiderweb, giving a breath of life to the fabric.

To his right, Hecate Serina stood tall by his side, her arm locked in his, wearing the elegant black dress that Freya had made for her. Her face was calm, her eyes were serious, and she stood proudly by her Lord, escorting him to the center of the room, chasing away the blush of embarrassment as her ears caught wind of the whispers, and instead taking joy in their envy, avoiding Antoinette's jealous green eyes.

As Dusk made his way to the piano, Port dropped the feather board, his playful exuberance turning into a serious and satisfied grin as the members of the House of Dusk assembled around him.

"Esteemed members of Evan Blood..." Dusk raised his hands, surveying the room. "...Council of Elders..." The Elders assented. "...And finally, Head of the Evan Blood Coven, Lord Jason Castille..." Jason stood up, sucking in his stomach and nodding affirmatively. "The House of Dusk, first participant of the Evan Blood Coven's House System... bids you a warm welcome." The room applauded, as did Freya, excitedly waving at everyone from her position around Dusk. "Before we carry on..." He nodded to the human servants, who approached all the tables with fresh goblets of wine. "I invite you to toast... to the legacy of Evan Blood!"

"Hear, hear!" several chanted excitedly as everyone raised their glasses, taking a collective sip.

Dusk smiled, looking out at the faces, eyes lingering on Antoinette a little longer, her proud look of approval urging him on. "Lastly... I would extend *our* leader, Lord Jason Castille... an opportunity to address his House and his Coven. Lord Jason?"

A few hesitant claps quickly spread as Jason proudly made his way forward, standing face-to-face with Christian Nikolai Dusk, a glass in his hand. As he neared, he realized just how small he was in comparison to Dusk now. Their roles were not reversed, but it felt like they were. Jason still stood in the center of the room and Dusk still had only a few allies, but the fearful man who'd knelt before him five years ago was gone, and a behemoth of a man, more reminiscent of Bruce Alazar stood in his place.

"Thank you, Christian." Jason clapped awkwardly while holding a goblet. "Five years ago it seemed unfathomable to me that you, a once-servant, could turn a handful of slaves and an errand boy into anything more... but here you are, much to our enjoyment." Jason raised a glass with a laugh. The collective faces of Hecate, Freya, Port, and Ilovo struggled to remain unfazed and Ilovo took another nervous drink from his goblet. "Remarkable as it may be for me to say... as I see you lot up here today, I think it would make for a more joyous occasion for me to declare that the House of Dusk has satisfactorily completed the task assigned to it. To celebrate this joyous occasion, another round of wine. To the success of the House Charter!"

"To the House Charter." Everyone clapped.

"To the House Charter," Dusk whispered under his breath as he drank.

Once Jason had returned to his table, Port took his seat back at the piano and began playing, leaving everyone to eat, drink, and approach the members of the House of Dusk individually.

Freya's hand reached for Hecate's and pulled her aside. "Sister!" she hissed for the second time in an hour. "Why are you wearing the dress? What did Lord Dusk say to convince you?"

"He..." Hecate blushed, playing with the dress nervously. "I'll tell you later."

"No..." Freya pulled her outside, where the sounds of voices were quieter. "You tell me now. I know you. I know you were going to change. What did he do?"

"He..." Hecate scrunched her nose. "He gave me something."

"The accessory? I overheard. What is it?" Freya took her hands, looking past the black nail polish on her fingers. "No ring." She pushed Hecate against the wall, looking at her ears. "No earrings." Her eyes went up to her hair, then down to her collarbone, then back to her wrists, then finally she shook the bottom of the dress to see her feet. "What did he give you? You're not wearing anything else..."

"It's not visible."

Without missing a beat, Freya crouched down, reaching up Hecate's legs until she got to her thighs, feeling Hecate's hand smack her over the head, but continuing on, feeling something on Hecate's thigh. After a moment of running her hands over the object, her face pinched up. "Really sister?" Freya crossed her arms angrily. "Really? Sister?"

"It's an... accessory."

"It's a..." Freya lowered her voice, "...knife! He gave you a knife on a garter."

"First of all..." Hecate began, wagging a finger in the air. "It's a gift. He reforged the knife that broke when we captured Mikey and added a silver edge. Second... it would be rude to turn it down and third... it... it makes me feel like me..." She tugged at the dress. "Even in this, okay?"

Freya shook her head, progressively smiling as she did. "Port hired an artist for this ball as a surprise... you and I are going to pose for a painting... and then you owe me a dance, okay? That is your penance."

Hecate pursed her lips and nodded. "Fine... but for the painting... can I hold up the knife?" She lifted her dress over her thigh, pierced by her sister's stare. "Joke! It's a joke."

96

ANTOINETTE FOUND IT HARD TO TAKE HER EYES OFF CHRISTIAN as Ausch paraded him around the room, meeting and mingling, smiling and nodding, repeatedly glancing her way as the night went on. From a common seat at a common table, she watched the man she knew he could be unfold in front of her eyes, exuding power and grace. Many members of Evan Blood celebrated the man who hosted them, unaware of the mask he wore and the weight of the toll it had on him.

While other members of the House of Dusk, like Port, Freya, and Marie were naturals to the socialization of the ball, others used the opportunity to appeal to a broader audience. A small gathering of younger vampires listened to Jeremiah's preachings as he tried to recruit more devotees, making headway with some, but increasingly less as the wine flowed freer.

Antoinette's hand traced the outline of the black and white curio around her neck as Christian made the rounds, absent Ausch, finally arriving at her table. "Lord Dusk." Antoinette could hardly stifle a giggle as she said these words, listening to the others around her table introduce themselves, leaning into the conversation, smiling and laughing with the other members of Evan Blood like it were one of the many parties that her mother had taken her to. It had always felt uncomfortable, but then again, Christian had never been allowed to attend.

Their conversation was interrupted as Port's silver knife struck his glass chalice three times, each time progressively quieting the room, prompting the humans to begin to shift the tables to the edges of the room. The guests collectively raised their eyebrows curiously.

"My fair vampires..." Port smiled, rolling up his sleeves, "...as the night beckons for the day, so does this piece beckon for couples. Find a partner to hold and dance with, as I play this, my latest piece... *The Heartbeat of the Red World.*"

Christian held out a hand for Antoinette to take, intercepted by Freya Serina who winked at her. "He's all yours after this... promise," she said with a gleeful smile. She took Dusk to the middle of the room then quickly pulled Hecate in and forced them together, giggling as they bumped into each other, grinning as her sister reached her arms over his head and felt his hands at her waist draw her closer.

With a satisfied grin, Freya reached for Ilovo, wrapping his arms around her and leaning against his chest happily as other vampires coupled up and joined them. Ausch extended his hand to Antoinette who happily took it, rotating him as they arrived on the dance floor so that she could watch Dusk and Hecate.

As Port began to play, the couples held each other closely, some closed their eyes, others giggled, and still others found waves of embarrassment wash over them. The music began slowly, a delicate smattering of scattered notes that were more akin to simple sounds. As Port played more, additional notes brought harmony to the composition, giving the couples something to sway to and rock against. Still, Port carried on, striking more and more notes until the music was a symphony, echoing from the walls and ceiling, breathing beautiful life into everyone who listened: an elegant melody repeating serenely.

But the longer Port played, the more notes he folded in, injecting chaos into the beauty.

Antoinette closed her eyes as Port's gentle and deliberate key strikes turned aggressive. The notes he played overwhelmed the piano, swelling into a chaotic and discordant barrage of sounds that made several of the couples stop altogether. The room turned to watch the madman at the piano as his fingers disfigured beauty into noise. His feet slammed down on the pedals, his hands ran amok at both ends of the ivory keys. His careful finger placement devolved as ten fingers controlled two keys each, striking in unison. He rocked back and forth on the bench, the swelling of the noise causing others to plug their ears as his forearms banged and banged, each key a snowflake swallowed into an avalanche of sound and then, at long last...

Silence.

Port slammed the feather board, rising to his feet with a satisfied sentiment of catharsis as Dusk looked on.

A single clap from the far corner of the room emanated from Marie who opened the room up to applause, joined first by Saya, then slowly by the rest of the House of Dusk. The Evan Blood Coven joined in nervously, unsure of what they had just witnessed.

"Thank you," Port said sincerely, eyes only upon Dusk, receiving a small nod of approval and making out the word *incredible* on his lips. He inhaled deeply. "And now!" he said loudly, addressing the entire room. "Let's transition to something more conventional."

With these words, he returned to his seat, lifted the feather board, and began to play, the nervous room of vampires returning or exchanging dance partners, a wave of relief washing over them.

Hecate brushed her cheek against Dusk and whispered something in his ear with a smile before she made her way off the dance floor. Just as she had with Hecate, Freya took Antoinette, matching up her hands with Dusk's, watching with a giggle as Antoinette fell into his arms, giving her another wink before running over to Port's side, praising him as he happily drummed away on the keys.

At the corner-most table of the room, Hecate took a seat beside Saya and stared at the back of a canvas as a painter in the corner surveyed the room, his eyes darting from Hecate back to the canvas several times as he applied brushstroke after brushstroke.

"Freya's going to have us pose later..." Hecate mumbled, pulling up the dress. "She'll probably want it hung at the entrance..."

"Would that be so bad?" Saya closed her eyes as the guests continued to dance.

"I..." Hecate's eyes narrowed as Jason Castille stumbled across the room, bound for the members of the House of Dusk he hadn't recalled meeting.

"Jason's coming." Hecate's whisper perked up Saya.

"Ladies..." Jason Castille's bloodshot eyes undressed his paranoid temperament, and the table served as his crutch, a sprawled hand resplendent with rings upon the fine white linen of the only table that, as yet, appeared undisturbed. "That was quite a spectacle, wasn't it?" His eyes glanced over to Port. "As you know, I am Lord Jason Castille, Head of Evan Blood... and I don't believe we've had the pleasure yet." His eyes climbed Hecate, from her dress to her collarbone, and eventually to the sour face that stared blankly at him as he wagged one of his fingers. "Wait... you were one of our slaves... weren't you?"

Hecate's tongue lapped the inside of her sharpened teeth. She could still remember his wanton torture of her when she'd been a slave. Her scars had healed when Michael had Turned her, but she hadn't forgotten how Jason had carved up her leg for joy, or how he'd toyed with Elise's flesh. "Indeed I was," she responded cooly.

"I remember you..." He pointed lazily. "I think." His eyes measured Saya in the same lecherous manner, starting at her feet and then up her simple dress to her statuesque face. "But you are new... But not a new vampire?"

"Quite perceptive, My Lord." Saya's soft voice and frozen stare made every action appear more jagged than it was.

"Is something wrong with your face?" Jason forced his eyes wider, leaning closer to Saya, looking at her unchanging pupils, his breath heavy with iron and alcohol.

"My eyesight is poor, My Lord... it's difficult for me to see you... you blend into the darkness."

"How exactly does a vampire have poor eyesight?" He raised a brow.

Hecate was about to interject from beside Saya, raising a hand, when Saya pinned it down. "An accident, My Lord. A jeweler was resizing a ring my betrothed had promised me. He was a poor man and believed the ring to be iron, which in fact was silver. The grinder shredded part of the ring, sending splinters of silver into both my eyes. They were removed... but as you are undoubtedly aware—if a wound inflicted by silver heals, it always leaves a scar."

"Tragic," Jason said monotonously, looking towards Dusk as he danced with Antoinette, then catching Ausch's eye as he made his way over calmly. "And... you... are...?"

"Ausch Enimor, My Lord." Ausch took a spot beside Hecate, trapping her between Saya, himself, and the wall. "An honor to..."

Ausch was about to bow when Jason scratched his chin. "Where did Christian find *you*? You seem to be the only one capable here between slaves, servants, dejected clerics, and invalids. Where do you come from?"

"Lord Dusk and I came to terms on a business proposition. A unique venture," Ausch said, holding Hecate's wrist as her hand reached for the blade on her thigh.

"Is that so?" he asked skeptically. "And what pray tell is this unique product?"

"Vampirism, My Lord. We sell... immortality."

Jason stood in stunned silence and a few of the human servants stopped in their tracks. "Surely you jest." He looked around the room nervously, the humans scattering back to their jobs, lending an ear to the conversation. "Christian's barely cobbled together the requisite number of vampires... you expect me to believe you've been Turning vampires for profit?"

Hecate's hand relaxed as she pulled it away from Ausch. "Not all who are Turned would make good housemates, but coin is coin. Ilovo could attest to it, if you wish to hear it from a more reliable source. How else would you expect the tax we regularly contribute? You said it yourself, My Lord. With songs and dresses?"

"I..." Jason cleared his throat. "Perhaps I *will* ask Ilovo. I should be getting back to my Coven soon. The last time a Head was gone too long... well..." He grinned mischievously, finishing the wine in his cup and heading towards the main entrance.

"...Do you think that was wise?" Hecate asked Ausch when Jason was out of earshot, crossing her arms over her chest. "Ilovo may cover for your lie, but what about the others?"

"Eventually he will ask. Eventually the future of the House of Dusk, your House, will require an explainable income stream. Better on our own terms than on his. Besides..." Ausch said with an innocent shrug, "...it *is* plausible. Isn't it?"

"Your prudence wanes with each drink." He adjusted his glasses. "No more for the rest of the night. Understood?" Ausch grinned. "Understood?" She reiterated.

"Very well..." Ausch said, his grin turning into a sigh. "Though I do not believe my state to be so far gone... At least my lies are believable."

"...What lies aren't?" Hecate asked fearfully.

"Ilovo's. I overheard him at another table just now saying that Lord Dusk is heir to the Evan Blood Coven." Ausch laughed awkwardly. "Isn't that absurd?"

97

As Jason Castille departed the House of Dusk, Hecate Serina unceremoniously pulled up at her dress to take larger strides, marching her way behind Dusk, faking a smile to the four Heads of Houses that surrounded a table that Ilovo was at, and sinking her nails into his wrist as she abruptly pulled him out of the ballroom, only releasing him when they were outside, hurling him onto the ground.

"Lady Hecate?" Ilovo blinked slowly as he stood up, the wounds from her digging nails healing as he did. "Is something the matter?" He stumbled as he got to his feet, nearly falling into the cellar doors leading to Michael Escoté's former underground holding cell. "What's wrong?"

Hecate folded her arms with disgust at the hunchback in front of her, his eyes bloodshot and veiny, a pitiful stare of abject indifference across his starry eyes. "What were you telling those men?" She looked around as she spoke, ensuring no one was eavesdropping.

"It's wonderful..." he smiled, brazenly placing a hand on her exposed shoulder. "If Lord Dusk takes his place... you can keep this House, and I can have one too!"

Hecate's mouth opened slightly, trying to connect the pieces to a puzzle she didn't quite understand. A moment later, Freya and Port appeared behind her in their bright red ensembles. "Sister... we saw you storm out..." Freya's bright smile was dashed by the ire on Hecate's face as she shoved Ilovo back. "What happened?"

"Your sweet Ilovo has been telling others that..." she lowered her voice to a hiss. "Lord Dusk is the heir to the Evan Blood Coven."

"It's true!" Ilovo announced with open arms. "It's true! And it's the answer to everything!" Port put a hand on Ilovo's shoulder nervously, walking him further away from the former Red Crescent Coven as Hecate stormed forward. "I've thought about it... Lord Dusk takes his rightful place. Hecate... you take over the House of Dusk. And I..." he patted his chest, "I get my own House and Freya... if you want to come with me... you can!"

Freya's face opened slightly, just like Hecate's, unsure of what to say when Port interjected. "Ilovo... you've had a bit too much again. Why not go and sleep it off."

"Wait." Hecate raised her hand. "Is there any truth to this?"

"I can't start a House of my own. Jason won't let me. But if Lord Dusk is Head of the Coven, he will. It's true."

"Does Lord Dusk... know?" Freya asked nervously.

"Does Jason?" Port asked quietly.

"Does Jason know?" Hecate asked sternly.

"No? I don't know?" Ilovo shrugged. "Does it matter?"

Hecate's hands rubbed at her forehead nervously. She felt hot for the first time in a long time, the voices in the ballroom interrupting the silence as her brows furrowed. Her chest rose and fell as Port and Freya watched on edge, waiting for her to break the silence. "If Jason knew... he wouldn't have let Dusk live." Port nodded slightly. "If Jason finds out... he might order him killed."

"Or change the line of succession?" Freya asked nervously, looking for an agreement from Port that didn't come.

"No one else can find out," Port said as Hecate brought a nail to her mouth nervously. "The four Heads of Houses... we need to make sure they don't know, or didn't take you seriously, otherwise we're all in danger. Ilovo, you can't say anything else. You have to convince them that it was all an elaborate joke."

"No," Ilovo said bravely. "I deserve this. I want this."

"Lord Dusk doesn't—he's made that quite clear. He wants to leave, and you want to put him front and center and in danger. How selfish can you be?"

Ilovo scowled. "Give me the House then."

"What?"

"When Lord Dusk leaves—give it to me." Hecate clenched her teeth. "I've known him longer. It should be me."

"*It should be me?* It could have been you!" Hecate growled. "We only had five years to prove ourselves. You had over a decade."

"Hec..." Freya put her hand on her sister's shoulder before it was shoved off.

"It could have been you if you were deserving. You're not. Not of this House, and not of any House according to Jason."

"Hecate..." Port tried to restrain her as she advanced, causing Ilovo to fall to the ground as she towered over him. Freya stepped between them and Ilovo's terrified eyes reflected the red from her dress for a moment before Hecate pushed her aside.

"Strike me," Hecate boomed. "Challenge me for it, Ilovo." She held her arms open as Ilovo retreated, wind swaying her dress. "You're a pathetic coward Ilovo... I hate it, but I tolerate it, for them, and for Lord Dusk, and for this House... but today you crossed a line that jeopardizes his life, and ours, and you don't seem to care. So, you will stand up... and you will go back into that room... and you will convince those vampires beyond a shadow of a doubt that you were joking. And then you will pray that they believe you and that no harm comes to this House because if it does, seek counsel from Jeremiah and his Gods—I will smite you where you are." Hecate turned around, her nails curled into her palms, a bloody trail on the floor beside her.

Ilovo got to his feet weakly, punching his leg to stop the shaking. "No! Not unless you give me the House... this is the only way I can have my own." His voice quivered as he spoke, interrupted by a hiccup, watching the back of the woman in front of him drop her head in frustration before turning around.

"Freya..." Hecate said sadly, turning to her sister as she reached under her dress. "We can do this my way, or we can do this your way."

Freya nodded slowly as Port sank his hands into Ilovo's shoulders, forcing him to his knees before Freya.

"Ilovo..." she said with a sad smile. "I'm sorry... but... you will go back into that room... you will do your best to convince those vampires and any who ask that you were joking, and you will not discuss this matter any further, with anyone." Freya's eyes flashed red as she finished speaking, a ring of compulsion from the Executive Command reflected on Ilovo's eyes.

"Understood." He said mechanically, rising to his feet and returning to the house.

98

"Y OU WERE A BIT HARSH." PORT WALKED IN LOCKSTEP WITH HECATE, back to the ballroom, trailing behind Ilovo who had already returned to the table with the four Heads of Houses, making small talk, laughing, and drinking deeply from a glass in front of him, ignoring the piercing stare of Hecate at his back.

"Is the gravity of this lost on you?" She returned to her table, absent Saya. "This could endanger everything we've built and our very lives... and for what... a whim?"

"He wants to be someone Hec. He's always wanted that."

"By gossiping? Or blackmailing? Or undermining?"

"Tell me you wouldn't do the same if Lord Dusk ordered you to."

"I..." she sighed. "Not at the expense of your lives. I am loyal to him, yes..." She held up a finger. "I would risk my life for his ambition... but not yours."

"Is it because you love us?" Port fluttered his eyes, leaning across the table. "We love *you*." He batted his eyes faster. "Hecate Serina... I love you." She couldn't fight the grin growing under her scowl. "Say it back... say 'Port, I love you.' Say 'Port, I would have your babies if I could.'"

Port pressed his nose against hers, attempting to reach her with his lips which she batted away playfully, shaking her head. "You're a real pain sometimes, you know?" He grinned and stole a kiss from her cheek before skipping towards the piano.

Freya approached her nervously, avoiding Ilovo's eye contact as he laughed and joked, unable to fight her Executive Command. "Sister..." Freya began, "are we really in danger?"

"Freya..." Hecate sighed. "I don't know, and that's why I'll be here... watching."

"Should I tell Lord Dusk?" Freya looked over at Dusk, Antoinette's table was finally vacant with just the two of them, a broad smile on both of their faces as they talked.

"No..." Hecate said sadly, looking at them. "Let him have this night. He's waited too long for it."

"And Ilovo?" Freya looked at his table with a deep feeling of guilt.

"Leave him be... he has his orders..."

THREE YEARS AGO

FREYA SERINA HUMMED TO HERSELF AS SHE CLOSED HER EYES, LAYING down in the setting summer sun looking up at the clouds. A simple flowery dress was all that stood between her and the grass, a delicate arm over her forehead shielding her eyes as her sister approached. "Hecate... do you think Lord Dusk would be mad if I didn't want to become a vampire?" She squinted to look up at her sister in her brown trousers and dirt-covered shirt.

"Where's this coming from?" Hecate took a step in front of the sun, her shadow falling over her sister. "Once Lord Dusk is back from his trip, he and I will be going after Michael... we've talked about this for almost two years."

"I think... I want to be a mom." Freya blushed nervously, fiddling with the bandages on her fingers. "I think I could be a good mom, and you could be a good aunt, and if I become a vampire... I can't be either."

"And who would be the dad in this arrangement?"

"I don't know... but I have time... and if I become a vampire... I lose that."

"...I don't see why there's any rush." Hecate turned to look up the hill to the House of Dusk. "I don't think it needs to be today or tomorrow... but once we get Michael... I *will* be Turning." Hecate paused as her sister sat up. "Do you plan to tell Ilovo?"

"He shouldn't mind... we're just having fun. He's even said that when I find the right person that he'd understand."

"If you say so... I'll head back inside. You coming?"

"Once the sun sets."

"Suit yourself."

"You'll miss them too, sister..." Freya said with a smile, laying back down. "Once you're a vampire, you'll miss seeing them. Sure you don't want to join me?"

"I'll join you next time... I'd better get up there before Port..." A loud thump from the piano shook the ground as Hecate sighed, stomping up the hill. "Never mind, too late."

"FREYA?" HOURS LATER, ILOVO'S VOICE BOOMED AS HE MADE HIS WAY down the hill, a broad smile upon his face. "Hecate is asking about you. Come inside!" His eyes caught sight of her signature red hair and he walked over with a grin. "Freya, you have a bed now. You don't need to sleep on the ground." His brown eyes looked to her closed eyes sweetly and he placed his hand on her shoulder. "Freya?"

He rocked her back and forth gently, his smile fading as he shifted her, a low hiss getting louder as he did, his brown eyes seeing through the darkness, clear as day, as a snake slithered away, the faint scent of Freya's blood still hot on its fangs.

"Freya... please wake up." His lips quivered and his eyes went wide, shaking her nervously. Her limp body cooled in his arms as his tongue retreated behind his own fangs, fearfully inching closer to her. "Freya... please... please wake up."

99

BEFORE THE CELEBRATION WAS OVER, AN ABSENTEE ANTOI-nette and Dusk were not missed. As the guests drank, night turned to morning and only a few carriages remained while the couple walked through the halls, hand-in-hand, broad smiles on their faces. "Once this is all over, I'll be going to check on your future home. To make sure it's ready for our family, for the day when Jason approves your own House."

Antoinette nodded earnestly, idolizing a man her mother would have chosen for her in a heartbeat. Here he was, in a palace greater than theirs, with more respect than any suitor, and without any of their ego, content to just exist by her side. "Are you worried?"

"What about?"

"The... thing," she whispered, too aware of how walls generally had eyes, ears, or both. "It's taboo... isn't it?"

"We're alone," Dusk said calmly, the Red World affirming it. "Resurrection has never been fully understood, but with the necromancer blood and with the knowledge I've spent these past years honing... I'm confident that if anyone can do it... it's me."

"Claire... and... our son?" Antoinette said nervously. "Is that everyone?"

Dusk paused for a moment. "No. Elise, and the others who have helped me... is that a problem?"

Antoinette gulped. "You love her, don't you?"

"I do."

"Like you love me?"

Dusk shook his head. "No."

"Does she love you, like I love you?"

He pressed his ear to the Red World. "...At times."

Antoinette looked down at her feet. "My father... Michael... and how many others? Women bore and men move on. Even my mother knew it when Aubrey came to live at the house. What kind of woman would I be if I wasn't bothered by the notion that you wouldn't need to go far to find someone waiting with open arms? What kind of wife could I hope to be if I willingly invited that?" He opened his mouth, but before he could speak, she continued. "And what kind of woman would I be if I forsook a once-in-a-lifetime chance to live a life stolen from her." She smiled somberly. "You put me in an impossible position Christian Nikolai Dusk: to trust you, where every other man has failed."

"You could command me," he shrugged. "You could command me to stay faithful to you if you do not trust me."

Antoinette exasperated. "I won't... I won't ever command you again and I trust you even in the presence of those I don't. You do these things to me Christian... surround yourself with women far more capable, often more beautiful, just as loyal, and even more truthful and expect me not to feel... insecure." She bit her lip. "It's not fair."

"What *is* fair?" He responded with a smile, continuing down the hall. "Eating scraps when the kitchen was bursting at the seams? Burying my sister for fear that she would have been burned like garbage? Sleeping under the same roof as another man took my spot on your bed? A chance encounter once a decade while we reminisce over all we've lost?" With each question, Antoinette's head fell further. "The Gods have cursed us sufficiently, we needn't do it anymore to ourselves, especially when there is a chance to take back what we've lost." He held both of her hands in his, his bright blue eyes looking into her glowing green ones. "Whatever happens Antoinette Katherine Schofield—I will love you always."

"Do you really mean that?" Her eyes twinkled. "Even if you don't like me one day... even if you hate me one day... would you still love me then?"

"I would never ha..."

"Christian?"

"Even then."

Antoinette leaned forward, wrapping her arms around him, kissing him deeply and passionately, holding his body as close as she could. "I'll always love you too. I hope you don't forget that."

"I won't... don't you forget it either." He grinned.

"I would never."

A pair of deliberately heavy footsteps announced Hecate Serina's presence before she turned the corner, finding the pair standing side by side with a guilty innocence that gave them away. "Forgive the interruption..." She said awkwardly, keeping her distance. "Only a pair of carriages remain, and the last one has been reserved for our other four guests."

"I'll take my leave." Antoinette reached for Christian's hand, squeezing it gently before running past Hecate, turning once more at the corner to catch his gaze again.

"My Lord," Hecate said with crossed arms as she approached. "I have good news and bad news."

"Let's start with the good."

"Though I suspect you may know it already... Saya and I were successful. We've located the site and her eyes confirmed it. We're confident we found it: the tomb of a necromancer."

"The key to resurrection," Dusk said with a smile. "Hopefully still intact. Were you able to recover it? A body? Blood?"

"No, My Lord. It's part of a property that's fenced off... Ausch has already been notified. He departed to attempt to acquire it so we may excavate without any prying eyes... unfortunately it's near a quarry."

"Ausch left?"

"Yes, My Lord... I may have had something to do with that..." Hecate said nervously. "That brings me to the bad news..."

"...Ilovo?"

"Ilovo."

As the four Heads of Houses departed on the final carriage bound for Evan Blood, Hecate and Dusk stood at a window, the former filling in the latter of the events that had transpired.

"...Did you know?" Hecate asked nervously as the final carriage rolled out of sight. "Did you know you were the heir?"

"I did," Dusk said plainly, trying to keep the Red World at bay. "But I made my plans clear to you. To you all."

"How do you want to handle Ilovo?"

"The sun is about to rise... the anger is high... and the wine has flowed. Difficult as it may be, we'll sleep on it and tomorrow, as a House, we come together and decide."

"If we wait..."

"...I'll be able to Listen. In the morning, I will find out if anyone has told Jason anything. We'll find out if we are in jeopardy. For now, get some rest. Tomorrow promises to be a long day."

As most of the House turned in, Port drew the curtains and continued playing a soft melody for the painter and human servants who hurried to finish up. The painter took the completed canvases to be framed while the human servants stored the remaining blood wine, picked up the dishes, covered the skylights, and tidied the ballroom before thanking Port and leaving the House of Dusk to its members once more.

Port gently struck the keys, finishing up his goblet of wine as the House slumbered, most accustomed to hearing him practicing at all hours, unbothered by his elegant melodies.

The sun was high in the sky when he finally played his final note, setting down the feather board and sprawling his body atop the piano, closing his eyes with a goofy grin of satisfaction on his face.

In the midday hours in the House of Dusk, every vampire slept, though some more soundly than others, until Christian Nikolai Dusk's dreams were interrupted by a panicked Claire.

"Brother! Wake up! Get out of the House now!" Her voice pierced the Red World, startling him awake. *"Get out of the house. You're in danger! Get out now!"*

100

"**B**ROTHER! *WAKE UP!*" CLAIRE SEFIRA DUSK'S VOICE PIERCED THE Red World, startling her brother awake. *"You're in danger! Get out now!"*

"Kill yourself!"

A spark from a fuse had been lit in the cellar.

The Red World collectively fed him information as the spark traveled down the wire. Dusk ripped his bedroom door off its hinges, standing in the doorway for only a second. "Wake up! Get out now!" he shouted.

Hecate Serina's door on the second floor of the House of Dusk was closest to his. In the moment between his booming voice calling out and the sound reaching her ears, she didn't have a chance to react. Her door was shoved off its hinges.

Hecate lay asleep atop her bed in only her short underpants with the blinds drawn, still happily wearing the silver blade garter she had been gifted. She didn't register the command before she felt Dusk wrap her in her bed-sheet and hold her close. Her eyes barely opened before she realized what was happening, as the sound of her room's shattering window deafened her, as the pair flew through it to the ground below.

The fuse's light traveled greedily towards an unmixed crate of alcohol below the parlor.

Dusk's solid frame cracked the hardened dirt below as he landed, Hecate rolling from his arms, wincing for a moment before Dusk covered her with her black bedsheet, shielding her from the sun. His leg didn't shatter this time, and as Hecate opened her mouth to wonder what was happening, the ground below her began to grumble as the fuse reached its first barrel.

"Launch me." Dusk took her hands and folded them on the ground so she would understand, stepping in her interwoven hands. "Tell the other wing to get out! I'll get this one."

Hecate panicked, raising her hands with all her force, throwing off the sheet she wore and sending Dusk flying over the second story of the Coven, landing on top of her room and crashing through the ceiling above. "The others!"

Hecate could feel the ground warping under her feet as she ran around the building, the sun beginning to bleed through the fibers of her bedsheet. Before she could make it to the opposite wing where Saya, Marie, and Jeremiah were, she heard an explosion and finally realized.

An elaborate network of aisles in the cellar ran underneath the castle. One of the barrels had ignited and exploded under the parlor.

Another explosion shook the ground and a frightened Marie opened the window to her room and jumped out with a shriek. Hecate managed to catch her before she landed. "Hecate?" she winced, clutching the shadows on the side of the wall, wearing a nightgown, trying to avoid the sun to no avail.

"Hide in the wheat..." Hecate tore her away from the wall and Marie made a beeline. "No wait... it'll burn. The carriage! Go to the carriage house. It's covered!" Marie changed her path, wincing with every step as she threw her arms over her head. "Jeremiah! Saya!" Hecate cried out nervously. "Get out!"

Another fuse branched with excitement on a journey all its own. The explosions multiplied.

Hecate winced as she looked up to Saya's window, still not opening. Jeremiah Ethan Andor appeared, bursting through his own and crashing onto the ground below with Saya in his hands. Hecate couldn't get under them quickly enough to soften the impact and Jeremiah landed on the ground with a loud thud, letting out a groan as his legs snapped.

"What's happening?" Saya held out her hand for Hecate to take, righting herself nervously, removing her shawl to cover Jeremiah's skin.

"I don't know. Get to the carriage house. I have to check on Freya." Saya nodded, scooping up Jeremiah with a strength that didn't fit her small frame and walking forward hurriedly.

Each explosion blew out more panes of glass, cracking the walls of the House of Dusk.

"Freya!" Hecate barreled back towards the spot where Dusk had landed with her, breathing a sigh of relief upon seeing Ilovo and Freya now on the ground with him. She threw her arms around her sister, tears in her eyes as Dusk patted the singed coat Freya had made for him that he had thrown on, wincing as the sun beat on his feet and face.

"Hecate... what's happening?" Freya asked, completely confused.

The former Red Crescent Coven turned House of Dusk began to crumble as the ground continued to quake.

In unison, a dozen explosions coming from underground blew out the windows, toppled the walls, and sent thunderous ripples over the floor. Hecate squinted to look past Dusk at the crumbling castle, then looked around nervously from under her sheets-turned-cloak. She looked to the carriage house where Marie, Saya, and Jeremiah were, then back to Ilovo, Freya, and Dusk. "Port! Where's Port?" She stared at the House of Dusk, two fireballs reflected in her eyes when Dusk turned around to shield her, bringing her into his chest as another explosion sent a chunk of wall hurling towards them, striking Dusk's shoulder, sending him toppling over Freya and Hecate.

"He wasn't in his room." Ilovo quivered as he retreated, looking at Dusk's battered frame as he righted himself.

"He must be in the ballroom. He's in the ballroom! We have to get him!" Hecate screamed, pushing Dusk off her before another loud explosion decimated the few still-standing walls. She threw off the bed sheet, ignoring the sun's glare and running forward, a violent explosion blowing her back like a ragdoll. A film of tears were on her eyes as she tried to get her footing again, but a powerful arm around her torso kept her from moving towards the House. "We have to save him!" she pleaded.

Her eyes had never been filled with so many tears. She looked back to Dusk, one shoulder shattered as he held her tightly with his good arm, her skin against his. She had yearned for a hold like this. But not this one. She didn't want him to open his mouth. She didn't want him to say anything. She had wanted him to hold her like this, her bare back against his bare chest. She had dreamed of an embrace like this for so long, but she would have given anything not to feel it now.

"We have to save him..." she whispered amidst the explosions and crumbling House.

Freya's lip quivered, wrapping her arms around her sister, looking from a nervous Ilovo to Dusk as he shook his head, letting Hecate fall into her sister's arms.

"It's too late," Port whispered from the Red World.

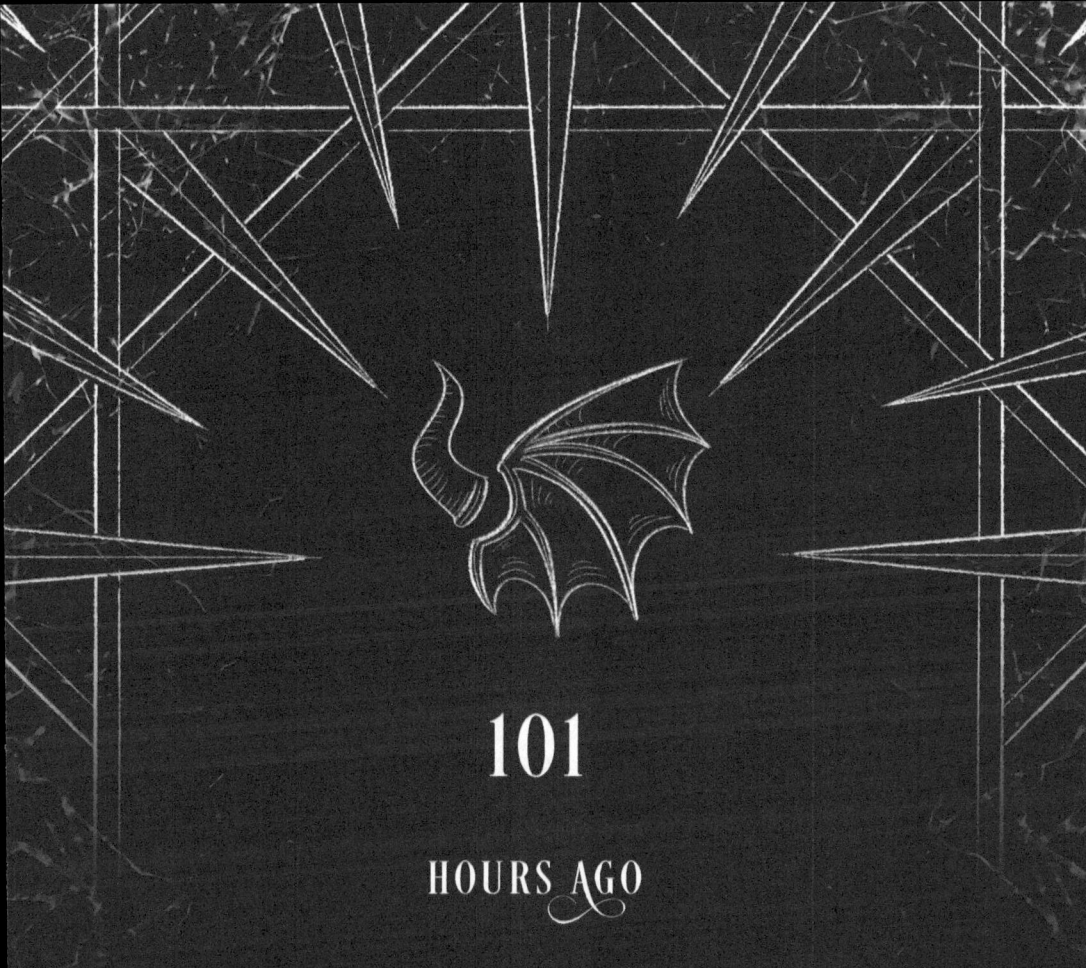

101

HOURS AGO

"**F**IRST, HE SPIES ON US. THEN, HE HAS THE NERVE TO MAKE *OUR* home his. Then he lectures us about how we can be successful. And to add insult to injury, he could very well claim Evan Blood as his own!" One of the Heads of Houses spat as their carriage, the final carriage, departed from the ball. "At least Jason was also a victim of Bruce Alazar."

The three other men nodded. "At the rate we're going we'll never take back our home, let alone give a second life to the name Red Crescent." He hiccupped.

"Just because we can't take it back, doesn't mean they should get to keep it." A wry grin overtook one of the four men. "I took a stroll through the wine cellar last night while everyone was busy... one fuse in the right place could erase it all."

"Are you serious?"

The man slapped on the side of the carriage. "Driver, stop for a moment."

"Are you really going to light it up?"

"If I wasn't..." the man reached into a small brown satchel at his side, "...would I have brought this?" The three other men grinned as they looked at a roll of wire in his bag. "Just cover for me until I'm back. For Red Crescent."

"For Red Crescent!" the others repeated drunkenly.

 THIS MORNING

HECATE COULDN'T REMEMBER EXACTLY HOW SHE MADE IT FROM THE wheat fields to the carriage house. She didn't remember when the explosions stopped, nor did she remember seeing the flames that toppled the House quickly erase their yearly harvest, stopping at the paved path around the structure they sheltered at. She couldn't remember Dusk leaving her side and nestling against her sister. She didn't know when the last time she blinked was, but her dry eyes fixated on the spot under the rubble where the piano had been.

A battered Dusk returned, sun blisters upon his face and a foreign body limp under his arms as Hecate's sadness turned to rage. "It was him." Dusk dropped the body in front of her. The man coughed as he sat up. A stream of blood spilled out of a corner of his mouth, revealing a crooked smile with shattered teeth as Dusk slipped deeper into the carriage house, his skin on fire. "A former member of the Red Crescent Coven... unhappy with us living in his former home."

"I have a name!" the man, one of the four Heads of Houses, spat. He looked at the House of Dusk circling him, unable to get it out before Hecate withdrew the silver blade and pierced his throat with a surgical precision. He fell to the ground, writhing in pain as Hecate stood up, pursing her lips and shaking away the tears that wanted to return, pressing her bare foot to his throat, harder and harder, until a snap made him go limp.

Saya watched with a morbid curiosity, Jeremiah bowed his head solemnly, and Marie looked away.

"Was it just him?" A pointed question matched the tip of her knife as she wiped the blood on his clothes, looking at Dusk for an answer.

"...Yes."

"The other Heads of Houses?"

"They knew."

"I'll kill them too."

"In time," Dusk said, slowly taking the silver blade from her hand. "In time."

"Lord Dusk..." Ilovo began nervously. "Is Port in the Red World? Perhaps Hecate could speak with him..."

"*...Present and accounted for.*"

Hecate swiped the knife from Dusk's hand, throwing off the bedsheet she'd been wearing. She pressed the tip against Ilovo's neck, pinning him against the side of the carriage house. "You! You're to blame. You're to blame for everything!" Her knife drew a drop of his blood as the House of Dusk slowly approached her. "If you hadn't invited them in! If you hadn't opened your big mouth! If you hadn't put us all in danger, I could talk to him now! I could see him now! I could tell his stupid face that I loved him like he begged me to last night!" Her grip on the knife tightened as everyone tried to calm her down, calling out her name quietly.

"I never wanted anyone to die..." Ilovo trembled. "I cared for him too."

"Not good enough!" Hecate's grip tightened around the blade, a cold emptiness in her eyes. In the moment when she wavered, Dusk pulled her away and pinned her to the ground. She writhed under him as he tried to wrestle away the knife, catching his wrist with the blade before Dusk snapped hers, a jolt of pain flooding over her body, desperately trying to overwhelm the anger and sadness.

"Freya." Dusk's voice was calm as he wrestled with Hecate, his forearm pinning her. "He has to leave."

"I'm sorry Ilovo."

"No. Freya. Not again." Ilovo trembled and he tried to run before Freya caught him. "Look at me." She commanded, his face turning to look at her, a flash of red as it did. It was a pitiable face, gaunt and afraid, attached to a weak frame. He retreated from her gaze as everyone except Saya turned away. "I can't protect you anymore..." Freya's own tears clouded her gaze. "You can't be here anymore." Her hands caressed his cheeks as his body, frozen in place, stared meekly at her. "As of this day..."

"Please, Freya. Please."

"Go, Ilovo. Go far from here. Go anywhere you want, but you are no longer welcome here. You are no longer a member of the House of Dusk, and you are forbidden from speaking our secrets aloud." She paused, seeing his eyes flash red. "Goodbye... Ilovo."

The red ring of compulsion faded.

His legs tried to keep him in place.

His eyes dared to look at Hecate who still flailed against Dusk as he pinned her down.

"I'm sorry," he called as his legs carried him away. "Please. I'm sorry." His arms shielded his head from the mid-day sun as best they could. "Lord Dusk. Hecate. Freya. Please. Please. Please!"

The further he went, the less Hecate writhed, laying on the ground nursing her broken wrist as Dusk stood up, draping his charred coat atop her body, wrapping a piece of fabric around his bleeding wrist, blue eyes taking in the smoldering mountain of their former home.

102

DUSK STOOD OVER A FRESH MOUND OF DIRT, NOW A PRACTICED veteran of gravedigging. Marie, Hecate, Freya, Jeremiah, and Saya stood around the grave, dressed in black. Three days had passed since the fall of the House of Dusk. For three days they had worked, moving rubble, scavenging a few personal effects, and eventually retrieving Port's body to give it a proper resting place.

"...What happens now?" Freya asked nervously, looking from the scar on Dusk's wrist to Hecate's healed wrist. "Even as vampires... this isn't something we can rebuild quickly... it would take years..."

"Ausch procured a house of worship in the city for me... you would all be welcome," Jeremiah said with a broad smile.

"Hecate and I have unfinished business... don't we, Hecate?" Saya said.

"We do," she said weakly. "Now more than ever. Lord Dusk?"

"These aren't the conditions I'd hoped to end on..." he said with a sigh. "...but it would be opportune to see how the House of Schofield is doing firsthand. It was constructed with many rooms... you would all be welcome there too."

"I..." Marie began nervously, "I'd like to accompany Hecate and Saya... if that's alright?" Saya looked to Dusk for approval, spreading open an arm to welcome her by his side. "Freya?"

"I think..." Freya said nervously, grabbing at her dress. "I would like to become a proper clothier... Is that alright, sister?" She nodded, putting her own arm around her.

"I would ask..." Dusk crossed his arms, "if one of you could wait for Ausch to return. He'll still be a few days."

Hecate nodded. "I'll inform him... Saya, Marie?"

"What's another day in the grand scheme of things?"

"I'll see if I can salvage any books..." Marie added.

"Does this mean you won't be returning?" Freya asked teary eyed, inviting herself to his side, wrapping her arm around him.

"No... If it's not an imposition, I'll be at the future House of Schofield with Aubrey. That's where you'll find me. Once Jason realizes what happened, I doubt he'll consider me a threat anymore."

With a firm handshake to Jeremiah, a light hug to Marie and Saya, a lasting hug to Freya, and what felt like an eternal embrace to Hecate, Christian Nikolai Dusk departed for the house that he had built for Antoinette, unaware that at the very moment that he departed on his days-long journey, Antoinette sat nervously at a desk, dipping her quill in ink, writing a letter to Christian, the address of the House of Dusk already on an envelope by her side, her hand trembling and eyes welling with tears as she wrote.

"Christian—I suspect that despite your relationship with Claire, she didn't have the heart to tell you, so it falls to me to be honest, to ensure that when the time comes for us to start a family again, it is with absolute honesty. First off, please don't be mad at Claire... I'm sure she had her reasons..."

After days of traveling, Christian placed his hand on the molding of the home he'd ordered constructed for the love of his life and knocked, waiting until Aubrey's tender hand opened the door, staring at the wide frame of the man who stood in her presence. "Christian!" She threw her arms around him happily. "Come in, come in! Dram!" she bellowed. "Dram! Put on some tea, we have a visitor!" A curly-haired teenager peeked out with his black eyes, looking at the behemoth who dropped a bag in the entryway of his home.

"...*I know that Claire has shared some of the tortures that Michael subjected me to. When I had the opportunity to speak with Hecate, she assured me of your vengeance, and though I wish you didn't have to put yourself in such a position on my behalf, your willingness to protect people is part of the reason that I love you. I love you so much.*"

"Christian! How long has it been? Three years?" Christian walked through the entryway to her home. The barren walls were now scratched and dented. The closets were now filled with clothes. The floors beneath the table were scuffed. As the timid boy watched the man who had killed his father from the stove, the happiness that Aubrey shone made him drop his guard. "Forgive the mess... if I had known..." She took a pair of socks from the chair and offered him a seat.

"I'm glad to see you're doing well." He looked around the room. The sparse house was now someone's home. It radiated love and emotion. Everything he tried to do at the House of Dusk unsuccessfully somehow lived in this mess, bringing a smile to his face. "Dram." Dusk smiled weakly as the boy's dark eyes looked at the powerful stranger.

"*When I ordered you away, I was pregnant with our son. I was overjoyed and nervous. Our plan was to raise him together under the auspices of the arranged marriage with Michael, but then we were attacked, and you were Turned, and I was Turned, and everything changed. I didn't know how to be a vampire then, and I knew only how to be afraid of what could happen if Michael realized the child was yours.*"

"Are you planning on staying?" Aubrey's warm smile still lit up the room. "I'll be honest, even though it's only three of us, we've spread out, but in a few hours we can have a room cleared for you..." She put her hand over her mouth. "Unless... are you kicking us out?" Dram spilled the tea as Aubrey said this, apologizing quickly and fetching a dishtowel to dry the table.

"Not at all," Christian took the towel from Dram, continuing to wipe up the mess, folding it neatly and placing it at the edge of the table. "This house is yours, in part, as long as you want it... though you should know, it is my hope that Lady Antoinette and I join you here in some time."

"Antoinette?" Dram asked excitedly. "Is Auntie Antoinette coming soon?"

"Soon is still to be determined, but for now, I come in her stead so that when she arrives, we have a room to stay in and a bed to our name."

"He didn't have your eyes, our son. Honestly, he looked a lot more like me than you. Perhaps that was for the best. Michael didn't suspect early on that he could be anyone else's. He was a clumsy child... He often dropped things or crawled into things. Michael got Aubrey pregnant shortly after you left and she had a son too, Dram. They played together all the time..."

"Come come!" Aubrey said, reaching out to take his hand. "Dram! Finish cleaning up!" Aubrey hurried up the stairs. "Take your pick!" She led him down the long line of rooms. "Whichever one you want... it's yours."

Christian looked down the line of doors. "Really Aubrey... any room is fine. We come from sleeping on floors, or have you forgotten?" He chuckled, as did Aubrey.

"We might... but Lady Antoinette doesn't. I'll clear out the largest room for you two. It's only fair. She'll still be the Lady of this house once she arrives."

"Eventually... Michael did find out he was yours. I didn't know about the Executive Command when I bit him... I didn't know how much more power he would have over me. One day, after I had Turned him, he compelled me to spill all my secrets to him, and one by one they came out: how I hated him, how you and I laid together, how the child was not his. His hatred towards me was solidified on that day. I stopped being his plaything and instead became his slave.

*Our child was three years old when he realized... when he killed him...
or so Claire had you believe...*

"Do you know when she'll come?"

"Not for the foreseeable future. A year or two is my hope. You have time.
It will be nice..." Dusk said, leaning on the side of the door to the room that
would become Antoinette's as Aubrey tidied up. "To live. To be part of a
family."

"Oh Lord Dusk!" Aubrey tossed the clothes aside and threw her arms
around him. "How insensitive I have been! To not offer my condolences for
the loss of your son, or my gratitude for this home you've offered us." Her hug
caught him off guard, but he smiled as she embraced him. "Thank you for
what you have done for us. We are eternally grateful. I know we both wish you
could have arrived in time to save your boy too, before Michael gave her that
disgusting order."

*"...I want to believe that somewhere deep-down Michael thought
I would find a way to break the Executive Command when he
ordered it so, but we both know it's not possible... not alone. I'm sorry
Christian—I'm sorry for not telling you sooner... but Michael
ordered me to kill him. I killed him... I killed our son."*

"...what order?"

"Brother—*it's best you don't know. Get out of there.*" But Dusk didn't move.
"*Brother please. Brother!*"

"He ordered her to..." Aubrey whispered sadly, "...strangle him to death."

*"I love you Christian. I will always love you. I'm sorry. I know
you said you'd always love me, but if you stop... if you stop loving me
that's alright. I'll never stop loving you, or our son, and wishing that
I could take it back. I would wait a lifetime for you.*

-Always yours, Antoinette Katherine Schofield."

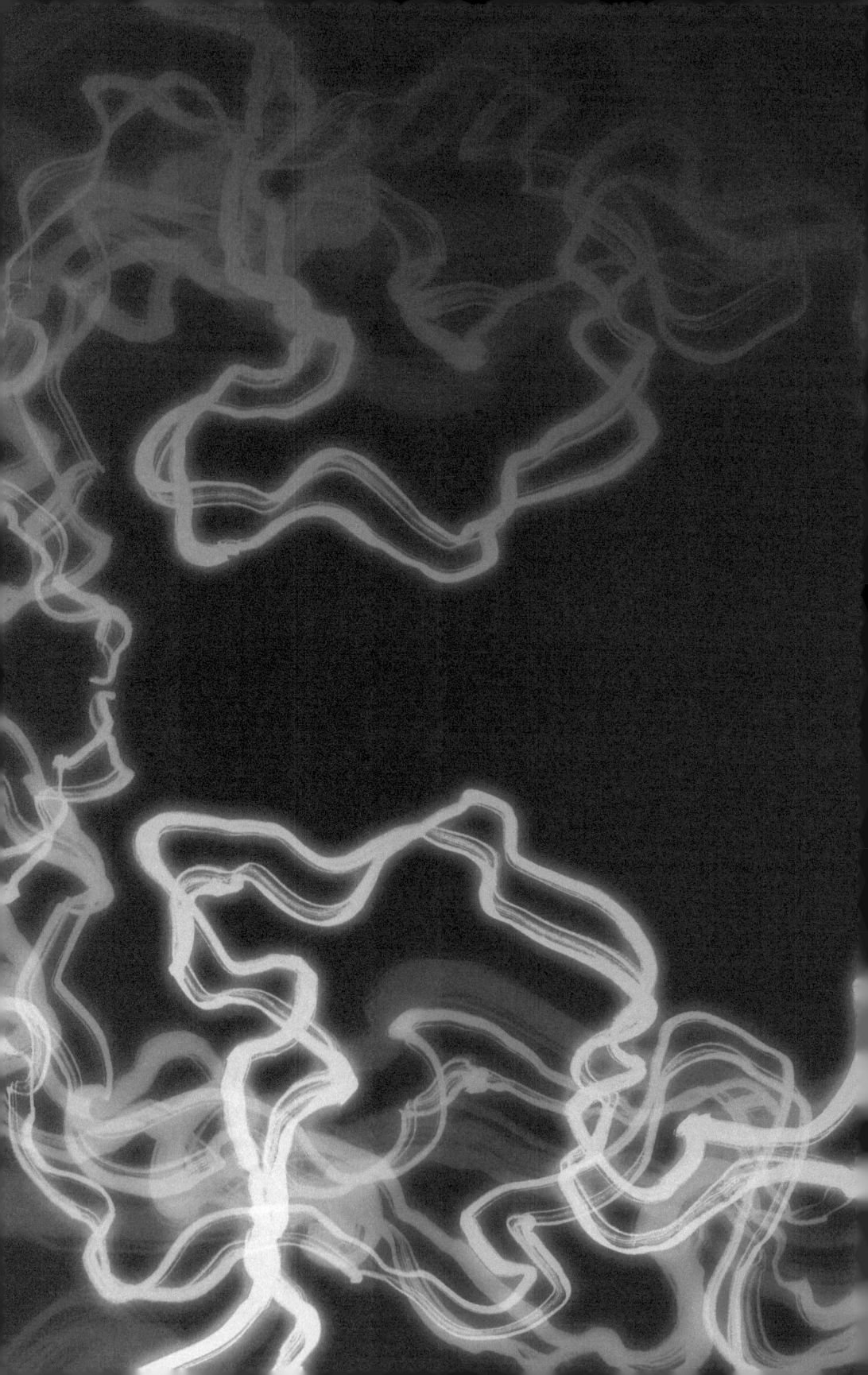

FIFTH REGRET

"I should have saved you."

-CHRISTIAN NIKOLAI DUSK

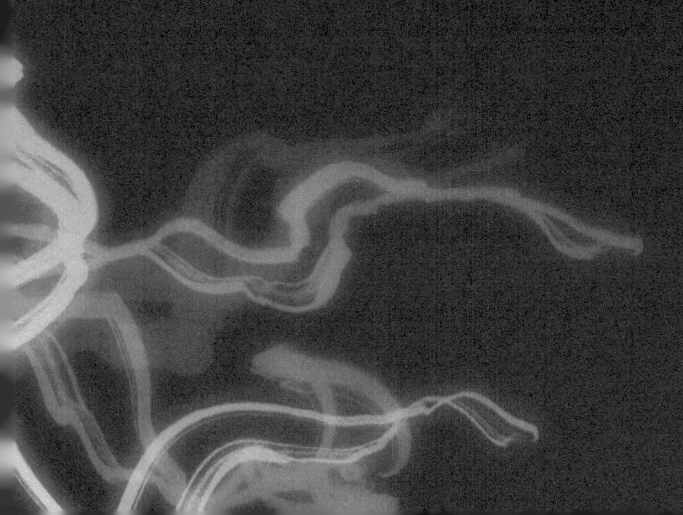

103

ONE HUNDRED SEVENTY YEARS LATER

Jason Castille, Head of Evan Blood, stood beside the prepared dining-room table in his Coven, adjacent to the split-level ballroom beyond the double doors from the Hall of Houses, surrounded by the allies he'd amassed over two centuries. Nearly two hundred years since he had allowed Christian to create his own House and welcomed Antoinette into his Coven, he now stood before a similar cast, ready to pass judgment again.

Despite digging Michael out of the grave he'd been left to rot in, Michael's testimony hadn't been enough to condemn Christian. Ilovo had taken the fall for his former Master and, with it, absolved him of any punishment. Or at least, any *direct* punishment.

Jason's face twisted as he presided over the trial of Antoinette Katherine Schofield. Her crimes were many: she had failed to report the new vampire she had Turned, Albedo; she had killed a fellow housemate, Arrah; she had maimed another, Orpha; and her once-housemates now defectors had caused her House to Fall.

You will not escape my judgment... and Christian... don't think you will get off scot-free either. Jason inhaled deeply, stowing his broken hand in his robes. "Orpha, you loved your arm. Didn't you?" She nodded woefully, playing the part he'd orchestrated for her. "And Antoinette stole that from you. So tell me, former member of the House of Schofield, what is something Antoinette loves? What has she revealed in the decades you have lived with her?" *Say it. Say his name.*

Orpha's face twisted, just as it had when she'd held Albedo against the headboard, blood spilling from his neck before Antoinette had intervened and Turned him. "Him." She pointed to Dusk. "She loves *him.*"

Jason folded his arms childishly. "Well, I believe I have an equitable solution..." *to punish you both.* Antoinette felt a cold shiver run down her body as Jason leaned over to Michael and whispered something in his ear, something that made his lips curl with delight. "Michael?" he asked gleefully.

"Blow out her ears brother!"

"I command you..." Michael began as Christian reached for the golden hairpins in Antoinette's bun, catching her eyes as he did, welling up with tears, "...Antoinette Katherine Escoté..."

"Run." Antoinette's eyes locked on Christian's for a moment as he reached for her hairpins, a ring of red in her eyes that caught his, that stopped him in his tracks. A ring of red that was mirrored in his eyes for an instant that forced him to bolt towards the door.

"Brother!"

Christian darted so quickly that no one realized. He flashed down the Hall of Houses, anger in his eyes, pain in his soul.

Run, she had instructed.

The Executive Command was absolute.

A BLUR OF WHITE ACROSS THE FARMERS' FIELDS OUTSIDE THE EVAN Blood Coven was easily mistaken for a patch of fog, and not a man. The former High Listener could scarcely see as his legs carried him through walls of water and over bogs of mud. The fine shoes he'd borrowed from Antoinette's departed housemate came undone as he ran. He wanted to turn back, but his body propelled him forward. He'd stop when it was safe. That was how it had happened when she'd commanded him to leave the Schofield Manor.

The scar beside his heart throbbed as the visage of the Evan Blood Coven disappeared behind his quick-moving body. He ran alone. For the first time in a long time he felt alone.

The Red World waited with bated existence to see what Michael Escoté would command his wife to do. Claire tried to keep an ear pressed to the Coven while staying by her brother's side as he raced through the land, further and further from Evan Blood, and closer and closer to the place he'd departed from hours ago. His breaths were shallow, his tear reserves empty, and he finally fell to his knees where Antoinette had fallen to hers when he'd lied to her and told her that Albedo was dead: the front steps of the House of Schofield.

"Coward."

"Brother, Antoin..."

"Silence!" For the first time in a long time, the Red World hushed at his hiss. For the first time in a long time, the Red World obeyed the High Listener as he balled up his good fist and struck a beam that held up the wooden porch, shaking the foundation of the home he'd ordered built for them so long ago. "You failed me sister. You failed her! You failed us! Again!"

"Lord Dusk..." Aubrey had whispered nervously to him all those years ago. "I'm sorry... I thought you knew. I can leave you alone..."

"Brother, I'm so..."

"She... strangled him?" A well-built Dusk of some two-hundred years ago looked up to the ether, as though trying to find Claire's voice in the future House of Schofield, his legs carrying him down the stairs to the wooden porch outside, grabbing the railing to steady himself, a panicked breathing setting in. "She strangled... our son?"

"He forced her to! She didn't do it willingly. It wasn't her fault!"

"You knew?" Both voice and railing cracked under his frame, his radiant *smile shattered, his blue eyes searching for meaning, for something real as Aubrey retreated. "I trusted you." A silent pause as he stared forward. "I trusted you!"*

Nearly two centuries later, the blacksmith rose shakily, leaning against the railing that had long since been repaired, looking down at his hands, one shattered and the other still clutching a single golden hairpin. He'd been too slow to deafen her; he'd been too weak to protect her from Michael. She was under his thumb again.

For the second time in as many days he was sopping wet; for the second time in as many centuries he was in the same place where everything had fallen apart; and for the second time in his life, Antoinette's command had chased him away.

Here he stood, burdened by a hope he'd been convinced to rekindle when it had taken him so long to move on. The red ring of compulsion had faded. His grip on the hairpin was tight. He could hear his heartbeat racing and the Red World waking, ready to make him suffer again...

"*Kill yourself.*"

"*Coward.*"

...and like he had been all those years ago, he was so very tired...

Aubrey held Dram by the shoulders as Dusk picked up the bag he'd carried with him from the House of Dusk, an uncertain vacancy to his movement as he left without a word, heading in the direction of his future shop, the expanse claimed by a thrush of trees, stronger and sturdier than he was.

"Brother, stop! This changes nothing," Claire called out to him. "You're on the precipice of something incredible. The prospect of resurrection can be made a reality. You'll bring us back to life and everything that's happened will pale in comparison to the joy ahead."

Dusk kept his face down. "And what if he returns with his memories?"

"He might not... he can't even speak... and if he does, we'll explain it to him..." she tried to sound optimistic. "He'll understand... It was an accident."

"His mother killed him, sister." He paused, his lip quivering. "His father abandoned him."

"...You had no choice... Things will be different. Michael's taken care of. You can still have your happily ever after if everything works out. Not even Bruce came this close!"

"We failed him Claire..." He dropped the bag and slumped on the ground beside a large willow. *"...And you failed me..."*

"I..."

"I want to hear him again..."

"...Yes, brother."

Christian closed his eyes, listening keenly to the Red World as best he could. There were no errant voices around to distract him in the desolation, only the light breeze whistling through the trees and a far-off babble from a child in the Red World struggling to bring a small sense of relief to a broken man, betrayed by the two women he loved, near the place he had planned to have a future.

104

T HE ONLY LIGHT THAT ILLUMINATED THE BLACKSMITH'S SHOP
came from a small bulb in the center of the room, struggling to fill the
space. The small window which rested at ground level, low and long,
called for the light of the moon, but the storm that had taken Antoinette
from him kept it at bay.

Two figures obscured the window temporarily as they descended the
stairs, pushing open the door which struck a bell, a single chime silenced by a
woman who reflexively stopped the clapper before it could strike again.

"Lord Dusk," the woman spoke into the blacksmith's shop, her hazel eyes
washing over the armaments until she spotted a pair of vacant blue eyes staring
forward at her from the opposite side of the smithing table.

Dusk rose to his feet, setting down the thick gloves he'd been wearing as
he neared the woman, the scar on his wrist throbbing as he approached her.
He stood toe to toe with her. She challenged him now. She stood fearlessly
before him now. *No,* he admitted to himself as his eyes locked with hers, *she
had always been fearless. That had always been her nature.* "Hecate."

She opened her arms, swallowing him in her cloak, stroking the head of the man who had rescued her from slavery, given her a home and a purpose, and cared for her so long ago. He was a shell of a man now. When once his powerful legs had managed to drop two stories to save her, now they were weaker. When once his powerful frame had shielded her from exploding rubble, now it would have been blown away. When once he towered over Michael, now they would have been on equal footing. His body was not the same, and neither was his mind.

He was similar now to when Elise had died, before his vengeance had motivated him to get stronger, before they had captured Michael, before his House had been built, and before it had Fallen. "I've brought someone."

"Marie."

"Marie?" Dusk's voice carried out of the shop to the stairs where Marie Elzunaga appeared in a matching cloak, slowly finding her way inside. She was thin, her hair wrapped in a tight bun and a satchel was slung over either shoulder. Her face was mostly the same as it had been some two hundred years ago when she'd woken up: curious and excitable.

She approached pitifully, as though nearing a wounded animal. "Lord Dusk...?" Her eyes adjusted to the darkness, taking in the man before her. "You look... just like your portrait." He smiled hollowly. "I'm sorry," she said nervously. "I... we didn't know what to expect."

"How did you know to come?" He turned to look at Hecate, taking in her features. Tall, thin, and elegant. Her muscles radiated as she folded her arms across her chest, her hair still short and tame. "How did you know to come find me?"

"We started a Coven..." Marie interjected before Hecate shot her a cold glance. "Sorry."

"We have a Listener," Hecate continued. "A few days ago, she began hearing your name: *Master Dusk, Master Dusk, Master Dusk...*"

"Eventually Hecate realized it was Elise. She couldn't tell us anything else, but I thought to ask her questions with one *Master Dusk* being 'yes' and two being 'no.' That's when we realized it was Elise. That's when we realized there was a problem... there *is* a problem, isn't there?"

"Michael got out... he's with Jason and they have Antoinette... She's..."

"...a prisoner."

"...being held hostage, but..."

"We're going to save her?" Marie asked excitedly, receiving another death glare from Hecate that humbled her, relegating her to walk around the shop with her head down, quietly exploring the swords, shields, and knives that hung from their cast-iron hooks.

Hecate leaned against the same table that Antoinette had sat at, looking towards the wall of knives, feeling the weight of the garter that wrapped around her right thigh and the silver blade still sheathed within. "We came... expecting to fight."

Dusk measured his arms against hers. Despite years of hammering steel, he was only stronger than the average vampire. His body wasn't as conditioned as it had been when he had trained to take on Michael. Today, Bruce Alazar could have snapped him like a twig, and perhaps that's why Jason hadn't pursued him. He was nothing to him: no longer the threat he had once been, no longer the Head of a powerful House, no longer heir to the Evan Blood Coven, no longer the wealthy High Listener and, absent Antoinette, no longer anyone worth fighting against.

Hecate's eyes shifted to the space behind Dusk, her hand instinctively reaching for the silver blade as a pair of brown eyes looked out at her from the darkness. She knew them instantly. She knew them before his body took a step towards the light, despite his hair having greyed, even though their last meeting had been almost two centuries ago. The timid and fragile man that approached from the back of the shop, Ilovo, still cowered behind his Master.

"What's Ilovo doing here?" Marie waved as he took a heavy step forward, his feet more shifting than walking, his gaunt figure stretched thin over his skeleton despite the oversized shirt he wore. His belt was tightened to a manually-created notch and his wrists buckled against his body.

"He came to stand by my side... perhaps for the last time."

Hecate looked him up and down. One hadn't aged, and the other had done only that. She slipped the knife back in its holster, returning to her relaxed posture, leaning against the table.

"I..." Ilovo's voice was horse. It could have been mistaken for an Elder's. His chords trembled before her sour glare.

"Ilovo, perhaps you shouldn't." Dusk placed a soft hand on his shoulder.

"I agree," Hecate said crisply.

"I..." His tongue struggled to salivate as his throat dried up, swallowing aggressively. "I was wrong." His oversized eyes, like those of a doll, looked on from below his shaggy brows as Hecate scoffed. "I'm sorry."

She looked from Dusk to Marie, and finally to Ilovo. "Port died because of you. Our home was lost, because of you. Some of us never recovered... because of you. And Freya..." Hecate tried to stand a little taller. "... What you set in motion affected us in ways you can't even imagine."

"Hec..." Marie interjected, silenced by Dusk's outstretched hand.

"It may come as no consolation..." Ilovo said, taking another step out of the darkness, "I never recovered either, but I am trying to make amends. It's why I'm here. It's why I left the Evan Blood Coven."

"For now." Hecate shook her head. "Until you betray us again, and like a dog with its tail tucked between its legs run back to your true Masters, or those that would offer you a treat." She ran her tongue over her teeth. "There's no Freya to make excuses for you anymore."

Ilovo looked down, his pained eyes unchanging. "Lady Hecate, there is no return for me this time. I have chosen the House of Dusk and I will stand by Lord Dusk's side once more, regardless of what you want. It's not much of a penance... but my life is all I have left."

Marie raised her hand timidly, "Ilovo... why exactly is there no return for you?"

"He took the fall for me." Dusk pursed his lips. "He escaped before the Coven could pass its sentence. Jason's ordered him killed."

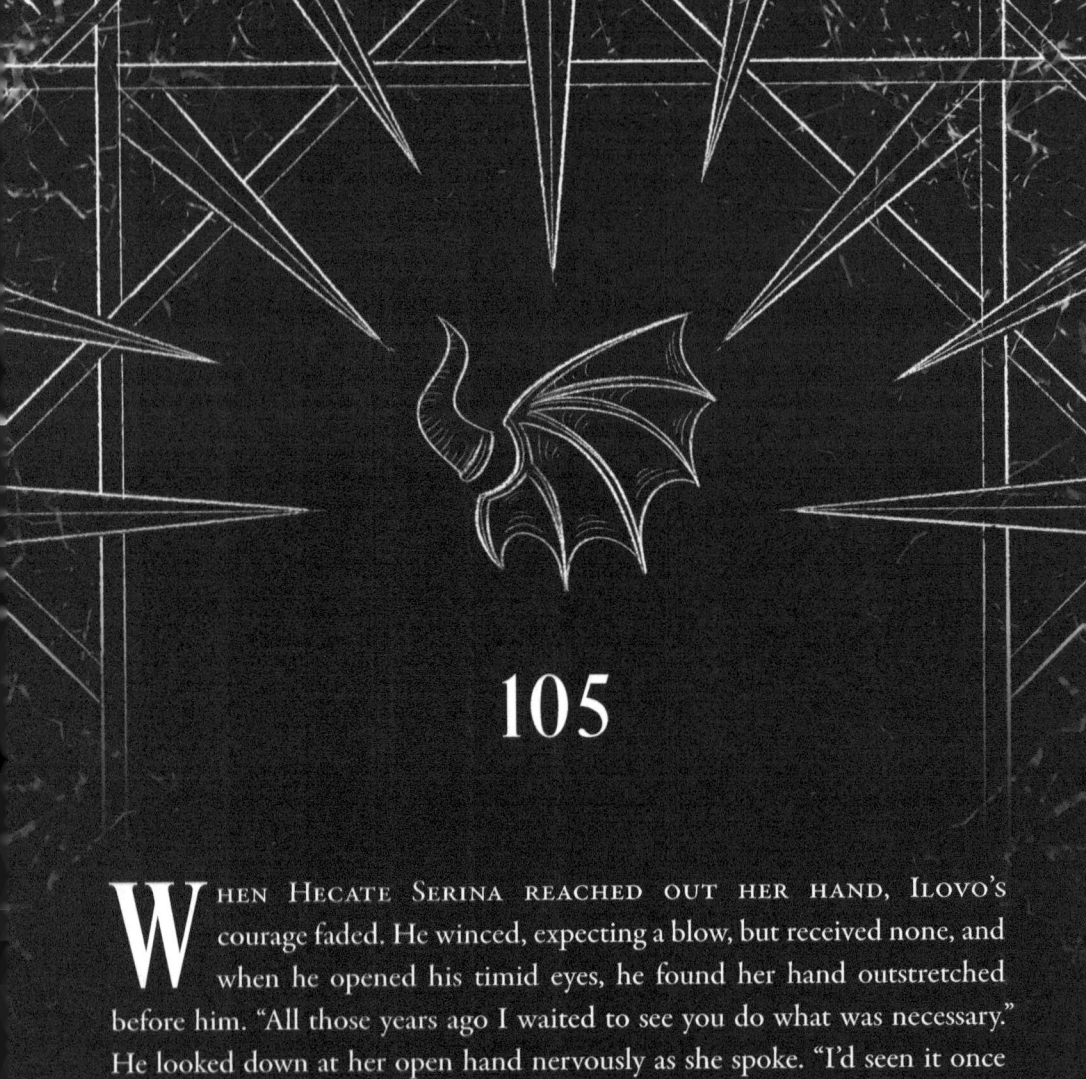

105

WHEN HECATE SERINA REACHED OUT HER HAND, ILOVO'S courage faded. He winced, expecting a blow, but received none, and when he opened his timid eyes, he found her hand outstretched before him. "All those years ago I waited to see you do what was necessary." He looked down at her open hand nervously as she spoke. "I'd seen it once with Freya, when you Turned her: doing not what was convenient, not what was easy, but what was difficult and necessary... but that was the only time. Every other play was at someone's behest, or someone else's fault. Even as you brought those men into our House..." she inhaled sharply, "...you were the victim of the self-imposed will of *Lord Dusk*. It's what I hated about you— your inability to accept the consequences of the actions you committed." Her lips curled upwards slightly as she stuck her arm further out, closer for him to take. "Until now. I can't believe that taking the blame was easy or convenient, but without a command you did what was necessary. Take my hand Ilovo. It's not forgiveness, but it's as close as you'll get."

His gaunt figure straightened itself, standing taller than it had in two centuries taking Hecate's hand in his own and shaking it, wanting to cry, wanting to bawl, but composing himself as he let go, the gleaming pride he once felt at the House of Dusk restored by her hand, years of regret melting away. "Thank you."

"So, is there a plan?" Marie asked, closing in on the group, entering the shared light.

"You haven't known him long enough sweet Marie, but the piece is already in flight... and the answer obvious." Port remarked.

"He's right," another voice spoke. *"I didn't make dresses just to put on mannequins. Or are all these weapons just for show?"*

"We do what's necessary." Dusk put on his gloves donning a grim smile, morose and frustrated, deep wells in his eyes as he gripped his trusted hammer, the wooden cedar handle impressed upon by his hand, and the rounded ends of the head hungry for steel. "I was at peace... in the Schofield Manor as a servant, in Evan Blood as a member, in the House of Dusk as its Head, and in this shop doing what needed to be done." The hammer twirled in his hand as the moonlight broke through the clouds, striking his cool blue eyes. He tied the straps of his apron around his back. "A hundred swords hang on these walls, crafted in the memory of a hundred souls filled with discontent, allowing me to channel their regrets into a new shape." He picked up his pair of goggles. "I have always been a Listener... but there is one more sword I must fashion before we rescue Lady Antoinette... before I hold Jason accountable for his crimes... before Michael reduces her to his plaything again. I won't take my regrets with me into the Red World..."

"Brother, every moment is another..."

"I know, sister..." Dusk walked over to the forge, "I know better than most that time is precious... but I don't think I can dig another grave for a person I care about... and I don't think I can watch over her from beyond if I fail..."

"You won't have to." Hecate nodded. "Tell us what you need."

"A plan... Ilovo, you we present for enough briefings with Bruce to know how it ought to be... and you know the Coven better than anyone else."

"...Are you expecting bloodshed?" Ilovo asked nervously.

"Never..." Elise whispered, *"But we always prepare for it."*

"We'll do whatever it takes." Dusk paused, looking around at his visitors. "And if you march with me... there may not be a return trip."

"I would have died in that cell if you hadn't saved me. I would have never known this life if you hadn't allowed it so." Hecate stood tall and proud. "I offer everything I have as repayment. And you would insult me if you turned it down."

Dusk nodded, his gaze shifting to Marie. "The last time I saw you, you looked away as Hecate killed the man responsible for Port's death."

"Some people stay the same..." Marie placed the satchels on the table, "...others grow. I never had a chance to surprise you, Lord Dusk, but however brief our exchange, being a member of the House of Dusk changed my trajectory too." She opened one of the bags, revealing vials of blood. "I didn't come all this way expecting to stay inside and read books."

"So be it."

"What do you need from us, brother?"

"Kill yourself."

"I need the errant voices of the Red World to quiet while I work..." His eyes turned away as he lit the forge for the last time, embers burning brightly in the enclosed shop.

106

H ECATE ADMIRED THE WALL OF BLADES AS DUSK WORKED, HER
hand running over them. Some were longswords. Some were barely
daggers. Some were rough, and others shone to a stunning precision. A
few had jewels on the hilts, but most were plain. There was little consistency to
any of the swords, each piece unique, some objectively good, others objectively
bad, but all hanging from the same hooks beside each other, a constellation of
artistry and the incarnation of *his* Red World.

"Lord Dusk. Perhaps you could select a blade for me as well." Ilovo's voice
hesitated in the spaces between the strikes, looking to the blacksmith who
nodded, eyes hidden, foot tapping twice before each blow, lost in thought.

A hundred years of strikes. A hundred years of blows. A hundred years
he had worked with only a fraction more power than a human. Now, as a
blood-fueled vampire, the metal yielded effortlessly. He wasn't used to it being
this easy. He wasn't used to the hammer taking just as much shape as the hot
steel, but he also wasn't used to working angry.

Ilovo's eyes looked to the wall of swords as he waited for his Lord to finish. He reached for a small dagger that ran perpendicular to the others, tip pointed down, slightly shorter than his arm.

From across the room, Hecate cleared her throat, removing her cloak, revealing a thin black shirt which fused to her toned body. "I could choose one for you instead," she said, strolling over, instantly feeling a wave of relief from the heat of the forge, looking towards the single open window that Ilovo stood under.

"Please," Ilovo said, hand retreating from his first choice.

Hecate took a lap around the shop, slowly and carefully judging each blade, unaware that one of Dusk's eyes followed her as she did. She finally stopped in front of a sword, the same one that the realtor had sliced his finger on days ago, confidently reaching forward and lifting it from its hooks, offering it to him.

"Good choice."

The sword was long and gleaming with a topaz gem on the hilt. When Ilovo took it, the heft of the steel carried his hand down. Beneath a layer of dust polished by Hecate's hand, it shone brilliantly, layered steel painting the dense blade with an intricate pattern. Ilovo struggled to swing it, at first offended by the choice. "You can't wield it as you are... but is that truly how you plan to fight Evan Blood?"

"Fight..." Ilovo repeated nervously, feeling the weight unsteady him as he tried to hold it level, the tip of the blade pointing down as it challenged his struggling arm. The hairs on his arm were white now, surrounded by liver spots that wrapped around his hand. The blade was strong and beautiful. He could swing it, but not enough to slice anything.

"I haven't drank for pleasure..." he felt shame as he said those words, "not since that day." Hecate paused, ready to say something, but decided against it, reaching out her hand to take back the sword. His nose scrunched as he held it up to her. "Perhaps something lighter," he said, offering Hecate the sword.

"Rude."

"Would you find an excuse with something lighter too?" Dusk hammered another blow, his anger escaping through his mouth.

"Lord Dusk?" Ilovo turned to look at the man between sparks of light, unsure of what he meant as Hecate reached for the hilt.

"You're afraid. For everyone but me, it's natural. I know where I'm going."

His foot tapped twice. "I could make you a butter knife, dull and common." He shifted his grip on the metal tongs that held his workpiece, forcing the end into the fires once more. "It would feel comfortable to hold. Inoffensive to brandish. Difficult to do damage with." His black goggles reflected the fire. "Jason would laugh at you if you held it up. He might even be so amused that he would offer you a way back." Dusk turned to stare at him, covered in soot, menacingly illuminated by the fire. "Is that what you want?"

"Lord Dusk..." Marie chuckled nervously. "You may not realize it but that was..."

"...no?" Ilovo said quietly, his grip on the sword tightening.

"Was that a hiss from my furnace?" Dusk squinted as he rotated the metal in the fire. "Or a whisper from the Red World?"

"No," Ilovo said a little more confidently.

"Then tell us what you want." Dusk pulled out the metal and rested it on the iron anvil. "Not what you think we want of you. Each one of these swords is a life lived with regret. Will I forge yours next?"

"No, Lord Dusk," Ilovo said angrily, pushing past Hecate, handing her the sword as his eyes looked around the room greedily, taking a powerful stride to stand before an elaborate longsword. "This one." He didn't turn back to look at them for approval. He dismounted the longsword with both hands before turning to face them. "This is the one."

"The king's sword." Dusk struck the steel in front of him. "Forged from the regrets of nobility. It's heavy. Two hands will be needed to swing it with a strength your frail body does not have. You'll need to drink to hold it. A sword that offers no defense." The metal chimed with each blow. "You'll be vulnerable if they come for you. You'll have no hand to serve as a white flag. No opportunity to beg for forgiveness. Do you think you're worthy to wield that sword?"

Ilovo trembled as the blade pointed forward, looking from Marie to Hecate. His eyes were illuminated by the fire of the forge and his leg twitched nervously. "I..."

"A king should be honored..." Hecate interrupted, smacking Ilovo on the back, "...to be wielded by a member of the House of Dusk. There is no greater call."

Ilovo nodded hesitantly.

Dusk struck again. "Some come to buy my swords... some come to buy my art. Which are you?"

"When the time comes, this body... these hands... I will be ready to swing this sword as it was intended."

Dusk nodded, as did the other members. "And what about you, Hecate?" She had turned around, ready to return the blade with the topaz gem to the wall where it had hung. "Will you go into battle with your sister's sword?"

Hecate looked at the shining reflection of herself in the blade she had polished. Her hand traced the outline of the topaz at the end of the hilt and her finger ran up through the layers of folded steel. "I should have known..." she said, batting away a tear. "It's hopeful... like her. Would she let me? Does she still hate me?"

"I never hated you..." Freya whispered. "I hated myself for what I did... and how much you reminded me of it... I love you sister. I love the woman you've become. Take it... I know you'll treat me well."

Dusk nodded. "She never hated you... she loves you... and she loves who you have become." Hecate looked away before she could shed a tear.

"I can take Port!" Marie said excitedly, looking at the wall of swords. She bounced around for a moment. "Uh... which one is Port?" she added nervously.

"Look for the most eccentric one," Hecate cleared her throat and whispered under her breath.

"Ah!" A voice from the Red World gasped exaggeratedly.

Dusk turned the sword he'd been working on, a hint of a smile as he plunged it in a barrel of liquid beside him, pulling up the goggles to reveal his vibrant blue eyes. "None of these is Port, I'm afraid."

"Uh... why not?"

"Each of these swords is a story told over time... of a life lived with regret... Port Chinda died with none."

"Well..." Port whispered, watching the solemn smiles around the room, "I wouldn't have minded..."

Dusk pursed his lips tightly, hiding a grin as Hecate held her sister's sword close to her chest. Her eyes caught his smile and the tender nostalgia was interrupted by a single cold word from her lips. "What?"

"Huh?" Marie asked.

"What did he say?" Hecate asked, a little annoyed.

"Who?" Ilovo turned around nervously, not having heard anything.

"Port. He's here, isn't he? He said something. Lord Dusk, what did he say."

"Is that true? Did he say something?"

Dusk turned away, a smile too large to hide as Hecate put Freya's sword on the table, the clang of the metal echoing through the room. She approached and rotated him with ease, forcing him to face her. "What. Did. He. Say?"

"Lady Hecate..." Ilovo began nervously, silenced by her glare.

"Was it about him seeing me naked?" She pressed her face closer to Dusk's. "No, he probably sees me naked every day. Little pervert."

"I do," He giggled.

"Me saying 'I love you'? He knows I love him. I love you Port... little weasel." Dusk kept his lips pursed. "Lord Dusk," Hecate inhaled sharply. "Tell me what he said... *or else.*"

"Or else what?" Port chuckled. *"She's bluffing. There is no or else. She loves you. She wouldn't hit you."*

"Apologies Hecate..." Dusk began innocently, watching her weigh her options for a moment.

Hecate gulped, suddenly daring to press her lips against Dusk's, reaching one arm around his back, pulling him closer as she did, kissing him for what seemed like an eternity as Ilovo wheezed and Marie looked away, turning back to peek through spread fingers.

"Go sister," Freya screamed gleefully. *"Huzzah!"*

"First base!" Port whooped.

"Stop!" Claire gasped. *"Stop encouraging her you two!"*

Dusk pulled away, looking at Hecate's satisfied grin as she licked her lips, scrunching her nose playfully. "Tell me what he said... or I will strip right here..." She reached for the bottom of her shirt, "...in this room, and then I will strip you down and we will put on a show for the Red World... and Lady Antoinette will not be happy when we rescue her..." Hecate lifted her shirt over her belly button. "I'm stronger than you right now Lord Dusk... I wasn't always, but I am now... you know it, and I know it."

"Go sister! This is your chance!"

"*Stop encouraging her! He loves Antoinette.*"

"*He loves her too. And she loves him back. And their relationship is complicated...*"

"Fine." Dusk held up a hand, quieting the Red World as Hecate inched the shirt up, about to pull it over her chest. "But you need to go over there." He pointed to the entrance. "Because otherwise you will strike me when I tell you. Go over there, where we are all safe." Ilovo put the longsword down on the table quickly and retreated behind Dusk, as did Marie, watching the pouting Hecate in the doorway.

"Okay. Now tell me." Hecate readjusted her shirt angrily.

"He said," Dusk held up both gloved hands defensively after setting down the unfinished blade, "and these are *his* words, Hecate, not mine. Not Ilovo's. Not Marie's. These are Port's words."

"Yes yes yes. Port's words. Out with it." She folded her arms, drawing attention to her flexed biceps as she did.

"He said his only regret was that the last meal you cooked for him was so inedible he can still taste it... despite not having a tongue."

"*Hehehe,*" Port chuckled.

Hecate's clenched fists matched her scrunched face as she resisted the urge to blow out the doorway she stood under. Ilovo looked away and Marie began fidgeting with a rectangular business card on the table in front of her.

"Porterfield Eloise Chinda," Hecate said, poorly hiding a wave of anger, her pursed lips taut with fury. "If you come back one day, expect to pay for this."

"*Aww...*"

"And if you don't. You'll still pay for this when I'm dead."

"*Oh no!*"

107

AN EMPTY VIAL OF BLOOD ROLLED ON THE TABLE BEFORE ILOVO, its contents already emptied into his mouth. The liver spots on his hands were already receding. His youthful appearance, the same he'd had when he'd served under the High Listener, was already returning, but his confidence faltered.

He was anxious. He was nervous. He was afraid. He hadn't felt such unease in a long time and, as he stared at the longsword before him, he wavered, reaching for another vial of blood, trembling hand struggling to open it, downing its contents greedily.

Hecate watched her former housemate's blank stare as he avoided their gazes, lost in a world all his own. His hand reached for a third vial from Marie's satchel. He had never been a fighter. He had never been a warrior. She didn't even know if he had ever used a sword properly, but soon that would change... or so she believed. "Ilovo?"

His trance interrupted, he spun around on the stool, turning to Hecate. "Apologies Lady Hecate... Lord Dusk... perhaps it would be best if I don't join you. I would only..."

Before he could finish, Hecate's closed fist struck his shoulder with so much force that it cracked. Ilovo spilled onto the ground and Dusk looked up from the forge, setting down the blade he'd been working on. "Do you remember Lady Daina?" Hecate flexed her fist calmly as Ilovo lay on the floor, dazed at what had just happened. "You told Freya that there was a time she barely tapped you and broke your shoulder."

"I..." Ilovo grabbed at the spot where Hecate had punched him, already feeling the bones healing, the human blood still working its way through his system, "...I don't understand..." He didn't get up. He didn't dare get up.

She teased another blow and he flinched, unmoving from the spot on the floor, knees curled up defensively. "You're not afraid of pain..." She took a vial of blood, squatting down to hand it to him, watching as he nervously swiped it. "Perhaps you're the only one here who's not afraid of pain. So, what *are* you afraid of?" He uncorked the vial and drank. "What's keeping you frozen in terror? Where's that courage you had an hour ago? You're better than this..."

"I'm not... I'm pathetic..." Ilovo's legs quivered. "That's what he told me. I'll always be pathetic."

"You're not... you're so much more," Freya whispered softly.

"Who?" Marie asked from a corner of the room, standing up.

"Before I met you... before I met any of you..." Ilovo's leg throbbed as he looked up at Hecate, his eyes flashing with rings of red. "...He said I'd always be pathetic."

"That's a lie. You're not pathetic!" Freya whispered angrily.

"Who?" Hecate narrowed her eyes.

"Before I met you..."

Dusk held up a hand to the room, quieting everyone, eyes fixed on Ilovo. "Say it again." He turned away from the unfinished blade in front of him, almost as long as Ilovo's sword, twice as dense as Freya's, and wider than either. "Say it again."

"Before... he told me... I'm pathetic..." Ilovo's eyes pulsed with rings of red.

"No," Freya repeated. *"You're not pathetic!"*

"Again." Marie and Hecate watched as Dusk approached him.

The former messenger of the Evan Blood Coven cowered on the floor of his shop. "I'm pathetic..." Ilovo teared up, his eyes flashing with rings of red.

"No," Freya screamed. *"You're not pathetic!"*

"No!" Dusk and Freya said in unison. "You're not pathetic." Ilovo's eyes, brown and teary, looked onwards, the essence of red in his eyes flickering, fading, and disappearing. "You're not pathetic," they repeated.

"I'm not... pathetic?"

"...Lord Dusk?" Marie watched as Dusk extended his hand and helped him to his feet. "...Lord Dusk... what was that?"

"I..." Ilovo's face relaxed. For the first time in over three hundred years, a sense of calm washed over him, clean and crisp like the waters of an undiscovered brook. "How..." He smiled, swallowing hard, throwing his arms around his former Lord, breathing out heavily. "I'm not pathetic..."

"An Executive Command?" Hecate folded her arms nervously. "An Executive Command to keep you in your place?"

"...But... how?" Marie watched as a newfound life filled Ilovo. His skin glowed and his features softened. He rubbed at his relaxing jaw as he smiled.

"Before you came along," Hecate began, "Port and I experimented with Michael... subconscious commands to have him forget certain things when we had him helping with the housework, but nothing like this." She paused, biting her lip. "Normally, a jolt will snap you out of an Executive Command if you're in the middle of an action, but this... How long? How long were you under this Command Ilovo?"

"I don't know exactly... Three hundred years at least..." Ilovo opened the door to the shop, feeling the light breeze over his younger skin, pulling off the shirt he was wearing and stepping into the moonlight, rolling his shoulders back.

"And Freya?"

"She didn't know..." Ilovo's smile filled the room. "I didn't either... it was a feeling... it was a weight that was heavy atop me. It came in waves... some days worse than others. I don't remember the first vampire I Turned issuing me this Command... I don't remember this torture."

"Lord Dusk..." Hecate looked at the former High Listener with confusion. "How did *you* break the Executive Command?"

"It was Freya."

"But... she's dead," Marie added awkwardly.

"*Saya...*"

"Saya once told me that the Red World sometimes moves through me... I don't understand it myself, but this isn't the first time an Executive Command bled through the Divide." Dusk placed a hand over his chest, feeling the throb of the scar near his heart. "It was Freya's will that canceled out the other Command."

"Freya..." Ilovo looked to the topaz sword on the table and smiled. "Thank you."

"*You're not pathetic... all those years... all those years and I never saw it...*"

"...So, does this mean you're brave now?" Marie raised a brow.

"No... but my fear..." He flexed his hand. "For the first time in so long... it's my own. It's mine... and it's so much lighter." He stood tall and proud, approaching Hecate, meeting her gaze. "I wish to challenge you, Lady Hecate... once we save Lady Antoinette... I wish to challenge you for the right to be the heir to the House of Dusk."

108

MARIE ELZUNAGA SAT ON AN IRON STOOL IN THE CORNER OF THE blacksmith's shop, the moonlight filtering through the singular window onto a notebook that she had open. A set of instructions bled from one page onto another, illuminated by the forge. "It seems overzealous..." She spoke in between the blows from the blacksmith as she reviewed her notes, "...that the four of us could rescue Lady Antoinette from anywhere other than the Silver Cell... Everywhere else is... risky."

"It's not impossible, but if we fail, Jason will ensure there isn't a second chance." Dusk removed his goggles, thick lines of soot darkening his face as he raised up the glowing blade to his winked eye.

Hecate took the journal from her, looking over the possible locations where she might be. "Right now, she's in Jason's room... but there's no guarantee she'll still be there when we arrive... so we plan for all possibilities. Lady Antoinette once told me you were overly cautious. It's nice to know some things never change."

Dusk smirked, setting the unfinished blade on the table before him, looking up. "When Bruce was the Head of Evan Blood, the Coven was a force to be reckoned with. Fierce warriors like Daina, Saber, Nier, and Bruce were ruthless. They slept in shifts and lived their lives preparing for an attack, but today, the Coven of Jason Castille is a far cry from what it once was. The longer we give them, the more prepared they become. But today their stronghold is a building of schemers and legislators willing to pass judgment, but unwilling to face the consequences themselves. They would run if they knew they were in danger." Dusk paused, a somber smile on his face. "There was a time that I would have too, but the warriors that remain are few. They are touted for sport. I saw them firsthand when Antoinette was brought to heel." His eyes measured the shaped steel, gloved hand running along the edge as the members of his former House listened intently.

"He's right." A refreshed Ilovo added, a harmony to his voice absent the normal quiver it hid behind. "The numbers won't be on our side... but we will have the element of surprise. Many of them will flee if it turns into an actual battle... I know them." He paused. "Will we pursue them if they run?"

"If you tried," Dusk looked to Hecate, "I think you could overthrow the Coven yourself." She beamed, a wide grin across her face. "But there would be nothing left when you stood at the top. You would kill the Jasons and the Michaels, and indiscriminately you would cut down the Elises and the Freyas alike." His eyes cast a heavy judgment on her, stripping away her smile. "There is no guarantee we can spare them from this judgment, my judgment, cruel as it is, subjective as it is... but if they flee, we won't pursue."

"*Coward... you didn't give me a coward...*" Albedo's voice sounded off.

"...and in spite of my selfishness..." Dusk closed his eyes, listening to the crackle from the fire in the forge. "If they don't resist, or if they pose no threat, or if they run, we won't give chase. We'll do only what's necessary to save her."

"Understood." Hecate took in a satisfying breath. "I must say... it has been ages since I've felt so anxious."

"So, what's our plan?"

"Assuming they do not move Lady Antoinette beforehand... Hecate and I will survey any vampires outside the Coven first. We'll use the newly constructed servant's entrance to make our way in. With the Red World at my ear, I'll guide and stand beside Hecate as we move through the Coven."

Dusk looked to Ilovo, his fists clenched, his liver spots gone, the color of his soul breathing life into him. "Ilovo, I would have you make your way in with us." He nodded nervously. "Marie, you would be posted at our entry point, receiving those we'd spare. We'll divide the blood you brought between ourselves." She nodded. "Once we've cleared the basement, Ilovo, you'll be stationed at the end of the Hall of Houses, blocking the only other entrance in and out of the Coven."

"It doesn't sound possible to do this without killing anyone," Marie sighed.

"No..." Ilovo said quietly, "... but we would do best to reduce the bloodshed as much as possible."

"Lord Dusk has spoken," Hecate warned.

Ilovo raised his hands with an unusual confidence. "I meant to say, we would be wise to strike without drawing blood. At the first scent, the Coven could stir. Our swords will wake them."

Hecate assented, her frustration subsiding. "Snapping their necks it is." She shifted her posture, facing Dusk. "How do you want to handle Jason and Michael?"

"Personally..." he said quietly, "...but the outcome is more important. Do what needs to be done, but keep Michael alive so we can make him recant his Executive Command..."

"Understood."

"Then all that's left is to sharpen this blade. Be ready to move out... From here on out, every moment wasted is a risk to Lady Antoinette."

109

MARIE ELZUNAGA FOLLOWED BEHIND THREE OF THE FOUNDERS of the House of Dusk. Beneath a shimmering black cloak, hanks of rope were strapped to her body and a pair of adorning daggers were sheathed on her hips. Octagon-shaped glasses reminded her of the human she used to be as she dashed towards the Evan Blood Coven that sat atop the hill in the distance, remembering the one other time that she had so excitedly begged Ilovo to let her come. Nearly two hundred years of standing at Hecate's side had readied her for anything, but a knot in her stomach still made her feel queasy: she was no longer the girl who needed to look away when someone was killed.

In front of Marie, a second hooded vampire moved through the land, his long strides barely disturbing the ground, nimble as a gazelle. His eyes were still sunken into his face, but the white hairs and liver spots were gone now. The longsword on his back no longer felt heavy. He flanked the man in the middle as they moved forward, for once not falling behind, eyes measuring the Coven that had been his home for almost three centuries, not once elevating him like Dusk had in the five years he'd served him. The prospect of redemption was in his future. The idea of regret was trailing behind. Today, he resolved that he would prove himself—even if it was the last thing he would do.

On Dusk's right, Hecate Serina kept pace with the two other men. Each step she took impressed upon the ground. Her right hand held steady the sword that Dusk had crafted: the memory of a sister forged in steel. A polished topaz stone at the end of the handle beckoned for clear skies, but the storm that had robbed Antoinette of her freedom wasn't done yet.

The first drop struck her face and she smiled earnestly for the first time in a long time. A hundred years of dedication had taken her to a place atop her own world as founder of a Coven all her own… and yet the view had grown stale. Tempered challenges and cautious moves had made her a force to be reckoned with, but the men beside her hadn't seen her rise, nor witnessed her glory. She was just Hecate to them, a fellow housemate with an unseen potential. It didn't matter though; today she would prove herself to them too.

Three black cloaks formed a triangle around Christian Nikolai Dusk, former Head of the House of Dusk, once High Listener, and now ousted heir to the Evan Blood Coven. A hefty black coat stitched with delicate red thread, still charred from the fire at his House, hid his body from view. Returned to the former High Listener by Hecate, it was a tarp on the man he was now, and though the man he had once been would have filled it out, it still felt right.

In his breast pocket he carried only one item, a memento of his life and of his father, a well-intentioned forgery, a copper coin with a poorly imprinted half-shield on one side. Against all odds, the coin had survived the fire that had toppled his House, preserved in the wreckage and extracted by him in the days they had searched the rubble for Port. It was a worthless piece of metal, better suited to be melted down, but despite all the bad that had come of it, the coin had claimed justice once before. Today he hoped it would do so again.

His coat's tail draped over an edge that ran parallel to the ground at his back. The sword was wide, thick, and stocky; the sheathed blade still remembered the whetstone that had sharpened it. The faces of the sword longed for such care against their rough finish. It was neither his proudest nor his finest work, but the vampires up the hill didn't deserve his best, and no soul in the Red World had ever celebrated being killed by something beautiful.

The four figures paused, three of them looking towards the man in the middle whose closed blue eyes heeded the words of those who loved him, attempting to silence the chaos from those who detested him, trying to quell those who were committed to impede him.

"Kill yourself."

With a simple nod, the group was on the move again, ducking low under the overgrown grass and sprinting across the fields to the back of the Evan Blood Coven, rain coming down more steadily as they sought shelter against a wooden door, an unsuspecting gateway to their revenge.

Dusk held up four fingers, he signaled three in one direction and the fourth in the opposite. A single hand at his side was the signal for *spare,* but Hecate still drew her blade, watching as Ilovo's unsteady hands rattled a keyring for a moment, taken by Marie who slowly opened the lock.

Four figures slipped into the basement of the Evan Blood Coven, walking past the former slave cells now turned human quarters, catching the eyes of a man, Brian Keet, who had escorted Antoinette and Dusk to their doom. His neck stretched upwards, about to scream when Hecate's forearm slipped underneath, a perfect fit to silently suffocate and lay his sleeping body down.

As Marie tied up the unconscious man, Ilovo unlocked each door, and, one by one, each human was rendered unconscious and tied up, making quick work of the basement.

Dusk stared at the jagged bars of the vacant Silver Cell that had once held him. "Where is she?"

"She's in Jason's room..."

"And Michael?"

"The Promotion room."

"Good luck." Marie handed one of the satchels to Ilovo and took her post at the basement door, carrying out the humans as Dusk headed for the staircase.

Hecate's eyes looked to the place where her cell had once been, trying in vain to remember the first time she had seen Dusk. She couldn't recall, but she distinctly remembered the moment she and her sister had held each other's hands, walking towards the man with Elise's death still fresh in their minds, wondering if the fate of serving under the High Listener would be worse than continuing to live in their cells.

Dusk's steps were light as he climbed the stairs. One hand gripped the hilt of the sword at his back, ready to draw it, Hecate behind him, and Ilovo bringing up the rear. He paused at the top of the stairs, holding out his other hand, Hecate's chest colliding into it, and then Ilovo colliding into her.

"*Second base!*" Port cheered quietly as Hecate looked down at her chest, Dusk's hand retreating from it.

"*Shh!*" Freya hushed.

The five founders stood quiet, synchronized in their silence as Dusk slipped onto the first floor, his eyes overlooking the Great Ballroom where Jason had killed Bruce, the same one where he'd been forced to kneel and start the House of Dusk, and most recently, where Jason and Michael had made a spectacle of him.

The room seemed larger now, absent the hundred pairs of eyes that gawked and gestured. The eyes were always the same, regardless of who they belonged to. They judged from afar, marveling at whatever the production of the month was. Today there would be no watchers. Every human and vampire wrapped within the four walls was an actor, willing or not, to the play that was about to unfold.

Hecate's heavy footsteps flanked Dusk, her eyes darting around cautiously, opting to stay in the middle of the room. Ilovo retreated against the hallway wall, the hilt of his sword climbing over his right shoulder, hands sweaty with anticipation.

Dusk was the first to notice a pair of vampire eyes grow large in panic. The prelude to a scream was all that came out before the vampire's head spun around with an unruly crack, Hecate's powerful hands cradling the body as it crumpled to the ground.

"*Good luck, brother,*" Claire whispered, watching as he unsheathed his sword.

110

MARIE ELZUNAGA STOOD ALONE IN THE BASEMENT OF THE EVAN Blood Coven. The immobilized humans had been moved outside and the morning sun had begun its ascent behind the clouds. The faint footsteps she had heard on the first floor above her were now replaced with more, slowly approaching from all directions, heading towards the center of the Great Ballroom. "Be careful," she whispered to herself as she reached into a bag at her side, making the preparations she'd been instructed to.

"H...!" A single aspirated sound threatened to echo through the Evan Blood Coven, silenced by a snapping neck, but not before it stirred others in their beds. The pitter patter of raindrops on the roof and windows had put some vampires to bed, but others couldn't shake the feeling that something was awry in the halls of Evan Blood.

The creaking floors of those who couldn't sleep announced their arrivals and, working in quick succession, Hecate would snap their necks and Ilovo would drag their bodies out of sight. Dusk directed her movement as he weaponized the Red World, half-awake vampires marching towards an unknown commotion, rendered unconscious or killed.

The body count was at twelve when someone finally emerged from one of the second-floor openings, stepping forward to the overlook of the Great Ballroom and the collection of fallen corpses. A sheer yellow nightgown flowed over her body as she leaned against the railing, unsure of what she was witnessing at first. Her eyes surveyed the room as Hecate killed another vampire on the floor below her, a sudden realization washing over the former member of the House of Schofield, Orpha deReville, as she caught the eyes of Christian Nikolai Dusk, his knees bent in the space below her.

He was airborne before she could process the action, but his legs didn't carry him as high as they once had. Hecate hadn't been there to propel him upwards like when the fire had burned his House. Instead, the sword held tightly in one hand had to manage the distance his body alone couldn't as he leapt up.

A pointed thrust slipped through the vertical bars under the second-floor balcony, impaling the chest of the woman on the other side. Ilovo and Hecate's eyes watered as they looked up, the smell of blood in the air as Dusk used the impaled sword as leverage, swinging over the railing, delivering a second slice to Orpha's throat to finish the job. His glistening blue eyes looked down to the other members of the House of Dusk.

Hecate's hesitation was nonexistent. The smell of blood was enough to wake her and the sword which had been at her side was now comfortably in her hand. With a nod of acknowledgement, Dusk was off, leaving Ilovo to retreat to his post by the Hall of Houses and Hecate to excitedly prepare for a challenge.

"Be ready sister..." Hecate whispered as her ears focused on the sounds of footsteps around her, "...it's time for that dance." Her eyes watched as Dusk retreated, deeper into the Coven.

When he had been the High Listener, Bruce Alazar's room had been the only room on the third floor of the Evan Blood Coven's west spire. It was an offshoot that was accessible from its own spiral staircase. Bruce had joked that the staircase itself was a deterrent. *Any man who would come to kill me in my room has twenty-eight steps to think twice, because when he arrives at the twenty-ninth, I'll make the decision for him.* **Now** it was Dusk who climbed those stairs, knowing that the man at the top, Jason Castille, who had tried in vain to order his execution at least twice, would finally meet his end. Contrary to Bruce's claim, each step served only to fortify his resolve until he arrived at the top, door already open a crack, almost inviting him in.

"Careful brother—he'll use her," Claire warned.

When Dusk pushed open the door he spotted the man in his bed, face down, one arm under his lavender pillow, trying to keep his breaths shallow. "Jason Castille..." Dusk whispered in the quiet of the room, "...would you have me kill you in your sleep?"

A pair of green eyes stared at Dusk from the corner of the room. Innocent emerald eyes draped in a torn bedsheet looked at him with a morbid curiosity. Antoinette Katherine Schofield remained immobile and quiet, paralyzed by an Executive Command.

Jason's smile was up faster than he was, keeping a hand under his pillow, a smug crooked smile hovering above his bare chest, eyes hungry for death. "Christian Nikolai Dusk—twice you've come into my sights... twice you've escaped... but you won't a third time... not this time Christian. There's no one here to save you... and your beloved will bear witness to it all." In a flash, Jason withdrew a hand from under his pillow, brandishing a brass pistol for only a moment before it went spinning in the air, attached to his severed hand, a trail of blood arcing between Dusk's sword and Jason's wrist, his eyes going wide as the realization of what had happened dawned on him.

The brass barrel's thud echoed in the room as Jason took a nervous step towards the far wall, brushing against the curtains as he did, staring down the empty blue eyes of the man before him—thinking, planning, scheming.

"Help!" he suddenly screamed at the top of his lungs, once, twice, thrice before his crooked smile returned, encumbered with a faint quiver. "They'll come now... even if you kill me, they'll come for me, for their Head... they'll kill her too." Jason's eyes looked from the empty gaze that Antoinette gave them to the pistol across the room. "I am Jason Castille! I am the Head of the Evan Blood Coven... my people... they will come for me... and they will kill you!"

The defiance of the former heir to the Alastair Coven was gone as a trail of blood spilled down the clean slice of his wrist. "You are mistaken Jason." Dusk looked to the sword at his side, brushing Jason's blood on his trousers. "They will not come. They will not save you. You can't hear it... but they can't even save themselves."

Jason looked past Dusk, to the door directly behind him, his own breathing interrupting the silence, listening for any sounds and hearing only the occasional slice or groan, panic settling in. "Christian... we can come to an agreement." He reached the stump of his hand towards the window behind him, slipping it under the curtain, feeling the sting of the morning sun break through a cloud for only a moment, failing to cauterize the wound. "If this is about Antoinette... I can order Michael to undo what he's done. We can waive this nasty business of her crimes... and as for Michael—have at him! I... we... we can make this right." He took a step forward, the open palm of his good hand facing towards the ceiling.

Dusk also took a step, the hefty weight of the pointed sword guiding him. "Have you ever bit someone? Have you ever risked putting your life in someone else's hands? Or have you always just been in it for yourself?" His grip tightened on his sword, raising it parallel with the ground.

Jason's nose quivered as he looked at the severed hand on the floor, eyes resting on his ring finger, standing taller than he ever had. "I didn't have a chance..." he snarled, expression turning. "Bruce killed her before I could... on the night of my wedding no less..."

"Maybe if you had... you'd understand. Recanting an Executive Command doesn't undo the damage."

"Perhaps I can still learn." He tried hard to swallow his rage. "And you can still walk away... before your vendetta becomes her burden." A man at odds with himself wrestled with how to diffuse the situation before him. "I can pardon you..." Dusk chuckled. "The Coven then! It's yours! Take it."

"If you knew me Jason... you'd know that I never wanted it."

Jason looked towards the pistol out of reach. "Tell me what you want then..."

"My family..." He looked to Antoinette. "And to deliver a message..."

"A message?" Jason asked with confusion, looking up at him.

"Bruce sends his regards."

"Christian!" Jason screamed, lurching for the pistol as Dusk swung his sword, a mighty blow slicing Jason Castille in two.

"Christian!" he bellowed from the Red World as his body fell with a thud. *"Christian!!!"*

Dusk let out a long exhale, lowering his sword onto the ground slowly, squatting down and coming face-to-face with Antoinette. He pinched her arm to shake her free from the Executive Command until she jolted.

She scurried back and her green eyes looked away nervously, away from him and away from the man who had been sliced in two before her. As Jason's killer towered over her and offered her his hand, she took it hesitantly. "My Lord?" Her voice was barely a whisper. "Who are you?"

"I command you Antoinette Katherine Escoté..." Michael had said after Antoinette had ordered Dusk to run, *"...as long as you live... forget Christian Nikolai Dusk."*

"You'll remember soon enough." He smiled as he took her hand, ushering her towards a closet. "Stay here and hide. I'll come back for you when it's over. I'll come get you when it's safe."

It was pleasant, she thought to herself as he took her hand, walking her into the closet and pulling the wooden doors closed, *and it was warm.*

111

HECATE SERINA STOOD WITH HER BACK TO ILOVO. HIS LONG-sword brandished away the increasing number of vampires who flocked to the Great Ballroom, the scent of vampire blood in the air. As Ilovo swatted them away, Hecate would use the opportunity to strike, but as the number of vampires grew, so too did their awareness, until fewer and fewer fell, a ring of vampires surrounding them.

A stark grin graced Hecate's face as she kicked some of the dead vampires at her feet backwards. Her face was drenched in sweat. Her body was covered in blood. And for the first time in a long time, the thrill of an unsurmountable challenge danced in front of her. She hadn't been this uneasy since she'd accompanied Dusk to capture Michael. She would have died in that circle if she were alone, but the man at her back, Ilovo, was finally proving himself.

His gaunt gaze paralyzed the swarm. The plaything messenger of Evan Blood gripped the longsword with a ferocious precision, and his ghastly eyes threatened to send them to the afterlife. Not even Ilovo knew he had so much backbone, but with a handful of kills amidst the dozens of dead vampires, fear was a thing of the past. There was nowhere to run now and, strangely enough, he had never felt so free.

"What do we do?" Ilovo whispered as he and Hecate continued moving in a circle, back-to-back. "They'll retrieve the pistols from the armory... and we'll be easy prey."

"You might be right." Hecate took a step back, pushing Ilovo towards the wall, scattering the vampires who regrouped and formed a semi-circle around her. "Shameful as it may be... there are just too many of them."

"We call for Marie?" Ilovo asked, his back to the wall.

"Brace yourself." She smiled, pulling out a few vials of human blood and hurling them against the far wall. "We go to her."

Hecate tapped her heel on the floor three times as the vials soared through the air, then raised her right foot to the sky. The vampires watched her carefully until the glass vials collided against the far wall, the scent of human blood overpowering the room, their heads turning away from her on instinct. In the moment their focus was torn, Ilovo leapt into the air and Hecate's foot struck the floor beneath her, shattering the ground and dropping her down to the basement below.

Hecate landed first, skipping back towards their entry point on her good foot, regrouping beside Marie who kept her fists closed and at her sides. "Ilovo! Come," Hecate called. He quickly took his place at Hecate's side in the basement, behind Marie, watching Hecate reach for a vial of blood in Marie's coat, still standing on one foot. "Don't move, Ilovo." She inhaled deeply, attempting to stand on the foot she had used to smash through the first floor, wincing as she did. "Stay behind Marie."

Marie remained still, watching as the bravest of the vampires in the circle above jumped down to the basement, looking to the trio by the back entrance, slowly encroaching upon them. They noticed how Hecate favored her foot and used Ilovo to support her. "Now?" Marie asked as Hecate surveyed the vampires on the first floor, seeing no one else jump down into the hole and hearing others make their way to the stairs leading down.

"Now."

Marie Elzunaga crossed her closed hands quickly, prompting a whirring sound that echoed through the basement. As the vampires on the first floor listened with confusion, those in the basement stood paralyzed for a moment, unaware of the razor-sharp silver thread trap that had ensnared them where they stood, cutting them in half.

As body halves fell, several of the vampires on the first floor screamed and others fled. Ilovo watched with abject terror as Marie's gloved hands began to wind back the wire until only a thin bleeding strip of silver was suspended in the space in front of her face. "How long do you need?" Marie asked as she looked up at the vampires on the first floor.

"Just a few minutes," Hecate said, placing some weight on her foot. "I still can't believe Lord Dusk was able to bring Vega down two floors..." She marveled at the single floor she'd been able to burst through.

"Ilovo?" Marie asked. "Are you staying?"

"No," Ilovo responded with a tinge of confidence. "I'll take the stairs."

"Then I'll take the first floor."

Hecate leaned her shoulder against the wall, still wincing as her foot began to heal, watching as Marie and Ilovo made their way to their respective posts, unaware of the slowly-opening door behind her, unaware of the empty black eyes raising a piece of blackened metal to her back, unaware of the full-force swing already in motion, ready to catch her off guard.

112

MICHAEL ESCOTÉ'S EMPTY BLACK EYES GREW WIDE AS HE SLOWLY opened the basement door. While the rest of the vampires had clambered down the stairs or gawked from the hole in the first floor, Michael had taken a blackened fireplace poker and a thick black cloak, quietly making his way around the back of the building, avoiding the morning light that began to chase the clouds away, slowly opening the back door to see Hecate Serina in his sights and within range of his strike. He silently gripped the weapon and swung with all his might as her head rotated around to see him, catching his eyes at the last second.

"Freeze." A grim smile spread upon her face as the Executive Command rang out, poker stopping in midair, suspended by an impossible force as Michael's body shook with anger. The limestone-colored hair of the Elder he'd been a few days ago had been replaced by his restored golden locks, but the harder he tried to bring the poker down, the more resistance there was.

Hecate's grin widened as she took the poker, tossing it aside. She slowly reached down to the small silver blade at her thigh, her eyes watching him struggle as she wiped it clean on her trousers. "Last time we fought... you broke this..." She held up the blade in front of his eyes. "Do you remember?"

He went pale as he realized the weight of her words. A bead of sweat ran down his face as Hecate gently shifted her weight to her previously broken foot. "Lord Dusk needs you alive for now..." Hecate looked at her reflection in the blade of her small silver dagger. "But when it's over I hope he'll let me do the honors." Michael's lip quivered in his paralyzed state. "You can speak."

His eyes pulsed red. "What did I ever do to you? You kept me prisoner for years... You buried me for over a century. I did nothing to you!"

"And what did Lady Antoinette do to you?"

"She lied to me! She wasn't *his* to have! I didn't want a Weather girl for a wife."

"And she didn't want a little bitch like you for a husband." Hecate balled her fist and struck his jaw, sending a tooth spilling out. She looked back to Ilovo fighting off the vampires who were coming down the stairs, and then up to Marie, wielding two swords and striking down the vampires on the first floor. "Stay put," she commanded. "And when next you see Lady Antoinette, recant the order you gave her. Restore her memories." Michael's eyes pulsed red, resisting to no avail. "Say 'Yes, Master.'"

"Yes, Master."

"Hec!" Marie called from the first floor as she was pushed back.

"There's too many!" Ilovo groaned as he failed to properly maneuver his longsword in the confines of the stairwell, feeling a sword cut into him.

"I'm coming." She smiled, moving her ankle.

113

WHEN DUSK ARRIVED TO ASSIST HECATE, ILOVO, AND MARIE, the Evan Blood Coven was beginning to make headway. They had been unaware that a fourth ally was also lurking in the Coven. The vampires had splintered off into three groups, one facing off against each known member of the Fallen House of Dusk.

When he arrived, he descended into the mob on the first floor which threatened Marie. The unaware vampires were mowed down by an indiscriminate blade. Before the group of vampires pushing Ilovo back at the stairs could comprehend what had happened, his descent meant their death. And when only Hecate remained outnumbered, standing amidst the half-corpses that Marie had severed in the basement, a sweeping strike from Dusk's blade created the necessary opening for her to finish off the rest.

As Marie and Ilovo regrouped with Hecate, Dusk's cold blue eyes surveyed the remaining movement, the Red World louder than it had ever been.

He measured the paralyzed Michael by the back door as he tossed a key to Hecate. "To the Silver Cell," Dusk said coldly. "Let's make sure he doesn't get away this time."

Hecate spun the key in the lock several times before the deadbolt retracted enough to open. With a single command, Michael walked into the center, one of the few structures far enough from the rubble that it wasn't disturbed by the broken floor. As she sealed him inside it, silver bars protruding from every direction, the man inside shook with anger.

Marie took a vial of blood that Dusk offered her, restoring life to her sliced up arms. "Good timing," she whispered.

"Agreed," Ilovo heaved, taking a vial all his own, clutching a deep wound at his side and paying no mind to the volley of blood that spilled down his legs.

"We were fine," Hecate chuckled, turning her neck back and forth, admiring the black cloak that Freya had made Dusk so many years ago. "Where is she?" Hecate wiped the blood and sweat across her face.

"Hiding in Jason's room." Dusk smiled. "I'll get her when the work is done."

"And Jason?"

"Taken care of."

"*Slaves, servants, and vagabonds...*" Hecate laughed, remembering how Jason had referred to them. "Done in by such a low bar."

The group watched as a few other vampires appeared, timidly stepping over the sea of bodies, looking down to the trio and turning tail. "We don't pursue... right?" Marie asked, her eyes glued to them as they scrambled.

"*Incoming.*"

"Not necessary."

Dusk reached his hand back, putting it on Hecate's shoulder. She looked over at it as he shoved her forcefully, sending her across the basement a moment before a thunderous bang exploded the ground where she'd stood. "Just a few Elders left to take care of... unfortunately... they won't run."

Hecate trembled as her eyes fixated on the blast of a silver ball lodged into the floor. If he hadn't pushed her, the bullet would have killed her instantly. For a moment she felt fear. For a moment she felt human. For a moment she remembered what it was like to be a slave again... and when that moment had passed, she felt anger. She wiped down Freya's sword against her bloodied trousers, peering up to the second floor where a frail old man rested a tired eye against a sight, breathing slowly as he readied to fire again.

114

ONE HUNDRED SEVENTY-FOUR YEARS AGO

"**I**S THIS REALLY NECESSARY?" A YEAR AFTER JASON CASTILLE HAD become the new Head of Evan Blood, and a year since the High Listener had been ordered to start his own House, Elder Versel watched as Elder Armand picked at a wall in the library behind the Promotion room. Versel's arrival had come in the aftermath of Jason's coup état, when Bruce had been killed, and another Elder had died in the chaos. "This strikes me as irresponsible," he continued. "One wrong move and the Coven could be destroyed." Armand turned around, mixing a slurry in a small bowl. "And from what you've told me... Jason and Bruce are very different..."

"Versel... you're young by comparison and new to Evan Blood, but I have watched as this Coven has transitioned... and we Elders were powerless when Bruce's ambitions threatened to thwart everything we sought to preserve. Our one detriment will always be the same as our strength: our years. I do not disagree that today it is unnecessary, but tomorrow another Bruce could overtake these halls, or a rival could attack, and we would again be powerless to stop it."

"...And no one will know of this besides us Elders?"

"Our role is to protect the Coven and preserve the order of the vampire world. We can always rebuild these four walls, but the legacy in that book..." he motioned towards the Evan Blood Charter on its silver chain in the center of the small room, "...could be wiped out in a single night... as was the case for Red Crescent."

Armand bent over a circular oak table in the library behind the Promotion room where the Charter was kept. Where once a sigil made of six circles had been inlaid in a beautiful copper on the tabletop, the patina had aged and turned a nauseating shade of green that infected the wood.

The Elder delicately ran a wire through a small chamber in the tabletop, through one of the six circles, then down the base, threading it and running it along the divots of the floor. He tucked it behind a bookshelf and connected it to another wire that disappeared behind the wall he had been picking at. Once the six wires were flush in the cracks, he began pouring a slurry over them, hiding them.

"If anyone finds out about this..." Versel began.

Armand chuckled. "Once it's set, who but us would know?"

"Where do they go?" Versel's eyes followed the different grout lines. Each hid a wire and was threaded through a different circle in the tabletop, neatly hidden in the wood by a mix of sawdust and paste.

"Memorize these Versel... when the time comes, we don't want to bring it all down... just the room with the threat." Armand pointed to the first circle and worked his way around. "Hallway. Great Ballroom. War Room. Kitchen. Head's Chambers. Promotion."

"Promotion?" Versel asked nervously, looking to the room just beyond the library they were in.

"Indeed... our last line of defense. The library we are in can only be accessed through the Promotion room. If they make it this far... we'll lock ourselves inside while we collapse the room outside."

"Ah..."

"It should be easy enough to remember that one at least... that circle is the one closest to the Promotion room."

TODAY

A SECOND SHOT EXPLODED BESIDE DUSK AS MARIE AND ILOVO SCRAMBLED to the walls, leaving Hecate to dart across the basement and seek refuge in the stairwell.

"Is it just him?" Marie asked, peeking out, narrowly avoiding another shot.

"For now." Dusk nodded to Hecate across the basement, watching her ascend the stairs. "Ilovo—you'll head to the library. Elder Versel is there, alone and afraid, attempting to remove the Charter from its silver chain. You don't need to kill him, stalling him will be enough." Ilovo nodded, throwing on his cloak and darting out the back door. "Marie... the kitchen is on the west side. I trust you remember from your tour?" She nodded.

"What about Hec?" Marie paused for a moment before a powerful yell interrupted the silence, the gasp of an Elder echoing through the halls as a blade pierced him. "Never mind," she said, jumping up through the hole and making a beeline through the ballroom of bodies.

"I'll take Armand..." Dusk whispered as he followed her, looking to Hecate on the second floor, pulling out her sword from the robed man. "You'll take the last one, on the roof. Cover up," Dusk warned as he approached a set of double doors to the War Room, memories of Bruce angrily tossing them from their hinges still fresh in his mind.

"The pistol is aimed at the door," Claire warned. *"Be quick."*

"Tell me when he looks away," Dusk whispered, picking up one of the swords off a dead vampire and hurling it across the room with all his strength, a loud clash echoing from down the hall.

"Now."

When Dusk burst through the double doors, Armand the Elder had only a second to refocus his gaze and aim. The recoil from the single-shot pistol sent a ripple through his hand and a bullet whizzed across the room, missing Dusk by a mile. As the Elder reeled, his foot twisted under his robes, unbalancing him for a moment, causing a guillotine of steel swung by Dusk to miss its mark and instead slice deep at his stomach.

The Elder fell to the floor, a torrent of blood spilling from his wound.

"Dusk?" For a moment, the man's face was utter shock and confusion. "You...?" He hadn't seen him creep in, he had only heard a commotion and seen his fellow Coven members wage war on a threat to Evan Blood. He hadn't known who would burst through the door, only that they were foe. Now, as Dusk stood over him, the confusion turned to anger. "What have you done?" The man groaned as he turned up to the cold calculating eyes of the former High Listener. "We gave you an opportunity... They'll kill you for this..."

"This," Dusk whispered as he rounded Armand, letting him see the Great Ballroom filled with bodies, "...is the aftermath. Jason is dead... his second in command too. Does the line of succession still fall to the High Listener or do you need to consult with the others?" Armand's parched lips trembled. "I'll tell you what I told him... I never wanted it." His sword pressed against Armand's back, emerging in front of his heart.

"They'll kill you for this..."

Dusk withdrew his sword from the Elder, unaware that Ilovo watched with confusion from the Promotion room as Versel climbed atop the table in the small library. The reinforced steel door that they had once left open was chained up. Ilovo's gaze through the bars didn't comprehend why the Elder began to grind away at the patina of the circle closest the door, madly scratching and digging into the wood.

"Versel?" Ilovo held out the longsword, too far to strike him, unable to burst through the door with ease. "What are you doing?"

"Goodbye, Ilovo." His smile turned sadistic as he pinched together the buried fuse, striking a match he withdrew from his robe, watching as the lit fuse disappeared into the wood, racing down the table and kicking up the grout before disappearing behind a wall.

Ilovo stood paralyzed as he watched, hearing an explosion a moment before he felt it.

115

ONE HUNDRED SEVENTY YEARS AGO

NEARLY FIVE YEARS AFTER THE CREATION OF THE HOUSE OF DUSK and two days before the ball, Ilovo had arrived at the Evan Blood Coven with Marie to pick up Lady Antoinette and the other failing Heads of Houses.

He looked to the lectern in the library behind the Promotion room, noting a silver chain that bound a book to it: the Evan Blood Charter. The book sat comfortably on the table with Marie's excited eyes peering into its pages. "That book is the only one that can't leave this room, Marie. Notice how it's the only one chained... We'll be departing soon."

A young Marie stood up, stretching her back, looking around at the other books. "I'll just find my way to a bathroom first and meet you at the entrance."

Ilovo closed the Charter and picked it up as Marie left. He walked around the round oak table to take the book back to the lectern. The silver chain had coiled upon itself and, as he tried to untangle it, it got caught on a slit at the edge of the table. As he tugged on the chain, the round table in the center of the room rotated clockwise until he wrestled it free, chain jolting towards him and catching his palm, causing him to stumble, tipping over the lectern and the book as he fell.

With a grunt and a sigh, Ilovo looked at his bleeding hand, wrapping it up in the handkerchief he carried in his back pocket. He read through the opened pages and learned that Christian Nikolai Dusk, the High Listener, was the rightful heir to the Coven.

He righted the lectern and returned the Charter atop it carefully, gently nudging the table until it returned to the outline of where it had been in the center of the room, unaware that the table had rotated...

TODAY

ILOVO STOOD PARALYZED AS HE HEARD A BLAST, CLOSING HIS EYES, waiting for an impact that was more akin to an earthquake from where he stood.

An explosion on the far side of Evan Blood rattled the Coven and startled the remaining members of the House of Dusk. In the basement, Marie and Michael reeled as the ground shook. In the Promotion room, Ilovo peeked his eyes open nervously, watching a silver dagger fly directly into Versel's forehead, quieting his frantic movements across the table as his blood painted it red.

Hecate appeared behind Ilovo, looking towards the origin of the sound that rattled the Coven elsewhere. "Ilovo, what was that?"

"I don't know..." he confessed as Hecate wrestled with the iron chains that sealed off the library, eventually shattering with their combined strength.

"I'll check on Lord Dusk." Hecate withdrew the blade from Versel, pushing his corpse onto the ground. As she quietly raced past a sea of bodies, she came to the War Room where Dusk stood in quiet reflection, lips pursed. "Thank goodness... I thought..." Hecate rounded him, his white knuckles clutching his sword, still decorated with Armand's blood, grief in his eyes. "My Lord?"

He shook his head sadly, placing his blade atop the table and taking the nearest seat, the one that formerly belonged to Bruce. "It was her..." he quietly whispered as the remaining members of the House of Dusk flocked to him. "The explosion came from Jason's room... where I told her to hide."

"Kill yourself."

"Is she...?" Ilovo crept forward nervously, unaware of his role in her death, unaware of the traps the Elders had laid while he was a member of the House of Dusk, unaware that the threat even existed.

"I was hiding like you told me too..." a voice whispered into the ears of the High Listener. *"I'm sorry I forgot you for even a moment."*

116

ONE HUNDRED SIXTY YEARS AGO

A DECADE AFTER THE COLLAPSE OF THE HOUSE OF DUSK, AUSCH Enimor stood at the edge of a large crater. Once a month he returned to the site he had procured. Each time it was the same: the rugged outline of the former Head of the House of Dusk, now absent his home, driving pickaxe against earth. On this night, he loosened a golden cravat to take in the breeze, dropping to his hunches to survey the progress. Occasionally, he would hear Dusk talking in the depths of the hole, but tonight there was none, just the sound of steel against dirt. Suddenly the steel struck another note, and the future blacksmith paused.

Ausch descended into the hole to join him, deeper than the former Red Crescent was tall, and just as wide. After years of digging, the former Head of the House of Dusk stopped, bending over to inspect what he'd struck.

A simple latch hung over the sides of a buried box. The intricate metalwork made the steel safe appear regal and delicate, but when Dusk pried it from the ground, his hand sank. The box was dense, like an unforged ingot, and his index finger reached for the latch as Ausch watched with a rare excitement.

The lid resisted his strength, eventually revealing a rectangular crystal container that was wedged inside, with only a few drops of a stark red liquid that seemed to glow unnaturally in the starlight.

"Is it...?"

"Necromancer blood." A shirtless Dusk held it to the sky sadly, moonlight highlighting its color through the crystal, a heartbroken laughter as he stared at it, finally in his possession.

"You found it..."

"My Lord... why are you not overwhelmed with joy?" Ausch's eyes looked from the container to his shirtless torso, observing a deep scar that went askew beside his heart.

ONE HUNDRED SIXTY-ONE YEARS AGO

LISTENING WAS AN ABILITY FEW VAMPIRES HAD, SOUGHT AFTER BY COVENS since the times when the Old Religion was at its zenith and the teachings of the Six Gods proliferated. The clerics claimed it was the Gods at one of the first Conclaves who first called it Listening and coined the term: Listeners. Listening was an ability that took a toll: the power to hear the dead and, in tandem, the inability to hear silence in any place where they clung. The voices of the dead echoed from beyond the Divide, from the Red World, where lives went, where events were recorded, and ultimately, where he too would go one day.

Christian closed his eyes, silver blade in hand, listening to the Red World as best he could.

Some carried their entire histories with them into the Red World; others took their regrets; still others, nothing. Some could learn beyond the Divide, but most were a broken record, repeating their last living moments, recalling their final circumstances, unable to say anything else. Some voices were louder, and others quieter. It was a coin toss as to what the former High Listener could glean from the Red World. Some would help, some would not. Some could be commanded to help, others could not.

There was only one errant soul to distract him in the desolation. *"Kill yourself,"* it said.

The voices from the Red World were varied. Some were quiet and others were loud. The stronger the will, the clearer the voice. Some lives had mattered more than others; some lives were solidified in the Red World, like pillars in the afterlife, holding it up and keeping it taught, loud and crisp. It was around these pillars that the most threads wrapped around—a spike through a chaotic web— the arteries of the Red World that seemed to keep it upright and living. Other lives straddled the opposite end of the spectrum: threads that dangled, dead ends that would eventually rot away and fall into the nothingness below, slipping from people's minds altogether, quietly withering, desperately wanting to matter again, but without a single soul to vouch for their worth or relevance, or too young to know how to hold on...

Claire watched her brother's pained face as he raised the silver blade to his heart, struggling to hear a babble she could no longer perceive. There was no Antoinette to walk in on him this time. There was no one to save him from himself. *"Don't do this brother..."* she tried to plead, fighting through her own mourning, fighting through the voices of others.

The transition from one side of the Divide to the other took a toll. Not all remained whole, and, for many, the journey to the Red World meant being stripped of almost everything. The voices of the Red World judged him. Some praised him. Some cursed him. Some comforted him.

Some persisted, but others slowly faded into nothingness, eventually disappearing from the Red World entirely...

...eventually disappearing from the Red World...

...eventually disappearing...

...entirely.

He steadied the blade against his heart, taking in a deep exhale, eyes overflowing. "I can't do this anymore, sister... Now that he's gone from the Red World too... I can't..."

"Kill yourself!"

"Shut up, father!" Claire screamed. *"He's stronger than you!"*

Christian couldn't see through the tears as he drove the silver blade towards his heart, steady and true. His eyes flickered red as the blade sliced through his flesh, narrowly avoiding his heart. He cried out, looking down in agony, attempting to drag the blade over, but he couldn't. His eyes flickered red as he wept, eventually pulling out the blade and tossing it to one side. "Please..." he pleaded, "I can't go on..."

"Don't let the sadness consume you..." Elise had said when she was alive.

The Executive Command was absolute.

TODAY

CHRISTIAN NIKOLAI DUSK STARED AT THE MAN IN THE SILVER CELL, unable to escape, measuring the hatred the former noble held towards him. The scar on his chest throbbed and Michael didn't need verbal confirmation to know that Antoinette was dead. The former servant's eyes were all the proof he needed.

"Brother..."

Jagged spears of silver wrapped the cell, pointing inwards like an iron maiden, containing him. Just like he had been for so long, the man was trapped again. And just as it had been for so long, Christian remained without his son or the love of his life.

"Another century of sleep?" Michael's words clawed at the bars that his hands would bleed to touch, feeding on the despair written across the faces of the members of the House of Dusk before him. "Is that your sentence, *servant*? For what I did to your bastard?"

"Kill yourself."

"Not this time," Dusk said sadly. "This time you'll die."

"Michael... I command you..." Dusk placed a hand on her shoulder, shaking his head. "Lord Dusk?"

"Once it's done, Hecate. Once it's done."

"*It?*" Ilovo asked nervously, clutching at his side as he approached them.

"It's time."

Marie's eyes lit up with excitement as she approached, out of breath.

"Time for what exactly?"

"To bring them back." Hecate smiled, looking at the sword in her hand. "To bring them all back."

"Not all of them..." Antoinette whispered weakly.

"...just those of us that remain."

AUTHOR'S NOTE & ACKNOWLEDGMENTS

IF YOU ASKED ME TO CLASSIFY WHAT KIND OF WRITER I AM, I WOULD tell you that I am an *experimental writer*. My craft is ever-changing: sometimes evolving, sometimes merely bifurcating.

Finishing this novel was one of the hardest things I've ever had to do.

Some days, the progress appeared intangible. Some days, the progress couldn't be quantified. Some days, I felt like Penelope, unraveling the work from days prior and going backwards. But those were just the bad days.

Other days, the writing flowed like a rushing river. Other days, I wrote something so profound it surprised even me. Other days, I wove together something so devastating that I hated myself for it—and stood in awe of myself at the same time.

Some days I couldn't bear to tell anyone that I had stagnated.

Other days I couldn't bring myself to share my clever idea for fear of spoiling the plot.

Balancing the loneliness of my failures and successes to complete this novel was one of the hardest things I've ever had to do. I wish I were strong enough to have done it alone, but I'm thankful that I didn't have to.

I am grateful to those family, friends, acquaintances, and strangers who helped me along my journey. For some, it was a single question or curiosity; for others, it was a *like* on social media; and for most it was simply Listening.

A Melody of Crimson Regrets is the culmination of a decade of world-building. It is the climax of ideas that ruminated in my head and demanded to be shared. It is my latest and greatest *experiment*. On most days, I couldn't imagine getting this far—but I believe it is what many of you always knew I was capable of.

"Thank you."

ABOUT THE AUTHOR

MANUEL CACHO IS A LIFELONG STORYTELLER. *A MELODY OF CRIMSON Regrets* marks the first entry in a fantasy series more than a decade in the making. A passion project in every sense, the novel is the culmination of years spent refining ideas, experimenting with structure, and crafting characters who live in the morally complex space between shadow and light.

Born and raised in Sacramento, California, Manuel holds a Master of Arts (M.A.) in Spanish from California State University, Sacramento. His deep love of language informs his layered and detail-rich style riddled with subtle themes and narrative 'easter eggs' that invite re-reading to reward the keen reader.

In his free time, Manuel enjoys spending time with his wife and daughter, pursuing hands-on hobbies, and traveling (with a particular love for Japan).

ABOUT THE ILLUSTRATOR

ELWIRA PAWLIKOWSKA IS A GRADUATE OF THE FACULTY OF ARCHITEC-ture at Warsaw University. She currently lives in Stockholm, Sweden, where she works as a freelance illustrator and concept artist. Her artwork is primarily created using traditional media, occasionally enhanced with digital techniques. Elwira draws inspiration from the works of the Old Masters as well as the rich worlds of the fantasy genre.

INSTAGRAM: HTTPS://WWW.INSTAGRAM.COM/ELWIRAPAWLIKOWSKA/

ILLUSTRATIONS DISCLAIMER

THE ILLUSTRATIONS THAT FOLLOW WERE LARGELY COMMISSIONED before the final version of this novel was completed. Over the past years they have quietly inspired me to continue.

Though some of the smaller details may differ from the final text, I hope you'll enjoy the curated pieces that still capture key locations and still reflect the essence of the novel.

TRISTAN NIKOLAI
DUSK FALLEN